The Cocoon Within

LIISA SABAH

First published in paperback by
Michael Terence Publishing in 2024.
This hardback edition published 2024
www.mtp.agency

Copyright © 2024 Liisa Sabah

Liisa Sabah has asserted the right to be identified as
the author of this work in accordance with the
Copyright, Designs and Patents Act 1988

ISBN 9781800947184

No part of this publication may be reproduced, stored
in a retrieval system, or transmitted, in any form or
by any means, electronic, mechanical, photocopying,
recording or otherwise, without the prior
permission of the publisher

Cover images
Copyright © Aquir, Daniil Lipin
www.123rf.com

Cover design
Copyright © 2024 Michael Terence Publishing

Michael Terence
Publishing

Emmanuel

For Ketta and for Faith

Prologue

Her heart pounded with fear. She didn't know whether she should stay hidden or climb out of the window and make a dash for it. Ariana could hear the intruders crashing into things downstairs. She had no idea if Granpey was safe or if they had hurt him. She longed to go downstairs and help him, but she was afraid. Whoever was downstairs, was set on destruction. Suddenly, she heard multiple footsteps racing up the stairs, and her heart nearly leapt out of her chest. Panicking, she dashed to the small window. She didn't know how she managed to squeeze through it so fast, but somehow, she did. Thankful that it wasn't pitch-black outside, with the moon shedding enough light to be able to see quite well in the darkness, Ariana stood on the narrow ledge, contemplating her next move, before carefully edging sideways and taking hold of the drainpipe, which she used to help lower herself inch by inch. She could hear the drainpipe starting to creak from her weight before she tumbled to the ground and landed with a thud. At least the grass broke her fall, and she didn't care that she was bruised.

She jumped to her feet and ran, and ran, she kept running, keen to get as far away from the intruders as possible. Fear drove her forward without even thinking about where she was going, other than the fact that she needed to get help. She needed help to go back for Granpey. Her heart was still pounding furiously, and she began to take in her surroundings when suddenly confusion and bewilderment hit her. Why was she in a forest? Where was her street, her neighbours, was she even still in Bloxham Vale? Where on earth was she? She felt clammy and faint, panic setting in, as she looked around wildly, and it dawned on her that she was in the middle of a forest at night, and she was all alone.

Ariana stopped running; she looked at the moonlight shining through the trees, her heart still racing, every rustle of leaves and snap of a branch made her jump. Where was she? And should she go back? But which way was back? Every which way she turned, the panic within her grew, it all looked the same, how could she even tell which way was the way back? She listened to the sound of her own breathing, which seemed amplified. Eyes wide, darting to every waving branch and rustle of leaves, she felt she was being watched but she couldn't see anyone. She ran to the nearest large tree and hid behind it, whilst her eyes scanned the moonlit darkness, frantically looking for somewhere better to hide. And then she heard it, a sound in the distance, it was getting louder. Ariana realised that she was holding her breath as she listened, frozen to the spot. It was the sound of something or someone moving through the forest and as the sound got louder, it became clear that it was something quite large; she could hear the furious snapping of twigs and branches and the sound of leaves underfoot and she imagined something running at speed through the forest. She dared not move, let alone expel a breath as the runner stopped nearby. Then she heard it, a strange sound like none she had ever known before, and that's when she realised that whatever had stopped nearby, wasn't human.

Ariana covered her ears at the sound of a succession of loud guttural cries, the creature was close by and unless she was mistaken, it sounded like it was calling for others. The same sound of fast running confirmed her thoughts; she could hear more runners, unknown creatures as though in response to the cries. She thought she might faint, she was trembling in fear, she knew that she was only yards away from the creatures and she dared not move and she was too scared to look around from where she was hiding. Instead, eyes forward, she stared into the dark forest. She was just about to close her eyes, ready to succumb to her fate, when she saw the stark, ghost-like face of a woman, almost hidden beneath a hooded cloak, staring at her from a gap in the trees directly opposite, arm outstretched, beckoning Ariana to come to her.

Taking her chances with the ghostly woman, Ariana ran towards her, but she could hear the creatures immediately in hot pursuit, too scared to look behind her, she didn't want to see what was chasing her. Heart pounding like never before, she made it to the trees and reached out to grasp the ghostly woman's outstretched hand, but just then, she felt something rip into her ankle and drag her backwards; she screamed in pain and instinctively jerked around. Ariana's mind filled with terror, as she saw the flash of angry amber eyes in the face of a giant creature that she couldn't identify, and in that split second that she tried to process what was happening, the creature opened its vast mouth revealing its sharp fangs as it lunged for her face.

Ariana sat bolt upright in her bed, it was a dream, a bad dream, heart racing, she realised she was sweating, her nightdress clinging to her skin. She couldn't believe that she'd had such a nightmare; it had all seemed so real! Normally, she slept really well. She looked at her bedside clock, 3 a.m. She had to be up in four hours. Rolling over, she hid under the duvet and hoped that her mind wouldn't pick up where it had left off. She would much rather dream about a handsome love interest or at the very least something much less terrifying than giant creatures chasing her through a forest! She shuddered as she replayed the moment that the grotesque creature had been about to bite into her face, and she quickly tried to switch her thoughts to happier paths, hoping she could influence her next dream should she manage to fall asleep.

1
The Book

It was one of those dreary September days, rain, rain, rain, and too drab outside to even want to bother getting dressed to venture outdoors. Ariana snuggled further into her pink fluffy oversized dressing gown, securing it around her with its soft belt. She padded across the living room floor towards the kitchen in her matching pink furry slippers. The constant patter of the rain against the window played a musical background beat.

"Would you like a cuppa, Granpey?" Ariana called over to the elderly man sitting in the wooden rocker in front of the blazing fire. The sound of gunfire blasted out from the TV as a scene from an old Western movie dramatically played on.

Granpey turned and looked over at Ariana from his rocker and smiled, a slightly toothless smile as his face crinkled into the most amazing smile. It was a smile that Ariana loved dearly; he was like a father to her, in fact, the only real father she had ever known.

"Aye, Sweetpea, that would be just tidy," he winked in approval and turned back to his Western as he began to fill his old pipe with tobacco.

Ariana smiled to herself as she thought about her beloved Granpey, the most upbeat person that she knew, and for as long as she could remember she had never heard a stern word from him. He had always been nothing but encouraging to her throughout her life, if a little challenging at times, but even then, his purpose was always with the right intentions, to help her become a better person. Granpey had moved to England from Aberfeldy, Scotland, some twenty years ago, when Ariana's parents had still been alive and being her only surviving relative, he had taken her in following their deaths and raised her as his own.

She beamed back at him and padded over to the kitchen to make the tea. She walked through the cosy kitchen, which was warm, from the continuous heat emitting from the large Aga, the centre piece and heart of the kitchen. Ariana had added a feminine touch to the kitchen over the years. Dotted about the kitchen hung bright wind chimes with blue, yellow and red patterned chrome, and wooden butterflies chiming a gentle melody as the slight breeze from the open window dictated. Being the main cook of the household and cooking being something that Ariana really enjoyed, the Aga had a seemingly never-ending supply of Scotch Broth simmering away in an oversized pot on most days.

As Ariana made the tea she thought about her parents, the parents that she had never known, yet had come to love in a memory created and kept alive by the stories that Granpey had told her over the years, stories that Ariana cherished in her heart almost as though she had known her parents; funny how dead people can live on in one's mind seemingly so alive. Her fingers instinctively felt for the small locket at her neck that held tiny photographs of her parents and she ran her thumb over the smooth silver casing; a habit whenever she thought of them or perhaps a comforting gesture.

"Granpey, tell me the story of how my parents met again please!" a beseeching request with an equally beseeching facial expression directed towards Granpey as she held out the mug of tea as though it were a bribe.

He eagerly took the mug and beamed his toothless grin. "Aye, you love that story lass. I can't count the number of times I have told and retold this one to you, my love."

"Please, Granpey!" cried Ariana as she settled on a large bean bag at his feet, snuggling into it as she slurped her tea, all the while smiling back at him with a cheeky *you just can't say no to this cute face* look.

He turned the volume down on the TV and then after much tea slurping, he proceeded to recount the story he had told on a multitude of occasions.

"It was a cold and dark November night," he cleared his throat, slurped some more tea and continued, "and your father had just left work after handing over to the night shift. As he was driving home, he decided to take Mayflower Way instead of going along the Hoover bypass to avoid the ongoing roadworks…"

"Granpey, you forgot to say that he worked at the hospital and it was his first permanent posting following graduating as a fully-fledged doctor and how proud of him you were. You always say that when you tell the story!" chided Ariana, keen to hear every detail exactly as before. She never tired of him retelling the story.

"Am I telling this story or not child?" he retorted with fake annoyance as he gave her that crinkled-faced look of being cross before he chuckled and began stoking his pipe. Ariana couldn't help but laugh every time he made that face. That was his intention to make her laugh; he was such a joyous soul, always ready to have a good laugh.

"Why, I'll be buggered if I don't finish this story before the hour is out! Now listen here child, your father worked at Falmouth Birch hospital as a doctor. It was his first permanent posting since he graduated as a fully-fledged doctor and I was so proud of him," he beamed at the memory. "Aye, Colin was a good lad so he was; he had loved his studies since he was a wee boy, and he always wanted to be a doctor when he grew up. He was determined so he was and he wouldn't give up till he succeeded! He was an intelligent man, full of charisma, and everybody loved our Colin, aye so they did." He had that faraway look in his eyes as he blew a cloud of pipe smoke. Ariana loved the smell of Granpey's tobacco. To her, it was the essence of home.

She felt like a child again as she listened to the rest of the oh-so-familiar story of when her parents had first met. "Granpey, can we look at the photos together please?"

"Aye, bring them over. You know where they are."

Ariana quickly got the photo album titled *Mum and Dad* from the shelf where it always sat, then she dragged her bean bag closer to his chair so they could look through the album together.

"Mum and Dad's wedding," she liked to give a running commentary of the photos on each page. Whilst Granpey nodded and grunted or gave a courteous "Aye," here and there as they sat together, amicably enjoying each moment captured by the camera.

"Mum and Dad's opening dance. She looks so beautiful in that shot, with her dress flowing."

"Aye, aye, so she was."

"Cutting the cake," Ariana looked wistful as she stared at the photograph, soaking up her mother and father's facial features. "There's you, Granpey, you look so happy."

"And so I was that day." Another cloud of smoke escaped Granpey's lips.

Ariana turned the page, "There's me as a new-born, Mum looks tired but overjoyed at the same time and Dad is so proud!" Ariana's eyes lingered on the photo; she loved this picture so much.

The mother that she had never known, held her in her arms and was staring intently, lovingly at her, she was loved, so loved and so wanted. She could look at that photo for ages. She used to do that whenever she got upset about anything as a child. Granpey would know where to find her, she would be sitting right here on the floor with the photo album out, and this photo plucked from the page, and there Ariana would stare for hours at it, mesmerised, reminding herself that she had been loved and wanted by her parents, and somehow that made everything right again.

She closed the album and looked up at Granpey as he rocked slowly back and forth in his rocker blowing smoke rings from his pipe.

"Granpey that day… did you… get to say goodbye?" Ariana knew the answer, but she just wanted to hear it again.

"Aye, lass, to your bonnie mam, so I did, but your Pa… well it was too late," his eyes welled up, "and they would want you to know how much they loved you, so they would, aye so they would," he said with a faraway look in his eyes.

"Do you think we've got any more photos of Mum and Dad that I haven't seen?" Ariana said almost as though she was thinking out loud rather than asking a question.

"There will no doubt be some up in the loft, so there will, aye, boxes of memories up there. I've been meaning to get up there and have a clear-out for years, but me old aching back puts me off every time," he sighed.

A loud knocking at the front door made them both jump and then as Ariana recognised the familiar beat being tapped on the door, she arose laughing out loud. "That'll be Jack then!" she exclaimed as she strode to the front door and opened it wide.

Holding a blue umbrella covered with white polka dots, stood Jack, Ariana's best friend and confidant. He was immaculately dressed in a royal blue suit complete with a white shirt, tie and waistcoat. He had his brown 'man bag' draped over his shoulder which didn't match the outfit, but none the less, that was Jack, and he took that bag almost everywhere he went. Ariana stared open-mouthed as her eyes trailed down to his feet, drawn by the sparkle radiating from the shiny, dark blue shoes that just shouted *look at me*.

"Wow!" just one word came out of Ariana's mouth as a smile tugged at the corners of her lips before she broke into a fit of giggles.

"Let me in then!" cried Jack with a wave of his hand as he closed his umbrella and edged past Ariana, ignoring her laughter.

"Afternoon, Granpey!" Jack smiled his winning smile. "Is there a spare bowl of Scotch Broth going for a weary lad who has just spent the last four hours of his life over at Barnsley Theatre, playing his heart and soul out, in front of an audience of three hundred?" Jack asked as he gave Ariana a dramatic look over his shoulder, rolling his eyes and emphasising his words.

Granpey laughed his deep bellow laugh, clouds of smoke puffing along with his laughter. "Aye, lad, there's always a spare bowl going for you, so there is!" His eyes twinkled as he watched the two friends interact, both chattering to each other at the same time and he thought that anyone watching them wouldn't be able to make head nor tail of what they were talking about, these youngsters talk so fast nowadays. Shaking his head, he turned back to the TV to see if there were any more Western movies about to start.

***

Ariana opened her bedroom door, padded in with her slippers and flounced straight onto the memory foam mattress on her double bed. Patting the other side of her bed, she signalled for Jack to join her. He removed his suit jacket, found a hanger in the wardrobe and hung his jacket on the wardrobe door. She watched as he undid his waistcoat and the top button of his shirt before coming over to join her on the bed.

"Much better!" Jack beamed as he bounced onto the bed landing neatly next to Ariana as he folded his hands behind his head and stared up at the ceiling, smiling. "Guess who was in the front row of the audience?"

"A talent scout?" asked Ariana, hopefully.

He turned to face her with a huge smile on his face, "Jessica!"

"And?" she asked, expectantly. She wanted to roll her eyes but thought better of it.

Jack was infatuated with Jessica Brown. What a plain name, Jessica Brown. However, she was the most talented, popular and (depending on whose opinion) the so-called most beautiful girl in the entire school. All the boys drooled over her, so it was no surprise that Jack did the same, though Ariana couldn't really understand why Jack, (her intelligent Jack) had to be the same as the rest of the dumb boys in class. Didn't any guys have real taste these days?

"And well, nothing... yet," he replied as he carried on staring up at the ceiling, as though deep in thought.

"Well, why don't you just ask her out and get it over and done with, instead of hankering after her without her ever really knowing? At least you will know either way," she said, slightly exasperated.

"You think she'll say no, don't you?" asked Jack dejectedly.

"Er... I never said that... it's just that you need to take some form of action if you want anything to happen. Think about it in musical speak, a language you understand," she smiled at him. "You are a very accomplished pianist, right? So how did you come to be so? By taking action... by practising right?"

"Right," he replied as he turned to face her, attentive to what she was about to say.

"So, apply this to asking girls out, to become accomplished at it, you need to take action and ASK!" she said with a fake stern look.

"Alright, alright, yes, yes I know." His smile faded and was replaced by a serious frown.

"Ok, practise on me, pretend I'm Jessica." Ariana sat up, grabbing Jack's hands in hers and pulling him to face her.

"Ok, let me think," said Jack, brow furrowed in nervous thought.

"Come on just try," she coaxed, rather impatiently as she got into character and started flicking her long red hair and inspecting her manicured nails.

"Hi, Jessica, I'm Jack, we are in music class together; how's it going?" Jack gulped nervously almost as though she really was Jessica.

"Oh, hi, erm yeah it's going well, thanks," she replied in a high-pitched voice, trying to mimic Jessica and she carried on looking at her nails.

"Er, Jessica… er I just wondered if… er you'd like to grab a coffee sometime?" Jack spluttered the words out awkwardly.

"A COFFEE! Jack! Come on think of something better than that, get my eye contact and make me notice you!" she cried.

Just then Jack grabbed her shoulders, making her face him. Surprised, a small involuntary gasp escaped Ariana's lips and she looked him dead in the eyes and was about to laugh, but seeing his expression stopped her in her tracks. He was looking at her with… intense longing in his eyes! Momentary shock… Ariana had never seen Jack in that way. They had been friends since they were four or five years old, they had adventured together through fun times growing up, and through challenging ones too, but there had never been anything between them other than just good friends.

They stared at one another, and Ariana felt a moment of confusion, and she saw the same momentary confusion in Jack's face.

"*Sweetpea! Jack! time for stew!*" Granpey's voice carried up the stairs loudly, a welcome interruption.

"Oh, I'm just absolutely starving, aren't you?" Ariana confessed as Jack immediately dropped his hold on her, his arms quickly falling to his sides and Ariana pulled her gaping dressing gown closed, suddenly becoming aware that Jack's eyes had been looking in that direction. Looking rather embarrassed, Jack's eyes darted to the bedroom door, and he swiped his hand through his dark curly fringe pushing his hair away from his face.

"Oh yes, me too, I'm ravenous, race you downstairs!" and with that, he was running down the stairs in a flash.

Ariana sat on her bed for a moment in stunned silence; she shook her head and laughed, convincing herself that she had imagined the whole exchange. This was Jack she was talking about, Jack who has always had a never-ending infatuation with Jessica

Brown for as long as she could remember. Jack whom Ariana had never looked at in a romantic way whatsoever, though she had never noticed before how broad and strong his shoulders were, nor how his eyes twinkled a sort of auburn shade of brown... or how his hands that played the piano so well, were also very masculine yet smooth...

"Sweetpea!" Granpey cried.

"Coming!" replied Ariana as she hurried from her room.

They ate Scotch Broth till they were bursting at the seams and played Trivial Pursuit and Cluedo until late that evening. Jack cycled home on Ariana's push bike. Jack was almost eighteen now and he had just passed his driving test, his uncle had bought an old Ford Fiesta and together Jack and his uncle were fixing it up, it was nearly ready, so Jack would be driving around soon and would be a "free man at last" as he liked to put it.

Ariana still had a few months to go before she turned eighteen. She and Jack were both in their last year of sixth form and Jack was a very accomplished musician. He was going to go to university to achieve his BA and become a college music teacher. Ariana's hopes for her future were also to go on to university with the hopes of becoming a veterinary surgeon. Ever since she was a small girl she had always loved animals and as soon as she was old enough, she got a part-time job at her local pet shop, where she worked a couple of times a week and weekends.

"Hey Sweetpea, I'm gonna turn in for the night now lass," Granpey yawned as he stood in the kitchen doorway, and watched Ariana pick up the tea towel and dry her hands as she padded over to him and gave him a hug and a peck on the cheek.

"Night, Granpey," she smiled fondly.

"Night, lass," and with that, he turned around and walked slowly towards his bedroom which was actually the dining room turned into a downstairs bedroom. Since Granpey's arthritis in his left leg had gotten worse last year, Ariana had suggested he sleep downstairs to avoid the stairs. Of course, he had resisted at first, but she wouldn't take no for an answer. She had enlisted the help of Jack and his uncle to move Granpey's bedroom furniture downstairs. He had quickly settled into his new bedroom and had come to appreciate the convenience of having a downstairs bathroom and kitchen close at hand.

She heard his bedroom door close and she looked around the spotless kitchen satisfied with her own handiwork. Then she smiled and switched the kitchen light off. Walking through the lounge, she checked the front door was locked.

"Meow," Ariana looked down at the fluffy bundle of fur rubbing against her legs.

"Hello, Flower, come here." She picked up Flower, her beautiful silver-furred Persian mix cat and made her way upstairs to her bedroom, carrying the rather large cat that looked like a huge ball of fluff. Flower purred loudly and leapt from Ariana's arms onto the bed where she curled up on Ariana's side of the bed and settled down to sleep.

"Hey, you cheeky, that's where I am going to sleep in a minute, so you'll need to budge over!" Ariana smiled fondly at her fluffy cat before her thoughts wandered to her parents as they often did, and she remembered that Granpey had said that there were more photos that she might not ever have seen up in the attic!

Her eyes sparkled with excitement; that was it! She was going to the attic. Besides she didn't feel tired, and she was up to date on all her course work. Being the organised person that she was, she didn't fancy watching Netflix especially as her favourite series had ended anyway. That would mean searching for a new series or a good movie, and she couldn't be bothered to spend her evening scrolling endlessly for something to watch.

Pulling herself up into the attic, Ariana made sure that the step ladder was secure so she could get back down easily. Shining the torch from her mobile phone, she found the light switch, flicked it on and watched as the attic lit up brightly. Granpey had put a light in the attic some years back when he had been more active. In those days he used to do quite a lot around the house.

"Hmm, now where are those old photos?" she muttered to herself as she carefully made her way over to the numerous boxes crowded on the far side of the attic and opened one box after another, going through the contents. She pulled out old shoes and clothes, ornaments, bits and bobs, and after over an hour searching through timeless memories of old, she stifled a yawn.

"I think that's it for tonight... time to turn..." Ariana's voice trailed off as something glinted in the light and caught in her peripheral vision; it was coming from a box at the other end of the attic. She walked steadily across the beams towards the box which had a hole in the side for a handle and she could see something shiny glinting through it. She carefully lifted a pile of records off the top of the box and laid them gently on top of a large black bin bag. Opening the box, Ariana discovered that the glinting object was a copper plate, one of those ornamental ones that you put on a wall. Sighing, she made a mental note that perhaps the records and the copper plate might sell well at the local antiques store in town. Picking up the copper plate, she inspected it and then looked inside the box and there staring right back at her was a pile of photographs.

"Yes!" she cried, elated at finally finding what she had been looking for. She quickly stowed away the pile of photos in her rucksack that she had brought with her. Reaching back inside the box, she pulled out a thick old leather-bound book and blowing the dust off the cover, she peered at the interesting swirling patterns and pictures on it, with writing that reminded her of braille, though it was clear that the writing was in a different language.

"Hmm this looks interesting," Ariana muttered to herself as she put the book in her rucksack with the photos and headed back out of the attic with her treasures.

***

Ariana mused at how very lucky she was to have an ensuite bathroom all to herself. She padded across the bathroom floor to her bedroom, towel wrapped around her head and feeling cosy in her bathrobe. As she stood in the doorway of her bedroom and towel-dried her abundant, lush red hair, she looked thoughtfully at her rucksack on her bed. Making a decisive move towards her bed, Ariana wrapped the towel around her shoulders and sat down next to the rucksack as she eagerly pulled out all the photos.

Leaning back against the pillow, she held up the first photo. It was indeed a photo that she had never seen before. Feeling elated, she settled back comfortably to enjoy these new, and some old pictures of the past, photos of her mum, dad and Granpey and pictures of her as a child growing up with Granpey by her side. Ariana felt warm and secure, as memories of her childhood flooded her senses and she savoured each moment captured in time.

She flipped through picture after picture and then she stopped at a photo of her dad; he looked so young, eighteen perhaps, maybe nineteen? She had never seen a picture of her father at this age. She peered closer at the picture, absorbing her father's young, handsome features, the hint of a moustache growing. He was sitting in Granpey's rocker, and he had an expression of intense concentration on his face. Ariana smiled wondering if Granpey had taken the photo or if someone else had. Her father was holding a book on his lap, looking down at the closed book with its leather-bound cover.

Ariana grabbed her mobile phone and took a picture of the photo of her dad holding the book and she zoomed in on the book. Just as she thought, it looked like the same book that she found in the attic. Ariana leaned over and pulled her rucksack towards her. Reaching inside it, she pulled at the old heavy leather-bound book, and it easily slid out of the rucksack into her hands. Ariana studied the cover of the book with its array of symbols, trailing her fingers over the raised patterns; now that she could see more clearly than in the attic, she noticed that the symbols had an ancient and mystical look about them.

"I wonder what they mean?" she said, as she let her fingers travel over the strange writings that were in another language, and some that reminded her of hieroglyphics. A double-headed eagle, a star, a lion and a five-fold symbol flanked each corner of the book. "Fascinating…"

She took one last look at the photo of her father holding the book and her heart warmed as she stroked the cover of the book, feeling a connection to her father at the thought of holding something that he had also held so many moons ago.

Ariana gathered up the photos and popped them on her bedside dresser, then dried her hair with her hair dryer, and decided she would do a little night-time reading. She turned on her bedside lamp and flicked her main bedroom light off, hopped into bed and settled into her lavender marshmallow pillows and matching quilted duvet, and opened the book for the first time. As she looked at the words on the first page that were in a strange language, the words began to change right before her very eyes! Ariana closed her eyes and then opened them and looked at the words again, but they continued moving, changing. She rubbed her eyes and looked again; the same thing was happening!

"*What on earth?!*" she said out loud and snapped the book shut, heart pounding.

Sitting in stunned silence for a moment as she absorbed what she had just seen, Ariana pondered that perhaps her eyes had deceived her; she was rather tired after all.

Ariana opened the book and let her eyes travel to the first page, almost waiting for the same thing to happen again, but instead, the words were no longer in an unknown language, they were in English.

She read:

*As the Stars are bright,
so can you light the world in a thousand days.*

*A wise man once said,
Where there is a beginning with no end*

*There is One afore the beginning,
A One who hath no end.*

A thousand upon a thousand eyes,
shall see where the symbols of power lead.

Was there something wrong with her eyes a moment ago? She was sure that the words had been in a strange language that she could not understand! Ariana stared at the page, and she started to frantically turn the other pages, second page, third page, fourth, fifth and on and on, the writing on every other page was in an unknown language!

Picking up her mobile phone, Ariana took several photos of the first page and some of the subsequent ones.

"Proof that I am not going mad!" Happy that she could not be fooled into doubting her own eyes again, Ariana re-read the verses on the first page.

She mused upon the rather poetic words; there were more symbols dotted around the page which seemed to be made of quite coarse, strong paper. She peered closer and could see the outline of patterns imprinted through the page itself. "Wait a minute, that's interesting…" Ariana took the torch on her mobile phone and held it under the other side of the paper and clear as day as she shone the torch directly at the paper, she could see the image of a young woman in battle with a sword drawn and shield at the ready and a mythical creature surrounded by some sort of gargoyle-type beings with angry faces. It was some kind of battle scene like something out of a mystical movie, an archangel-type of being was in the air holding a chalice and a blazing arrow as if about to aim that fiery arrow at the gargoyles.

Ariana yawned, "That's enough strange book reading for tonight!" and she put the book down on the carpet next to her bed, snuggled into her duvet and switched off her bedside light.

***

Ariana grabbed her rucksack and stooped to hug Granpey as he sat at the dining table reading his morning paper, as he did every morning. The local grocery store still offered deliveries for a small weekly fee, a bit of a community service so to speak taken up by the local townsfolk, mostly the OAPs. Despite her best efforts, Granpey was just not interested in using her I-pad or laptop. The internet and worldwide web were like a foreign entity to Granpey and he was happy for it to stay that way. He still had the old mobile phone that Ariana insisted he have and even that he only used for emergency calls and messages.

"Have a bonnie day, lass," he smiled affectionately.

"Thanks, Granpey and remember, I am doing a couple of hours at the shop after school, so I should be home by eight o'clock. There is stew in the fridge; you just need to heat it up and text me if you need anything. Love you!" Ariana beamed her winning smile at Granpey as a car horn tooted outside and after giving a final wave, she was out of the door.

It was the first day back to school after half term and Ariana was looking forward to it. This signified the final chapter of life at school. Sixth form final year was almost complete, a last lap of hard graft, final exams and then the doors to the future would be open!

"Hi Jack," she said, climbing into Jack's blue Fiesta and noticing how clean it looked inside. "Someone has been busy cleaning then, smells nice in here too."

"Yep, finally finished restoring it so I am taking care of this baby, my pride and joy! Obviously, first car pride written all over it," Jack flashed his winning smile as he crunched the gears. "Oops, sorry ha ha!"

"I had the weirdest dream last night though," Ariana had so much to tell him. "I dreamt that I was on my way to work and as I passed Abbot's corner, I looked down the alleyway, you know the short cut to the underpass, and there were two guys down there and they were trying to take this woman's handbag and she was screaming. I ran down shouting to them to stop and leave her alone, and then one guy ran towards me and he pulled out a flick knife and I stopped dead still and he marched towards me with intent. He raised the knife to me and I raised my hand to block his attack and I shouted to stop and it was like an explosion of power shot out of my hands and both the guys flew backwards and hit the ground! And then I woke up!"

"That's a pretty random dream, have you been watching M*urder on the Southern Coast* right before bedtime again?" Jack asked, laughing.

"No!" Ariana rolled her eyes, "but I did find another strange thing that I forgot to mention. I went into the attic to find old photos last night and I found some, and there is this one of my dad holding this ancient book and guess what? I found the same ancient book in the attic with the photos, and it's got all these weird symbols and writing on it. But that's not even the strangest part, no word of a lie, the writing in the book is in some strange language but when I was looking at the page, the words started changing and then the writing turned into English!" Ariana's face was flushed and fully animated as she recounted the astonishing event, waiting for Jack's reaction as she stared at his profile whilst he drove the car confidently through the narrow streets of Banbury town centre.

Jack glanced at Ariana quickly and back to the road ahead. "Hey, I hope you're not getting stressed about final coursework and exams. I hear the pressure can sometimes turn one's mind loop the loop!" his laughter filled the air, the deep tone of his voice vibrating as he openly chuckled aloud, his infectious laughter overflowing.

"Oh, shut up Jack! I was actually being serious…" but Ariana couldn't help but burst out laughing too, realising how ridiculous her story sounded. "Oh God, no one will believe me anyway!" she declared through her laughter as she sat back in her seat exasperated.

Jack turned expertly onto the campus driveway and into the student car park.

"So, when are you going to start learning to drive?" he asked, flashing his winning smile and turning to face her, clearly proud of his own driving skills and newfound independence.

Ariana studied Jack and as usual, her face crinkled into a big smile. He always made her smile. She couldn't be in his presence without smiling or for that matter without laughing at some point. Well, he was just so funny. That's why he was her best friend, but then the other night that had been… well, kind of weird, but she didn't know why her heart was racing right now as he held her gaze with that big, charming smile, those smouldering amber eyes and his lips… sensuous… *Stop it!* Ariana snapped her thoughts back to reality.

"Er, soon… I mean I am saving up a bit more first," she quickly responded before throwing him a light punch on the arm. "Come on, race you!" and with that she was out of the car and trotting up the campus drive to join the throng of students making their way to their respective classes, leaving Jack fumbling around for his car keys and bag before racing after her.

***

Rubbing her eyes might help, yes that must help surely. Ariana rubbed at her eyes and then looked at the words written on the blackboard, nope that didn't help. She rubbed at her eyes again, but it was futile; sighing, she focussed on the words again.

Mrs Roberts carried on talking whilst continuing to write on the board. Ariana glanced around the classroom. Her peers were all writing, copying what was on the board just as the teacher had asked. She looked down at her own notebook, apart from the date that she had written at the outset of the class, it was blank. She looked up at the board and it was happening again, the words just didn't make sense, they were changing, moving, floating and suddenly two words floated towards her:

"Power Symbols"

Ariana's hands instinctively reached up to touch the words and in an instant, they disappeared. Mrs Roberts turned to face the class; she was talking but Ariana wasn't listening. What had just happened? She looked at the blackboard and everything was as it should be. Ariana sat through the rest of the class, but she couldn't concentrate; maybe she needed to see a doctor. But she felt fine.

The Cocoon Within

Ding, ding, ding, ding, the continuous ringing of the school bell signalled that the day was over. Ariana hurriedly packed up her things and made a quick exit. She had to go to work, which was good, that should take her mind off these strange happenings! She hurried off campus and walked briskly. She put her ear pods in to listen to her favourite playlist, that's better, she jigged to the beat and sang along feeling uplifted. As she walked towards Abbot's corner, she suddenly remembered her dream and smiled and shook her head at the thought. She couldn't help it, she didn't want to look down the alleyway just in case, but she felt compelled to look. She came to a complete stop and removed her ear pods and slipped them in her pocket.

"Oh dear," her heart sank as she softly uttered the words.

The scene of her dream was happening right before her very eyes; two men were trying to take a woman's handbag and the woman started screaming.

Ariana's reaction was instant. She couldn't even remember deciding to run down the alleyway. "Stop! Leave her alone," she cried loudly.

Both men immediately turned to face her and one in a red hoodie ran towards her, then he stopped and pulled out a flick knife and marched towards Ariana with intent. He raised the knife and Ariana lifted her hand to block his attack and in an instant both men flew backwards with force and hit the ground as though a lightning bolt had blasted them.

"Oh my gosh! Are they dead?" Ariana hurried over to the men and looked at them, they were out cold, but she could see they were breathing. She looked over at the woman who was standing with her back to Ariana, the sound of her crying softly was audible.

"Are you alright? Did they hurt you?" Ariana asked.

The woman turned to face her, and Ariana gasped at what she saw. A face as white as snow, almost ghost-like, piercing green eyes the colour of the brightest and sharpest jade that Ariana had ever seen. But the most striking and unusual thing about the woman was that her face was covered with symbols; they didn't look like tattoos, instead, the symbols were formed by raised bumps of skin. On the woman's forehead, the raised bumps of skin were in the shape of a vivid, circular five-fold symbol.

Ariana continued to stare at this ghost-like woman's face, and for a fleeting moment she felt like she had seen her face before somewhere, but where?

The woman opened her mouth to speak and it was like she spoke in slow motion, as she vocalised the words,

"Power Symbols" the actual letters began to float out of the woman's mouth: P…O…W…E…R…S…Y…M…B…O…L…S and each letter floated towards Ariana in a steady line.

Ariana opened her mouth to speak but the woman's words floated right into her mouth, every last letter before Ariana could speak. Did the woman just say power symbols? Ariana turned around to check if the two men had started to come to, but they weren't there, they had disappeared. Where had they gone?! She turned back to the woman but now she wasn't there, she had disappeared too!

"What the…?"

Ariana was all alone in the alleyway. Feeling somewhat creeped out she decided not to hang about. She hurried back out of the alleyway, and she couldn't even remember how she got to the pet shop as her mind was a complete muddle over what had just happened.

"Hiya, you're a bit late, that's not like you. How was school?" Lara had her hands in the fish tank she was cleaning, and she glanced at Ariana as she walked into the shop, the little bell on the shop door jangled at the same time. "You ok?" Lara paused and turned with a furrowed brow as she peered over her glasses at Ariana. She liked Ariana she was such a vibrant and intelligent youngster, good company too and she had held many an interesting conversation with her over the couple of years she had worked for

Lara, and Lara was very fond of her, though today Ariana looked a little out of sorts.

"Oh, ha-ha, yes I'm fine, thanks. Sorry, I'm late it's just that there was… erm… just I had to stop to help er… rescue a bird that was in the road." Ariana cringed inside as she wondered why she couldn't think up a more plausible reason for being late.

"Oh, poor thing, you should have brought it in, we could have seen what we could do to help it," Lara turned back to cleaning the fish tank.

"Oh, I think it was just stunned. Once I picked it up it flapped a bit and then flew away." There, that sounded plausible.

Feeling better in Lara's company and busying herself with feeding and cleaning out the animals and serving the odd customer, Ariana began to relax again, though she still couldn't shake off what had happened in the alleyway. Who would believe her? It had been as real as day; she wasn't losing the plot, she was just about the sanest person around. She couldn't burden Granpey, he would just worry. She would tell Jack, make him listen and show him the evidence about the book. Yes, that's it, she has the photos on her phone and she could show him the book too; all of this started because of that darn book she was certain of it.

Mind made up, Ariana finished all her jobs with ease and stood back and admired her handy work. A car horn tooted, and she knew it was Jack coming to pick her up.

Lara looked up from the till, she was cashing up, "that'll be Jack then, are you not walking out with that lad yet?"

"Eh?" asked Ariana as she gathered up her things and popped them in her rucksack.

"Walking out, dating – the same thing," Lara smiled, fishing as she pushed her glasses up on her nose and peered at Ariana.

"Oh, ha-ha, what Jack? And me? No, we are just good friends." Ariana laughed awkwardly as she waved goodbye to Lara and hurried out the door and the little bell jangled.

The Cocoon Within

Lara watched thoughtfully as Ariana greeted Jack and climbed into his Fiesta.

"Hmm, if that's the case, then why are you blushing, my dear?" Lara softly voiced the question out loud, with a twinkle in her eye as she watched the two friends drive away.

"You're quiet, what's up with you?" asked Jack as he glanced over at Ariana and then back to the road as he flicked on the indicator and then pulled into Ariana's drive, before coming to a halt right outside the front steps.

"Come inside and I will tell you; just not out here and not in front of Granpey either." She was out of the car already.

Jack, sensing her urgency and serious tone quickly followed. "Why? What's wrong? You sound serious."

"Something happened today. I'll tell you when we are in private, but I will warn you now, I am not even sure where to begin."

He watched as she tried to open the front door with her key, but she was hurrying, and her keys dropped to the ground. "Oh, darn it!"

"Calm down and give me the keys, less haste more speed, Arry."

She visibly relaxed, only becoming aware of her heightened sense of urgency upon hearing his words. Funny, he was the only one who called her Arry. It had started as a joke when they were kids and he had called her a tomboy and started calling her Arry, which sounded like Harry, which he said was appropriate considering all she ever wanted to do was try to beat him at all the action stuff, like cycling, and karate, and every single X-box and Play Station game that they ever played.

Jack opened the door and Ariana followed him in. They could hear the sound of voices coming from the sitting room.

"I wonder who's here?" she gave him a surprised look, they hardly ever had visitors.

Ariana was very surprised to see two suited men rise from one of the sofas as she walked into the sitting room with Jack.

Granpey was sitting in his rocker. "This is my granddaughter, Ariana and her friend, Jack. I told you they'd be home soon," Granpey smiled at Ariana reassuringly.

The taller of the two men said, "I am Detective Inspector Jones, and this is my colleague DC Peterson."

"Nice to meet you," Ariana responded quite taken aback and curious as to why they were here.

"Hi, I'm Jack Johnson."

They all sat down and waited for the detectives to speak. After a short silence, Detective Jones explained, "You are no doubt wondering why we are here, so I will get straight to the point. I am sorry to have to say that there has been a serious knife attack on a young woman in the area."

Ariana gasped and her hand flew to her mouth. She felt Jack's arm move around her lower back in response to her reaction as they sat together on the old blue sofa opposite the detectives.

"Aye, it's a grand shame so it is. This used to be a safe neighbourhood, times are changing so they are," muttered Granpey, shaking his head and looking solemn.

The detective continued, "The attack took place earlier this evening at around six o'clock or just after, in the alleyway by Abbot's corner."

Ariana couldn't believe what she was hearing. She began to tremble, and she knew Jack could feel her trembling. She felt his gaze on her, but she dared not look at him. He rubbed her back gently.

"We found something of yours at the scene," said the detective, holding out his hand and in his palm was her locket!

Her hand flew to her neck; the chain was still around her neck just minus the locket.

"My locket, I didn't even know it had come off!" she cried as she stood and reached out to take it from the detective's hand. "Can I have it back? I mean you don't need it as evidence, do you?" she asked uncertainly.

"Yes, you can have it back now we have taken photos and samples for any DNA matches. We have established that this item is unrelated to the incident."

"Luckily the woman is recovering in hospital and is doing well. We were able to speak with her and she confirmed that her attackers were two young men, so we have good descriptions. We know that you were in the alleyway just before the attack; did you see anything suspicious or see any men in the area lurking around or sitting in a car anywhere nearby? Anything at all that you can remember?"

She couldn't tell them her story as it would sound too farfetched, and what if the two were not related? In her encounter the two men disappeared from the alleyway, so how could she explain that? No, better to keep silent on the matter.

"I don't remember seeing anything suspicious, but if something comes to mind, can I get back to you?" she asked.

"Of course, here is my card," the detective stood looking directly at Ariana as she took the card that he held out to her.

Granpey showed them out, leaving Jack and Ariana alone in the sitting room.

"You're not telling me something, what is it and why were you shaking? What happened?" Jack whispered to her looking concerned and still with his arm around her. Ariana felt safe with Jack; she was so glad he was here.

Granpey walked back in shaking his head and Jack stood up. Ariana immediately felt bereft and wished that Jack was back next to her with his arm around her. Oh God, why was she thinking about him in this way? Everything was just so confusing. She quickly shook her thoughts away.

"Granpey, how about a cup of tea?" asked Jack. "I'll put the kettle on."

Ariana listened to the sound of Jack filling the kettle and making tea. She looked at the card the detective had given her.

"Aye child, it's a wicked thing that was done to that poor young lass, so it is. If I could get my hands on those lads, I would teach them a lesson so I would," Granpey looked cross as he shook a fist in the air in anger.

"I know, it's just so awful," she agreed.

As Jack brought out the tea in mugs, he said, "You mustn't walk that way to work anymore, at least not until they find the culprits. You should have waited for me, I'd have dropped you. I don't mind taking you on your workdays, Arry," he looked intently at her.

"You're a good lad, Jack, it makes me feel a whole lot better knowing you are taking care of Ariana," said Granpey, visibly relaxing.

The three of them drank their tea in amiable silence until Granpey yawned and retired to his bedroom.

"Let's go to my room, I have to talk to you," said Ariana, grabbing Jack by the hand and literally yanking him up. He hurriedly drained the last of his tea and followed as instructed.

***

Behind the closed door of her bedroom, Ariana quickly relayed everything that had happened, leaving out no details. Jack sat down on the little vanity stool opposite Ariana's bed, a frown on his face, deep in thought.

"Well?" she asked, impatiently.

"Well, I'm just trying to get my head around all of this," he replied, looking intently at her. "I do believe you, ok, but not many would, so in terms of keeping silent, that makes sense at least for now while we figure out what is going on." He continued to look at her thoughtfully. "Hey, maybe you have developed some sort of strange ability to see into the future right before it happens; next time how about focussing your mind on where to buy a winning lotto ticket or something like that?" his face crinkled into laughter.

"Oh, Jack, stop it. this is serious!"

His laughter was contagious. Why he always made her laugh so much she could never fathom; this wasn't even a funny situation, but she thought it better to laugh than cry!

After their mad moment of laughter had passed, Ariana became serious again, and she pulled the book out from under her bed. "Look."

He came over and sat next to her on the bed and lifted the book from her hands. Holding it in his lap, he studied it.

"Wow, you weren't joking about it being an ancient book, and it's quite fascinating too, quite unusual," he remarked as he studied the cover with intensity and turned the pages to peer at the writing. "This is one of a kind by the looks of it."

"But Jack, see how the first page is in English and the rest are in a foreign language." She reached over and turned the pages back to the first page that had transformed before her very eyes when she had first opened the book.

He looked at the page. "It's not in English; is this the right page?"

"Huh?" Ariana looked again and turned the page to check if it was the first page. Perhaps she had missed a page, but no it was the first page. "What is going on? Why has it changed back? This is getting weirder now!"

"Are you sure you weren't dreaming this bit about the book?"

"No, Jack! Hang on, I have a photo. Let me get my phone."

She scrolled frantically on her phone. The pictures had better be there... yes! They were!

"Look, see I told you! Zoom in, see for yourself." She thrust her phone at him urgently and peered over his shoulder as he looked at the photos, "See?"

He kept swiping to and from each photo and zooming in to get a closer look at the text on each page. "Wow, well you definitely weren't dreaming then."

"Well, what do you think I should do?"

After a thoughtful pause, he replied, "Nothing." He looked at her quite seriously which seemed strange for Jack, as he was always such a fun, happy-go-lucky guy pretty much all the time. "Just do nothing. You haven't got anything to tell really. I mean, it's all an experience that has happened to you; no one can verify your story, and no one will believe you, except me of course, plus you don't want anyone thinking you've lost the plot. I say do nothing at least for now."

Later that evening, when Ariana was alone and sitting in bed, thinking about everything that had transpired in the last twenty-four hours, she concluded that Jack was right, there was no point saying anything to anyone especially when she had no idea what was going on herself. Feeling restless, she decided to look through the book again. Perhaps she could find clues or something to help her understand what this all meant.

She supposed she should feel scared of this book after all the strange goings on of the day, but she didn't. Oddly, she felt a sense of peace as she held it. She had noticed it the first time she had held it. Kind of strange, but she also felt something else that she couldn't quite put her finger on. She pondered what she was feeling inside as she held the book in her hands. And then it suddenly dawned on her that the feeling she was experiencing was as though she had been away for a long time and had finally come home. How bizarre! But that was it; holding the book gave her an undeniable sense that she was home, that she belonged, and that she was meant to have this book.

Sitting in silence as she looked again at the intricate cover of this unusual book, Ariana remembered that her father had held this very

The Cocoon Within

book in his hands and she smiled as she turned the page. There it was again, she watched as the foreign words on the first page transformed into English just as before. Ariana quickly turned to the next page and the same thing happened, she read the words:

Awaken, awaken o sleeping one,
Arise from your slumber and become one that is known,
Run with lions and let the transformation begin,
Arise o sleeping one,
Let the battle begin.

"What does this all mean?" she asked under her breath, as she read and re-read the words.

A loud knock on her door made her jump. She slipped the book under her duvet. "Come in!" she called, knowing it would be Granpey checking she was ok after today's events, though he usually avoided climbing the stairs due to his arthritis.

He popped his head around her door and asked, "Are you ok, Sweetpea? I just wanted to check up on you. It's been a heck of a day."

"Thanks, Granpey, I'm ok. Are we still going to the dog shelter tomorrow?"

"Aye, let's go as planned, eh? Something to brighten us all up a bit. Don't stay up too late, lass."

"Thanks, Granpey, I won't." She smiled cheerfully at him.

He closed the door and she listened to his slow footsteps as he descended the stairs. She strained to hear his bedroom door close so she could relax, knowing he was safely in his room.

"I had better get some sleep, you can go back under my bed for now," she said to the book, popped it under her bed and switched her bedside lamp off. As she snuggled into her duvet, she returned to mulling over the poetic words of the book, though it wasn't long before she drifted off to sleep.

2
Let the Battle Begin

Toot, Toot! Ariana grabbed the large wicker basket that she had borrowed from the pet store; Lara had said that she could take whatever she needed as long as she returned it intact.

"Ready, Granpey? Jack's here!" she called loudly.

"Aye, Sweetpea, I'm coming." Granpey walked with a slight limp out of his room, pulled on his brown anorak and opened the front door holding it wide for Ariana so that she could get the basket and herself through it with ease.

"Thanks, Granpey!" Ariana's face lit up as Jack strode towards her taking the wicker basket from her and placing it in his open boot. He shoved some bits and pieces aside to ensure it was in properly.

"Did you sleep well?" Jack asked as he cast a sideways glance at her. "No funny dreams?" he smiled at her.

Ariana's heart melted at his smile. Why does he look so handsome? And how come she is only just starting to notice this recently? She averted her eyes and pretended to focus on what he was doing as he closed the boot securely.

"Oh yes, thanks and no strange dreams thank goodness! I think I am done with self-fulfilling prophesies!" She laughed and their eyes locked in laughter. Did she catch a fleeting glimpse of emotion on his face as he studied her? She shook her head, gosh what is going on with her lately?

"Well, that's good, now let's go and choose you a dog!" Jack beamed, his gaze lingering on Ariana as she returned his smile and climbed into the back seat of the car.

He shook his head and turned his attention to Granpey who was already climbing into the front seat of the car, then he hopped into the driver's side and off they went.

They chatted animatedly and laughed at Granpey's funny stories all the way to the dog shelter. Ariana was so excited; this was a late birthday gift from Granpey. He had wanted to buy her a puppy, but Ariana had insisted on getting a homeless dog instead. The background checks, home visits and application process had taken a while, but it was worth it. Ariana looked over at Jack and Granpey as they chatted happily to one another. When Jack eventually pulled up outside the dog shelter and they all climbed out of the car, Ariana could sense their excitement too and this was turning out to be a lovely day out together. She loved that when the three of them were together, it felt like her family was complete. She had never told Jack that, nor how important he was to her as her closest friend.

Jack already had the dog basket out of the boot in seconds and strode ahead to the dog shelter entrance. Ariana walked with Granpey at his slower pace, and she looped her arm through his to give him a little support as the arthritis in his knee was playing up this morning.

"Hey, Sweetpea, today is turning out to be a good day so it is. Are you happy, my love?" he asked as they walked together.

"It really is a lovely day, and I am very happy and excited that I am actually going to be a dog owner today! Our very own dog; this will be great for you too, Granpey, good company whilst I am out all day."

"Aye, lass, I think so too," smiled Granpey, happy to see Ariana so joyous. "Now don't you worry about those detectives last night; they'll catch those nasty buggers to be sure."

"I hope so." Ariana was thoughtful for a moment and wondered at her own experience in the alleyway mirroring an identical crime in the same spot that took place an hour or so later. Had she imagined the whole thing? Yet it had been so real to her.

Jack was stooped down talking to one of the dogs through the mesh door of its cage. "Hey, Arry, what about this little fellow?"

She looked at the little brown and white fluffy dog that was bouncing around with so much energy, its wriggling body seemingly uncontrollable, as its little tail wagged with furious enthusiasm in response to the attention from Jack.

"Aww, he is so cute, though I just know that I'll know the one when I see him... or her." Ariana was sure she would feel a connection as soon as she saw the right dog for her, she would just know which dog was the one. She left Jack bemused with his little playmate and wandered on.

She strolled by the identical cubicles that held dogs of all different sizes and breeds and eventually, she stopped, caught by the gaze of a rather petite, somewhat scruffy-looking terrier. It was the unusual stare of the dog with one blue eye and one molten brown eye, and head cocked to the side with intent eye contact, that immediately captured Ariana's heart. The little dog ran to the mesh door as she approached, holding her gaze with its intelligent stare, tail wagging animatedly.

Ariana put her fingers through the mesh and the little terrier immediately nuzzled them, straining for her touch. "Aww, hello there, aren't you just so adorable!" The terrier yapped a greeting and stood on his hind legs, front paws on the mesh door as if trying to force it open. "You're the one," she whispered softly as she held the little dog's gaze and he immediately rolled over and then sat up obediently, demonstrating a well-trained and intelligent nature. Ariana beamed with joy as she felt that spark of yearning inside her and she knew that she was completely decided upon this little terrier. There was just something about it. She looked around for Jack and Granpey, they were looking at another dog further down.

"Granpey! Jack!" she called with urgency, "this is the one I want."

She bent down to read the sign on the mesh door of the terrier's cage:

"My name is Leo. I love people and children. I am friendly and loyal, and I like to play. I might chase small animals so keep an eye out for that, I might have different coloured eyes but no need to worry about that as I can see perfectly well. I'll be a friend for life, and I won't ever let you down."

"What's wrong with his eyes?" asked Jack as he stopped next to Ariana and looked at little Leo.

"Nothing, the sign says he can see perfectly well, he was just born with different coloured eyes. I think it's endearing and suits him; his name is Leo a perfect name! I definitely want him, I'm sure I have a connection with him already."

"Leo it is then!" smiled Granpey.

The paperwork was all signed and they were out in under an hour. Jack carried Leo in the wicker basket and popped it onto the back seat of the car. Ariana sat beside Leo talking to him and encouraging him, wondering if he was a little nervous, though he didn't actually seem to be as his little tail was wagging all the time.

"He looks really happy," she stated matter-of-factly.

"I'm sure that he is, Sweetpea," responded Granpey from the front of the car.

"Hey, we can take him for walks together. I know some great walking spots," Jack was already planning where they could take Leo. "He's gonna love it and he won't be bored, that's for sure."

"We can take him to Botswood forest; he'll love that!" cried Ariana. She had always wanted a dog ever since she was small and now her dream had come true, she was over the moon.

The three of them chatted enthusiastically non-stop all the way home. Yes, today was a happy day, a truly good day.

Leo made a great addition to the family and both Ariana and Granpey were surprised at how quickly he settled in. Flower the cat was completely indifferent to Leo, she just went about her usual business unperturbed. They had been given Flower by an elderly neighbour just before she had to move into a care home and she had also had a little dog, so Flower had been accustomed to living with a dog for many years, though the little dog had died just before the lady had to move. So, Flower was pretty much unaffected by Leo's presence and carried on with her cat life as usual. Meanwhile, Leo was Ariana's shadow; wherever she went, he followed, and to Ariana, it seemed as though he had always been with her, and she now couldn't imagine life without him. She wondered why they hadn't gotten a dog much sooner.

"Granpey, I'm just taking Leo out for his walk!" called Ariana loudly. She paused as she waited for the reply, her hand suspended in mid-air holding onto Leo's leash. Leo was in an identical mode of pause, waiting for Granpey's reply.

A couple of coughs later and the reply came, "Aye, Sweetpea, no walking through the forest alone at this hour and take the main roads!" he called in return from his bedroom. Ariana knew Granpey was worried about her, what with the recent attack on the young woman and the culprits still at large.

"I will, bye!" And with that, she was out the door with Leo at her side happily trotting along.

"Ah, boy this is the life!" Ariana was happy; she was doing really well at school, she had aced her mock exams, her coursework was on track, and she felt pretty proud of herself for being really disciplined in her studies. Granpey had said how proud her mum and dad would have been if they could see her now. She felt for her locket around her neck, and smoothed her thumb and forefinger over it as was her habit, smiling to herself as she thought about them being proud of her.

She remembered how often she had felt envious of people that still had their parents around. She used to sit in the shopping mall and people-watch, and there she would observe mothers with their daughters, and she would feel a deep-seated yearning for what they had as they shopped together, laughing, linking arms, trying on clothes and thoroughly enjoying one another's company on girly days out. She would watch doting fathers with their daughters, that special relationship that only daughters had with their fathers. She often pondered how safe and protected those daughters must have felt whilst they walked beside their big strong caring fathers, as they held that special place in their father's heart. Ariana sighed as she remembered herself being obsessed with watching others in that way. She hadn't been to the shopping mall in ages and that was intentional. She still looked on wistfully whenever she encountered a mother and daughter or a father and daughter, but nowadays she only allowed herself a fleeting thought of what could have been. The luxury of a single brief moment before she switched her thoughts to something else, no dwelling allowed, no what-if's.

She had decided one summer's day, after crying her eyes out in the public toilets in the Addeson shopping centre, that it just wasn't fair to herself or to the memory of her parents to keep dwelling on what could have been, and from that day onwards, she had never allowed herself more than a fleeting moment to reflect on what could have been.

Realising that she had pretty much walked to Jack's house without even thinking about where she was going, she thought that she might as well knock for him.

"Let's go see if Jack's about, come on boy!" Leo responded wagging his tail eagerly, his eyes on Ariana as he matched her pace as she opened the iron gate that led to Jack's place. Leading Leo down the little garden path that was set in the middle of one of the most beautifully kept front gardens that led to a fine Victorian house, nestled in a rather swanky cul-de-sac situated in the village of Bloxham Vale. She had noticed Jack's car parked out front behind his dad's car, so he must be home.

Ding dong! The doorbell chimed loudly when Ariana pressed it and after a rather long wait, the immaculately clean white front door with its intricate stained-glass windows, in keeping with the house itself one might add, swung open to reveal Jack wearing nothing but a pair of blue-grey boxer shorts, sports socks, and an oversized dressing gown. Ariana's eyes travelled from Jack's face as he munched on a piece of toast, slowly down the entire length of his body and back up to his face, a smile crinkling on her lips at the same time.

"Well, at least you're not wearing a onesie!" she laughed, as she admired Jack's brown-skinned complexion, of which she had always been envious considering her own rather pale skin.

Jack's smile lit up his face and with a glint in his eye, he did a little twirl and a bow with a dramatic sweeping arc of his arm. "Jack Johnson at your service, ma'am! I sensed you were coming so I thought I'd keep it low-key," he winked at Ariana as he munched the last bit of his toast and licked and sucked the butter from his fingers, making popping sounds as he went along each finger.

"Eew, how old are you again? Five?" Ariana rolled her eyes in fake disgust. "Get dressed and let's go walking, come on!"

Leo barked excitedly as if on cue to say *hurry up let's go!*

Jack threw his head back and laughed. "Give me five and I'll be with you," he said, signalling for them to come in as he dashed upstairs to get changed.

Closing the front door behind her, Ariana looked at herself in the large ornate mirror in the hallway. Her green eyes were bright, set in a beautiful oval face with perfect cupid bow lips, framed with her bouncy, long red curls. She cocked her head to one side as she studied her own reflection and thought how much she looked like a little pixie. "Well, a cute pixie at least," she said to herself.

"A beautiful pixie," Jack whispered behind her, making her jump, heart pounding.

"Jack!" She turned around wanting to give him a thump, but she misjudged how close he was standing to her, and she ended up in his arms taking them both by surprise with her sudden movement. His arms immediately went around her to steady them both from stumbling over.

Suddenly, Ariana's heart was thumping in her chest at his proximity. She raised her eyes to look at Jack's face just a few inches from hers. Was he going to kiss her? Jack's eyes were holding her gaze intently, and then she saw him look at her lips and she felt a sudden surge of excitement as she watched him lower his head towards her...

"Oh, Ariana, how lovely to see you!" it was Jack's father!

They jumped apart, Jack brushing his hand through his hair and Ariana noticed his face redden slightly.

"Hi, Mr Johnson, how are you?" Ariana smiled enthusiastically, her heart was still racing, unsure if she was glad for the interruption or not.

"I am very well, my dear. How's your grandfather? And I see you have a little friend with you too." As he looked down at Leo, he approached and gave him a little stroke. Leo wagged his tail in response.

"Granpey is good, thank you. His arthritis has been playing up a bit lately but other than that, he's fine, thanks for asking."

"Tell him hello from me," Jack's father smiled.

As they said their goodbyes and left, Jack closed the front door behind them.

"This little fellow seems to have settled in with you guys really well," Jack observed looking at Leo and giving Ariana a sideways glance before bending down to pet Leo.

"Yeah, he is no trouble at all, follows me everywhere. I think whoever he lived with before has trained him really well. He fetches things, sits, heels and even stands on his hind legs to open doors, a great help for Granpey by the way and he can do little tricks too. Look..."

They stopped as Ariana demonstrated with a few waves of her hand and some commands and Leo responded by rolling over, then jumping up and lastly, he ran and collected a gift of some sticks and heeled.

"Very impressive!" Jack was rather amazed.

"Hey, let's go through Botswood forest for a bit. He'll love that."

"Sounds like a plan."

Together Jack, Ariana and Leo walked in the direction of the forest, Ariana and Jack chatted amicably about their future plans for Uni amongst other things.

"So, you haven't spoken about your love interest in quite a while?" Ariana smiled cheekily at him but secretly she wanted to gauge how he really felt. Did he still have a piping hot crush on Jessica Brown or not? She pondered at the signals he had been giving her lately, ever since their moment in her bedroom the other day, and he had been about to kiss her just a moment ago too.

"Jessica who?" Jack's eyes were dancing with humour as they met Ariana's eyes and almost involuntarily, they both burst out laughing.

They reached the entrance to Botswood and Ariana unclipped Leo's leash and watched as he sped off through the forest like an excited child, exuberantly crashing through piles of autumn leaves and bouncing over fallen trees. Together Jack and Ariana walked further into the forest with just the sound of leaves rustling underfoot, birdsong in the trees, and the odd squirrel scurrying around.

Ariana thought about how Jack was the only other person apart from Granpey, that she could be with in total silence without any awkwardness, just natural, easy, amicable silence, and it dawned on her how much they just understood one another. She didn't know why she had felt so ecstatic when Jack had replied, *'Jessica who?'* just now, even though he had been kind of joking, he could have meant it too. Ariana pondered if it was because she wanted to be romantically involved with Jack now. Had their friendship shifted across the line and into the romantic arena? And if so, was it real or was it just a spark of passionate interest that might fade once tried? Ariana really wasn't sure, but one thing she was sure of was that she didn't want to ruin the amazing friendship that they had.

The bright autumn sunlight penetrated through to the forest floor up ahead signifying they were approaching the open clearing that was known as the Sparrow's Nest. Ariana wondered why it was given that name. Leo had already darted like a bullet through the clearing minutes before.

"Race you to the Sparrow's Nest," and with that Ariana raced off ahead of Jack taking him by surprise, though he quickly caught up and overtook her, leaping over a log, looking at her and laughing as he sped past her.

He waited for Ariana to catch up with him, as he stood in the clearing that they call the Sparrow's Nest, arms stretched wide and face heavenward, enjoying the autumn sun rays beaming directly on his upturned face. "Ah, this is amazing, there is nothing like the sun on your face," he said as he stood still in the large circular clearing which was surrounded at the edges by thick trees that led deeper into the forest.

Leo must have sped across the clearing and into another part of the forest somewhere as he was nowhere to be seen.

"Mmm, I love it," said Ariana and did the same as they stood together soaking up the early morning autumn rays in the suntrap of the Sparrow's Nest.

"Hang on a minute, is that Leo barking in the distance? Listen," Jack lowered his arms and looked around.

"It is Leo!" cried Ariana as the barking got louder and then it sounded quite frantic and before they could react, far off in the distance two people burst through the thicket of trees, running in their direction at high speed.

"They are running pretty fast, I'm not sure if we should run too," said Jack as he grabbed Ariana's hand and started pulling her backwards. "They look like they are either running away from something or running at us…" Jack's voice trailed off as he tried to understand what was happening.

Ariana's heart was racing, adrenaline pumping, she knew something was wrong but what was going on and where was Leo?

They both started edging backwards as they watched the two men. How were they running so fast? They had covered distance like they were bionic and were getting closer as Leo's barking grew louder. Then she saw Leo bomb into the clearing chasing after the two…

"What the…?" cried Jack and at the same time Ariana's sharp intake of breath could be heard as she gripped Jack's hand tightly.

The faces of the two men running at high speed towards her and Jack now came into focus and what she saw astounded her. The men's faces looked… distorted… and then as they got close enough to make out their appearance, Ariana could see that they didn't look like human faces! Their heads were large as were their muscular bodies, and they were really, really, tall, they looked like they were eight or nine feet tall! Their faces looked a sort of strange, pale greyish colour, with eyes, nose, mouth and ears just like a human, set in their oversized uneven heads, their wide jaws were open, snarling, exposing rows of ferocious-looking jagged teeth. They looked quite terrifying, and angry amber eyes focussed intently on her and Jack as they raced towards them.

"Oh, my God!"

"Get behind me; we can't outrun them!" Jack tried to shield Ariana and as one of the beings reached out its huge hand complete with talons to take a swipe at Jack, Leo came out of nowhere, jumped into the air with lightning speed and as he did so, a mighty roar could be heard and he transformed instantly into a gigantic, winged, silvery-golden lion that proceeded to maul and kill the greyish being with one precise bite to its neck!

Ariana and Jack both fell backwards to the forest floor as they watched in shock at the scene unfolding before them. The other being drew a translucent sword from nowhere and Leo, now a giant majestic-looking silver-gold winged lion, struck out harshly with his claws making contact with the giant being across its chest and face, ripping its greyish-coloured torso open, blood streaming from its chest and face. The lion struck viciously again and again until the grey being dropped to the ground, severely wounded and the lion delivered a fatal bite to its neck.

Ariana and Jack watched open-mouthed as the two bodies began to melt away before their very eyes until there was no evidence left of their existence. They stared at the huge, majestic lion as it walked rather regally towards them and then sat down in front of them, towering over them at a great height of six or maybe even seven feet. Its beautiful, silvery-golden feathered wings spread wide and began to fold inwards until they rested neatly on the lion's back. Ariana couldn't stop staring at the lion's huge silvery-gold mane. It appeared to shimmer with every subtle movement and was undoubtedly the most beautiful creature that she had ever seen in her entire life.

Suddenly, the lion appeared to melt away, fading subtly until it became nothing but an apparition which was replaced in bodily form by Leo, her beloved and faithful little terrier. Ariana and Jack still sitting on the grass in stunned silence, watched as Leo got up, casually walked over to Ariana, curled up by her side and rested his head in her lap, before staring up at her lovingly with his mismatched eyes.

"What the… I mean what just happened?" Jack was first to speak, his eyes wide and with an incredulous look on his face.

"I… I… don't know," Ariana shook her head slowly as she stroked Leo, looking at him in awe, yet half expecting him to roar. "I mean you saw them too, didn't you? Two strange people, I mean they weren't people in the human sense but creatures… I mean, I don't know what they were! And they were running for us, they would have killed us if not for Leo! I mean who'd have thought… no one would believe us." She stood up and paced up and down, her voice rising as she spoke, "So, this little terrier that I have had living with me and Granpey all this time, is not really a dog… well he's a dog on most days… but a lion on days when crazy creatures from another dimension or somewhere are trying to kill us!" Ariana sounded near hysterical as she paced up and down, while Leo sat up staring at her calmly. "And look, I'm shaking!" She held out her arms, which were shaking from the fright.

"Ariana, stop!" commanded Jack as he stood and held Ariana's arms giving her a little shake to calm her ranting. "Yes, I saw Leo turn into a giant lion with wings and kill those crazy things, but we are both ok, no harm came to either of us and now we just need to figure out what to do and if we should tell anyone what just happened."

"Yes, yes you're right. Ok… but what if they come back?"

Jack stared from Ariana to Leo and back. "They looked pretty dead to me, at least up until the point that they melted away," he shrugged, and they stood looking at each other in silence for a moment before bursting into laughter.

After laughing hysterically for a good full five minutes or so, they composed their thoughts on the matter.

"The only good thing about this experience is that you saw it all too," declared Ariana. "Not like the last time in the alleyway when I saw the strange woman with the symbols on her face."

"What do you think it all means?" he asked, keen to get to the bottom of it. That was Jack's way, he was a natural problem solver. To Jack, it was never a matter of the impossible but a case of there always being a way forward, a solution, you just had to find it.

"I don't know," she shrugged, thinking about the strange encounters of late. She looked down at Leo as they began to walk back the way they had come. Ariana, half expecting Leo to transform again, kept straying her eyes back to check every few seconds or so, but nope, he was still a regular dog.

"Hey, didn't you say that the pale ghostly woman with the symbols spoke words that floated into your mouth?"

"Oh yes, I forgot about that. I was too busy trying to get over other worldly beings trying to kill us to remember those weird details. Seems so long ago now." It was rather ironic how that didn't seem to concern her so much now after this crazy experience.

"Yes, but what were the words, Arry? This could be a clue to what is happening," Jack was insistent.

"*Power symbols*, those were the words and… the book has symbols of an eagle, and a fivefold symbol the same as on the woman's face and then a lion and something else I can't remember."

"Hmm, ok let's check out the book when we get back to yours?" He said and then stopped suddenly.

"Jack, what is it?"

"We've been walking for about twenty minutes, so we should have reached the road by now… but we are still in the forest, that's weird." He looked around and they were still in the thick of the forest. "What the…?"

Ariana looked around at the trees, "Erm, I think it's this way," she said, pointing to her left. She felt sure that was the way they had come, it looked familiar. No, wait, or was it that way? She looked to her right, but now she wasn't so sure, though she had come to the forest many times and she knew her way home, but right now it all looked the same whichever way she turned.

"Give me your scarf, Arry," Jack ordered.

She complied, removing her scarf before handing it to him. Then she watched as he tied it tightly around a branch on a nearby tree.

"Right, that way if we come back full circle, we'll know. Ok, now let's get out of here." He took hold of Ariana's hand and they set off. Jack led the way determined to get them both out of the forest before any more strange beings decided to appear out of nowhere.

They walked and talked and walked and talked, on and on they went but the forest seemed never-ending. Their conversation began to slow down until it petered out as they grew weary and the reality of the fact that they could be lost dawned on them.

"Leo, why can't you lead us home? C'mon boy, take us home!" Ariana was ready to try anything; she wished she had trained Leo on what home meant so he could lead the way.

"We have been walking for over an hour now, this is ridiculous!" cried Jack as he swung around looking at the trees surrounding them. "It feels like we are just going deeper and deeper into the forest!"

"Jack, look, it's my scarf!" Ariana cried pointing to her scarf that Jack had tied to a tree over an hour and a half ago.

"No, no, no!" he ran to the tree and lifted the scarf as it hung from the branch that he had tied it to. "What is going on? Why have we found ourselves back in exactly the same spot after walking for over an hour?" Ariana had never seen Jack so exasperated, as he scratched his head in confusion.

"Jack, look," she whispered, "we're being watched."

Jack immediately froze on instant high alert as he scanned the trees. Ariana knew he was half-expecting another attack of the giant grey creatures as was she, her heart was racing in anticipation.

"Just there, through the trees, keep watching and you'll see someone is trying to spy on us," she whispered, nudging Jack in the direction straight up ahead.

Someone or something was peeping from behind a tree in the distance. Suddenly, what looked like a person peered again; Ariana got a much better look and she saw that it looked like a person with a pale white, ghost-like face. The person stood apart from the tree stared at them for a moment and then turned and ran.

"It's the woman! I swear it looks like the woman from the alleyway!" shouted Ariana, and taken by surprise at seeing her again, began to run after her, not wanting to lose her.

"Arry wait! It could be dangerous!" cried Jack as he ran after her.

"I have to catch her, I just have to!" she shouted back as she continued to chase and suddenly the forest opened up to a clearing which was actually at a cliff top, with nowhere else to run other than to turn back and return the way they came. Ariana watched as the woman ran to the edge of the cliff top, stopped and turned to face Ariana who by now had stopped several metres away. Leo was barking frantically and pulling on his leash. Jack emerged running through the clearing and stopped at Ariana's side.

"Who are you?" shouted Ariana in desperation as she looked at the woman whose piercing green eyes stared unwaveringly back at Ariana, her strange symbol-covered face and pale ghost-like skin creating an eerie figure against the backdrop of the sunset behind her.

Leo's leash slipped from Ariana's hand as he pulled with strength. She gasped and watched as he immediately stopped barking and ran to the woman and to Ariana's surprise, sat obediently at her side.

"What on earth…?" Jack's voice trailed off, just as surprised.

Then the woman spoke, *"Matato shokarat Eriat, berimata shorut shapiedah, halo et shadeia!"*

"Who are you?" Ariana cried boldly, asking again in frustration at not being able to understand the woman's words.

Jack lay his hand on Ariana's arm as though to steady her or restrain her frustration, she wasn't sure which.

"I am Eriat! The one sent to answer the call," the woman's shrill accented voice rang out loudly.

Both Ariana and Jack were visibly taken aback by the high-pitched response, this time in English.

"Who sent you?" Ariana quickly asked with determination. She wasn't going anywhere without some answers; her heart was beating wildly as she waited with bated breath for the response.

The woman spread her arms and the cloak she was wearing fell aside and as she opened them wider, she spoke again, "The one afore the beginning, the one who hath no end…" And with that, she leaned backwards over the cliff's edge, arms stretched wide and allowed herself to freefall backwards over the cliff edge.

"No!!" cried Ariana in shock as both she and Jack ran to the cliff's edge and looked down, but they couldn't see the woman; she had vanished.

"Quick, let's get away from here," Jack took hold of Ariana's hand, picked up Leo's leash and together they hurried back through the forest, and this time they quickly found their way out and back to the sunny streets of Bloxham Vale.

Ariana looked at her watch, "It's only eleven thirty in the morning!" she looked at Jack, her expression incredulous. "But we were in the forest for hours and hours and we even saw the sun begin to set and I don't even know how the time passed so quickly in the forest, so unless my watch is wrong, how can it still be morning?"

"My phone says eleven thirty-two, so we can't both be wrong. After everything we have just seen, nothing surprises me now!" Jack walked up to a passer-by and asked for the time and then he walked back to Ariana and Leo.

"Your watch and my phone are right, I knew it! We must have entered some kind of parallel universe or another dimension where time moves quicker or slower… I am not even sure which, but surely that's the only possible explanation," Jack shrugged. "But right now I'm starving, let's get food, all this crazy stuff is giving me some sort of brain fog and I need to eat, come on!"

He was right, they needed to get some food and downtime and try to figure out what on earth was going on, what the woman from the alleyway was talking about, and what they needed to do next.

Jack half-dragged her and Leo to Marco's chippy and they sat at one of the plastic tables to enjoy their crispy battered cod and chips in amiable silence, just the sound of the radio playing softly in the background. Ariana hadn't realised just how hungry she was, it must have been all that walking in the forest for hours that had built up her appetite. She was never usually able to finish a whole portion of chips from Marco's, he always gave such generous portions. They had bought Leo a couple of sausages, and he was happily eating them just outside the shop door. He would wait obediently outside for them, and his leash didn't even need to be tied to anything.

"So, we have to come to terms with the fact that Leo is actually a lion in disguise, how amazing is that!" said Jack. "And he's not even a regular lion… oh no… he is a giant-sized lion that can fly. I mean was that even real? Could we somehow have both imagined it all?" He scrunched up his empty chip paper and threw it neatly into the bin as though taking a basketball shot and then leaned back in his chair folding his arms in front of him.

"Nope," she replied, "definitely not imagined, that's for sure. I know what I saw, plus our brains can't imagine the same thing at exactly the same time, right?" Ariana carried on munching the last of her chips.

"I know, I know, wishful thinking I guess, but clearly this all means something. We need to get back to yours, I have a feeling the answers are in that book," Jack enthused.

"Yep, let's go." Ariana quickly popped the last bit of her crispy cod in her mouth before passing Jack her scrunched-up chip paper which he proceeded to throw in the bin making another perfect shot.

The plastic chairs scraped noisily on the floor as they pushed them back and stood up.

"Bye, Marco!" Jack called loudly, and he got a thank you from Marco, accompanied by a huge smile, as larger than life Marco stood behind the counter, shovelling more chips into the fryer, and Ariana waved to him as they left.

Back at Ariana's, and after a hurried greeting to Granpey, who was in his rocker in front of the TV, indulging in his favourite pastime, fully engrossed in an old Western film, they went straight to her room to see what clues they could find in the book.

Sitting side by side on the bed, Ariana opened the book and started from where she had left off, and as if on cue, the unknown words on the next page transformed before their very eyes into

English. Ariana slowly read the words aloud savouring each sentence as though by reading slowly some revelation might come to them:

"For we do not wrestle with mere mortals,
Flesh and blood is not our enemy.

How then do we earn victory o'er those that fight against us?

Do they perish by the edge of the sword?

Or do we take hold of the power bestowed upon us gracious ones,
to tear down immortal strongholds and fortresses alike?"

"Well, that's it then," decided Jack, "this book is the cause of all this chaos, quite literally. Maybe we should burn the book? That might put a stop to any more strange creatures showing up?"

"Then we might never find out where this all leads," she argued. "I mean think for a moment, Jack, we could be the only two people on Earth that have discovered that there are living things outside of our everyday earthly lives. That's a momentous discovery in itself!" she looked at him, wide-eyed in amazement.

"I suppose… though I wasn't thinking that when one of the giant creatures tried to kill us," he said rather ironically as he looked back at her with that twinkle in his eyes, and after a moment's pause, they both fell about in a fit of laughter.

"Oh, Jack, what does this all mean? It's kind of exciting yet scary at the same time," she asked after finally catching her breath after all that giggling.

"I don't know, but at least you have Leo the Lion to protect you if you ever see any more of those giant creatures." They both looked at little Leo sleeping on Ariana's fluffy pink rug in the centre of her bedroom. He looked so sedate and harmless, quite the opposite of the roaring lion they had witnessed some hours ago. "Meanwhile, I need to get going. I promised Dad I would go with him to pick up my Aunt Jenna from the airport this afternoon."

Jack stood and smiled cheekily at Ariana. She smiled back, and that weird heart pounding started again, which she tried to ignore.

He held out his hand to her, she put her hand in his, and he pulled her up to stand facing him. He towered over her at just shy of six feet with his athletic build and handsome young face. She noticed a slight hint of stubble around his jaw line as she smiled at him as she always did whenever she looked at his familiar face.

"So, Miss cute red-headed pixie girl," Jack winked at her mischievously and to her embarrassment, she blushed, "I'll be off then, thanks for the strange adventure and text me if anything else happens." With that, he gave her a quick affectionate hug and left.

Was she disappointed that he hadn't taken the opportunity to kiss her just now? She wasn't sure. Her racing heart began to return to normal.

"Bye Jack!" Ariana called loudly as she listened to his footsteps running down the stairs. She sat back on her bed and allowed her thoughts the luxury of replaying in her mind the strange events of the day.

Putting the unexplainable aside, a few things were pretty clear to Ariana. One of those things was that Leo was no ordinary dog and that she had chosen him because she had felt a strong connection to him, from the moment she had clapped eyes on him. She now strongly believed that it wasn't a coincidence that she had chosen him. Perhaps he had been sent to protect her and Jack from those creatures, but sent by whom? Ariana watched Leo as he yawned and stretched out on her pink rug, looking as relaxed as ever. She shook her head in disbelief, no one would believe all that they had encountered in the last twenty-four hours.

Another thing that seemed pretty clear to Ariana was that the woman from the alleyway was probably not a foe which would mean that she must be some kind of ally. The fact that Leo had protected her and Jack from the creatures and he had also sat obediently at the alleyway woman's feet, validated Ariana's conclusion that the woman must have been sent to help in some way. But then why the backwards dive off the cliff? Why not stay and tell all? It kind of didn't make sense; none of this made any sense. There was something about the woman that seemed familiar, as Ariana pondered this, suddenly realisation dawned on her that she had seen the ghostly woman before! Yes, the exact same face, she was sure it was the woman in a dream she once had, where she had been chased by terrifying creatures with amber eyes! How could she have forgotten about that dream? Or rather… nightmare! It was the same face of the woman in her dream, that had held out her hand to help her! Ariana felt frustrated that she didn't have all the answers, but what she did know was that she was so glad that she had Leo, and she would make sure that he slept in her room every night from now on. Feeling a lot safer with the thought of a great lion watching over her, she smiled to herself as she walked to her bathroom to take a shower. After all that traipsing through the forest, she certainly needed one.

***

Toot, Toot! The sound of Jack's car horn outside made Ariana jump.

"You alright, Sweetpea?" Granpey peered at her over his morning paper, a concerned look in his eyes. "You're a bit jumpy of late; it's not because of the attack on that young girl still making you worried, is it?"

"No, no I'm fine Granpey, really I am." Ariana grabbed the last slice of toast on her plate and picked up her rucksack, hoisted it over her shoulder and quickly gave Granpey a hug and a peck on his cheek.

"Now, now, be gone with you and have a good day at school," Granpey smiled affectionately as he watched Ariana leave and close the door behind her. Leo had followed her to the door as he always did, and he sat down obediently and watched her leave before lying down right there in front of the door. Granpey stared at the closed door and his gaze dropped to look at Leo and he shook his head and went back to reading his newspaper.

Ariana stood for a moment on the front doorstep and looked at the closed door behind her, and then turned to wave at Jack who was sitting in his car, watching her walk towards him. She suddenly became very aware of her every movement, the sway of her hips in her skinny, figure-hugging jeans, the bounce of her freshly washed red curls, long and swishy, the swell of her ample bosom against her fake cashmere sweater that couldn't conceal her curves as she walked. Ariana felt herself blush as she continued walking; she knew that Jack was looking at her and probably capturing her every movement from his perfect viewpoint as he lounged in the front seat of his car. She dared not look at him for fear of seeing that male appreciation in his eyes. They were meant to be friends, just friends, but the disturbing thing about it all wasn't the fact of Jack admiring her in a non-platonic way, but it was the fact that deep down she liked it, and she wanted him to admire her in that way.

"Hi, Jack!" Ariana flounced into the passenger seat, her blazing mass of red waves bouncing around and emitting a sweet floral scent of freshly washed hair. She threw her rucksack on the back seat and flipped her hair away from her eyes to look at him. She was struck by his expression and her heart began to pound as she looked into his eyes. He looked… mesmerised… could it be that he was mesmerised by her? The thought of it made her heart race even faster.

"Arry," Jack said softly, "I… you look… so…"

Just then they both jumped at the sound of a loud tapping at Jack's window, it was Granpey and Leo was jumping up and down beside him. Jack pressed the button and the glass rolled down.

"Now look what the young lass has forgotten, so she has. You won't be getting far without these now, will you?" Granpey held up Ariana's door keys. "Remember, I'll not be home for you today as I'm down to bingo tonight with old Ned and Jake, so I am. So you'll need to be having your door keys, lassie, in case I'm late home." He chuckled as he handed them over.

"Oh, silly me, thanks Granpey!" Ariana laughed and took the keys as Jack passed them across to her and she popped them in her jacket pocket.

She watched Granpey and Leo walk back to the house as Jack clicked the car indicator left and pulled away, driving in the direction of their school.

As Ariana walked to her first lesson, she thought about the interrupted moment between her and Jack, and how for the rest of the journey in the car they had just talked about everything they had experienced from the book to the forest, the creatures, Leo and the alleyway woman; over and over they tried to pick apart and analyse every key moment, hoping to come to some sort of conclusion. She thought it a good diversion from the growing feeling of attraction sizzling between them, wholly unexpected, but she knew without doubt that Jack was experiencing the same attraction. She could see it in the way he looked at her and it was definitely growing stronger, at least on her part, of that she was certain. She shrugged off her thoughts of Jack and hurried to class.

"Good morning, class. I want you to get into pairs and work on this experiment together. Turn to page twenty-one of your workbook and follow the instructions. You have thirty minutes starting now."

Miss Dean began chalking instructions on the board as the classroom started buzzing with dim chatter and the students bustled about organising themselves into pairs and set about getting all the necessary apparatus to begin the experiment. Ariana looked around for a potential partner, pretty much everyone appeared to be already paired up. Her heart sank as she scanned the classroom but just then the door opened and in walked none other than Jessica Brown.

"It just had to be his original crush, didn't it?" Ariana muttered to herself as she made a beeline straight to Jessica. There was no one else to pair up with so she may as well bite the bullet and ask.

"Hi, Jessica, do you want to partner up with me as everyone else is paired up right now?" Ariana made it sound like a casual request rather than a desperate one, her voice and expression gave it that *'I don't really care whether you say yes or no'* feel.

"Well, I suppose so, as it looks like we are the only two without partners then it would make sense." Jessica raised a quick token smile, though Ariana was convinced that she knew a fake smile when she saw one and it was duly noted.

They set about getting their equipment and ingredients ready for the experiment and Ariana quickly and adeptly set up the Bunsen burner whilst Jessica busied herself with getting the pipette, litmus paper and other condiments needed to conduct their experiment.

Ariana already had her goggles and overalls on, and she proceeded to read the instructions to herself so that she was clear on what they needed to do. Together, they set about starting the experiment, determined to complete it within the allotted time. What did surprise Ariana though, was how well they worked together. She could only describe it as effortless, and though she wouldn't admit it if asked, she was actually enjoying working with Jessica.

"Funny how we have been in the same chemistry class all year and not once worked with one another," observed Jessica as she looked up at Ariana whilst using a pair of tongs to carefully hold a test tube that held a purple substance that was beginning to fizz after being dipped in a bowl of ice water.

"Until now," Ariana replied. She thought that Jessica looked like a mad professor with the lab goggles making her eyes appear extra-large like a cartoon character, Ariana laughed thinking she must look the same just with big red hair.

"What's funny?" asked Jessica smiling as she continued the task of taking each test tube and dipping it in the ice water after Ariana had filled them to the right level with the relevant substance and heated it over the Bunsen burner.

"Oh, just that you look like a mad scientist," Ariana chuckled.

"Funny that, I was just thinking that you look like a nutty professor," Jessica smiled broadly at Ariana and they both started giggling at one another.

"Five more minutes, class!" Miss Dean called loudly and immediately everyone began rushing to complete the finishing touches to their experiments which reminded Ariana of the contenders on an episode of Master Chef that she had watched the other day with everyone scrambling around to plate their dishes, just like she and Jessica were rushing around now to complete the last steps of their experiment.

Miss Dean blew the whistle when the time was up. Ariana was convinced that Miss Dean took real pleasure in blowing that whistle. She would always walk around the classroom and inspect everyone's efforts. She would make strange cooing sounds when she was impressed, and her voice would elevate with joy as she gave praise for work well done; sometimes she would even clap her hands as she beamed at you in ecstasy. On the flipside, you could always tell when she was disappointed with your efforts as you would get the shake of her head and she wouldn't hold back in telling you that you needed to try harder next time.

As Ariana sat at the lab workbench next to Jessica Brown (of all people), happy with their team effort and their results written up with a clear conclusion displayed next to the array of test tubes lined up in their holders ready for their turn to be inspected. Ariana watched Miss Dean as she inspected the results at the first workbench, at which sat Mary-Jane and Thomas, closest to the front of the class, their expressions full of anticipation for a positive result.

Just then, something caught Ariana's peripheral vision. She turned to look in that direction and she saw a quick movement through the glass window of the classroom door and what she saw next astounded her. Two human-like creatures, not unlike the tall beings that she and Jack had encountered in Botswood forest, entered the classroom, but the difference with these creatures was that they were much smaller. In fact, these creatures were about the same height as an eleven-year-old child, and they appeared almost translucent, having walked right through the classroom door like ghosts.

Ariana stifled her gasp, as she watched the two beings wandering around the classroom together, going up to individuals at their workbenches, peering at them and inspecting them intently. Their greyish-white translucent bodies made them appear like strange aliens. They held up small thin arms with large hands that had weird claw-like nails; they had large heads and Ariana noticed that their faces had the same raised skin markings as the creatures in the forest. Miss Dean carried on talking to Mary-Jane and Thomas, praising their efforts, before moving on to the next pair. Ariana watched as one of the creatures walked in the same direction as Miss Dean, but instead of colliding, it walked right through her as she continued to her next inspection.

Ariana began to wonder if she was imagining this; everyone was carrying on as normal, so no one could see the creatures except her it seemed. Perhaps the book has caused her to imagine these strange things, after all, they were not dissimilar to the forest creatures. Just then the two creatures separated, going in different directions in the classroom. One went directly up to Eddie Marskall who was at the workbench directly in front of Ariana. Eddie Marskall was a school bully, an angry lad known for picking on anyone weaker than him. He liked to make himself look big and strong by preying on those who were smaller, younger, and timid. Ariana saw the creature stand really close to Eddie as it cupped its strange hands and puckered its grey lips, it blew a cloud of smoke in the direction of Eddie's ear. She watched and saw that the puff of smoke contained letters that formed words that had emerged from the creature's mouth in a flurry, and they floated with speed directly into Eddie's ear!

Eddie immediately picked up a pair of scissors and dropped them on the floor, somehow it seemed like he did it on purpose. Hearing the clang of the metal hit the tiled floor, everyone turned to look in Eddie's direction.

"Sorry, Miss, I knocked my scissors on the floor, pardon me," Eddie gave Miss Dean an apologetic look.

Miss Dean resumed her inspections and the class turned back to observe. Meanwhile, Eddie got off his stool and picked the scissors up from the floor, but instead of going directly back to his seat, he stopped behind one of the boys who was seated at a bench adjacent to him. Ariana didn't know the boy's name, he was a quiet lad and rather small for his age. Eddie began cutting the back of the boy's shirt as it had come loose from his trousers. He snipped away a large square piece of the boy's shirt without him noticing. Ariana heard some boys behind chuckling. The small boy turned his head to look round as though sensing someone behind him and Eddie held the scissors to the boy's neck and whispered a threat in his ear before quickly going back to his seat. Miss Dean turned around too late to notice what was going on. Ariana felt the anger rising inside her. She watched as the creature observed what Eddie had done, and it laughed and laughed, its little strange grey thin body shuddering with laughter as it slapped itself on the thigh as though enraptured with the output of its evil efforts and enjoying the results. Ariana looked over at Eddie, he was now making faces at the boy, tormenting him using mean scare tactics.

Ariana looked over at the other creature and saw it blowing a cloud of words into the ears of a girl called Miriam who was sitting closest to the classroom door. Miriam was a troubled girl; she had been in and out of foster care all her life and had no friends. Ariana had spoken with her briefly on a few occasions, and she seemed to want to genuinely pursue her studies, but she just got side-tracked by the anxiety that she constantly battled with. Ariana watched as Miriam immediately raised her hand after the cloud of words from the creature had entered her ears.

"Miss, please may I be excused to use the toilet?" Miriam's voice was shaky.

"Of course, you may," responded Miss Dean.

Miriam quickly left the classroom, her body hunched as she clutched her small bag and the creature hurried after her.

"Miss, please may I also be excused?" Ariana asked boldly, feeling a sense of urgency.

Miss Dean peered over her silver-rimmed glasses, seemingly disappointed at being interrupted again so soon. "Of course, you may and come straight back please," she replied somewhat reluctantly.

The Cocoon Within

Ariana hurried to the girls' toilets. No one was in there, but one cubicle was locked, and she could hear small snuffles, as though someone was crying softly. It must be Miriam. Ariana tapped softly on the door; the snuffling immediately stopped but there was no reply.

"Miriam, it's me, Ariana. We have spoken a few times before. I don't know if you remember me?" Ariana asked very softly.

Silence...

"Miriam, er I just wanted to check that you are alright, as you seemed a bit upset."

Ariana heard the door bolt slide, and the door opened a peep and then a little wider. Feeling encouraged, Ariana went to the open door and gasped at what she saw. Miriam was sitting on the closed toilet seat, looking deathly pale and with a bewildered and scared expression on her face, which was blotchy with tear-stained cheeks and black mascara streaks; her equally black hair was wild, making her look like something out of a horror movie as she gripped a small razor blade in one hand, and her other arm, skin exposed, had cuts all the way along it. Small streams of blood trickled from the individual cuts on her arm, and the tips of her fingers were also bleeding from the blade.

The grey creature was crouched in the corner next to the toilet seat. Unbeknown to Miriam, it lurked beside her, its eyes stared for a moment directly at Ariana noting the interruption and then it turned back to Miriam and cupped its hand towards Miriam's ears.

"NOOOOOO!" Ariana cried in shock, instinctively putting her hands out as though to stop what was about to happen, and immediately she felt some sort of electrical shock fire through her arms and hands and what can only be described as a shocking blue-white ray of light sped from her hands and zapped the creature which immediately just melted away!

"What the...?" Ariana looked at her hands; they were fine, she was fine, and her arms didn't hurt, she felt... great. "Did you see that?" she asked astounded as she looked at Miriam wide-eyed.

Miriam dropped the razor blade to the floor in horror. "What am I doing? I don't know why I have been doing this!" she stood up horrified, looking at her bloody arm and hands.

"Did you see that? The blue light?" Ariana was still in shock at what she had just done.

"What? No, I didn't see anything," said Miriam and she walked to the sink, threw the razor blade in the bin and washed her hands and her arm. "Ariana, isn't it?"

Ariana nodded still thinking about the blue light from her hands that zapped the ghostly creature.

"Please don't tell anyone about this," begged Miriam. "I… I… don't know why I was cutting myself. I feel fine now and I…"

"Don't worry, I won't say anything, but you can always talk to me if you ever feel down anytime, ok?" Ariana smiled, noticing that Miriam stood taller and more confident, and her face looked radiant; it was almost as though she had somehow been set free.

Miriam looked at Ariana and smiled back, "Thank you, let's go back to class."

"I will catch you up in a bit, I just need to use the toilet."

She watched as a much happier Miriam went off to class. She didn't need the toilet, she just wanted some time to process what had just happened. She knew that she hadn't imagined the creatures! The only conclusion she could come to was that she must have powers, magic powers, and the woman in the alleyway must have given her the powers when she spoke those 'Power Symbols' into her mouth! Yep, that had to be it! She had a dog that was a secret powerful winged lion and now she could zap invisible alien creatures with her hands… so she must be… a real-life superhero perhaps? She grimaced to herself at the thought and inspected her hands again, but she didn't feel any different.

"Stop!" someone shouted from the corridor. She quickly ran to the door and let herself out into the corridor to see what on earth was happening now.

The Cocoon Within

The other creature from the classroom was standing in the middle of the corridor making angry faces, and directly opposite, facing it stood Jessica Brown!

"You have got to go!" Jessica shouted, holding out her hands like weapons and that same beaming blue-white light that Ariana had seen from her own hands, shot out of Jessica's and zapped the creature to smithereens!

Ariana couldn't believe it! She watched in amazement as Jessica swiped her hands together as if dusting them off and turned around to see Ariana staring at her open-mouthed.

"Hiya, oh I wondered where you had got to…" Jessica muttered, her voice trailing off at the look on Ariana's face.

"Jessica, I saw that!"

"What did you see?" she asked with a curious look, half-hopeful and half-suspicious.

"I can see the creatures too and I saw you zap that one just now. I just did the same and zapped the other one that was harassing Miriam!" Ariana watched as the revelation dawned on Jessica's face.

"Oh my gosh, this is awesome!" Jessica's face broke into a huge smile. "I have been dealing with this stuff on my own for months, I never thought I'd meet someone else like me!" To Ariana's surprise, Jessica flung herself at her and gave her the biggest hug ever.

When Jessica finally released Ariana from one of the most enthusiastic hugs that she had ever had, Jessica stood back beaming and said, "Let's go and zap some more. They seem to come and do a school round of tormenting at this time of the day, but it's not every day that I see them, but randomly a few times a month or so, but it feels like it's getting more frequent lately. I call them *the Tormenting ones*. Come on, I'll give you a tour. I'm still trying to figure out why some people don't get tormented whilst others do."

The school bell rang signalling it was time for lunch. Jessica grabbed Ariana by the hand and led her in the direction of the canteen whilst giving a running commentary as they walked. Ariana was only half-listening as Jessica let go of her hand and pushed the double doors of the canteen wide open.

"Now, take a look at the midday chaos," said Jessica, standing back and holding the door for her.

Ariana strode into the canteen, and she stood and looked on in horror as a multitude of the greyish translucent tormenting creatures prowled all over the canteen. Everywhere she looked there was at least one of these creatures blowing words into an innocent pupil's ears and immediately the evil effects could be seen as the victim started misbehaving in some way. Ariana looked from person to person and after receiving the words in their ears, one boy got up and spat in someone's food, another started a fight with someone on the next table, another girl started a food fight and others began picking on some younger pupils. The canteen erupted into chaos which was growing worse by the minute!

Ariana looked on in shock; she had never really paid that much attention before and to be honest she didn't often come to the canteen for lunch, but when she had, there was always some kind of troublesome stuff going on, bullying or a fight here and there kicking off. And now she could see that there was more to it than met the eye.

"Watch this!" Jessica announced as Ariana continued shaking her head in disbelief at what she was seeing.

Jessica strode over to the nearest groups of creatures, zapped them with her hands and they instantly melted away. She continued zapping the creatures as she strode confidently through the canteen. No one else could see what was happening except Ariana and Jessica. To others, it just looked like Jessica was walking up and down the canteen holding her hands out every so often and no one was bothered or interested enough to ask what she was doing.

Ariana followed suit, she may as well see if she still had the zapping power or if it was a one-off. Holding out her hands towards one of the creatures as it jumped through the crowded canteen, she immediately felt the electrical sensation fly through her arms and out of her hands, zapping the creature in an instant!

"Yes! It worked!" cried Ariana and she continued zapping the creatures with Jessica until they had got rid of them all.

"Wow, that was easy!"

"Yep, and thanks for the help," said Jessica. "I have been doing this every month by myself for at least the last three months! Let's grab some lunch and you can tell me how you found out about your powers."

Found out about her powers? Wow, did Jessica really just say that? This was mind-blowing stuff; how on earth did she go from being a regular seventeen-year-old girl, to one with powers? Ariana thought she ought to sit down because this stuff was just getting full-on crazy.

After quickly grabbing a plate of food each and a carton of juice, Jessica and Ariana found a secluded table at the back of the canteen and sat opposite each other. Ariana listened as Jessica enthusiastically recounted her own story, which was not dissimilar to Ariana's experience, including the discovery of an ancient book which set off a bizarre chain of events leading up to today.

Ariana studied Jessica's beautiful face as she chattered on. She was quite stunning and Ariana couldn't deny that fact. It was kind of obvious really why the boys all swooned over her. Jessica quite literally had model features. She was tall but not too tall and had natural golden skin all year round, the kind of skin that glows and puts every other girl standing next to her in the shade; her mixed-race Egyptian and Brazilian heritage accounted for that. Her hair was just so lush, thick and long with beautiful tendrils of dark, curly waves framing her perfect face. Her unusual exotic features were offset with perfectly shaped, long-lashed, glowing brown eyes, her nose was aquiline and her cheekbones and jaw line exquisite, with cute, dimpled cheeks. Jessica was perfectly the envy of any female onlooker, and she was outgoing and confident. Ariana knew that Jessica came from a wealthy family, or rather, she had been adopted by a very wealthy family hence her very British name considering her heritage, and she was an only child, a very pampered, cherished and much longed-for only child.

"So how did you discover your powers?" asked Jessica as she forked a mouthful of salad into her mouth and began chewing.

"Where do I start?" she replied, looking thoughtful.

"Try the beginning? I'm all ears," Jessica pushed her empty plate aside and sat forward, resting her chin in her hands as she looked at Ariana, elbows on the table, eager to hear all.

And that's what Ariana did, she started at the beginning and told Jessica all, from the book to the woman in the alleyway and the floating words, to Leo, and the forest and of course, Jack.

"Wow! A dog that transforms into a flying lion! I don't have one of those." Jessica's eyes were wide with amazement "So, Jack knows about all of this too? And he saw the giant creatures in the forest, but he hasn't got powers?" Jessica looked thoughtful.

"That's right, though I suppose we can't presume Jack hasn't got them," Ariana pondered if Jack too might have powers but not know it yet.

"Jack hasn't got what?" asked Jack, making Jessica and Ariana both jump as he stood by their table holding a tray of food.

"Jack! You made us jump!" cried Ariana as she smiled up at him giving a little nervous laugh.

"Jumping Jack, I like that," said Jessica mischievously as she smiled her beautiful smile at him. "Take a seat." She patted the seat next to her and watched him sit down as instructed, placing his tray on the table next to her.

Ariana could feel her heart beating wildly. She looked from Jack to Jessica and wondered if he still had a crush on her. How could he not? She was stunning.

"Well, you two must kind of know each other?" said Ariana as she sucked up her feelings of not wanting Jack to be sitting next to his forever childhood crush and wanting him to be sitting next to her instead.

"Not well enough," purred Jessica and she turned to study Jack as he took a swig of his orange juice.

He looked at Jessica and gave his winning smile, "Jack Johnson at your service ma'am!"

Jessica laughed, "Witty too! I like it, and a cool name, nice to meet you, Jack Johnson."

Ariana didn't like the way Jessica said Jack's name. "Jack, there have been some developments," she interrupted. "In class today, we saw more creatures similar to the ones in Botswood but smaller and translucent, ghost-like. They came into the Chemistry lab and started causing havoc, and guess what? Jessica can see them too."

Jack's mouth was open wide, and he put his forkful of food down. "No way!" he looked at Jessica and then back to Ariana.

"Yes, and I have powers to zap the creatures away and so does Jessica!"

"Powers? And don't tell me Jessica has a book just like yours?" Jack asked, already steps ahead.

"Yep, I sure do, it's in my locker," replied Jessica, matter-of-factly.

"Damn! Where can I get one of those so I can have magic powers too!" he chuckled.

"Maybe you do have powers and just don't know it yet?" said Jessica. "You saw the giant creatures too, didn't you? But so far no one here can see the smaller ones, except Ariana and I, and we don't know yet if you can see the smaller ones as we zapped them all before you got here."

"Thank God for that! I have had my fill of crazy creatures for one day that's for sure!" responded Jack as he wolfed down his chips and bit into his burger hungrily.

"Guys, I think we should get both our books," suggested Ariana. "We may be able to piece together some clues as to what this is all about and what to do next." Ariana needed to know more, they all needed to know more.

Jessica stood up, "Good idea, let's go get it from my locker."

"Great, then we can all go to my place and compare your book to mine." Ariana stood, and Jessica led the way as they cleared their table and put their empty trays away.

3

Elopia

"It's not here!" cried Jessica as she rummaged around inside her locker, frantically pulling her stuff out as she double-checked every nook and cranny.

"Someone's picked the lock, but why? And more to the point, who?" asked Ariana as she and Jack inspected the locker door. No signs of a break-in though, so, either someone was an excellent lock picker, or they had the spare key.

"Did you have a spare set of keys? We normally get two keys with a locker," asked Jack.

"No, I was only given one set," Jessica sighed as she began to put her stuff back in her locker and then closed and locked it.

"Don't leave anything valuable in there, because whoever took the book probably still has the other key if that's the way they got into your locker," warned Ariana, suddenly worried that her home might be the next target if they were after both books. "Guys, we had better get to my place. I'm worried that whoever stole your book will be going for mine next!"

As the three of them headed down the hall, Ariana picked up the pace, suddenly feeling a wave of panic as she imagined intruders attacking Granpey in their pursuit of the book. Just then, three giant creatures the same as the ones they saw in Botswood forest, bounded into the corridor awkwardly, slightly hunched to avoid hitting the ceiling; one of them skidded on the floor, and all three were heading towards them. But what was strange was that the pupils in the corridor were all frozen mid-motion as though time had stopped. The ugly-looking giant creatures with angry grey faces, their muscular grey torsos visible underneath some kind of metallic armour and their bulging great arms covered with symbols and markings, weaved in and out of the frozen pupils with surprising ease, intent on their targets.

"*Run!*" cried Jack.

Ariana, Jessica and Jack did just that. They sped down the hall in the opposite direction to the creatures.

"Quick through here!" urged Jack. "Let's take the fire exit at the bottom of the stairs."

He pushed the heavy metal door open and Ariana and Jessica bolted straight through and down the stairs with him following fast behind. When they reached the bottom of the stairs, they heard the metal door upstairs being opened and then heard it slam hard against the wall. They looked at one another in fear and ran. They ran out into the parking lot in panic, and everywhere they looked, everyone was frozen in mid-motion.

"Oh my God, what is happening!" cried Ariana as she ran faster than she ever had in her life.

"Quick, my car's over there," Jack signalled racing ahead and fumbling with his keys at the same time.

"These really are giant beasts!" said Jessica. "I haven't seen these before. Are they the ones you told me about from the forest?"

They reached the car; Jack quickly unlocked it and they scrambled in, locking the doors behind them as he started the engine.

"Oh my God, hurry! Hurry!" screamed Jessica as the three creatures sped out of the building and began running at high speed towards them.

"Step on it, Jack!" cried Ariana, her heart beating out of her chest in fear.

Jack accelerated and the car flew forward as he swerved around one of the oncoming creatures just as it tried to dive at the car. Jessica had opened the back window and thrust her hands towards one of the creatures that had almost reached the car, an electrical shock of blue-white rays shot from her hands and zapped the creature which fell backwards. Jack was able to drive away, accelerating at the top speed of his little Fiesta. Ariana poked her head out of the window to look back at the creature Jessica had zapped and she saw it get back up and carry on running after them, she couldn't see the third one.

Jessica and Ariana wound up their windows and sat back as Jack continued driving like a formula one driver, heading for Ariana's place.

"Wow that was so close!" he shouted.

"When you zapped that creature, Jessica," said Ariana, "it didn't die, these are a lot stronger than the smaller ghostly ones." Her heart was pounding as she spoke, "My hands are still shaking."

"Mine too," Jessica replied. "Perhaps it was the armour that protected it, maybe if I had zapped its body, it might have melted away like the other ones."

"Why do you think everyone is frozen except us? This is crazy," said Jack.

"Oh my God, I hope Granpey is ok." Ariana was really worried now.

"Are they still alive? And do you think the creatures have stopped time?" asked Jessica.

Jack swung the car into Ariana's drive, and they all jumped out.

"Jack, look out!" shouted Ariana.

One of the giant creatures had appeared out of nowhere. When it tried to take a swipe and grab Jack with its massive claws, Ariana screamed and grabbed Jack's hand to yank him out of harm's way, but she was too late! She watched in terror, but in that split moment, instead of grabbing hold of Jack, the creature's claws hit an invisible barrier that made a loud scraping noise on contact. Jack fell backwards towards the house and Jessica and Ariana quickly helped him up. The three of them backed towards the house watching as more and more of the creatures began to gather, lunging at them with great claws and teeth striking the invisible barrier.

"Oh my God, this is an army!" cried Jack.

"How many of these things are there? And why are they after us and the books?" said Ariana.

Just then, one of the creatures ran forward and head-butted the invisible barrier which made a loud noise at the impact and a vibration could be felt as though the invisible barrier shuddered. More of the creatures started doing the same, trying their hardest to break it down.

"We'd better get inside and get the book. Who knows if that barrier or force field or whatever it is will hold," Jessica urged.

Ariana unlocked the door, and they hurried inside. Jack went to the window to watch the crowd of creatures, as more and more of them were trying to break through the invisible force field.

"This is crazy," he said. "They are still trying to break through! It looks like there are forty or fifty of them outside. Thank God for whatever or whoever has put that force field around your house." He continued to keep watch.

"Granpey! Granpey, wake up!" Ariana cried.

Granpey was frozen in time, sitting at the kitchen table, holding an open newspaper in his hands. Ariana waved her hand back and forth in front of his face, but he was like a mannequin.

Jessica stood in the kitchen doorway, "Ariana where is your book? The clue to helping Granpey and no doubt my parents and Jack's too, and all the other innocent people frozen in time, is going to be in that book. It must be very important for a whole army to have been sent from another place to find it."

Jack strode into the kitchen and put his hands on Ariana's shoulders. "Come on Arry, Jessica's right let's get the book and see if it can help us find the answers. The three of us are being protected for a reason, come on." He put his hand on Granpey's hand. "Arry, he is warm, he is still alive, seems he is just frozen in time, he might even be able to hear us. This will mean all our families are like this; we need to find a way to set things right and the answers must be in that book."

He gently took Ariana's hand and led her out of the kitchen as she wiped tears from her face and she called out, "I'll be back to rescue you, Granpey. Don't worry, I will be back for you!"

Jack was right, Ariana thought to herself; she needed to be strong for Granpey, and they needed to find the answers so they could unfreeze him and all the others and get things back to normal.

"I'll keep watch," offered Jack, "you guys go and get the book and see what you can figure out." He went to the front window to keep watch on how the creatures were progressing, trying to penetrate the barrier. So far so good, none were through, yet. "Go quickly!" he called. "Hurry, and if you hear me shout, you know we are in trouble!"

Ariana ran upstairs to her bedroom with Jessica following close behind. She grabbed the book from under her bed and opened it where she had left off, and as she turned to the next page with her hands shaking, the unknown words immediately transformed into English and lifted off the page. The golden words sparkled and hovered in front of them, as Ariana and Jessica looked on in amazement and together, they read the words aloud:

"Arise, Go-betweens, fear not, for the one with no beginning and no end goes afore ye. Walk forth into unknown lands, take up your armour and conquer those that stand in your way, for the righteous ones cometh in the name of the Mighty One that none can stand against. Find first your footing and strength, endurance must be fulfilled, hear ye I sayeth, go forth into the land unknown, you will seek and you will find where the bridge meets the sky near the place where the birds rest."

Jessica and Ariana looked at one another for a moment as the golden words melted away before their eyes.

"Look!" cried Jessica, pointing to the words on the page in the book. Ariana watched as they changed back to the unknown language.

"So, the book must be talking about us, Jessica; we must be the *'Go-betweens'*, which would mean we have to go to an unknown land and take up our armour and conquer these creatures; this must be our destiny!" she looked at Jessica wide-eyed.

"I always wanted adventure, but this is something else! How on earth do we find the unknown land?" asked Jessica.

Looking at one another they both said simultaneously, "*Where the bridge meets the sky near the place where the birds rest.*"

"Yes, but that could be anywhere," said Jessica, shrugging her shoulders.

"I think I know where it is," said Ariana, certain that it was somewhere near the Sparrow's Nest because that was where she and Jack had first encountered the giant creatures, so the portal or doorway to another land had to be somewhere around there.

"Guys we have to go, now!" Jack yelled up the stairs, his voice frantic.

"Bring the book!" Jessica commanded as she headed for the door.

Ariana stuffed the book in her rucksack and sped down the stairs two at a time. Jack was holding the back door open and desperately motioning to them both with his hands, panic showing on his face, "*Come on! Come on! Come on!*"

Jessica shot through the back door. Jack was beckoning Ariana furiously. She could hear the clattering and crashing sounds behind her. She dared not look back; she knew the creatures had penetrated the barrier and were in hot pursuit, destroying her beloved home in the process. She continued to run; she reached the back door. Jack was stretching his hand out to her, she grabbed it and felt his strong tight grip, as they ran together out the back door and into the garden.

The Cocoon Within

To their surprise and joy, was Jessica seated on the mighty lion, Leo! His wings spread ready to take off, waiting for her and Jack. Ariana's heart soared with relief. Jack reached Leo first, grabbed onto his mane, hoisted himself up and turned to offer his hand to Ariana to help her up onto Leo's back.

"Ariana, look out!" Jessica shouted.

Ariana felt herself fall back and she realised that one of the creatures had reached her and caught the strap of her rucksack with its claw. She turned and faced it, looking at its hideous snarling face as it frothed at the mouth, angry amber eyes staring back at her, and then just as it was about to take a swipe at her, Jessica raised her hands to fire a blue-white ray of power, zapping and blasting the creature backwards.

Ariana heard Leo's mighty roar as more of the creatures raced through the back door towards her. She grabbed the rucksack and ran towards Leo as he swooped towards her, both Jack and Jessica grabbed hold of her arms, and Leo soared into the air just in time as one of the creatures leapt up to try to get hold of Ariana's feet, missing her by inches.

"I've got you!" cried Jack emphatically as he pulled her up, his grip vice-like. Ariana hoisted her legs over onto Leo's back, taking hold of his mane. She could feel Jack's arms around her as she sat in front of him, and Jessica was secure at the back, holding onto Jack tightly.

"Thanks!" gasped Ariana, catching her breath.

"You're welcome. I couldn't lose you, Arry," he whispered to her. She could feel his heart pounding into her back, as was hers, the adrenaline pumping furiously with the fight-or-flight situation they had all just faced. Looking down at the crowd of terrifying, angry-faced giant beasts gathered in her back garden, Ariana shuddered as some of them continued to leap and thrust their clawed hands in the air, as they watched them soar out of harm's way.

"Thank you for saving my life, Jessica!" Ariana yelled loudly hoping she could hear her at the back.

"You're welcome!" Jessica yelled back at her.

Ariana lifted her eyes to the heavens, the clouds above looked glorious, the sky so blue and clear. "*If someone is listening up there then please let Granpey be alright, please, please, just keep him safe till we can get back and rescue him,*" Ariana repeated over and over in her mind. She remembered Granpey always used to say to her whenever she had experienced a setback, "*Never lose hope, Sweetpea, there is always hope and it will keep you going in tough times, so it will!*" As she remembered Granpey's encouraging words, she could almost hear him, and suddenly she felt the hope rising inside her.

"Where do you think Leo is taking us?" asked Jack.

"No idea, but Jessica and I had a clue from the book. It said we need to go to an unknown land, so maybe Leo is taking us there?" Ariana put thoughts of Granpey aside for now, determined to cling to the hope that he would be fine until they could find a way to get back to him and make things right.

'*Chosen One, what did the book say?*' Ariana heard the question pop into her mind, but she knew it wasn't her own thought. Slightly confused, she ignored it but then she heard it again, more insistent this time, '*Chosen One, what did the book say?*'

In her mind, Ariana asked, '*Who is that?*'

'*It's me, Leo, what did the book say?*'

"Guys, I think Leo is talking to me," Ariana called out, feeling a bit freaked out by the fact that she could hear the lion's thoughts questioning her or at least that's what she was being told in her mind.

"What do you mean?" asked Jack and Jessica simultaneously.

"I mean telepathically, in my mind."

"Wow that's cool; what did he say?" asked Jack.

"He asked me what the book said."

"So, tell him, maybe he can help?" Jessica shouted.

"Ask him why this is happening," suggested Jack.

The Cocoon Within

"Wait, let me tell him what the book said first."

Ariana quickly responded to Leo in her mind, reciting the words from the book as best she could. Leo immediately changed direction, swooping in an arc and heading towards Botswood forest.

"I knew it! I was right!" Ariana exclaimed.

"Right about what?" asked Jack. "What did he say?"

"The book told us that we need to go to the place where birds rest to find the bridge that meets the sky to go to an unknown land. That's the Sparrow's Nest, of course, where we first saw the giant creatures!" Ariana explained.

"Woah! Hang on a minute; are you saying the book told you to go to the land where all these giant creatures live? The same giant creatures that have been trying to kill us all day?" Jack asked in disbelief.

"Well, when you put it like that it does sound crazy, but I think we are being guided and the book told us not to be afraid, and I don't see what else we can do but follow its guidance."

Ariana was certain that it made sense to follow the book's guidance. What other choice did they have after all, if they were to find a way to save Granpey and the others? Had they stayed, they surely would have been destroyed by the creatures, but Leo had been there to rescue them as if on cue, that was no coincidence, of that Ariana was certain.

"No way! Not a good plan! Jessica, back me up here," Jack shouted over his shoulder to Jessica just as Leo swooped down towards the clearing of the Sparrow's Nest, which Ariana thought looked beautiful from the sky. The green expanse was surrounded by majestic silver birch and oak trees, and from up above they looked like huge strong keepers of the forest, with their broad canopy of branches stretching high and wide.

"Sorry, Jack, Ariana is right. Following the book is the only way. Nothing else makes sense."

"Fine! Bullied by two girls! Well, I hope I won't have to say I told you so," Jack stated wryly as they landed in Sparrow's Nest, and he hopped off Leo's back onto the grass, holding out his hand for Jessica and then Ariana as he helped them down one by one.

The three of them stood in silent awe and admiration of the mighty lion standing on all fours in front of them. Large silvery-gold feathered wings made slow swishing movements on each side of his body, whilst his magnificent golden mane glistened with every subtle movement. Ariana, Jack and Jessica stood captivated by Leo, the magnificent lion, as he shook his beautiful mane, then opened his mouth and let out a low rumbling, deep roar and stretched his body at the same time. Ariana was suddenly reminded of her cat, Flower, when she would stretch herself out just like that in the mornings, and she briefly wondered if Flower was also frozen in time just like Granpey. Leo's eyes, one blue and one molten amber made him look all the more unusual in his magnificence, like nothing any of them had ever seen before.

"And to think that we just rode on the back of this wonderful, majestic creature!" Ariana said, shaking her head in wonder.

"Arry, ask him which way we should go," Jack urged softly as though not wanting to speak too loud in the presence of such greatness.

As though on cue, Leo began walking towards the great oaks directly opposite them, his gigantic paws padding silently on the grass. Ariana looked at Jack and then Jessica and shrugged her shoulders, "I guess we'd better follow him," she suggested as she hurried along behind Leo.

Jack looked at Jessica and shrugged his shoulders, "Well, we'll be a heck of a lot safer with the big guy," and they both hurried after Ariana, falling into line beside her.

"Guys, we are literally following a gigantic lion that can fly. Can you even believe this is really happening?" Jessica asked in awe as they walked together, eyes fixed on Leo, not really expecting an answer to her question which was more a statement of wonder.

"I still can't believe we are going to the place where the angry giants live that tried to kill us," said Jack, still preoccupied with their previous near-death experience.

Ariana was admiring Leo from behind as he led the way. His enormous, majestic legs strutted across the forest floor easily, wide padded paws with claws retracted, stealthily silent. His ginormous, strong, muscular frame emanated magnificence and power, and his beautiful silvery-gold coat, wings and mane, shimmered with every movement.

After walking for some time, Leo stopped and sat down. Ariana recognised the spot; it was where the woman from the alleyway had launched backwards over the cliff's edge. The three of them stopped beside Leo, who had an air about him, as though he was waiting for something. Ariana was close beside him; she could hear his breathing and turned her head sideways to look at him, feeling mesmerised by his sheer magnificence and power every time she looked at him. She stared at his glorious mane and felt the urge to reach out and touch it. His face was concentrating intently, completely still, staring straight ahead, poised, and waiting. He was beautiful to watch, so strong, so graceful, and yet with all that magnificent might he exuded, Ariana could not help but feel an overwhelming sense of undeniable peace in his presence as she stood close to him.

"Isn't this where..." Jack began.

"Oh my God, look at that!" cried Jessica.

Ariana turned to look, and she saw that the sky was changing colour. The most glorious sunset reflecting swirling shades of purple and orange merging together, and beautiful as it was, that wasn't what Jessica and Jack were staring at. It was the dazzling lights, just like lots of brightly sparkling diamonds that were appearing to grow out of the middle of the sunset far in the distance, forming what looked like a lengthening arc that seemed to be travelling over a long distance, moving quite quickly. It seemed that it was coming from further than the eye could even see. Ariana watched in awe as the dazzling arc formed itself into a bridge, complete with sparkling railings, all the way to the cliff's edge right in front of them, as if beckoning them to step onto it.

"Wow!" she said.

Leo immediately stepped onto the bridge and began walking forward.

"To the land of the unknown where the bridge meets the sky!" said Jessica excitedly.

"Oh no," Jack muttered, "I haven't got a good feeling about this."

'Step forth now, hurry,' Ariana heard Leo say to her mind and she felt an urgency in his command.

"Hey, we have to go now. Leo said to hurry, come on," she urged and the three of them hurried onto the bridge after Leo. Jack turned back just as an army of giant creatures burst through the oak trees and raced at speed towards the bridge.

"Look!" cried Jack.

Ariana gasped in fear, as did Jessica and all three of them began running across the bridge as fast as they could, not daring to look back, hearts pounding, half expecting to be set upon by the beasts. Ariana could see Leo far ahead just sitting watching and waiting for the three of them to catch up. She wondered why he hadn't dashed back to their rescue like before.

"Hey, guys, look at the bridge; they can't catch us!" Jessica had stopped.

Jack and Ariana stopped running and turned to look back. The bridge had literally melted far away from the cliff edge and stopped just in front of where they stood. The giants stood at the cliff's edge, with angry faces disgruntled and frustrated, some paced up and down and just then one giant leapt off the cliff's edge and across the chasm, no doubt thinking that it could make the distance to catch them. Jack, Ariana and Jessica watched in horror as three, four and five of the giants leapt and fell one after another into the chasm, arms flailing as they tried to reach for the edge of the bridge and failed.

"Watch out the bridge is disappearing!" cried Jack as he stepped backwards, pulling Ariana and Jessica with him and they both looked down to see the bridge slowly melting under their feet! "Run!" he shouted.

They finally reached Leo who had been sitting patiently and calmly waiting for them. *'Climb on,'* Ariana heard as Leo stretched his front paws forward so that it was easier for them to climb onto his back.

They flew with Leo for what felt like many miles, all three of them silent as they looked on in wonder. Looking down at the unfamiliar landscape, Ariana knew that they must have crossed into the unknown land that the book had told them about. She concluded that the disappearing bridge must be some sort of magical gateway to this land, so whatever, or whoever lived here was most definitely going to be completely different from what they were used to, so they would need to be ready for the unexpected if the giants were anything to go by.

As Leo began to descend, they could see the land more clearly; trees and grasslands covered the ground, and hills and mountains towered above the coastline of the surrounding sea. Everything looked so much brighter in colour, dazzling almost, with richer greens and blues. It was strange, it looked like Earth but more colourful, more vibrant. But what they hadn't seen yet were any houses, cities, villages or living creatures.

"Leo, what is this place called?" asked Ariana aloud taking in the glow of the trees as Leo made for landing, "and why are the trees glowing?" she asked in amazement.

'Welcome to Elopia, these trees are life-givers, that is why they glow,' Leo replied with precision to Ariana's mind.

"What did he say?" asked Jack, the first to jump off Leo's back and landing on the grass but as he did so, he bounced straight back up into the air, taking him by surprise, arms flailing. "Whoa, what's happening?" he cried.

Every time his feet landed back on the grass, he bounced again and again and again, like a bouncy ball until finally he slowed down to a standstill, hands outstretched as though to keep his balance. Jessica and Ariana remained seated on Leo, not wanting to get off yet in case something weird was about to happen to Jack.

The land here overflows with nutrients from the life-giving trees, do not be afraid, it is good.'

"Guys, Leo said it's ok, and that the trees are life-giving, so we are all good to go. Come on Jessica," Ariana held out her hand to Jessica and they both hopped off Leo's back together holding hands. They bounced a few metres off the ground and continued bouncing.

"It's like being on a trampoline!" laughed Jessica as she bounced in the air.

Ariana was giggling as they continued to bounce up and down on the grass and Jack joined in, springing on the grass again.

"Look, you can bounce forward. Hey, it's easy to go fa… aaar!" yelled Ariana as she bounced along the grass like Tigger from Winnie the Pooh.

"Look at me, Jumping Jack, ha ha ha!" cried Jack jubilantly as he copied Ariana bouncing forward as if on springs, flying high into the air and making star shapes as he leapt and laughed.

Leo walked past them through the trees with a very subtle bounce in his stride. *'Come on children, let's go, I'm hungry.'*

"I think Leo has a sense of humour, he just called us children," laughed Ariana as she steadied herself, letting her bounce slow down to a stop. "And he wants us to follow him, he said he is hungry, and come to think of it, so am I."

"I wonder what he eats?" asked Jack tentatively.

The Cocoon Within

"Not humans I hope," replied Jessica and they looked at one another before they all burst out laughing and half-ran, half-bounced their way to catch up with Leo.

Jack, Jessica and Ariana stood at the water's edge, staring at the river which was like none they had ever seen before. A myriad of swirling colours of blue, pink, gold and silver encased within the water itself were shimmering, sparkling and dazzling. Little waves surfaced and dipped as though the river itself was dancing and alive. Rainbow-coloured fish swam beneath the surface and flying bright yellow fish broke the surface, opening their enormous bright blue eyes wide to look their spectators in the eye before quickly diving beneath the surface again. Everywhere they looked, brightly coloured insects were flitting to and fro, and luminous lizards scurried about on leaves, branches and trunks of the abundant glowing trees. Oversized rainbow-coloured birds of all shapes and sizes could be seen and heard up above, singing musical songs that sounded like a beautiful symphony of melodies like nothing they had ever heard before. Flocks of tiny red and blue birds flew in formation, whizzing up and down over the river.

"This is amazing! I don't know where to look next, it's just all so... beautiful!" cried Jessica.

"Leo has been underwater for some time now; do you think he's drowned?" Jack asked rather concerned as he stared at the river hopefully.

Just then, Leo's glorious head broke the surface of the multi-coloured river, shaking his soaking mane as he rose from the water with a large rainbow-coloured fish in his mouth, that was thrashing its body about furiously, yet unable to escape from Leo's jaws.

Ariana, Jack and Jessica stood back in awe as they watched Leo bring the huge fish onto the riverbank; it must have been at least a metre and a half in length. Leo sunk his teeth into the flesh of the fish, biting its head clean off, they watched as he crunched the giant fish's head several times before swallowing.

'Build a fire, cook and eat,' commanded Leo as he picked up the headless fish in his mouth and set it down in front of them.

"Don't tell me, Sushi anyone?" Jack suggested with irony.

"Let's make a fire, that's what Leo told us to do and then we can cook it," said Ariana and she started gathering some sticks; Jessica followed suit. "I'm starving; grilled fish sounds good to me."

"Hey, how are we going to light a fire? anyone got matches or a lighter?"

'Use your powers, Chosen One,' Leo commanded Ariana.

"Leo said to use my powers to start the fire. Let me try it; stand back."

Jack and Jessica stood back as Ariana lifted her hands towards the pile of sticks that they had put together. She aimed just like she had when she had blasted the Tormenting ones, but nothing happened. She tried again, but nothing.

"It's not working!"

"Let me try," said Jessica. She tried and also nothing happened.

"Why aren't our powers working?" Ariana asked Leo in frustration.

'Concentrate!' he instructed.

Ariana tried again; still nothing.

'Concentrate, harder, close your eyes and see the fire, think it, believe it, speak it.'

Ariana held her hands out towards the pile of sticks and closed her eyes, doing as Leo instructed. She focussed her mind and repeated his words to herself, 'see the fire, speak it,' and suddenly a vision of the sticks catching alight floated clearly to her mind and she felt that electrical surge through her arms and out of her hands, "Fire!" she said loudly and opened her eyes to see sparks flying as the rays from her hands lit up the pile of sticks with a blazing fire!

"Yes! I did it!" Ariana jumped up and down as Jack and Jessica gave a round of applause. They were all feeling pretty famished by now.

"Right, let's get this fish on the fire!" Jack said. He had a large stick that he had sharpened with his pen knife; he cut large chunks of fish and skewered them onto the stick, then held it over the fire to cook.

'We rest here,' Leo instructed Ariana as he stretched out his magnificent body on the soft grass and closed his eyes. Ariana studied his glorious lion face and thick silky mane for a moment and watched his side rise and fall with every breath he took, and she thought that she would be happy to just sit and watch him forever, her admiration would never wane.

The evening was closing in; Ariana hadn't even noticed how quickly the sunset had arrived and the daylight began to fade. Taking her rucksack off, she slipped off her jacket, folded it over her rucksack and lay back against it. She hadn't realised how tired she was. She watched the flames as Jack busied himself roasting the fish over the fire, it sure smelled good. Jessica plonked down beside her.

"Good idea, I'm shattered and hungry," she said as she plumped her own jacket as a pillow and propped herself back on it, next to Ariana. "What an eventful day, our lion friend is taking a cat nap, but I do hope he is only half asleep in case any giants or anything else nasty tries to come and get us in the night."

Ariana could barely keep her eyes open, feeling sleepy and mesmerised by the fire. "I think we'll be fine," she said. "Animals always sleep with one eye open. Wake me up when the fish is ready," and with that, she drifted off to sleep.

"Arry, wake up, come on Arry wake up, time to eat!" She slowly opened her eyes to see Jack staring at her with a big grin on his face, which was lit up by the flames and glowing embers of the fire behind him.

"What time is it?" Ariana yawned and smiled back at him. "Was I snoring?" She sat up, eagerly taking the fish on a stick that Jack was holding out to her, before biting into the tender flesh.

"Like a train!" Jack laughed at Ariana's wide eyes as she poked him in the arm with her elbow and continued munching on her piece of fish. "Where's Leo?" she asked casually, more interested in food right now which tasted fantastic. She was trying to identify the flavour, it was the best food she had ever tasted but she couldn't begin to describe it. As she continued gobbling down the scrumptious fish, she absently wondered where Leo had got to; it was difficult to concentrate on anything else whilst eating this delicious-tasting fish, but she just hoped that Leo hadn't abandoned them in this strange, unknown, yet beautiful land.

Jessica had propped herself up on her side, leaning her head on one hand, elbow to the ground, supporting her weight as she looked on at the pair of them. "You two are like a pair of love birds!" she joked.

Jack spat his drink out in surprise and started coughing and spluttering.

Ariana immediately blushed, feeling rather awkward especially with Jack nearly choking on his bottle of water. "Er, I don't think so," she hurriedly replied, laughing in an attempt to make light of Jessica's remark. She wondered if Jessica had never known about Jack's secret crush on her throughout school, but she ought not to mention it, and Jack had seemingly changed his tune on that front very recently, which Ariana secretly hoped was going to be a long-lasting thing.

Jessica rolled onto her back, folded her hands behind her head and crossed one leg over the other, wiggling one shoe-clad foot in the air, inspecting her own movements idly as she spoke, "Well our protector Leo wandered off around twenty minutes ago, not sure that he said where he was going and as our translator was fast asleep, we couldn't ask!" Jessica smiled wryly as she looked from Jack to Ariana.

Jack was about to respond when suddenly Leo burst through the night sky with such grace, like something out of a magical movie, and landed with an almighty thudding of his paws to the ground. Ariana only noticed now that this grass wasn't the bouncy kind that they had landed on earlier when they had first arrived.

"Come we must go now, we are being pursued, I must deliver you to Eriat and the others."

It was a clear message from Leo, they needed to go, and they needed to go now.

"Let me guess, we need to go now?" asked Jack, guessing at the telepathic exchange as he looked from Leo to Ariana, taking in her somewhat bewildered expression.

"You guessed right! Let's go!" cried Ariana as she gathered her rucksack and hoisted it over her shoulder.

"Here we go again!" said Jessica as she quickly stood and dusted herself off.

"We had better put the fire out then," said Jack, kicking dust over the fire and Jessica joined in.

"No time for this, raise your hands and quench it!" commanded Leo. *"You, have a lot to learn!"*

Ariana did as commanded and as she thought about quenching the fire with her hands outstretched towards it, it just happened! The fire extinguished in an instant as the power zapped from her hands straight onto the flames.

"How did you do that?" asked Jack with a mixture of surprise and awe.

"Leo told me to, and I just did it and it worked!" she replied, staring at her hands as she turned them over and inspected them.

"Wow, I wonder if I can start fires and put them out too," said Jessica, looking thoughtfully down at her own hands.

Leo moved between them and lowered himself to the ground. He didn't even need to tell them what to do next. Jack gave them both a bunk up onto Leo's back and he had barely hoisted himself up beside them before Leo soared up into the sky, flying with the great force of his majestic silvery wings pushing himself forward.

Ariana could somehow read the urgency in Leo's movement. She thought it must be the telepathy between them. It seemed like it had grown stronger, as though she could sense his feelings, his demeanour and even what he was about to say to her next. It was quite strange; it was almost as though she was connected to his mind in some way. Ariana looked over her shoulder and saw that Jack had his arms around Jessica this time. It just happened that way when he had given them a bunk up; he had ended up behind Jessica and then Jessica behind her. Jack smiled at her, his hair flying backwards, pulling away from his face and his face looking like a vacuum cleaner was sucking his cheeks out because of the force of the wind. He looked funny, Ariana smiled back at him, thinking she must look just as funny. Jessica smiled at her too, thinking that Ariana was smiling at her. Ariana turned to face forwards as she chuckled to herself at how ridiculous they all looked with their hair blowing everywhere and their contorted faces from the G-force of the wind. And to think that twenty-four hours ago, they had been in school having a normal day, until the abnormal happened. Ariana shook her head at the thought as it barely seemed possible that the impossible was happening to them right now, who would believe it?

In the darkness, Ariana could see lots of lights in the distance, and as they moved closer, they seemed to be approaching some kind of city. She could just about make out structures, buildings of different shapes and sizes dotted all about the broad expanse of land. Her heart pounded in anticipation at the thought of encountering its inhabitants. She felt excited, more alive than ever, but oddly she didn't feel afraid despite everything they had experienced so far.

As Leo descended to land, the towering structures became hidden behind large trees. They landed in what looked like an open field and they climbed off Leo.

"Guys look at the sky!" cried Jack, pointing upwards.

What they saw next was a complete phenomenon to them, the sky was changing colour and bright lights just like the Northern Lights were appearing, swirling and dancing, moving before their very eyes, blues, yellows, purples and reds. The spectacular Aurora display in the night sky continued to dance before them as Jessica, Jack and Ariana looked up in admiration.

"This is the city of the lights in the sky called 'En Arias' which means Sky Lights," Ariana heard Leo explaining to her mind. *"Follow me,"* and with that Leo began walking with purpose.

"Guys, Leo just said this city is called *'En Arias'*, which means 'Sky Lights' and we have to go, come on," she said, grabbing Jessica and Jack by the hands.

They hurried after Leo, following him through the field and then at the edge of the field, Leo stepped onto what looked like a stone path which lit up the moment his paw touched the surface.

"Oh, wow!" exclaimed Jessica in awe.

With every step, the pathway lit up, with sparkly, silvery glowing lights that shimmered all around their feet, and then disappeared when they lifted their feet off the path and shimmered brightly again as they stepped back onto it.

"Arry! This is like a PlayStation dance mat!" cried Jack as he skipped on the path, watching it light up furiously with every step he took.

"It's amazing!" Ariana declared as she hopped and jumped on the path, watching the shimmery lights glow with each movement, "This is great!"

Leo stopped further down the path and watched the three of them jumping around on the path and laughing loudly, so engrossed with hopping around and watching the lights on the path react that they looked like they were having some sort of crazy dance-off competition. Leo shook his head and roared loudly. The sound made all three of them immediately stop in their tracks and look at him, and then he turned and began walking again, his message to them clear.

"I'm starting to understand this guy now, and if looks could kill, well I'll say no more," said Jack giving Ariana and Jessica a wide-eyed look.

"Come on," said Jessica, marching forward after Leo, and Ariana and Jack did the same.

Leo took them along the shimmery path, which led through sparkling bushes and undergrowth with rather lively trees surrounding them. The trees were lively for several reasons, there were creatures of the night scurrying around the branches and then as for the trees themselves, well, they were moving around too.

"Jack, I think there is a tree following us," Ariana whispered. They all turned around and a medium-sized tree with a multitude of roots rather like legs, scurried behind them and stopped when it realised it was being watched. Jack, Jessica and Ariana looked at one another in surprise.

"Well, that's not something you see every day!" cried Jack with a half- scared, half-amused expression on his face.

"Er, maybe we should just go a bit faster? I think we ought to keep up with Leo," said Jessica as she half-ran, half-skipped backwards, keeping an eye on the tree and then she turned and ran after Leo.

"Yeah, I think Jessica's right, we'd better catch up with Leo," said Jack decisively as he began to edge backwards.

"Yes, this is all getting a bit weird!" Ariana agreed and they both walked backwards and then began speeding up until they finally turned and ran.

As she ran, Ariana could hear rustling branches behind her and the scurrying and rustling sound of what she imagined was the tree running behind them, which made her, and Jack, run all the faster and she dared not look back till they had caught up with Leo and Jessica.

They stopped next to Jessica and looked on in amazement as they faced a pair of gigantic, silvery gates that towered in front of them and were set in the centre of a huge wall that looked like it was made of steel bricks. The wall appeared to surround the entire perimeter of the city that seemed to go on forever. The steel wall was patterned all over with writing and symbols, just like the symbols in the book. A large fivefold symbol was on either side of the gate, and above which, was also the symbol of a large golden star which radiated brightly, illuminating the area. Behind the gates, Ariana could see the peaks of buildings, roof tops and tall, towering buildings that reached up into the sky, set against the backdrop of the beautiful swirling lights in the sky, the sight of which was astonishingly breathtaking. Ariana heard Jessica's intake of breath as she said, "It's so beautiful."

The three of them stood looking on in silence and complete awe.

At the city gates stood two huge black panthers, though they were somewhat smaller than Leo by comparison, and they appeared to be sentries on guard duty. Both black panthers leapt forward, and then immediately recognising Leo, they lay down in front of him, heads low to the ground, one twisted his face to Leo and with deep growling and utterings, eyes intent on Leo's face, it appeared to be talking to Leo.

Leo responded, his head moving as he growled and roared as though emphasising whatever it was that he was saying to the panthers. Both panthers stood and walked to opposite sides of the gate, and each pushed the gate apart with a nudge of its head. They walked forward opening the double gates wide apart so that they could all pass through. Leo looked back at Ariana, Jack and Jessica, inclined his head and then walked through the gates; realising that was their cue to follow him, they hurried through. Ariana cast a tentative sideways glance at one of the panthers holding the gate open nearest to her and the moment she glanced at it, the panther's eyes locked with hers and it immediately bared is large canines at her, and with a formidable scowl, she heard its low rumbling growl which made her heart jump in fear. Its fiery green eyes gave her a dangerous, heart-stopping, intense look of warning that made Ariana want to freeze on the spot. She felt her heart palpitate furiously and she couldn't wait to get as far away from it as possible, so she hurried along with the others.

'These are the Fearsome ones, for they strike fear into every heart, they are the gate keepers of En Arias, and they will lay down their lives for the city and all who abide in it.' As Leo spoke to her, Ariana could sense her connection with him more and more and she knew that he had sensed her fear just now.

As the panthers closed the gates behind them, the three took in the beauty of the city, great buildings that shone and shimmered like precious stones, and beautiful plants with all sorts of unusual-looking fruits in abundance surrounded every building and pathway. The sky began to grow brighter and brighter with the early dawn of the sun beginning to rise, and still, the radiant colours of the sky continued to dance. Leo was walking purposefully towards a large shimmering building of gold which looked like some sort of surreal golden castle from a fairy tale. Ariana wondered what or who was inside it.

The three of them followed Leo inside the golden castle and they walked through the open double doors which were beautifully ornate and looked like they were encrusted with precious stones of sparkling colours that followed the pattern of a wonderfully carved vine, adorned with flowers throughout its design. They stood in a very large hall that looked like the inside of a palace. Then what can only be described as little fairies with shimmering wings, and smiling bright faces, came flying out of nowhere. There were four fairies in a group, three of them were each carrying a champagne flute, with a pink potion, that fizzed and bubbled, one each for Jack, Jessica and Ariana. Ariana looked at Jessica and Jack next to her as they beheld the little smiling fairies that were babbling in an unknown language, clearly the language of Elopia and shoving the champagne flutes at them, encouraging them to take it.

Jessica took hers from the little fairy that was fluttering in front of her, and Ariana did the same.

"Well, I guess it would be rude not to," said Jack enthusiastically as he took the little champagne flute and was just about to drink it when Jessica stopped him.

"Why don't you ask Leo what it is before we drink it?" she suggested as she sniffed at the potion and sneezed as the bubbles went up her nose.

"Good idea," said Ariana.

She asked the question in her mind and watched as one of the fairies was trying to push the champagne flute to Jack's lips, and another was trying to push his jaw towards the drink. Ariana smiled as she watched Jack laughing, finding the whole thing rather amusing. She looked at Jessica who appeared to be trying to fight one fairy off her champagne flute, as it was desperately trying to get her to drink it. Ariana felt a tiny tapping on her cheek, and she looked at the little fairy that was staring at her with a rather cross expression, whilst chattering away and pointing frantically at the potion. It began lifting her hand that held the drink, upwards towards her lips, using all its might to do so, judging by the straining of its little face as it tried to heave the glass. Ariana chuckled, the fairies did look rather funny and cute, it seemed to be very important to them that they drank whatever was in the flutes!

'A potion to give you understanding, drink, it will not harm you.'

"Guys it's okay," said Ariana. "Leo said it's a potion to give us understanding."

"I'll go first then," said Jack eager to get the little fairies to stop hassling him; and as he drank, they gave a little cheer and began clapping their tiny hands as they fluttered around him in joy.

"Do you feel any different?" asked Ariana as she studied Jack intently, hoping he wasn't about to grow any strange appendages.

"Nope, I feel fine."

"Let's do it then," said Jessica as she looked at Ariana. "On three. One, two, three!"

They both drank every last drop, much to the fairies' delight as they began cheering and clapping, dancing and fluttering around in joy.

"Well, they are easily pleased," observed Jack, smiling.

One of the fairies flew forward, signalling to Ariana, Jack and Jessica to come nearer to her. She seemed to be the leader of the little group as the other fairies lined up behind her. Jack, Ariana and Jessica looked at one another, then, shrugging her shoulders, Ariana moved closer to the fairy as requested and Jack and Jessica did the same.

The little fairy spoke, *"Herubas En Arias, eles atus maros indulads,"* Ariana and Jessica looked at one another again shrugging shoulders. The little fairy gave a cross look as she spoke again, *"Herubas En Arias, eles atus maros indulads."*

It was clear the little fairy expected them to respond, it seemed rude not to, even though they didn't know what the fairy was saying, Ariana thought she ought to say hello or something.

"Ostuda," Did that word just come out of her mouth? The little fairies cheered and started clapping and fluttering around jubilantly. Jack and Jessica looked at her like she was crazy, but she was saying hello in English, or at least that's what she was thinking in her head when she said it. She tried again, *"Ostuda."* Ariana clamped her hand over her mouth in shock and then burst out laughing.

Jack and Jessica started talking and their words came out as gibberish too. Eyes wide they too burst out laughing, much to the delight of the little fairies that were becoming most excited by all this.

Then the lead fairy flew up to them, clapped her hands, cleared her throat and said, "Welcome to En Arias, the city of Sky Lights, it is an honour to welcome mankind to our land."

"Oh my God, I understood her!" cried Jessica in amazement. The fairies roared with laughter amid many tiny claps and miniature joyous cries.

"Me too!" cried Jack laughing. "This is crazy!"

"I know, right!" Ariana was full of laughter.

"I am called Nulia," said the little leader fairy and she began introducing the other fairies who each in turn performed a little bow and fluttered up and down at the mention of their name. Ariana, Jack and Jessica greeted each one with a nod and a hello.

"Come, children of mankind, we must go, I need to take you to Eriat, she will show you all you need to know." It was Leo! He was speaking to them in growls and roars, but they understood every word as though in English, this was fantastic! The sound of his voice was just amazing, deep and smooth with such authority and clarity in every word he spoke through growls.

They waved goodbye to the jubilant fairies and followed Leo across the large hall. Ariana looked up at the high ceiling, it was covered with spectacular artwork, displaying battle scenes, just like she had seen on the pages of the book when she had held a light beneath the page.

"This way," growled Leo as he led them through an archway at the end of the hall and they followed him through a dimly lit, rather wide corridor.

They heard what sounded like men marching. The sound grew louder and louder until a troop of humanoid soldiers rounded the corner at the other end of the corridor and marched down the hall towards them. They looked like they were dressed for combat in glistening suits of some kind of metallic, silvery substance that appeared to cling to their bodies almost like a second skin, They also wore sheathed silvery yet translucent swords at their sides and their bodies were large, muscular and strong. Ariana noticed that each humanoid had the same fivefold symbol on its forehead just like the woman in the alleyway. The soldiers stopped in unison and saluted Leo who nodded, and his glorious mane shook in acknowledgement as he stopped directly opposite the troop.

"Commander, we are at your service!" the humanoid leading the troop said in a sharp, clear voice.

"What are your orders?" asked Leo.

"We are to secure the perimeter at the north border; the Higher Order of Celestials are to defend the east and west corners, and there are troops already engaged in battle in the south as we speak, Commander."

"What about the Arc Celestials?" growled Leo, his expression fierce.

"They are en route south, my Lord," the soldier bowed his head.

Leo put his gigantic paw on the shoulder of the soldier for a brief moment and then the soldier raised his head.

"I will go south and join them in battle," growled Leo, and the soldier saluted before marching his troop by.

"This sounds really serious, Arry," Jack whispered.

"I hope it's not that army of giant creatures," said Ariana, thinking it probably was, but she hoped wasn't.

"I bet it is," said Jessica, articulating what they were all thinking.

They hurried after Leo as he walked on and then came to stand at a pair of great golden double doors; each door had a large emblem of a double-headed eagle with a golden star just above it.

"Just like the book!" Ariana whispered to Jack who nodded in agreement.

Leo stood on his hind legs and pushed both doors with his paws and they flew wide open, revealing a great room that was full of activity. Animals and humanoids were talking amongst one another, humanoids with fivefold symbols on their faces and arms, with shimmering skin, some looked almost translucent, others had a bluish complexion, and some had dark ebony skin whilst others had bronze-like skin. Their hair was just like human hair but of striking and vibrant colours of gold, blues, reds and all different textures. Ariana thought it was just like the rainbow river. They looked like they were all busying themselves, getting ready for some great event. There were lions, a little smaller in size than Leo and without wings.

There was even a giant sabre-toothed tiger in conversation with a blue humanoid with bright red hair and she was telling him to be still as she tried to adjust a saddle on his back. He growled at her that it was too tight, she called him a baby and adjusted it and then hopped fluidly onto his back and together they rode off through a large archway exit.

"Follow me," instructed Leo with authority and a growl for good measure as he strode through the busy crowd, his magnificent, muscled lion's body cutting an imposing figure as animals and humanoids quickly moved aside to let him through, and each one greeted him with a nod or a salute or acknowledged him as Commander. They followed him as he approached a rather long table at the far end of the room. At one end of the table sat two very large leopards, a large warthog and another great creature with a broad dark face and piercing eyes with large antlers atop its head, though its features were much like that of a bear. At the other end of the table sat several humanoids, and in the centre sat a humanoid that Ariana recognised.

It was none other than the alleyway woman, Eriat. She was dressed in a suit of armour which had a silvery breastplate with a golden symbol of a large star and beneath it a double-headed eagle was engraved, and the faces of the eagle were fixed on the star above it. The suit of armour appeared to be clad to every muscle and sinew of Eriat's body as though a second skin. It looked comfortable and pliable as well as strong and protective, and Eriat cut a fine figure that any onlooker would recognise without doubt, that she carried an air of authority that would certainly not be ignored wherever she went. Her stark, snow-white face was topped with a crewcut of silvery-white hair, and that vivid fivefold symbol etched on her forehead seemed to glow or shine, Ariana couldn't tell which, as she looked on in wonder at everything and everyone around her. Yet her eyes kept being drawn back to Eriat, the brightest jade eyes stared back at her, and strong features told a story of boldness and fearlessness, and she gave off an intense energy of immense strength just like Leo. Ariana wondered how it could be that she could look at someone and sense their overpowering energy of fire and strength; she had never experienced this before.

Eriat turned to face them, she looked them over and her eyes moved to lock with Leo's. "Welcome Commander you finally arrived, and you brought the Go-betweens but also a Child of Mankind I see."

Everyone around the table fell silent and listened attentively to the exchange. Ariana looked from Jack to Jessica, she knew Jack had caught her glance as he gave a sideways look and then smiled at her, and at the same time she felt his hand reach for hers and he gave it a reassuring squeeze. She felt her body relax, that's right they were in this together, she needn't worry with Jack by her side; whatever happens at least they have each other.

Leo nodded and let out a low roar as was his custom before speaking,

"Yes, I believe this was not part of the original plan, but it may have its benefits; children of mankind have never had the gift of sight, but this one has."

A humanoid seated at the table raised her hand; she was smaller than the others, her skin was dark ebony and she had beautiful striking features with the brightest blue eyes and that all-familiar fivefold symbol on her forehead that all of the humanoids here seemed to have, though Ariana had noticed that Eriat had more symbols which were all around her face too, on her cheeks and jaw line.

"Speak," commanded Leo with a growl as he looked at the small one.

"Commander and Eriat, may I take our visitors and provide them with some replenishments and hospitality, for they are weary?" asked the small humanoid.

"Food, hopefully," whispered Jack.

"Mmmm," Jessica agreed.

Ariana wondered that they must look a bit of a state and hoped she could freshen up too, a nice shower or hot bath would be amazing.

"Of course," Eriat responded, and she looked at the three visitors, "please forgive me for my lack of hospitality. Welcome to En Arias. This is Jara, she has the gift of benevolence, please allow her to escort you and provide you with sustenance and comfort where you can rest and then we will talk tomorrow."

Jack smiled, "Thank you and er… nice to meet you all."

Ariana and Jessica thanked Eriat, and Jara sprang to her feet and flitted around the table to greet the three of them with a broad smile before leading them away.

They heard Leo say as they left, "Let us walk and talk Eriat, we do not have much time. I will need to join the troops tonight, they need reinforcements, and you will need to enlighten the Go-betweens."

Out of earshot, they didn't hear Eriat's reply, as they followed Jara out of the great room and through various corridors in anticipation of getting fed and watered, and hopefully, a shower and a good night's rest in comfortable surroundings was also on the agenda.

4
The Place of a Thousand Eyes

Ariana slowly opened her eyes to the sound of birds outside; or was it really birds she could hear? Still half asleep, she tried to register the sound. Yes, it sounded like a faint bird song. As she roused herself from her slumber and rubbed her eyes, she realised she had enjoyed the most amazing, if not the best night's sleep that she had ever experienced in her life. She pulled herself up and propped herself in a sitting position, leaning back into the most wonderfully soft pillows. She scanned the room that Jara had told her was called a *Sleep room* and one could see just why. Everything in the room was designed to give the best sleep experience, from the décor to the curtains, to the extra-large and super comfy bed. The moment Ariana had laid her head on the soft pillows, it was as though nothing else existed, all troubled thoughts dissipated, and her mind floated off into peaceful sleep.

Everything started coming back to her as she remembered the events of last night. Jara had taken them to the West Wing where she told them that the wish-helpers were busy preparing food for them. They had been surprised to see a wonderful spread of all their favourite foods. Jack had shouted with joy at the sight of a piping hot plate of steak and kidney pie with chips and mushy peas, laid on the table for him to enjoy, knife and fork at the ready. There had even been a little name tag beside it that said, *'For Jack, the Child of Mankind'*. Jessica had wasted no time getting stuck into a plate of her favourite pizza, and even Ariana had been pleasantly surprised to see an all-time favourite dish of lasagne waiting for her, complete with her name tag which read *'Ariana, the Chosen One'*. Jessica commented that as she also had powers, why couldn't she be a Chosen One too? Ariana tried to reassure her that both she and Jack had a very special place in all of this, otherwise, they surely wouldn't be here. However, Jessica just shrugged her shoulders, clearly not convinced, then flung her own name tag, *'Jessica, the Go-Between'* aside, and got on with eating her pizza. Ariana sighed; she felt too tired to deal with Jessica's disappointment, so she had carried on eating her lasagne, grateful for Jack's constant chatter as they ate.

They all agreed that the food tasted wonderful, far better than anything they had ever eaten before. They also discovered that the "fairies" were not actually fairies but known as *'wish-helpers'*. The little wish-helpers had prepared all their favourite foods; they also learned that a gift of the wish-helpers was that they knew what was wished for in the mind of any living being. Ariana asked Jara if the wish-helpers always granted what someone wished for, and she was glad to hear that the answer was no, as one could only imagine what the wishes of an evil mind would conjure.

There it was again, the sound of singing. Ariana's reflections on last night were interrupted by what sounded like birdsong, coming from the other side of her sleep room door. She reluctantly got up out of the wonderfully cosy bed and opened the door. There she saw five very cute wish-helpers, brightly dressed in sparkling outfits and singing the most beautiful of songs in such harmony, sounding just like the melody of the most talented of songbirds. They offered her freshly made tea, with steam rising enticingly from the hot cup.

"Oh, thank you so much! I was just thinking how much I would love a cup of tea!" Ariana clapped her hands together in glee.

The little wish-helpers flew swiftly inside the room and put the teacup on the bedside table and then two of them busied themselves drawing back the curtains and tying them back with sashes, letting the bright sunlight flood the room.

"I know, we heard your wish," replied one of the little wish-helpers, as she took hold of Ariana's hand and led her to sit on the bed. "Pippy at your service," and with that, she did a little bow followed by a quick twirl and smiling broadly, she instructed, "Now drink your tea whilst it's nice and hot."

Another little wish-helper flew at Ariana as she sipped her tea. "Did you like our singing?" smiling the brightest little smile, she twirled in the air and as she did so, lots of sparkling dust sprinkled all around her.

"Yes, it was beautiful, just like birdsong," Ariana responded, smiling back, feeling rather captivated by these tiny creatures. She looked around and saw the other three busy tidying her room.

Suddenly, Nulia flew in and clapped her hands. Ariana noticed that Nulia's wings were bigger and brighter than the other wish-helpers.

"Come on, chop chop! No time to waste! Hurry girls! Eriat has summoned an audience with our visitors within the hour!" and with that, she flew right up to Ariana's face. "Apparel has been provided for you and a bath is ready just down the hall. Everything is waiting for you and we will prepare some morning sustenance. Pippy will show you and your friends the way once you are ready." And just as quickly, she flitted out again before Ariana could barely say thank you.

∗∗∗

"What do you think, Pippy?" asked Ariana, standing in front of the full-length mirror admiring her reflection. She couldn't stop staring at her appearance; she looked positively radiant, but it was what she was wearing that amazed her the most.

Pippy had told her that the gold and green suit hanging in the bathroom was her very own personal *Suit of Ultimate Truth;* it wouldn't fit anyone else, and when she wore it, it would become a part of her, enabling her to express her ultimate truth, the truth of her inner self and who she really was. Ariana did not really understand what Pippy meant, however now she had the suit on, she felt... well, kind of different, everything seemed clearer, her vision, her thoughts, even her movements more precise. It was strange, as though she had somehow become a more advanced version of herself. As for the suit, well it fit like a glove and made her look, for want of a better word, sexy. It was like a second skin and felt extremely comfortable, yet strong and pliable, with a type of armour on the outside. She felt like a new person, but she wasn't sure just yet who that new person was. By contrast, without the suit, it seemed as though she had been but a shadow of her real self without ever knowing it till now. The black, gold and green boots that came with it looked rather like a boxer's boots and when she stepped into them, they automatically clicked into place, locking comfortably around her ankles and calves. Ariana thought that boots like these that did themselves up would be all the rage with her generation, and she hoped she could take them back with her and show Granpey.

Granpey! Oh God! She felt awful for not thinking about him at all in the last twenty-four hours and her hand flew to her mouth in horror. Tears started to prick at her eyes and then she remembered what Jack had said, that Granpey was alive and that they were the key to saving him. She had to cling to that hope!

Her thoughts returned to the room at the sound of Pippy clapping her tiny hands in glee. "Positively super-sonic!" she cried, as she did a little twirl in the air, her wings fluttering so fast they reminded Ariana of dragon-fly wings. Pippy's hair, tied in two little bunches, bounced around furiously and her tiny oval, pixie-like face lit up with joy. She beamed at Ariana and they both started laughing.

Just then there was a knock at the door. "Come in!" cried Ariana, hoping it was Jack so she could show him her suit.

The door flew open and in strode Jack, looking exceptionally handsome in his own outfit not dissimilar to Ariana's, only more manly of course. Jack's suit clung to his physique in ways that Ariana didn't think possible, and she drew her eyes over his chest in appreciation. The suit was predominantly black with gold and green trim around the neck and arms. It looked like it was made of leather but with metallic armour over the chest area, like a gladiator.

"Have you been working out?" blurted Ariana before she could stop herself.

He flexed his biceps and winked at her, "You noticed!"

They both burst out laughing, Pippy too. Jack started doing strong man poses as he grinned enthusiastically, spurred on by his keen audience.

"Arry, I am loving your outfit too! Very… ahem, fitting," he raised his eyebrows up and down with emphasis and grinned hugely as he gave her the once-over. This set them both off laughing again.

Pippy looked from one to the other, "I can hear your wishes you know," she said with a knowing smile, followed by a very cheeky grin that turned into a chuckle.

"Hey that's not fair!" cried Jack, looking away from Ariana rather embarrassedly, before being saved by Jessica as she poked her head around the door.

"Guys, we are being summoned. You both look great by the way and what do you think of mine?" Jessica swished into the room and did a few poses as they all admired her silver and gold suit.

Ariana thought Jessica looked stunning, there was no doubt about that and she felt a slither of envy surface, but it soon disappeared when she remembered how upset Jessica had been last night when she found out that Ariana was the Chosen One, whatever that really meant. The momentary envy quickly changed to compassion; so what if Jessica had a better-looking suit than hers anyway? Let her at least have that, it seemed to make her happy and that was a good thing.

"You look fantastic, Jessica!" Ariana beamed at her, determined to be friends. She liked Jessica now that she had gotten to know her a bit better. She was forthright and pretty straightforward, rather resilient and courageous too, just what they needed if they were to help Granpey and the others.

"You look fab, Jessy," said Jack who loved to shorten names.

"Thanks, guys, now let's go!" said Jessica, beaming with joy from the compliments.

Jessica ushered them out and Pippy led the way back through the great room and to what appeared to be a private suite which was covered with a luxurious white carpet and large comfy white sofas around a centre piece, a large yet low wooden tree stump table with a glass top, on which was a variety of breakfast dishes. The walls of the room were interestingly adorned with paintings of different battle scenes. Jack was the first to zone in on the food as he grabbed a freshly baked Danish swirl and bounced onto one of the sofas, propped his arms behind his head and took in the surroundings as he chomped away. Jessica was already looking at one of the paintings on the wall.

"Ariana come take a look at this," she said, surprised.

Ariana joined her and even Jack got up and followed. They realised that in the painting Jessica was looking at, the people and animals were moving.

"It's live art," explained Pippy, "a snapshot of the past that tells the truth of what happened, lest anyone forgets."

Just then the double doors opened wide and a pair of giant leopards entered the room. They could have been the same ones from last night that had been at the large table in the great room. Both leopards slinked into the room, acutely watching the three of them. One of the leopards sniffed at them and stared for a moment before taking up station at one end of the room all the while watching their movements. The other leopard pounced on one of the sofas and lay down keeping its eyes on them.

"It feels rather intimidating, I must confess. I think we ought to sit down," said Jack as they all edged to the other sofa like naughty children and sat down and waited.

At that moment, Eriat strode purposefully into the room. She cut a stark yet commanding figure with her silvery hair and pale white face covered in markings. She was dressed in her combat gear, and her stance was militant and as she strode into the room, she looked impressive. Both leopards instantly rose and flanked her on each side. Ariana found it difficult not to stare.

"At ease, Fearsome ones," she commanded, and the leopards instantly left her side, taking up their former positions all the while keeping their eyes on the three visitors.

Eriat looked the three of them over and said, "We have much to discuss, though I am pleased to see you each have on your Suits of Ultimate Truth, and a very good fit for you all too. Now please help yourself to replenishments," she made a sweeping motion indicating the spread of food on the table. At the same time, a group of wish-helpers flew through the open doors with a pot of tea and fresh juice that they set on the table and silently busied themselves with serving.

As they gratefully began to eat and drink what was set before them, all so rich and wonderfully tasty, Eriat slowly paced in front of them as she began talking,

"I am Eriat, Arc Celestial of the highest order of celestial beings from the seventh realm, I am a servant of the Mighty One." Both leopards and the little wish-helpers all bowed their heads at the mention of the Mighty One. Jack, Ariana and Jessica looked at one another briefly in surprise and then turned their attention back to Eriat.

"There is a great and evil age-old enemy at work, that is determined to destroy the children of mankind. This enemy's name is not spoken on the lips of Elopians nor the lips of any celestial being for that matter, for to utter the name itself is an abomination! He has many pseudonyms, one of which he is well known by in Elopia, *'The Destroyer',* and his ultimate goal is to seize the power of the Chalice of Fire, destroy the sacred books and gain control over Earth and the seven realms. This will never happen, not on my watch!"

They jumped at the fury in Eriat's voice. As she spoke loudly with vehemence, both leopards growled in agreement, their faces scowling and eyes flaming.

"Ariana and Jessica," she continued, "by bloodline you are Go-betweens and that is why you are here."

Ariana and Jessica looked at one another, confusion on their faces as they listened to Eriat.

"What does that mean? What's a Go-between?" Jessica piped up.

Eriat looked at her and paused for a moment. "Both you and Ariana are half-human and half-celestial."

"What? So, does that mean one of my parents was not human? Or they were not my real parents? I'm confused," Ariana frowned as she tried to figure it out.

"Well, I'm adopted so it doesn't make much difference to me, as I never knew my real parents," Jessica shrugged. "I think all parents probably hide stuff from their children, and anyway, I don't mind being different, I'm used to it."

"Ariana, you are of a royal celestial bloodline, the bloodline of the highest order of Seraphim from the seventh realm, mixed with human blood means you are a Go-between, and you can enter all realms," Eriat continued. "Jessica, you are half-human and half-Elopian and you can move freely between the Earthly realm and all six realms, but you cannot enter the seventh realm. Only the highest order of celestial beings can enter the seventh realm. Go-betweens have always lived on Earth, but most have remained dormant with no knowledge of who they really are. Only by reading from one of the sacred books can a Go-between be awakened, and you have both been awakened and now is the time for you to be enlightened. There is much for you to learn."

"Part celestial being? Woah, that's a lot to take in," said Jack, seeing that Ariana was grappling with this news, while Jessica on the other hand, seemed unfazed.

"As for you, Child of Mankind," said Eriat, looking directly at Jack, "you are a mystery. No Child of Mankind has ever had the gift of sight nor entered Elopia until now. I believe the Mighty One has a plan for you outside of the Earthly realm, for you to have been entrusted with the gift of sight."

His face lit up at Eriat's words. Ariana was glad that Jack was included in all of this. One thing was for sure, she needed him by her side now more than ever. To think that she was half-celestial, and no one told her! Granpey! Surely Granpey knows! But then that would mean he hid it from her for all these years, but why? No, Granpey must be in the dark about all this too. What if she was adopted too, like Jessica? Or what if one of her parents wasn't her real parent? Gosh, this was too many what-ifs, she would deal with the immediate, and then ask Granpey after they find out how to unfreeze him and get everything and everyone back to normal.

Eriat continued, "Many moons ago, there was a great war between the armies of the Destroyer and the celestials of Elopia. Many Elopians were taken captive and have never been seen since, but we believe they are still held in captivity to this day, bound in chains of darkness, their location unknown. Now a new war is beginning to wage, and you, Ariana, are at the centre of this war."

"Me! But why?" Ariana asked, eyes wide.

"Do not fear Chosen One! Go-betweens have not set foot in Elopia for over a thousand years. When you and Jessica opened the sacred books, we felt it. We knew that a Go-between had been awakened in the Earthly realm. But there are forces of evil that since the beginning of time have set themselves against the children of mankind, tormenting them and spreading evil in the hearts of the children of men. Many dark deeds of the children of mankind are the direct result of the control of the forces of evil. The Destroyer whose name is an abomination to us, cultivates this evil force which grows ever more evil. Thousands of years ago, Righteous Celestials were first sent to Earth in human form to multiply, and Go-betweens were the result, they were the protectors of the children of mankind, and they kept the forces of evil at bay, their powers in combat were second to none. But as the years went by, the Go-betweens became humanised and lost their understanding and knowledge of their powers and they became dormant. So, the forces of evil have ruled the Earth with an upper hand ever since. The Mighty One sent the sacred books to Earth to draw any last Go-betweens out of their dormant state, for their awakening, and that is how you came to rise up in the power of your true state." Eriat looked at Ariana and Jessica intently, she had their full attention.

Eriat went on, "The Destroyer has set his forces against Go-betweens on Earth; these forces have always managed to prevent any Go-betweens from awakening and entering Elopia to achieve their destiny, until now. The legend of the Go-betweens tells us that there is a Chosen One that would one day come to take up the Chalice of Fire from the sacred Mountain of Peace, use its power to defeat the Destroyer, restore Earth to its former glory of peace and set the captives free on both sides of the Earthly realm. You see, Earth is the middle land, the land of the living between the realms, we are connected in more ways than you can understand right now."

"Can you help us understand?" asked Jessica, voicing the question in Ariana's mind.

"Your understanding will come when you have attained a higher level of wisdom, this must be earned through trial and discovery. Ariana, you are the Chosen One and you must journey to the Mountain of Peace and retrieve the Chalice of Fire. We do not have any time to lose as the armies of the Destroyer have already entered Elopia's borders, and the celestials are in battle with them as we speak. Leo has gone south to join his troops to defend our borders with the might of the Arc Celestials. Meanwhile, you need to prepare for your journey and be equipped with all that you need. The journey to the Mountain of Peace will take you through the darker realms first and you need to be ready."

This was mind-blowing stuff to take in, but there was barely any time for the three of them to process it all before they were whisked off to get ready. Upon Eriat's instructions, the fearsome leopards took them to a combat arena where they observed rigorous battle practice between celestials that were faced in combat and fought one another aggressively, honing and practising their skills with their powers until one yielded to the other.

Jack, Ariana and Jessica were each given a translucent sword which they were told was called a Lifeblood sword. They were shown how it functioned and how easily they could store it safely at the hip of their Ultimate Suits without effort. They were told that the sword had the power to destroy any being, whether of spirit or of celestial form that opposed them from beyond the Earthly realm, and they were to use it as needed. After some rigorous sword practice, Jessica and Ariana were given lessons in controlling their celestial powers. It was easier than before, and they were told it was because of their Suits of Ultimate Truth. Surprisingly, the lessons involved control of their thoughts which they both quickly grasped; the concept was to think it into manifestation or to say it aloud and then the power easily flowed from the mind through their arms and out of their hands, slowly at first and then with lightning speed the more they practised.

"You are ready," said Eriat who had been observing them. She strode over to them as the three arose from their resting positions, following their rigorous training.

***

"I kind of miss Leo, I do hope he is alright," said Ariana, studying the two fearsome black panthers that Eriat had commanded to go with them as far as the river's edge; this would lead them to the ancient tombs and from there, they were on their own. Pippy would accompany them on their journey but Eriat said they ought to rely on their own powers and skills, and that the sacred book would guide them.

"I'm sure Leo is just fine, Arry. Can't you speak to him in your mind and say, *'Hey how are you doing? Hope you're winning the battle'* or something like that?" Jack was fiddling with his sword at his hip, adjusting its position. He looked at Ariana waiting for her reply, "Well, can you ask him? See if he hears you?"

Ariana looked over at Jessica, stunning in her silvery-gold figure-hugging suit as she strode beside the panthers trying to make conversation with them. Pippy was fluttering beside Jessica's face trying to get her attention.

"I didn't think of that, yes, I'll give it a go."

The Cocoon Within

"*Leo, can you hear me?*" Ariana paused, listening in her mind for a reply. "*Leo, are you there?*" And then she heard it, a faint response in her mind that slowly became clearer,

"*Chosen One, you must retrieve the Chalice! We battle hard, and many more enemy challengers are on the way. We need the Chalice of Fire to end this war and set all things right. Go quickly, Chosen One.*" Ariana could hear the urgency of Leo's voice in her mind.

"*Yes, we are on our way to find the Chalice! Leo... hello? Leo, are you still there?*" She waited but nothing came; all communication seemed lost.

"Well?" asked Jack, keen for any kind of response.

"He sounded urgent, urging me to get the Chalice; they need it. He said more enemies are on the way, so we need to hurry and then he went quiet. I hope he is alright."

"I am sure he is. Let's do this, Arry, together!" Jack held her eyes, his smile full of confidence. Ariana felt reassured and smiled in return.

"Race ya!" cried Jack as he bounded away, looking like a superhero in his slick gold and black suit. "Watch this Arry! I discovered I can do amazing manoeuvres in this suit!" He leapt high into the air and literally somersaulted in the sky, grabbed onto a really high tree branch and swung from it like Tarzan, as he moved quickly from tree to tree, finally coming to a stop on the peak of a rather large cluster of rocks. "Tah dah!" he sang with a bow.

"Guys, look at me!" Jessica cried as she ran at superfast speed and leapt up into the air and zig-zagged around one tree and then another, backflipped into the air and landed in front of Ariana, perfectly.

"Wow! Ok my turn," said Ariana. She ran and felt herself accelerate to a super-fast speed, leapt up and felt so free as she flew up into the air, higher than she thought she would go. She used her arms to propel herself forward and began doing acrobatics in the air too. "Oh my gosh, this is amazing!" she cried. "Why didn't they tell us this when we were in training? We could have done so much better in combat practice! Pippy, why didn't you tell us we could do all these amazing things in our suits?" she asked, turning to Pippy expectantly.

Pippy fluttered up to Ariana's face so she was at her eye-level. "I did tell you. I said that the suit would become a part of you and would enable you to express your ultimate truth, the truth of your inner self, who you really are." And with that, Pippy fluttered away to catch up with the panthers that by now were quite some way ahead of them, leaving Ariana thoughtfully mulling over her words.

"So, what do you think she means?" asked Jessica as she admired herself in her golden suit and did a few backflips with such overwhelming ease.

Jack had come down from the top of the rocks. "I think she means that everything we can do in these suits comes from our true selves. Now, that is amazing and means that we are capable of much more than we realise!"

"Wise words, jumping Jack," said Jessica as she somersaulted and landed right in front of them both, hands on her hips as she swished back her hair and grinned broadly, clearly pleased with her gymnastic display.

"Well, I am certainly not complaining but I have a feeling that we are going to need these abilities if we are to get the Chalice and get back to En Arias in one piece," warned Ariana. Her serious words brought them back to Earth with a bump, and they both looked at her with sombre faces.

"Come quickly!" called Pippy, fluttering up and down and waving her hands at them furiously.

The panthers were nowhere to be seen. Pippy flitted out of sight behind some thick brambles and trees up ahead. They couldn't see what lay beyond. The three of them hurried after Pippy and when they reached the edge of the bramble, their sharp intake of breath said it all. They were confronted by a tremendous valley, covered with the most beautiful green grasslands and forests, lush bright green foliage of different shades adorned the landscape, almost glistening in the sunlight. The view from where they stood was amazing and there was a sparkling waterfall like no other, that teemed with shiny fish, leaping in and out of the shimmering water as it gushed into a beautiful river that literally glowed silvery gold and flowed as far as the eye could see. Far in the distance, stood a mighty blue mountain range, snow-tipped and shrouded in mist. All around them, and everywhere they looked there was life, unusual insects and creatures scurrying around, birds and flying reptilian creatures zipping around in the sky.

Suddenly, one of the panthers leapt out from the undergrowth, making them jump. With eyes wide and fiery, and after a rather ferocious growl, the panther said, "We are being followed. My fearsome warrior brother has stalked the enemy and together we will head them off and destroy them, but more may come, so we will stand firm here to hold our ground and buy you time. You must follow the river northwards to its edge, and there you will find the way to the ancient tombs; the sacred book will be your guide from thence. May the protection of the Mighty One be with you." He bowed his head, turned and was gone.

Ariana took the lead; she had the book in her faithful rucksack. "That's our cue to pick up the pace, let's go!" She hurried after Pippy who was already fluttering down the hillside and ushering them on furiously with tiny frantic hand movements.

"Thank God we've got these suits," said Jack. "I feel pretty invincible, and I think I can make it down this hillside in no time, watch me!"

He leapt onto the hillside and proceeded to spring down the hill like some sort of crazy jack-in-the-box. Ariana couldn't help but chuckle, and she found herself easily making fast work of racing down the hillside, barely touching the ground. These suits really did make you feel invincible; what would have normally taken them the best part of half an hour to walk down such a long, steep hill, they achieved in a matter of seconds. Jessica was already at the bottom of the hill; Ariana swore that Jessica must have somersaulted from the top of the hill to the bottom in one large swoop.

"I feel so energised!" said Jessica, looking exhilarated in her golden suit, like something out of a retro Sci-Fi movie, only a better, super updated version. Ariana laughed to herself.

"Me too," said Jack, "I feel great! Like I could run a marathon right now!"

"Me three! I could run ten marathons!" Ariana joined in, smiling broadly. "Why do we feel so great, Pippy?"

Pippy zipped up to each of their faces. She looked angry, her wings furiously flapping. "We haven't got time for idle chatter! Just because you can't see them doesn't mean we are not being watched; we have to get to the river's edge!" With that, she folded her arms and puffed out her chest at them crossly before swishing around and zipping off again.

Ariana looked from Jack to Jessica, their smiles about to break into a laugh as they covered their mouths to stifle their laughter, so as not to infuriate Pippy further as they hurried after her. Together, they ran along the riverbank, following the length of the river in the direction that Pippy was leading them, which she said would take them to the river's edge and from there they should make their way to reach the ancient tombs. Pippy kept talking about retrieving a key that she had been told was somewhere in the ancient tombs.

The riverbank was beautiful; there was so much to see, plant life that was alive, moving and wriggling, swaying with gloriously bright flowers, some were star-shaped, pear-shaped, and others were continually unfolding with multiple layers of blossoms before their very eyes. Small creatures, frogs and reptiles of different shapes, sizes and colours, stunning birds that put birds of paradise in the shade, flitted about in all their fine glory. It was much like the rainbow river where Leo had taken them when they first arrived in Elopia, except this place was even more abundant with life. It was like some kind of technicolour paradise.

"Pippy, what is this place?" Jack asked as his eyes flickered from one spot to another, trying to keep up with all the plants and creatures that were swaying, wriggling, hopping and flying from place to place. Ariana and Jessica were doing the same, they could barely look in one direction without seeing multiple things moving, capturing their attention with every glance.

Pippy hovered mid-air and faced Jack. She seemed to have gotten over her fury from earlier. "The Rainbow River of life flows into this one, they are joined together, sister rivers, and along these banks, here the life-giving trees are at their most ripe stage of reproduction. This means the land itself is over-flowing with life-giving nutrients and that's why everything is so bright and so alive. Can't you just feel the joy of life here?" Pippy started singing in her beautifully sweet voice, and she somersaulted happily in the air, she looked positively radiant, a stark contrast to her annoyance moments earlier.

"Yes, actually now you come to mention it, I do feel rather joyous," Jack enthused smiling broadly as he bounced upwards and did a forward roll in the air and began laughing.

"Ha-ha, me too!" cried Ariana as she leapt up. "Come on Jessica!" Ariana was giggling and Jessica joined her somersaulting in the air, laughing and shouting with joy, whilst Pippy sang loudly in the background, though her version of loudly was just so cute with her mini high-pitched voice! None the less she was belting out a little tune and fluttering around the three of them as they messed around, jumping up in the air, full of the *joie de vivre*.

"*La, la, la, la, la, la, and this is the way we sing and dance, sing and dance, sing and dance,*" Pippy was doing a little spin in the air totally absorbed in her singing, whilst Ariana, Jack and Jessica were now all rolling about in fits of laughter on the grass, giggling so hard they ought to burst.

"*WHO GOES THERE?*" a loud voice boomed, immediately silencing them mid-laughter. Ariana and Jessica's hands flew to cover their mouths in reaction as they all froze; even Pippy looked bewildered by the unexpected interruption as she sidled up to Jack, who quickly stood, looking around for the source of the voice.

The Cocoon Within

"*I SAID WHO GOES THERE, CAN'T YOU HEAR ME? OR DO I NEED TO SPEAK LOUDER?*" the deep voice shouted again.

"Where are you? We can't see you!" Ariana stood up and bravely challenged the voice as they all looked around, trying to see where this voice was coming from.

"A question with a question! Wrong answer! *I ASKED WHO GOES THERE?*" the voice boomed even louder.

"We come in the name of the Mighty One," Pippy piped up as she flew forward and hovered in the air. Ariana presumed Pippy flew forward to make sure she was heard. "I am a wish-helper, I come from En Arias and these are my friends."

"You have another with you, who is by blood, not a celestial," the voice responded.

Just then what was invisible suddenly became visible in front of their very eyes, and they gasped as they realised they were standing before a group of large, mighty warriors, both male and female creatures of humanoid bodies and faces but with reptilian skin and features that glistened and shimmered, and snake-like tongues flickered in and out of their mouths as though tasting the air. They wore armour and held weapons that appeared in one moment as though made from stone, wood and iron, and the next, they shimmered as though metal and translucent. The warriors looked mighty and fearsome, and they sat on beasts that looked like large reptilian horses.

One of the mighty warriors was clearly the leader. His large muscular, and thickset reptilian body was seated on a great beast that shook its head with vigour, and scraped its webbed claws across the ground, appearing eager to race forward. Its master kept it under control as he spoke to them.

"We are the Gnetic, the keepers of the river's edge. What do you come seeking?" asked the leader of the group.

"Oh, great warrior," responded Pippy, fluttering in the air and giving a little bow as she cast a quick sidelong look at the others, signalling to them to do the same. Ariana and Jessica quickly bowed too, and Ariana nudged Jack and he did likewise.

"We only want to pass through the river's edge to the Ancient Tombs, if you please your greatness. We will just pass quietly through," beseeched Pippy on their behalf.

"What is your business in the Ancient Tombs, wish-helper?" asked the mighty warrior, scanning each one of them keenly, taking in their attire. His gaze paused at Ariana.

"Our business is by the command of the Mighty One, oh great warrior, we seek only to pass through, we bring no trouble." Pippy's little voice held a desperate note.

The great warrior paused before speaking again, "Why do you bring another with you that is by blood, not celestial?"

"He has the gift of sight, and he entered from the earthly realm with the others."

The other warriors reacted with mutterings of surprise as the great warrior stared at the three of them thoughtfully before raising his webbed hand to silence his followers, and responding,

"So, he is a Child of Mankind, yet their kind have never walked the other realms, interesting." He studied Jack for a moment before gazing upon Jessica and then Ariana. "Celestial beings, which order are you from?" he asked them directly.

"I am Elopian," replied Jessica, thinking that ought to do, as Eriat had told her she was half-Elopian, but she didn't remember her saying anything else other than her being a Go-between.

"And I am from the highest order of Seraphim in the seventh realm," said Ariana, remembering what Eriat had told her. The crowd muttered amongst themselves again in reaction to this news.

"A celestial being from the seventh realm has great powers and has no fear," said the great warrior, looking at the She-warrior to his left and nodding.

The She-warrior dismounted and withdrew a sword from its sheath at her side. The metal of the sword glinted and as the She-warrior raised her sword, it appeared translucent one moment, and steely silver the next. The She-warrior had muscled legs that were thickset, and strong arms just as muscled; she wore armour on her body and her exposed skin was reptilian. Her face was broad, eyes green and black just like snake eyes, her features were surprisingly regal with smooth reptilian skin and long dark hair braided with golden beads interwoven. Her snakelike tongue flickered in and out of her mouth; she had markings on her reptilian-skinned humanoid face, just like tribal marks that made her look even more fearsome. The She-warrior's eyes were fixed on Ariana as she motioned for her to step forward and fight, legs spread in a warrior stance as she held her sword at the ready.

Ariana looked at Pippy for guidance, but Pippy just shrugged her shoulders, fluttered close to Ariana and whispered, "Remember your training."

Training! Ariana wasn't sure what to expect from this opponent, training never really prepares you for the real thing. But before she could dwell on the matter any longer, the She-warrior was running at her with her sword, zigzagging at speed and as she came in for the attack with her sword lifted high about to strike, in an instant Ariana's sword struck the She-warriors sword in defence. Surprised at how fast her own reflexes had been, Ariana didn't even remember pulling her sword out, let alone with such precise speed. The clash of translucent metal on metal was loud. Ariana was surprised at how easily she pushed the She-warrior backwards with her sword against sword. The She-Warrior stood back and paced on the ground from side to side, getting ready for a second attack, yet with every strike, Ariana struck back faster, stronger, bolder, harder. Ariana realised she didn't feel afraid at all, she felt stronger and stronger the more she fought, it felt... easy. She could see her opponent becoming weary, yet Ariana was more and more energised, as she somersaulted, dived, and outmanoeuvred her opponent at every angle in every moment. Ariana realised that she could easily have killed her opponent many times over, but she didn't want to. When the She-warrior's strikes became weakened, Ariana struck her opponent's sword so hard that it forced the She-warrior to fall back, and at the same time the sword flung out of the She-warrior's grip, clanging to the ground. Ariana stood over the She-warrior and held her sword against her opponent's throat, and everyone fell silent.

Ariana withdrew her sword and sheathed it; she held out her hand to her opponent and pulled her to her feet. The She-Warrior bowed to Ariana in acknowledgement of her defeat and then climbed back onto her reptilian horse.

"You have proven yourself a superior opponent, therefore it rings of truth that your bloodline is of the seventh realm," acknowledged the leader and he turned to his group, "Stand aside and let them pass."

The group divided in two, riding their beasts outwards, to reveal a glistening tunnel. It looked like a giant wormhole, translucent, shimmering and pulsating as though it were alive.

"This portal will take you to the ancient tombs. Take these with you and keep them safe, you will need them to return," said the leader and threw a small pouch to Ariana. Inside were opulent crystal pendants on silvery chains, one for each of them.

"Thank you," said Ariana, putting the pouch in her rucksack which she zipped up, and hoisted onto her back. Then she bowed her head at the great leader and led the others to the edge of the wormhole.

"You kicked butt like I've never seen butt kicked before," Jack whispered, smiling at Ariana as they stood together staring down the opening of the strange pulsating wormhole, a great wind seemed to be blowing within it, creating a whooshing sound in and around it.

"Jack, it was just so easy, and I didn't feel afraid at all. I don't even feel afraid to go down this portal." She looked at Jack, their eyes met, smiling at one another and she could sense his adoration of her. They clasped hands as though their hands had a mind of their own and found each other.

Jack turned to look at Jessica standing behind them, with Pippy hovering next to her. "You ready?" he asked with a huge grin.

"I was born ready!" Jessica flicked her hair and gave a winning smile, just as Pippy perched on Jessica's shoulder and held onto the collar of her suit, ready for the ride.

"Ok, on three we jump!" Ariana squeezed Jack's hand and together they counted, "One, two, three!"

They all jumped into the wormhole and immediately it sucked them into what felt to Ariana like a supersonic downward free fall. The wind was gushing all over the place, she could barely move as they were going so fast. Her face and hair felt like it was stretched backwards tightly, she still had a grip on Jack's hand. She managed to move her head an inch to the left, and as she looked down, she could see stars whooshing by at speed beneath her, as she looked through the translucent pulsating walls of the wormhole. And then she saw a familiar sphere beneath her, for a moment she was confused and then realisation dawned, it was Earth, planet Earth! Her heart raced in response; her own reaction surprised her, because she immediately felt an overwhelming sense of love and yearning for the planet she adored, after all, it was home, and they were so far away from it. Involuntary tears streamed down her face as the sudden yearning besieged her, and she longed to be home with Granpey. Wonderful memories flooded her heart, memories full of Granpey and home.

She barely had a moment to dwell on those feelings as they shot past Earth, into space beyond, surrounded by clusters of the most stunning stars and nebulas that gave her a momentary sense of floating and time standing still. They headed straight towards a great nebula at such speed that the whooshing sound intensified. Ariana shut her eyes at the brightness and then suddenly the whooshing stopped, and she felt herself being thrown vigorously from side to side before landing on solid ground with a bump. Ariana opened her eyes to see a red rocky canyon; they were surrounded by a dry and arid landscape, it was sunny and hot. Ariana rubbed her eyes and looked at the ground, it was red, dry and dusty. She smoothed her hand over the ground and felt the crumbly dirt as she let it pass through her fingers.

"It looks like we're in Australia," said Jessica, as she stood and dusted the dry flaky dirt off her golden suit.

"That was some ride!" said Jack. "I mean who knows how far we travelled. I keep wondering if this is really a dream but it's as real as ever," he said and stood dusting himself off quickly. "These suits adjust their own temperature to suit the environment, have you noticed?"

"Yeah, no wonder I don't feel immediately hot and sweaty," replied Ariana. "Well, that's a good thing." She dusted herself off as she stood up and looked around, "Hang on, where's Pippy?"

"She was on my shoulder for the journey," replied Jessica. "She must have lost her grip at some point. It was rather windy in that wormhole tunnel thingy." She scanned the nearby rocks for Pippy.

They all began searching amid the dry rocks, calling Pippy's name. Suddenly, they heard the small sound of coughing and spluttering from behind a nearby rock. They raced over and Jack was the first to kneel down. Pippy was sitting down leaning on a rock. She looked up at them with a sombre expression on her cute little face.

"I have hurt my ankle, and my wing is torn," she said, twisting sideways to show them her right wing which had a little tear in the middle, the veins in the wing bulged slightly.

"Aww, does it hurt?" asked Jack with concern.

"Well, would it hurt if your arm was torn?" retorted Pippy grumpily.

"I guess that's a yes then," Jack stated wryly as both Jessica and Ariana chuckled and Pippy crossed her arms in a huff and turned her face away from Jack and pouted, at which point Jack had to stifle his laughter.

Ariana bent down and with her fingers, she gently rubbed Pippy on the arm to encourage her. "I'm sorry you're hurt..." her voice trailed off as a blue light shot out of her fingers straight onto Pippy and her wing restored itself in an instant.

Pippy turned to look at Ariana and her face lit up brightly as she flew straight up in the air and leapt about, crying, "I'm healed! Oh, thank you! My ankle feels great too!" She spun around kicking her little legs about. "You have the gift of healing, that's a beneficent gift!"

Ariana looked at her hands in amazement.

"Wow, Arry, that's just super cool, you really are the Chosen One!" Jack said with an awestruck expression on his face.

"What about me, do you think I might have the gift of healing too?" Jessica asked as she studied her own hands intently.

"Only celestials from the highest order have the gift of healing," Pippy confirmed as she fluttered about happily.

Ariana saw Jessica's face drop slightly.

"Well, we both have our own special powers, it would be pretty boring if everyone was identical," said Ariana, making light of it. "Let's try and find these ancient tombs. The Fearsome one said the book would be our guide."

Ariana pulled the book out of her rucksack; a bright white light shone from the pages and it glowed.

"The sacred book!" said Pippy, kneeling on the ground before it.

The others looked at one another and as Ariana was about to open the book, it opened by itself, the pages flipped with speed and then stopped at an open page. It glowed so brightly and then it began to dim until what was on the page became visible to them, glowing softly.

"It's a map!" cried Jessica excitedly. "I always wanted to go on an adventure like this; we'll be just like treasure hunters!"

"Bagsy me being Indiana Jones, then!" grinned Jack.

Ariana and Jessica both looked at Jack and burst out laughing.

The Cocoon Within

"Look!" Pippy had their attention, hovering over the book and pointing. They all peered closer.

"Look, I think this is the canyon where we are, and the Ancient tombs are all the way..." Ariana began.

"Here!" cried Jack pointing at the opposite end of the map.

"So that means according to this map, we have to follow the route straight through the canyon, and just beyond the red dust hills and there we will find the Ancient Tombs," Jessica finished.

Pippy clapped her hands with glee. "Then, when we get there, all we have to do is find the invisible key!"

"An invisible key?" Ariana, Jack and Jessica cried in unison with disbelief written all over their faces.

Jessica started laughing, "Pippy did you say that we need to find an invisible key? I mean if it's invisible, we can't see it, so we'll never find it; that doesn't make any sense whatsoever."

"I reckon it's called an invisible key but it's not actually invisible, right Pippy?" Jack half-asked, half-stated as he looked at Pippy with a hopeful expression.

"Well actually..." began Pippy but by then no one was listening to her as Jack and Jessica were arguing over whether the key was invisible, and Ariana was trying to be the voice of reason.

Pippy flapped her wings furiously and yelled at the top of her voice which sounded rather shrill, "Listen to me!" They all stopped and gave her their full attention. "As I was trying to explain before you all got so carried away, just remember nothing is impossible if you would only believe, and the key thing here... pardon the pun... is that I have the gift of seeing the unseen!" Pippy crossed her arms smugly, sticking her chin in the air as she waited for their reaction.

"Ok, so that means you see invisible things, right?" asked Ariana.

"Correct!" declared Pippy, quite proud of her gift as she did a twirl and gave a little bow. "Pippy the all-seeing at your service. So, what you can't see, I can see!"

"Hang on, so how come you didn't see the group of warriors earlier?" asked Jack not convinced.

"I did see them, but they had already seen us so there was no point saying anything," retorted Pippy.

"Guys come on, let's just get a move on and get the key and then get to the Mountain of Peace to retrieve the Chalice as per the mission!" Ariana was resolute as she reminded herself that this was the only way to save Granpey.

"Yeah, let's get a move on," agreed Jessica. "Remember the Fearsome ones had said that we were being pursued by an enemy, so for all we know they might be on their way to find the wormhole too."

"This way!" Pippy flew ahead leading the way through the canyon in the direction of the red dust hills that stood starkly against the backdrop of the clear sky.

As they journeyed across the dry rocky landscape, they encountered very little life other than the odd dry plant struggling to sprout a green bud or two, a few succulents that looked like cacti, the odd beetle and some flies. There appeared to be two suns in the sky, a greater Sun, and a lesser one, both emanating great heat that felt like thirty degrees plus.

Finally, after hours of walking, they stood in front of a giant structure with humanoid faces carved into a red rocky cliff face. It reminded Ariana of the famous faces of the Grand Canyon, but the difference was this carved rock was sparkling, they had to squint their eyes because it was so bright, but it was breathtaking. Looking up at the enormous cliff face, they could see the craftmanship had such detail. There was a great arched entrance that led directly into the cliff, which no doubt held many caves. The fascinating thing was that the carvings in the rock face shone and glistened and had the appearance of precious stones. Above the arched entrance carved into the precious stone rock face, the giant humanoid faces looked just like the faces of the giants that had pursued them back at the campus and in Botswood forest. The detail in the carved faces captured their ferocious expressions, sharp teeth exposed, and angry eyes. All around the archway etched in the sparkling rock were different creatures, leaping as in battle, some were slaying humanoids with five-fold symbols on their faces and likewise humanoids with five-fold symbols on their faces were slaying giants and creatures. It was a momentous battle scene etched in stone that sparkled as though cut from diamonds.

"Wow! The Ancient Tombs, right Pippy?" asked Jack, staring up at the great monument.

"Amazing, but I wonder what we'll find inside the caves?" said Jessica. As always thinking ahead, she stood with hands on hips in her golden suit and Ariana thought she looked like a real-life superhero.

"Is it cut in diamond I wonder?" Ariana looked on, completely awe-struck by the beauty of the monument.

Pippy fluttered up high to the rock face. "It is just as the legend foretold; this is a precious stone of three blends of celestial rocks, this will be seen at night from the cosmos when it grows ever brighter."

"Wow!" Ariana, Jack and Jessica declared together as they all continued to stare at the cliff face, such a sight to behold they didn't want to stop looking at it.

Pippy flew directly up to each one of them, clapping her hands in each of their faces, "Come on, don't allow it to mesmerise you, let's go find the key!" and she flew to the entrance and beckoned to them frantically to follow her.

"Pippy knows best, so let's go, guys," said Ariana, pulling Jack and Jessica away. Now that Pippy said it, she had been feeling herself lulled into a trance the longer she stared at the shiny rock carvings. She shook her head and felt clear-headed again. Jack and Jessica were both rubbing their heads too.

"Well, that was weird," said Jessica as she shook her head.

"You could have warned us, Pippy," Jack called ahead as they followed Pippy through the giant archway and into the cave.

"You could have asked!" retorted Pippy.

The caves were dark, and the only light was from Pippy as she glowed brightly in the darkness from the tips of her wings all through her body to the top of her head and the tips of her toes; she was like a little lamp light guiding them.

"Thank goodness we have Pippy for a light to guide us in this darkness," said Jessica, trudging after Pippy, keen to see what was up ahead as much as she could.

They followed Pippy through the cave which seemed to go on and on endlessly. Pippy stopped up ahead, her hovering wings making a flapping noise that echoed through the cave. Jessica was right behind Pippy.

"Guys, look we have three routes to choose from."

Jack and Ariana caught up with them and they stood together as they deliberated on which way to go next.

"Look, this way you can see the tunnel narrows quite thinly," said Ariana peering at the next route. "The middle cave looks wider but if you listen you can hear water, so I'm not sure that would be a good route." She looked at the final route. "Pippy, can you hover in the last cave so we can see better?"

Pippy flew into the mouth of the last cave entrance and as they all peered down to get a better view, they could see that the cave led to a tunnel that was not too narrow, the inside of it was lined with markings and symbols and it was different from the other two.

"Let's take this one," said Pippy enthusiastically. "This is the way! The symbols speak of hidden treasures."

"Great! Let's do this!" Jessica said eagerly and they all hurried after Pippy as she zipped down the tunnel rather excitedly.

"This is getting more and more like a cross between an Indiana Jones adventure and a Space Odyssey!" cried Jack with just as much enthusiasm, as he smiled at Ariana broadly and grabbed her hand.

Ariana liked this side of Jack; she had noticed he was becoming very tactile towards her since they'd left home, and it was making her heart flutter. She smiled back at him, and they continued forward following behind Jessica and Pippy. Jessica stopped up ahead, but Pippy carried on fluttering forward, illuminating the upper part of the cave which appeared to be getting narrower.

"Guys, I'm not sure about this place," said Jessica turning to face them.

Meanwhile, Pippy was quite far ahead by now and was ushering them to come forward, "I can see the tombs, it's this way, you can climb downwards to the actual tombs that's where the hidden treasure is, and the key is sure to be there too!" she shouted excitedly far in the distance, her little voice echoing.

Jack and Ariana reached Jessica. "What is it?" asked Ariana, seeing the concern on Jessica's face.

"I don't know... I can't put my finger on it, there is just something in the atmosphere here that I don't like."

"Ok, but we have got to get that key. Pippy said the treasure is just up ahead, I think we should move forward," said Jack decisively.

"Let's go forward slowly, follow in my footsteps," said Ariana.

She wasn't afraid, so she took the lead and began to move forward. The ground was crunchy and squelchy and with each footstep they took, they could hear and feel the crunching and squelching beneath their feet.

"Gosh, what is in this place, is it mud or something?" Jack asked.

"It sounds like we are squishing lots of snails, it's so crunchy underfoot," Jessica said, and she tried to examine her boots, but it was too dark.

The Cocoon Within

"Hang on, what's that noise? Listen!" Ariana stopped and after taking a few more crunchy footsteps, Jessica and Jack stopped too, right behind her.

"Sshh listen carefully!" Ariana commanded and they all went silent and then they heard it. It sounded like faint moaning but then it stopped.

"Come on, let's go; we can't even see Pippy now, just a dim light in the distance. I hope she is waiting for us," said Jessica, keen to get moving.

They all continued walking slowly again, crunch, squish, crunch, squish, crunch… and then the moaning again, so they stopped.

"Where is that moaning sound coming from?" asked Jack, scratching his head.

They started walking slowly again, crunch, squish, crunch, squish, crunch… and there it was again the moaning. They stopped again and the moaning stopped too.

"Pippy, Pippy, get back down here, we can't see and something isn't right, Pippy!" cried Ariana.

Pippy flew back towards them, down the narrow tunnel until she reached them and hopped onto Ariana's shoulder, her light illuminating their faces in the darkness of the cave.

"Pippy, hop onto my hand so we can see what's under our feet?" said Ariana.

Pippy hopped onto Ariana's hand and she lowered it to illuminate the ground of the cave. To their horror, what they saw staring back at them from the cave floor were lots and lots of eyeballs, bulging bloodshot eyes embedded in the cave floor, staring and blinking at them. They were horrid-looking bulging eyes in flattened faces with small moaning mouths, just about covering everywhere they could see on the cavern floor from Pippy's light.

Pippy screamed and hid her face in Ariana's hand. Jack jumped backwards and almost slipped over but Jessica quickly grabbed hold of him and steadied him. Ariana waved her hand sideways to use

Pippy's light to illuminate the area behind them and it was just as she thought, there was a trail of squashed eyeballs that they had unwittingly crushed as they had crunched and squished their way across the cave floor.

Jack began heaving several times at the sight of the bloody, crushed, eyeballs and Jessica and Ariana jumped out of the way as he threw up all over the place. He wiped his mouth with the back of his hand and looked down at the bulging eyes that were now covered in his vomit, and he muttered a courteous, "I'm sorry," and looked sufficiently contrite, though he began to heave again.

"Quick, let's get out of here or we'll all be throwing up!" yelled Ariana, covering her nose and mouth with her hand, as she hopped in between the bulging eyes and faces, trying to avoid squelching and splattering them. She could hear the moans as some collateral damage was inevitable.

They finally made it through the tunnel which led them to an opening of a large cavern and down below in the heart of the cavern they could see the ancient tombs surrounded by shiny treasures of gold, silver, precious stones and numerous ancient artefacts.

Pippy fluttered up and down with excitement, "We've made it! I'll search for the invisible key!" and she immediately dive-bombed down the length of the cavern to the treasure and began searching frantically for the key.

"Be careful Pippy!" cried Jack, ever the concerned one.

"I am being careful!" shouted Pippy from the cavern floor.

Ariana thought that Pippy was reminding her more and more of a rather petulant child and she chuckled to herself as she made the comparison. One minute she could be jovial and playful and the next she was stroppy and stubborn; it was all rather amusing.

"Look, we can climb down this way," said Jessica, leaping over a ledge and climbing down the wall of the cavern swiftly and easily.

She led the way and Jack and Ariana quickly followed. They all reached the bottom and could hear Pippy scrambling around, lifting item after item in her search for the key.

Ariana noticed that Jack had one hand leaning on the cavern wall and the other on his stomach as he took a few deep breaths. "Are you ok?" she asked looking at him with concern.

"Yeah, yeah, I'm fine, just a bit squeamish, taken by surprise. If there are any more gruesome surprises, I'll be ready now, though I really hope there won't be any more," he said, managing a smile.

"Well, that was pretty gross," said Ariana, making a face and then turning to see if Pippy had any luck yet, but it didn't look like it.

Meanwhile, Jessica was busy inspecting the treasure and Ariana noticed Jessica had slipped a handful of precious stones in her pocket and draped around her neck what appeared to be a silver and gold, diamond-encrusted necklace. "Jessica, I'm not sure we should be taking any of this stuff with us," she said, not convinced it would be a good idea. "As you said earlier, there is a really weird atmosphere about this place, and who knows where any of this stuff came from, or what it can do."

"We are part celestial, I don't see what it could do to us or why we shouldn't take it," argued Jessica, brushing off Ariana's comments. "Look, look at this, it's gorgeous and I have never seen anything on Earth like this and I think I deserve it." Jessica's eyes looked almost wild with greed as she held up a brooch covered in what looked like rubies.

Ariana shook her head and turned to see what Jack was doing, he appeared to be messing about on the wall. "Jack, what are you doing?" Ariana was getting rather exasperated with everyone acting oddly. Pippy was now going out of her mind, shouting about not being able to find the invisible key and she was even throwing stuff about in her frantic search. Meanwhile, Jessica was wearing every piece of jewellery she could find and wildly pocketing the rest, and now Jack… what on earth was he doing?

The Cocoon Within

"My hand is stuck in the wall!" Jack cried as he craned his neck round giving Ariana a desperate look.

She rushed over and Jack was right, his hand had disappeared into the wall! "Oh my gosh, does it hurt? What happened?" she asked in disbelief.

"I don't know, I felt my hand slipping as I leaned on the wall and now it's stuck and I can't pull it out, but the weirdest thing is it doesn't hurt, thank God, but I just want my hand back!" He looked bewildered as he tried with all his might to twist his arm and yank his hand out of the wall. It was as though his hand had been cemented into the cavern wall.

Ariana looked round for some support from Jessica and Pippy, but there was no point, as Jessica was now rolling around in the treasure, and Pippy looked like she was about to have a fit as she threw stuff about angrily, she clearly wasn't winning her search for the key. Ariana took hold of Jack's arm and pulled hard.

"Hey, you're gonna give me a really bad Chinese burn!" he cried.

"Oh sorry!" they both laughed, "let me try again." Ariana grabbed Jack's arm and tried to pull but it was no good. "Grrrr, this is so annoying!" she shouted and slapped the wall, and that familiar blue light of power shot from her hand, directly into the cavern wall. In an instant, what appeared to be a mouth in the wall spluttered and spat Jack's arm out, and both Jack and Ariana fell backwards onto the ground. They watched the mouth in the wall splutter and cough and then just above the mouth, a pair of giant eyes appeared, and they blinked, and then more and more eyes appeared all over the cavern walls and ceiling, hundreds and hundreds of blinking eyes staring at them, and making loud squishy sounds as they blinked. Jack quickly checked his hand and wriggled his fingers around and he looked to see if there were faces and eyes on the cavern floor. He visibly relaxed seeing that there weren't any.

"Guys... erm look, we're being watched!" Ariana warned, hoping that Pippy and Jessica might stop their antics.

"At least I have my hand back," whispered Jack.

"Whatever happens, this has been one hell of a journey!" she said, reaching for his hand. He squeezed her hand and winked at her. Why she felt the urge to laugh even now she had no idea, but that was the effect Jack always had on her.

Ariana looked at the hundreds of eyes everywhere, grotesque bulging eyes of all different shapes and sizes, blinking in unison, it was pretty creepy, but she wasn't afraid. She realised that the warrior leader had been right, she didn't feel fear, and it was pretty amazing to experience things that should cause fear and not feel afraid. It was extremely liberating. She stood and addressed the mouth in the wall,

"We seek the invisible key; can you tell us if it is here?" she asked boldly.

The giant mouth in the cavern wall began laughing, a deep bellowing laugh that turned into a high-pitched cackle and then a deep laugh. Again and again, its voice changed into a different sounding laugh and another and then another. Ariana realised that the mouth had a multitude of different voices. It was pretty eerie, with the ever-changing laughter from the mouth in the wall, coupled with the hundreds of bulging, blinking, bloodshot eyes; it was enough to make anyone want to make a swift exit from this place. Jessica and Pippy had stopped their frenzied search and had moved to stand alongside Jack, as they watched the interaction between Ariana and the mouth in the wall.

"You intruders bring a Child of Mankind here to desecrate this place, and yet you command answers from me!! Ha ha ha ha ha…" and on and on the gross laughter continued, getting louder and louder, as the eyeballs bulged and blinked at them continuously.

Ariana turned to look at the others for support, hoping for a suggestion on what she might say or do in response as she shrugged her shoulders, hands open wide. Jessica gave an encouraging smile and motioned with her hands to Ariana to carry on, Jack gave a winning grin and a thumbs-up, and Pippy silently clapped her hands as she smiled and nodded furiously, all to encourage Ariana. Ariana turned back to face the mouth as her mind grappled with what she might be able to say to get the result that they needed.

"That may be the case, but I am a celestial from the highest order of Seraphim from the seventh realm! And I command you to tell me where the invisible key is!" Ariana persisted defiantly, hoping that assertive aggression might win out.

To her surprise, the mouth in the wall pursed its lips together, then the lips trembled, and spat out its next words in a terrified voice, "Trapped! Trapped is what we are in this filthy cave wall! Accursed is what we are!" and then the voice changed to a feminine, yet screeching cry, "Oh celestial from the highest order, do not torment us for we are entrapped and there is no way out for us, help us, help ussss!" the voice echoed and was followed by great howling cries in multiple pitches of different voices which grew louder and louder. Ariana and the others quickly covered their ears at the awful cries.

Not wanting to take the sound of the cries anymore, Ariana had had enough of this cry-baby mouth. She was beginning to feel impatient, and a surge of anger rose within her. They were hungry and tired of this malarky of crazy eyes in this claustrophobic cave and they just wanted to find the key and get out of this damned place!

Ariana yelled, *"STOP IT NOW!"* and she put her hands out towards the giant mouth. "If you don't tell us where the invisible key is, I will blast your mouth closed so that you can never speak again!"

The mouth stopped screaming immediately, the lips began to quiver and to Ariana's horror, it began crying, literally wailing like a five-year-old. She felt a splash on her head as though someone had just thrown a bucket of water over her. She was drenched and as she looked up, another huge droplet of water splashed onto her face. She could see Jessica, Jack and Pippy getting splashed too as they tried to avoid the giant raindrops. Ariana looked up again and wiped her eyes so that she could see, and it dawned on her that it wasn't raindrops but tear drops! Huge teardrops were falling on them from the great mass of bulging eyes on the ceiling!

"Let's get out of here before we get soaked or worse before the cave fills up, look!" said Jack, pointing at the floor of the cave that was already starting to fill up. Meanwhile, Pippy was already heading back the way they had come and was at the top of the cave. She waved at them furiously to follow her out.

"Come on guys before it gets waterlogged!" Pippy cried as she waited up high back where they had first entered this eye-filled cave.

The others began leaping up the wall after Pippy. Ariana tried one last time, determined not to leave without having the answer. She aimed her hands at the sides of the mouth and concentrated on commanding the power to shoot from her hands. The blue rays immediately shot from her hands and cracked the rock at each side of the mouth.

"Now tell me where the invisible key is?" she yelled.

The mouth trembled and spat its reply, "The sacred eagles took it!"

"Where? Where did they take it?" yelled Ariana as she became drenched from the furious tear drops pelting down at her.

"Beyond the Edge of Reason!" spat the mouth before resuming its wailing cries.

That was enough for Ariana, she leapt against the cavern wall and sprinted up to the top of the cave in seconds, her soaking hair dripping. The others were in the cave entrance waiting for her. Amidst the echoing eerie wails of a multitude of voices, they scrambled back the way they came. They heard the squelching of the eyeballs underfoot and the groans of pain, but they had no time to stop and apologise, they just wanted to get out of this freaky place. Pippy lit the way as she zipped through each twist and turn, the wails fading as they put distance between them until they finally reached the entrance and flung themselves out onto the hot dusty sand, in the open air at last.

They followed Pippy as she flew over to a nearby cluster of rocks under a couple of arid trees that created a degree of shade. They made themselves comfortable leaning on the rocks as they got their breath back and took stock of events.

"Well, I feel bad for the eyeballs we squashed not once but twice," Jack said, slapping his hand on his forehead. "You just couldn't make this up!"

"Don't feel sorry for them, they're evil spirits and spies for the enemy," said Pippy casually as she admired herself in a tiny handheld mirror and pulled out a miniature hairbrush and began brushing one pigtail and then another, before snapping her mirror shut and shoving both brush and mirror back in her little purse that was strapped to her belt. They all looked at Pippy in horror.

"Are you telling us that the eyeballs have told the enemy exactly where we are?" asked Ariana, eyes wide already anticipating the answer.

Pippy looked up at them in surprise and said, "Oh, yes I didn't think about that!" with both hands on her cheeks as she looked at them rather sheepishly.

"In that case, we need to get going now," urged Ariana. "No time to sit around. Remember the Fearless ones said they would head off the enemy, but more may follow, so let's go." She was resolute and the others agreed. The map in the book should show them how far they were from the Edge of Reason and beyond.

5
Beyond the Edge of Reason

How strange to see a little house, or rather what appeared to be a small cottage in the middle of the dry red barren land hidden between two large clusters of towering rocks. Smoke was billowing from the top of its chimney, so it looked like someone must be home. They had made a hasty exit from the ancient tombs, putting a great distance between themselves and that strange place. Having travelled for several hours at pace, and hardly stopping along the way, they were all hungry and rather weary by now.

Looking at one another in amazement, Jack was the first to pipe up, "Do you think it's a mirage we're seeing?" he asked half-jokingly, but by now they had all accepted that the unexplainable was the norm in these parts.

"It's real!" Jessica sounded overjoyed.

"Well, it's a sight for sore eyes after all those blooming bulging eyes that's for sure! Pardon the pun!" Ariana grimaced with emphasis.

Pippy was off already, fluttering ahead to get to the little homestead first. Ariana had noticed that Pippy always wanted to be the leader; until things went wrong, she chuckled to herself.

"Do you know what I could really do with? A plate of fish and chips, fizzy pop and then a nice comfy bed to sleep it all off!" Jack declared.

"I'm hearing you, Jack, that sounds both delicious and dreamy!" cried Jessica in agreement. "Oh please let whoever is in there be friendly and hospitable and have food!"

"Well, if they're not, then they've got two fearsome Go-between warriors and a very handsome Child of Mankind who is a dab hand with a sword to contend with!" said Jack, unsheathing his sword and thrusting it about as if in battle, before he sheathed it again and bowed, grinning from ear to ear and looking from Ariana to Jessica expectantly.

Ariana and Jessica laughed and gave a quick round of applause. Ariana knew that was the reaction Jack was waiting for, he was such a big kid at heart, not to mention very caring and easy on the eye too… Ariana's mind was starting to wander.

"Come quickly!" Pippy was calling them from outside the cottage, waving her little hands at them with fervour, having found something of interest.

They rushed over and Ariana could hear Jack beside her repeatedly muttering, "Please let there be food, please let there be food…" she looked at him and he turned to her, and they both smiled at one another. She was so glad she was on this strange adventure with him; she wouldn't have chosen anyone else to be by her side.

They reached Pippy, and peered through the window to see what all the fuss was about, and to their surprise, and joy, they could see a table laden with a feast of food both savoury and sweet, and a pot of something brewing over a fireplace. The room looked cosy and welcoming with a very inviting living space, and leading off the living room were a couple of open doors through which Ariana noticed some very comfortable-looking beds.

"Jack, this looks just like what you hoped for!" Jessica was ecstatic, she clapped her hands and to everyone's surprise, she turned the door handle, opened the door, and walked right in.

"We should have at least knocked first!" Ariana said as she hesitantly walked in after Jessica, feeling like an intruder.

"Hello! Anybody home?" Jessica called loudly.

Ariana sure hoped they would be welcomed if someone was home, though there was no reply, and she thought perhaps that was rather a good thing.

"Mmm, this food tastes amazing!" Jack said between mouthfuls.

Ariana swivelled around and was rather horrified to see Jack sitting at the table, gorging on what looked like a pie of some kind and at the same time, he grabbed a handful of cake and stuffed his mouth with that too. Pippy was hovering over the table and appeared to be picking out some sort of round wafer-like things and she began munching on them. It suddenly dawned on Ariana that she had never seen Pippy eat before.

"What's that you're eating Pippy?" Ariana asked curiously as she pulled up a chair at the table. She noticed that Jessica had started to tuck in too.

Pippy looked at Ariana, her little hands holding a bunch of the wafers and her mouth moving really fast, cheeks full of wafer, with bits sticking out of the corners of her mouth as she ate furiously. "Mmm, mmm… it tastes so good… it's… erm… celestial food," Pippy gulped her food down before continuing, "In case you're wondering, wish-helpers don't need to eat as often as earthly beings."

Ariana couldn't resist the urge to eat. She grabbed a large slice of pie in front of her and took a giant bite; the more she ate, the more she wanted, and the food tasted wonderful. She hadn't realised that she was this hungry. Ariana stuffed herself with everything she could get her hands on, chicken drumsticks and pizza, cake and slices of apple and rhubarb pie; it didn't matter what it was, she just ate and ate, then wiped her mouth on her sleeve and let out a loud burp. She looked across the table and Jack had food all around his mouth and was still gorging; it looked like he had moved on to a pasta dish. Jessica was pouring peanuts down her cake-filled mouth, half of them falling all over her and on the table, and Pippy was now lying in a bowl full of the wafers she seemed to like so much and was still stuffing her face with them, her stomach bloated and protruding.

Ariana reached across the table for a slice of cake. She lifted it to her mouth and took a large bite, chewed and then stopped, it tasted funny. She looked at the cake in her hand and it started to change colour, and hey, did she just see something move in the layer of cream? She peered closer and then she saw something white moving in the cream, she poked at it with her finger and to her horror it started wriggling. The whole cake started to move, wriggling maggots began dropping out of it! Ariana instantly spat the cake out of her mouth and threw it down. She grabbed the glass of water from the table, but the water was putrid with bugs floating around in it, she shuddered and quickly put the glass back down. Ariana looked at Jack and Jessica and she saw them spitting black beetles out of their mouths and Pippy was throwing up maggots on the table.

Suddenly, the walls of the room began to bulge and move, as though something was creeping on the inside of the walls, it was happening all over the room. Ariana signalled to the others to gather beside her. They followed her lead, unsheathed their swords and to Ariana's surprise, even Pippy had a tiny dart gun at the ready.

They watched as cracks began to appear in the walls and a black shiny giant insect head came through one of the cracks with its munching pincers making short work of breaking through the wall. The giant creature wriggled through the gaping crack in the wall, its glaring large pincers wide, its multitude of sweeping legs making a clacking noise as it crawled swiftly down the wall towards them.

"Eww, it looks like a giant centipede!" declared Jessica as she pounced onto the table to avoid being set upon by the creature. She slashed at its head with her sword and severed its giant head which flew across the room just missing Jack's face by inches.

"Whoa, watch out!" cried Jack as he jumped backwards.

The wriggling body of the creature reared up and blood spewed and spurted from the exposed veins and arteries. Jack and Ariana slashed and stabbed at the creature's headless body and even Pippy blew tiny little darts which seemed to help subdue the writhing creature, but there was no time to rest in their success as they put one gruesome creature out of action, another grotesque wriggling creature emerged from the other side of the wall, then another and another and before they knew it, the walls were cracking apart and they were fighting off three more ferocious giant insects.

Ariana somersaulted across the table and sliced off the head of one of the huge maggot-like creatures with a great sweeping strike of her sword before it reached Jack from behind. Jack fought another giant centipede and as he slashed it repeatedly with his sword, you could hear the crunch of its shell as Jack's sharp blade made impact and the creature's insides splurged all over the floor.

Meanwhile, Jessica was battling with a giant beetle, its clacking arachnoid-like legs moving twenty to the dozen, as it charged towards her, with giant horns protruding from its black and green shell of armour, and its large scissor-like pincers gaping wide ready to crush whatever it could get hold of. Jessica pounced upwards and backwards onto the table, landing expertly out of the beetle's reach, then she withdrew her sword and jumped in the air and landed on the beetle's back as she struck with force and jabbed it right through its outer shell, before leaping out of the way. The beetle reeled in pain and ferociously snapped its pincers and butted its horns into everything around it, sending two chairs flying. Ariana leapt in the air and then slashed the beetle with one great sweeping arc of her sword splitting the giant creature in two.

As they stood with swords at the ready, breathing heavily amidst the blood, guts and remains of the giant creatures scattered everywhere, there was a great rumbling sound. They looked upwards and the ceiling began to crumble and then the walls too and they quickly ducked and dived out of the way of falling rubble.

"Quick this way!" Pippy flew through an opening in the wall, just large enough for them to get through and they quickly dived towards the opening, before they heard the entire cottage collapse in a heap behind them.

They spent a few minutes coughing and spluttering from the dusty rubble and as they gathered their bearings it became clear that they were in a cave.

"What the..." said Jessica, looking around the cave, "how did we go from being in the cottage to a cave? What happened to the great outdoors?"

Jack was at the other end of the cave trying to check for a way out. "Guys," he called, "I see a faint light through here."

"Hey, I have just had a thought, what is this place called?" asked Ariana, looking thoughtful as she tried to piece together what might be happening.

"What do you mean?" Jessica asked, scratching her head.

Pippy flew up to them and said, "She means this is the place called *Beyond the Edge of Reason* of course!" Seemingly glad to be the first to give a proper answer to Ariana's question, she did a little twirl and then crossed her arms and pouted in her usual superior manner.

Jack joined in the conversation as he made his way back over to them, "And that can only mean one thing then, right?"

"That we are all going mad?" said Jessica flippant as ever.

"Pretty much," grinned Jack, "to be fair I thought I was descending into madness the moment I saw those giants back in Bloxham... and a dog transform into a flying lion!" Jack made a face; dry humour was his default setting when he couldn't make heads or tails of what was going on, equally he would shrug stuff off with sarcasm.

"Guys, just be ready for psychological warfare so to speak," warned Ariana. "I think we may encounter some stuff that could take us to the edge, and I think we would do well to remember that all might not be quite as it seems," she suggested wisely.

"I think you're right," said Jessica. "The name of the place in itself is a dead giveaway, so I guess we need to expect the unexpected."

The Cocoon Within

Ariana pulled the small pouch from her rucksack that the Gnetic warrior leader had given to her, opened it, took out the crystal pendants and handed one to each of them. "Here, in case we get separated or lost then we can use them to get back to Elopia."

Pippy put the chain over her head and like a snake that was alive the chain and pendant shrunk itself to fit comfortably around her tiny neck. They all did the same and watched as each chain looped itself to fit their necks perfectly.

"Pippy, how do we use these things to get us back?" asked Jessica.

"You won't need to do anything," replied Pippy as she fluttered about and her crystal pendant shone and changed colour. She flew up to Jessica and lifted the pendant around her neck in her tiny hands. "These are thought-reading crystals, they are hard to get hold of and can be used to get from one place to another. The crystal reads thoughts, so it will know when you are in grave danger and you need to escape, and it will immediately transport you back to the place where the crystal was first given to you." And with that, Pippy flitted off to peer down the other end of the cave that led to a tunnel.

"That's amazing!" Ariana and Jessica both said at the same time each looking at their own crystal pendant around their neck.

"Will anyone believe us, Arry, when we go back home and tell our story?" Jack shook his head in wonder as he turned the crystal around in his hands and watched it change colour.

"If we ever get back," Jessica said shrugging her shoulders.

"We will get back and we'll save Granpey and the others and we will go back to normal life again!" Ariana was determined not to believe otherwise; Jessica could doubt all she liked but there was no way on earth that Ariana was going to let a jot of doubt enter her mind!

"Hey, Jack was right, there is light coming from down there. I think we should try to find a way out," said Pippy, beckoning to them.

"Come on let's go, lead the way, Pippy!" Ariana commanded as she strode after Pippy who fluttered ahead towards the faint glimmer of light.

Jack heard Jessica mutter, "Why has she got to be the boss of us all?"

"Come on, Jessy, let's get out of this place. I think these caves are making us all a bit stir-crazy!" Jack caught Jessica's eye and gave her an encouraging smile. She returned his smile and together, they followed Ariana and Pippy.

"Guys, look it's getting smaller," said Ariana. She and Pippy had stopped at the place where the tunnel narrowed substantially, and the light could be seen shining much brighter through the narrow opening, signifying that they had almost reached the way out.

Pippy fluttered up and down excitedly. "I can fly through and see what's down there," she offered and hopped onto the ledge of the tunnel, but before they could utter a word, Pippy disappeared down the narrow tunnel with such speed as though some force had gripped her and whisked her away.

"Oh my God, we have to go after her!" cried Ariana in shock at what had just happened. She looked at Jack who was just as shocked as her.

"What just happened?" he asked, looking bewildered.

Jessica approached the edge of the tunnel and yelled, "Pippy! Are you alright?" but there was no reply. Jessica leaned forward, "Pip..." before she could even finish her sentence Jessica was sucked headfirst down the tunnel just like Pippy.

"Woah! This is getting weird, Arry!"

"We need to go after them," said Ariana resolutely, but she waited for Jack's response.

"Are you sure that's a good idea?" he replied. "I mean we don't even know what's down there, we might be able to find another way to rescue them." He held out his hands and Ariana placed her hands in his and the moment she looked at him, Jack instantly knew that they were going down that tunnel. "Arry, where you go, I go," finished Jack.

"Great, then let's go after them." Ariana turned and climbed feet first into the narrow tunnel and in the blink of an eye, she was gone.

Ariana thought it was just like she was on one of those water slides and she felt herself zoom out of the other end of the tunnel at great speed, emerging into the daylight, but oddly, she didn't drop to the ground; it seemed she was… floating. As her eyes began to adjust to the daylight, she saw Jessica inside a giant-sized bubble, floating up high a few metres away from her, and in a much smaller bubble floating nearby, was Pippy who was frantically waving at Ariana and making gestures with her hands and face. Ariana realised that she was also inside her own giant bubble, floating in the sky, her eyes met Jessica's as they floated in their respective giant-sized bubbles, and she mouthed the words *'what the heck?'* Jessica responded mouthing words that Ariana couldn't really make out and she was pointing downwards. Ariana looked down and saw Jack fly out of the tunnel and shoot straight into a vacuum that created a giant bubble around him and he began to float upwards towards them.

Ariana looked around, they were in what looked like some sort of a small cove, floating in the sky in their individual bubbles. Ariana poked the bubble and kicked at it, it was no good, it was just like soft springy rubber. She unsheathed her sword and slashed at the bubble, but it simply closed back together the moment it was sliced, jabbed or chopped. It didn't matter how she attacked it, the bubble simply would not burst. Jack floated into her line of vision. He smiled at Ariana and shrugged his shoulders before showing his palms to her and pointing at each palm before pointing at her. Ariana knew what he was saying, though she was sure Jessica must have already tried using her powers to escape. Still, she decided that she might as well give it a go.

Think it, speak it…

Ariana held her palms outwards at the ready, mind focussed, she yelled *"I COMMAND YOU TO BREAK!"* and the familiar blue and white rays of power blasted from Ariana's hands and disintegrated the bubble in an instant. Ariana immediately began to fall, and she spread her arms wide in the sky, went into a dive position and braced herself for landing. She rolled onto the ground and finally leapt to a perfect standing position. Half-expecting to be set upon by an enemy of some kind, she held her hands out poised at the ready. Ariana scanned around but couldn't see any danger. She looked up and signalled to Jack, then blasted his bubble and he fell from the sky but landed well. She did the same for Jessica and Pippy.

"I tried to burst mine with my powers, but it didn't work! I don't get it!" Jessica scratched her head, totally confused as to why her powers hadn't worked.

"You need to think it and speak it, Jessica, remember our training. So, I guess if you didn't, then that could be why."

"Whoa, what is that?" cried Jack as they felt the ground begin to shudder violently, and they all swung around. "Guys, look at the ground!" he yelled and stepped backwards as cracks started to form. Jessica and Ariana hopped out of the line of the cracks and Pippy fluttered overhead with her little dart gun at the ready. Jack drew his sword, in defence mode, as they watched the rubble begin to crumble away as though something was about to emerge out of the ground.

One giant, greyish, gnarled hand with sharp black claws burst through the rocky ground and started frantically pulling the rock away. They watched as another giant hand emerged and then followed the muscular grey heavy-set forearms, and then a large grey creature's head appeared as it began to heave the rest of its body out of the ground, climbing out to a standing position. They hadn't seen one of the giant creatures as close up as this before. Its grey gnarled face was wide with raised cheekbones and amber eyes stared at them with fury. Large, sharp pointed canine teeth that looked like a row of great fangs and almost resembled that of a shark's teeth, were dripping in drool. Its ugly face was twisted, distorted and covered in raised markings that formed rows all over the top of its gnarled over-sized grey head. Its face kept twitching as though in constant spasm, and its mouth growled and snarled intermittently, baring those lethal fangs. For a moment it took its eyes off them and raised its head and then made a succession of loud, deep, guttural cries; it was clear that it was calling for others.

"Uh-oh, I think we should have stayed in the bubbles," Jessica shook her head and drew her sword.

"Er… Arry, perhaps we ought to run… like now!" Jack said, edging further and further backwards.

"I think we need to stand our ground and use our powers and swords to fight, there isn't anywhere obvious to run to," she replied.

"This looks like one of the same kind of giants that chased us around the school, this won't be easy!" said Jessica. "I sure hope my powers work when I need them to. I couldn't burst the bubble, but I seriously hope that was just a one-off user error, thank God I've got a Lifeblood sword!"

Heart racing with adrenaline, but ready for battle, Ariana eyed up the giant, standing at a height of eight or nine feet, its muscular body protected by some kind of metal armour with head, arms and legs exposed. It didn't appear to have any weapons, but she remembered that one in the forest had drawn a sword, though its teeth and claws looked lethal enough.

"Why is it just standing there staring at us?" asked Jessica, but then the ground began to shake, and the rubble began to move.

"No time to lose, more are coming!" warned Ariana and immediately aimed her hands at the beast and her power shot out from her hands and struck it, blasting its left arm away. Still, the creature ran towards her like a charging bull. She somersaulted backwards and used the force of her body to slide along the ground, parallel to the creature's legs; sword drawn, she sliced its legs in two and watched as it collapsed to the ground and then tried to pull itself to a standing position and failed, all the while its hideous face frothing at the mouth as it howled, angry amber eyes still set on destruction. She leapt in the air and thrust her sword through its back and immediately its body disintegrated until there was nothing left of it.

Ariana turned around to see Jessica and Jack each battling a giant beast, and more were emerging out of the ground. Pippy was firing darts which immobilised them as they climbed out of the ground but not for long, though it gave Ariana the chance to strike a fatal blow with her sword. Ariana worked in sync with Pippy and struck each beast with a fatal thrust of the edge of her sword, slicing easily as if through butter, cutting through each creature's toughened hide, as soon as Pippy had immobilised them with her darts. Ariana looked to her left and saw Jessica somersaulting through the air like a flying ninja and she began slashing at many of the giants with a fatal strike through their necks, as they fell to the ground and disintegrated. Jack joined in the battle and together they struck many of the beasts one by one, with force, springing into the air to ensure a good aim so as not to leave any standing. Their Lifeblood Swords were living up to Eriat's description. Ariana noticed the sword was light in her hands, yet it felt heavy, she couldn't explain it. The sword was heavy enough to strike with force, yet light enough to wield skilfully, and that she did without thinking, working with immense speed and agility, ducking from the enemy's blows, lunging jaws and claws, and easily killing each beast in front of her. Some of the creatures that began to emerge from the ground, now had swords like theirs, and they each fought with the clash of translucent sword against sword.

The problem they were having now was that every time they struck one creature down, another climbed out of the ground and another and then another until there were just too many, and now each creature coming out of the ground carried a Lifeblood sword.

"Arry, we need to retreat!" cried Jack as he was being forced backwards in battle by a huge angry giant creature, that roared at Jack before lunging forward, and the mighty clash of swords rang out.

Ariana turned to see Jack fall backwards to the ground with the creature looming over him about to strike.

"Noooooo!" she yelled and swiftly slashed the beast that she was battling against, and as it disintegrated, she raced towards Jack thinking she might be too late, and in that moment, everything seemed to be happening in slow motion. She saw Jack about to reach for his crystal pendant around his neck, but just then a tremendous screeching sound echoed loudly and immediately the creature standing over Jack covered its ears, turned and ran towards the hole in the ground, and jumped straight in. Every single giant creature and beast did the same, they all turned and ran back towards the hole in the ground, pushing one another out of the way to get into the hole first and escape.

But escape from what? Ariana turned towards the sound of the screeching; as it grew louder, her eardrums began to hurt, and she quickly covered her ears. And there in the sky swooping towards them, yet still in the distance, was what looked like not one, not two, but three giant birds of prey. As they loomed closer, Ariana and the others could see that they were tremendous giant-sized, two-headed eagles, and they were approaching with speed, heading straight for them.

"What shall we do?" Jessica asked, holding her hands over her ears. "Ouch! it hurts."

"Should we stand and fight? Use your powers?" Jack asked as he flinched and covered his ears as the eagles' cries got louder.

"No! We must yield to their authority, they are sacred beings, kneel, quick!" cried Pippy as she knelt on the ground with her tiny hands covering her ears and urged them to do the same. Ariana, Jessica and Jack quickly followed suit and kneeled beside her, heads bowed low.

"Don't look at them," whispered Pippy.

They all stayed still, poised in a kneeling position. Ariana could hear the tremendous beating of the eagles' wings as they came in for landing and she felt the force of a great whooshing of the wind from their wings. At the same time, she felt an overwhelming sense of their power and strength, and she knew she was in the presence of

The Cocoon Within

unusual greatness. She felt a sense of *deja-vu* and realised that it was the same feeling that she had experienced when in Leo and Eriat's presence.

Ariana listened to the multiple sounds coming from the eagles. They had stopped the awful screeching and now it sounded like they were communicating with one another with whistles and clicks. Ariana could see their giant talons striding beside her and the others, as the eagles walked around them noisily chattering amongst themselves. Then suddenly, their chattering stopped, and instead came the spoken word from the voices of the eagles,

"Celestial beings rise!" commanded the eagles, all three eagles with six voices spoke in unison.

Ariana saw Pippy immediately stand, so she did the same, as did Jessica. There was a great bright golden light surrounding the heads of each eagle, and their eyes were of the brightest jade, beautiful feathers shimmered, shades of gold, silver and bronze. The birds looked fearsome and mighty, and just looking at them took Ariana's breath away, and she had to keep moving her eyes away and squinting because of the glorious and pulsating light, emanating from them.

The six voices of the eagles continued to speak in unison, as though of one mind, "You come looking for the sacred key. Only those that are worthy can take up the key; who among you is worthy?"

They all looked at one another unsure of how to answer. Ariana hoped Pippy might know but she gave a tiny shrug of her shoulders. After a moment of silence feeling obliged to speak, Ariana said,

"Er your highness, majesties, not quite sure how to address you… er… we are not really sure who is worthy, please can you tell us?" Ariana asked in honesty, she thought she ought not try to blag on this occasion, pretty certain they would see through it straight away.

The six voices of the eagles responded, "Humility befits you Celestial, to establish a worthy one, you each must enter a trial of fire. Child of Mankind arise."

"Jack!" Pippy whispered harshly when Jack failed to respond. Urged by Pippy, Jack quickly rose to his feet and stood looking at the giant eagles with an awestruck expression on his face before squinting his eyes.

"Step forward," the eagles commanded in unison and Jack quickly obeyed. "Receive the gift of inner strength." And with that, the eagles formed a line, one behind another and the two that stood behind the first eagle suddenly merged into one and then finally merged again into the first eagle so that there now stood only one eagle before them. The two heads of the eagle spoke together, and their words began to float from their open-hooked beaks towards Jack,

"Wisdom in the inward parts"

Ariana and the others watched the words as they floated into Jack's open mouth one after the other.

"Excuse me, O' sacred ones, please may I have a gift too?" Jessica piped up bravely.

Ariana looked at Pippy dubiously. Pippy put her hands over her face and that confirmed Ariana's thoughts that Jessica probably shouldn't have asked for a gift. Ariana looked over at Jack who had an incredulous look on his face, and Ariana knew that he was probably thinking the same thing as her too.

"Step forward Celestial child," in unison the eagle spoke with its twin heads staring directly at Jessica, and she stepped forward eagerly. The eagle spoke words that floated with speed from their open beaks straight towards Jessica, but as soon as she realised what the eagle had said, she clamped her mouth shut hoping to avoid swallowing the words, but her mouth involuntarily opened, and the words slid inside.

"CONVICTION OF FOLLY"

"Oh, Celestial child, you have much to learn. Because you first rejected the words, you will stumble on your own folly." The eagle's words left Jessica speechless, and at that moment, the eagles separated back into three, and they all screeched loudly, causing Jessica and the others to cover their ears for the sound was excruciating.

The eagles spread their wings and flew up into the sky, and Ariana and the others only took their hands from their ears when they could no longer hear the eagles' pain-inducing cries, and they could be seen far in the distance soaring on high.

Pippy immediately flew at Jessica, hands on hips, brow furrowed and said, "Why did you think to ask for a gift? You shouldn't have done that and now look; you will bring trouble upon us all, I tell you!" Pippy pouted angrily.

"Well, how was I to know? It's your fault you should have warned us not to ask for anything, and anyway, I don't feel any different, so I'm sure I'll be just fine!" Jessica retorted just as angrily, planting her hands on her hips and staring at Pippy with her lips pursed.

Pippy turned her face away from Jessica and held up her tiny hand to Jessica's face. "Clearly you have no sense of wisdom, well you are only half celestial after all so it's just as I expected!" and with that, Pippy flew off.

"Oh... whatever! And I'm sure I have got the best of both worlds so there!" yelled Jessica as she stormed over to a rock and sat down and crossed both arms in an angry huff.

Jack and Ariana looked at one another, both stifling their laughter. Jack pointed to a cluster of rocks out of earshot of Pippy and Jessica, but close enough to keep an eye on each of them. Ariana sat next to Jack on the cluster of rocks.

"Let's just leave them be, I'm sure they'll both kiss and make up in the next five minutes or so," said Jack, ever the glass-half-full kind of guy.

"Yep, I agree, it's not worth the aggro, anyway how are you feeling? Any different?" asked Ariana as she peered at Jack intently.

"Nope, I feel fine and no different," he shrugged.

"That's good then, so what do you think about what they said about the key? That we have to go through trials of fire to see who is worthy, what do you think that's all about?"

"I don't know, Arry, but what I'm worried about is if those giants come back now the eagles have gone, then we certainly will be in a trial of fire!" he said emphatically as he looked towards the hole in the ground for any signs of movement.

"Oh yeah, I forgot about that. I think I was mesmerised by the eagles. I mean they were something else, absolutely breathtaking!"

"Isn't everything in this place!" agreed Jack as he took Ariana's hands in his and just stared into her eyes. Ariana's heart began to beat wildly in her chest, and she felt herself start to blush.

"Guys, look!" Jessica cried pointing over to Pippy.

Jack dropped Ariana's hands and they both immediately turned to see that Pippy had been sucked into a bubble, and they watched as she floated up into the sky. Pippy looked down at them from inside her bubble, gave a sad little wave and shrugged her shoulders.

Just then three more giant bubbles zoomed towards them and each one sucked first Jack, then Ariana and lastly Jessica inside their own giant bubble.

"Not again!" Ariana said aloud to herself as she punched the transparent wall of her bubble, but it just bounced back into shape. She contemplated using her powers to break them all free again, as she watched Jack and Jessica float up high into the sky in their bubbles alongside her own bubble, and then she heard voices speak in unison in her mind.

"Celestial do not break it! Let the bubble take you on your journey."

"The eagles," Ariana said softly to herself in wonder that she could hear them just like she had heard Leo in her mind telepathically. She decided she ought to obey their instruction and mentally prepared herself for whatever her nemesis or trial of fire was to be. Ariana's thoughts turned to Granpey and how much she missed hearing his reassuring voice and she hoped he would be alright till she returned with the others to rescue him. What could her nemesis be? Perhaps it would be a battle with ogres and giant creatures, a test of her celestial powers? Yes, that must be it; well, she wasn't going to let anything stop her from rescuing her Granpey, that's for sure. She would do everything in her power to pass this trial of fire so that she could get the key and go to the Mountain of Peace and retrieve the Chalice of Fire to stop the Destroyer, rescue everyone and get everything back to normal!

Ariana suddenly remembered where she was. She looked around wildly, her hands pressed against the soft and squidgy wall of the bubble, as she desperately looked across the sky to the left, to the right, up and down, but she couldn't see the others anywhere. She experienced a momentary sense of panic as she wondered where Jack had floated off to in his bubble. She realised that she felt worried about him, responsible even, should anything happen to him. She quickly shook off such negative thoughts. So, what if Jack didn't have any powers, he had a Lifeblood Sword that could easily slice through any being, and his Suit of Ultimate Truth made him stronger and more agile, and he moved like a ninja in that suit! Plus, the eagles gave him the gift of inner strength, so Ariana told herself that she had no reason to worry about Jack.

It was weird, she noticed that her bubble was moving faster and faster and it continued to gain momentum; everything was whizzing by, trees, forests, hills, getting further and further away as she was lifted high into the sky, until the land below appeared like a tiny map in the distance. Onwards and upwards she went in her bubble until she penetrated the atmosphere above, and suddenly there she was in space, whizzing through the cosmos in a bubble, star clusters and celestial bodies appearing to move past her at great speed, and on and on this went until she saw that fantastic familiar blue and green

The Cocoon Within

sphere, suspended in outer space, it was getting closer and closer, as she sped towards that beloved planet… Earth.

Ariana's heart was pounding hard with anticipation at the thought of going home. The sight of Earth invoked such a deep yearning within her heart that she thought it might burst and unexpected tears of joy trickled down her face. Would Jack be there? Did his bubble take him home too? And what of Jessica? And Pippy, could Pippy even go to Earth? Thoughts raced through her mind as she tried to figure out what to expect.

Ariana's bubble soared towards Earth at supersonic speed, and as it burst through Earth's atmosphere into the bright blue cloud-covered sky, she felt an amazing sense of happiness overwhelm her; she hadn't realised how homesick she was until now.

The bubble zipped downwards at great speed towards the land that she knew was England; it was taking her home. As cities and towns began to come into vision in the distance, her bubble took her straight down, heading towards a town and she could see the streets and lots of buildings and the bubble began to slow down. Ariana couldn't quite believe what she saw, as she travelled through the streets, she realised they were kind of familiar to her. It was Bloxham Vale, but it looked different. The bubble took her through the place where her old school should have been, but instead, an old factory was in its place. Marco's chip shop wasn't where it was supposed to be either, a regular house stood in its place. Everything was different.

Ariana frowned, feeling somewhat confused, why had everything changed? She peered through the bubble at everything she passed, wondering why it was all so different on the streets where she grew up. Even Lara's pet store wasn't there!

The bubble zipped all the way to the front door of her beloved home. Hang on, why was the door different? The door opened and the bubble took her inside. Granpey was in his rocker! But he looked different… less grey hair, less wrinkles… he looked younger!

The Cocoon Within

Ariana bashed against the walls of the bubble and shouted, "Granpey! Granpey, it's me, Ariana! Can you see me?" Ariana's heart pounded desperately at the sight of her beloved Granpey, she wanted to break free and throw herself into his safe, warm arms and tell him how much she loved him.

And then she saw a little girl, a toddler about two years of age run towards Granpey and fling herself at him. She was smiling and laughing, the little girl was so happy, her two little pigtails of red curls bouncing about as she tried to climb onto Granpey's lap. Tears streamed down Ariana's face as she recognised her younger self, and she watched herself as a tiny child. Granpey was laughing as he stood, picked her up and swung her around. Ariana watched as the little girl threw her head back in laughter.

Granpey didn't have a limp, he was walking about just fine. A woman walked into the room; she was beautiful. Ariana knew instantly it was her mother. Ariana's face and hands were pressed against the bubble walls, her eyes glued to the woman's features, she couldn't take her eyes off her. She couldn't believe how beautiful she was. Her mother, her mum, her mummy, all those things and more. She had never seen her mother before, other than in photographs, but when she was tiny, she had known her mother, but she didn't remember, why couldn't she remember her?

Granpey put the little girl down, and she ran and leapt into her mother's arms, her little chubby arms wrapped tightly around her mother's neck, and she was smiling at her mother and her mother's face beamed back at her with such love.

Ariana could feel tears streaming down her face, and such a deep yearning within her that it hurt. It hurt to watch the scenes unfolding before her, yet at the same time, it gave her such joy. Her mother and Granpey were talking, but she couldn't hear what they were saying from inside her bubble. Ariana watched every movement and gesture, she watched as her little chubby hands played with her mother's long red curls and she leaned her little chubby cheek against her mother's shoulder, snug in her mother's arms. Her mother kissed her cheek lovingly.

Then in walked her father! He was laughing, saying something, and he walked over to Ariana's mother and kissed little Ariana on the cheek before planting a loving kiss on her mother's lips. They looked into each other's eyes and smiled, they loved each other, and they loved her too and it was beautiful to watch. Ariana had been part of a loving family, with a mother and a father. Ariana wiped her eyes as she looked at her father's handsome face, he was tall and had broad shoulders and intelligent green eyes. His face was strong, and he had dimples when he smiled.

Ariana continued to watch as her parents were getting ready to go out, they said goodbye to Granpey, and her father held the door open for her mother who still carried little Ariana in her arms. Ariana's bubble followed them to the car outside and she watched as her mother got in the back seat of the car with little Ariana, and her father hopped into the driver's seat and off they went. Ariana's bubble followed behind them as they drove out of Bloxham Vale, through winding country roads, on and on they went through the countryside as dusk fell.

Ariana wondered where her parents were going. She tried to think of the places Granpey had said they used to take her when she was little, and the friends he told her that they visited. Suddenly Ariana's thoughts were brought to an abrupt halt, and she watched in horror as two giant humanoid creatures, just like the ones that Ariana had encountered, raced down the hillside and collided with her father's car, catapulting it into the air.

Ariana screamed and thrashed at the bubble, but she knew that she was just an observer, she couldn't change a thing. For some unknown reason she was being shown the past, the truth of what had really happened. Ariana's bubble zoomed forward, to where the car had rolled to a halt, and her hand flew to her mouth as she saw that, she and her mother had both been thrown from the car. Little Ariana had been thrown underneath some thick bramble and her mother was on the ground opposite her. Little Ariana was whimpering, she was hidden in the bramble her little face covered in scratches, her eyes wide and scared as she lay still, and her eyes met her mother's gaze as she lay on the grass opposite little Ariana, unable to move from her injuries. Ariana's mother's expression was desperate, she put her finger over her mouth to signal to little Ariana to be quiet and still. Tears filled her mother's eyes as they silently beseeched little Ariana to remain silent and one of the terrifying giant humanoid creatures raced towards them, grabbed hold of Ariana's mother and dragged her away from the bramble. Screams of pain could be heard as the creature mauled her mother over and over until there was silence.

Ariana's father was fighting the other giant beast and he blasted it with familiar blue-white rays of power from his hands and then used a translucent sword to finish the creature off and then he quickly ran to strike the other creature that was mauling her mother, slashing it through the neck until it melted away like the other one. Ariana's father gave an excruciatingly deep cry of anguish as he threw himself to the ground and cradled her mother in his arms.

What happened next shocked Ariana; out of nowhere a dark shadow emerged behind her father, and out of the shadow crawled a hideous creature with deep sunken, piercing amber eyes, in a face that appeared like it was carved out of raw flesh and bone. It had two coiled horns on its head, one on either side. It struck Ariana's father with great long knife-like claws right through his back, slicing through his flesh and piercing through his chest. Ariana screamed right where she was in her bubble and burst into a flood of involuntary tears, she sobbed as she looked on at her poor father, and the hideous creature's face contorted in fury as it twisted its knife-like claws further inside her father's chest. The beast's terrifying face was one that she would never forget. Through her tears, as Ariana sat on the floor of her bubble, she looked over to the bramble scanning for a sight of her child self, and there she saw through a small gap in the bushes, those tiny little green eyes, hidden, yet all-seeing, and they were overflowing with tears.

Ariana was shaking, she looked down at her tear-stained hands and they were shaking. Why couldn't she stop her hands from shaking? Was she about to have some kind of fit? And why did she have to see that, why? Thoughts continued to race around in Ariana's head as she sat on the bubble floor, just staring at her hands. She looked up and realised that her bubble was on the move again, she was heading back to Bloxham and it seemed she was heading home. The front door was open, her bubble flew inside, and there at the kitchen table she watched a much younger Granpey desperately trying to spoon-feed little Ariana, but she turned her face away from the spoon in Granpey's hand. Little Ariana shoved the entire plate of food towards Granpey and it tipped all over his shirt. Watching the exchange between Granpey and herself as a child was so moving, and in such a way that Ariana didn't think she would ever be able to explain to anyone exactly how it made her feel. She felt the tears prick at the corners of her eyes and the tug of her heart as she watched the scene in front of her play out. Granpey spoke to little Ariana as he wiped his shirt with a tea towel and he watched little Ariana's lips tremble and then her face began to crumple, and chubby little hands gripped the table, before climbing down from her chair and the little clatter of her shoe-clad feet on the hard floor could be heard as she ran out of the kitchen in tears.

From inside her bubble, Ariana watched Granpey bury his head in his hands. Ariana felt the tears roll down her cheeks, and she longed to reach out to her Granpey and put her arms around him and tell him that everything was going to be alright, that he did a great job raising her, and if only he could see her now.

The bubble suddenly whisked her along through the open kitchen door and into the next room. Ariana's heart skipped a beat as she watched her child self, lying on the floor with photographs strewn everywhere and in her chubby little hands she was holding her favourite photograph of her beautiful mother holding baby Ariana in her arms, and her father's arms were around her mother as both parents looked on lovingly at their beautiful baby daughter. Little Ariana was staring intently at the photograph of her mother and father that she held in her little chubby baby hands, and she remained motionless, captivated as she continued to stare at the photograph, and then she held the photograph up to her tiny mouth and she kissed it.

As Ariana watched from her bubble, involuntary tears burst forth from deep within her as though a dam had just burst. Her own voice sounded strange to her, deep guttural cries emerged from inside her and she felt as though she couldn't contain her heartache and sorrow and it all needed to come spilling out and that's just what it did. Ariana didn't know how long she cried as she lay on the floor of her bubble, nor how these strange-sounding cries from deep within her had been unleashed to let out all this pain and sorrow that had been unconsciously hidden and buried so deep for so long.

Ariana, still lying on the floor of the bubble and curled in a foetal position, her body shuddering intermittently as her sobs began to slow down, her mind was racing over and over the events she had just seen. She never knew that she had witnessed her mother and father's death when she was a young child. No, correction, she had witnessed their horrific murder! What a traumatic thing for such a young child to go through, she had survived it and yet she must have blocked out the events from her psyche. As Ariana tried to process everything, she began to feel a surge of intense anger rising inside her. It was an overwhelming fury that made her want to exact revenge on the evil ones who had done this to her parents and her. Ariana raised her head and suddenly she realised that she wasn't inside the bubble anymore, beneath her hands she felt soft grass.

"Where am I?" she softly asked herself, and she snuffled and wiped her eyes with the back of her hand as she looked around. Ariana hadn't even noticed that her bubble had travelled and had disappeared leaving her in what looked like the middle of a forest.

"Oh no, not another forest!" she muttered to herself, momentarily forgetting her sorrows as she raised herself to a sitting position.

The forest floor was covered in tiny plants that sprouted little red berries, making the forest look a little less gloomy. As Ariana's eyes swept across the forest floor, her eyes were drawn to the sparse rays of sunlight that penetrated the canopy of giant trees, and she noticed something glinting subtly through the trees in the distance, but she couldn't quite make out what it was. Her interest piqued, Ariana stood and dusted off a few remnants of grass and berry bits that clung to her suit, and she walked towards the trees up ahead, to get a better look at what it was that had caught her attention.

As Ariana got closer, she brushed hanging branches aside and was surprised to see one side of a hidden building with double doors that opened and closed as people entered it. Ariana stood in amazement and looked at the people who were walking through the double doors that opened silently, and closed again, and opened and closed after each person walked through them. She noticed that in each group of people walking through the doors, there were children, parents with their sons or daughters, mothers with their children and fathers with their children. Ariana followed, curious to know where they were all going, so joining the throng of people she walked through the automatic doors. As soon as Ariana went through the double doors, a loud bleeping sound, just like a shop alarm went off. Immediately everyone turned to look at her, all the groups of parents with their children, just staring at her in horror as though she had committed some awful crime. Ariana felt herself blushing with the multitude of eyes on her, she shrugged, her expression contrite, as she walked through the crowds. Looking around she realised that she appeared to be in a shopping mall, of all places! Ariana heard a chuckle behind her and whispering and she looked round to see the people were laughing at her, a small boy eating an ice cream was laughing and pointing at her. Ariana looked at the boy and gave him a stern look, but the boy spat words at her,

"You have no mother and no father, you freak!" the boy started laughing at Ariana loudly, with his mouth covered in ice cream. The little boy's face looked contorted.

A girl approached Ariana and threw an empty can at her, jeering at her, "No one loves you, no one wants you after you murdered your parents, it was all your fault!" The girl's face looked evil and when she started laughing, Ariana noticed her teeth were sharp and pointy.

One of the mothers stood forward and yelled at Ariana, "You should have done something to save your mother! You are to blame for their deaths!" The woman's face was contorted in anger, her eyes were a stark amber colour and she wagged her finger at Ariana for emphasis.

The rest of the crowd began to join in, hurling things at Ariana as she ducked her head and used her arm to shield her face. Her heart pounded furiously; she felt such overwhelming hurt and shame, as the crowd ostracised her. They were right, she didn't have any parents; it was her fault that her parents were murdered, she could have done something to save her mother but she didn't. As Ariana stood in front of the crowd, she was shaking and she felt such pain deep inside the pit of her stomach, believing she had let her parents down. Tears streamed down her face as she stood there in the middle of the evil crowd of parents and children as they hurled insults at her. As she wiped her eyes and looked around the crowd in panic, they continued to laugh at her, but they no longer had human faces, and even their bodies were transforming! She looked on, confused for a moment and then she realised that they were all turning into Tormenting ones, those strange alien creatures that she had encountered at school! She stared at the jeering faces set in the large greyish-white oversized heads of the creatures, their small thin arms with large hands and sharp claws waving around and punching at the air as they taunted her.

Ariana came to her senses and remembered where she was. She began to feel the fury rising inside her and she reminded herself that she had powers! This was her trial; she should have known! Ariana raised and aimed her hands at the creatures.

"No! I am not responsible for my parents' deaths! It was YOU, you evil creatures who killed them!" and with that, she began blasting the Tormenting creatures and she watched as they disintegrated one by one, the remaining ones were running about wildly trying to avoid being blasted.

Suddenly a thundering sound could be heard, and as it got nearer, it sounded like heavy-footed running. Ariana could see three giants approaching fast, racing through the crowd of Tormenting ones and she quickly drew her Lifeblood sword from her side. The Tormenting ones had formed a circle around her and they chuckled in glee as they took up positions, seemingly pleased at the giants' arrival on the scene. She realised that the Tormenting ones had taken up positions as spectators, some of them even appeared to be eating popcorn, jeering and laughing together. Ariana shook her head, as she reminded herself that she could blast them away when she had finished with these giants. Feeling glad that she had her old *'fire'* back, she reminded herself of her purpose, exact revenge for her parents, get the Chalice of Fire and rescue Granpey and the others.

She stood, feet planted apart and Lifeblood Sword at the ready as the three giants shoved their way through the Tormenting ones into the circle and stood opposite her. The three giants drew their own Lifeblood swords, their muscular bodies heaving as they each took up position, their angry faces twitching and snarling at Ariana, their amber eyes enraged. But Ariana was not afraid, she matched their rage, she could feel it deep inside her, a natural fury and disgust towards these evil creatures.

She looked at the breastplate of armour on the beast directly opposite her and she twisted her head slightly as she realised that it had writing on it, she read what it said:

"Orphan Spirit" what? As Ariana read the words, she felt shocked, like the words were a punch to her stomach.

The beast ran at her, and the clang of sword against sword rang loudly. Ariana had swiftly struck her sword in defence without even thinking. She hurled the beast backwards and it swiftly came at her again, its mouth drooling through those sharp teeth that it gnashed at her, as she sliced at its arm and her knife went through its skin like butter. The beast screamed at her, the first time she'd heard one of the giants speak, its voice was deep and coarse.

"Orphan! Is that all you have got?" scorned the giant. "You are nothing but an unwanted orphan, your mother screamed for your help, but you did nothing, and you watched your father get killed and you did nothing, Orphan!"

The beast's words invoked such rage in Ariana, that she threw down her sword and ran at it, raising her hands in fury and blasting the creature with her hands, whilst screaming at the top of her lungs at the creature, to die. She watched as the beast disintegrated in an instant. Ariana swung around and grabbed her Lifeblood sword from the ground just in time to defend herself against both strikes from the other two giants. Knocking one of the beast's Lifeblood swords from its hand, she ran and picked it up, then somersaulted backwards and leapt in the air, springing up high before striking the heads of both beasts simultaneously, slicing the head off one beast with its sword and the other with her sword.

Ariana landed on the ground and flung the beast's sword into the crowd of Tormenting ones, as they looked on in disappointment at their counterpart's defeat. The heads of both beasts rolled to the ground and both their heads and bodies quickly disintegrated.

Ariana stood breathing heavily, feeling victorious, justified and invigorated, as she held her sword at her side and watched the Tormenting ones, booing at her and jeering, some of them doing a thumbs-down signal with their oversized clawed hands. An involuntary laugh escaped Ariana's lips, at the sight of the creatures' human-like display of disappointment, it struck her as rather funny. The strange Tormenting ones began to fade away, and oddly Ariana found herself running, she was running through streets in what looked like Bloxham Vale.

"Remember, this isn't real, it's not real," Ariana said to herself as she ran, "and hang on, why am I running? Or rather, what am I running from?" She looked around and saw that she was being chased by more giant beasts. "Surprise, surprise!" she muttered to herself.

"Ariana, Ariana quick, hurry!" It was Jack and Granpey, both calling to her furiously and waving their hands at her from inside Jack's car.

She raced towards the car; the passenger door was already open for her and she jumped in and yanked the door shut as Jack slammed his foot on the accelerator, and they sped off just in time as the giants lunged for the car, missing it by inches. Ariana turned back and saw the angry giants still pursuing the car as Jack sped on, and they faded into the distance.

"Wow! That was so close! I never want to be tha…" Jack was stopped mid-sentence by a great crashing sound, and before Ariana even had time to process what was happening, she heard herself, Jack and Granpey scream aloud in shock simultaneously, as the car overturned and rolled down a hillside.

Ariana tried to brace herself and she reached her hand out towards Granpey at the same time, but she didn't know where he was. She saw the car door go flying as they tumbled further down the hill; she felt herself being flung through the open car, and she felt herself rolling through bramble, twigs and branches that felt like sharp needles and whips beating against every inch of her body. When she finally came to a stop, she tried to push her tangled hair from her face to see where she was and hopefully see if Jack and Granpey were alright, but her hair was stuck. She began to panic as she tried to yank her hair free from the branches it was caught in; she couldn't see properly, and she needed to find Granpey and Jack. Ariana swiped her hair from her face, and she tasted her own blood which covered her hands. She felt pain all down her legs, but she didn't care. She snapped the twigs that had her hair tangled up, and she crawled through the thick bramble and flinched as thorns dug into her arms and legs. She could see the mangled car up ahead, but where were Granpey and Jack?

Ariana felt her heart plummet in fear when she saw three of the giants prowling around the car. She struggled furiously to free her legs, but they were tightly tangled. She looked around to see what was restricting her movement and to her horror, she could see that one of her legs was entangled in some barbed wire. Blood was oozing down her legs, but she didn't seem to feel the pain. She looked back at the giants and one of them held Jack's limp body by the scruff of his collar. It was staring intently at Jack whose head hung limply, and his arms flopped about as though lifeless. Ariana stifled a cry with her torn hand covering her mouth and tears streaming down her face. Her eyes scanned frantically for Granpey and she saw him lying lifeless on the ground a few yards from the mangled car. One of the giant beasts approached Granpey, dragged him by the sparse white hair on his head and flung him in front of the other two giants. She heard Granpey groan in pain, and his hand moved feebly to his head. When the giant nearest to Granpey saw the movement, it instantly leapt forward and struck Granpey with force, sending him flying further down the hill towards the bramble where Ariana was hidden.

Ariana was frozen to the spot, terrified for her beloved Granpey and Jack. It was happening all over again. She felt like that helpless young child again, flashbacks of her parents' deaths paralysed her in fear as she looked on. The giant beast thudded its way down the hill towards Granpey, its gaze intent on destruction and its drooling mouth exposing its large sharp horrific-looking teeth, as its face twitched and grimaced. Just like the other giant she had faced, there were words on this giant's breastplate of armour. Ariana stared at the words that read, *'Greatest Fear'*. Her heart pounded wildly, and her mind raced as she tried to break free from the paralysing fear that was gripping her.

And then she heard it, a faint voice, just like a whisper in her mind,

"Remember who you are."

Hearing those four faint words was like a catalyst activated within her body and she immediately felt herself repeat the words as though in agreement in her mind, and then she said out loud, without even thinking,

"Yes! I am the Chosen One and I am not simply a helpless human! I am part celestial being of the highest order of Seraphim! and I am powerful!" As she uttered those words to herself, she felt the fear dissipate from her entire being and it was replaced with a feeling of intense rage towards the evil creatures in front of her.

Ariana's hands lit up with the now familiar blue-white rays of light, but this time the light encircled and covered her hands as though they were a continuous power source. The blue-white light was dancing and swirling powerfully, and the giant that had now reached Granpey, immediately upon seeing Ariana's powerful hands outstretched from the thick of the bramble, changed direction and headed straight for her. The other giant threw Jack to the ground and ran for her as did its counterpart, so that all three giants were coming for her. But they were no match for her; it was as though her power had reached some kind of unstoppable pinnacle, for Ariana simply pointed her hands at the giants and all three were immobilised. As she lifted her hands in the air, the three giants were lifted in the air, fixed in motion unable to move. Ariana blasted them backwards into the sky with a thrust of her hands and all three giants disintegrated with minimal effort. She realised that she wasn't bleeding anymore; it was as though all the cuts and grazes had disappeared, she was free from the barbed wire and had no injuries. She immediately ran to Granpey and as she knelt beside him and lifted his head in her arms, his entire body just faded away, as though disintegrating right through her hands.

"No! Granpey, no!" Ariana cried as she tried to grasp him, but he was gone.

Ariana ran towards Jack who was still lying lifeless on the ground, but he too disintegrated before she got to him. She stood there staring at the spot where Jack had lain, feeling defeated with tears rolling down her face. She suddenly felt exhausted, she couldn't cry anymore. She dried her eyes and that's when she noticed that there was the tiniest of flowers, a little bluebell all by itself. It reminded her of a summer's day when she and Jack had taken a walk through Botswood forest, and Jack had picked a bunch of bluebells, danced around and performed a mock marriage proposal to her, which had her in stitches at the time.

"No, no, this won't do! This isn't real, remember, it's not real," Ariana told herself as she dried her eyes. "Hang on! I'm floating again!" She looked down and could see she had floated high in the sky, and she realised that she was back in a bubble again, not sure whether she should be relieved or not. She wondered if this could mean that her trial was over, she thought rather hopefully, though of course she also hoped that she hadn't failed the trial, and she still felt rather dubious about where the bubble was taking her to next. She sat on the bubble floor and leaned back against the transparent bubble wall; at least it was comfortable.

Feeling emotionally drained, Ariana thought about how awful it had felt at the moment that she had witnessed her parents' deaths, it had felt so real, it was traumatising for anyone, let alone a child so young. Ariana buried her head in her hands, and to think that she then had to face losing Granpey and Jack too, though she felt certain that was part of the test. Number one, she saw Jack leave in a bubble and go off in a different direction and number two, Granpey was frozen in time back at the house. Yes, Granpey and Jack were just visions in the trial, she was sure of that; she hadn't really lost them. She sat up, feeling somewhat encouraged, and surmised that talking to oneself always did serve a great purpose.

Ariana sat on the floor of the bubble and watched the ground move further and further away from her, as the bubble zoomed upwards into the sky. It felt as though the bubble suddenly accelerated to great speed and took her back along the exact same journey to get here, but in reverse. All the way back through the streets of Bloxham Vale, past trees and hillsides and up higher and higher into the sky, until she cut through Earth's outer atmosphere and the cosmos at great speed. Ariana soon realised she was back in the land where she had started, only the bubble zipped past the Edge of Reason, and she found herself cruising towards an isolated island that appeared to be in the middle of a vast ocean.

Ariana crouched on all fours to peer down through the transparent bubble floor, trying to get a proper look at the island. Sheer technicolour beauty sparkled back at her, and she could easily have put on sunglasses to shield her eyes from the glare of the colourful and shimmering reflections that shone back at her. She looked up at the sky above and she could see the greater sun and the lesser sun, both shining brightly. She squinted her eyes and looked back at the colourful island as her bubble got closer and closer until it bounced softly onto the beautiful bright white sandy shore and then just melted away, leaving Ariana standing on the beach.

She felt her suit adjust its internal temperature, and if there was one thing that she was glad about, it was that her suit self-regulated its temperature to keep her comfortable, regardless of the external heat or cold.

She scanned the beach, squinting her eyes as she took in the beautiful giant palm trees, in bright shades of greens, pinks and blues. Colourful lizards scurried around on the sand, zipping in and out of rock crevices, tiny beady eyes looking up at Ariana as she slowly trudged along the sand. The sea created that lovely loud whooshing sound of waves lapping at the shoreline, ever-increasing just a little bit more in fervour, as it ebbed and flowed back and forth.

Something caught Ariana's eye as it moved far in the distance and she tried to make out what it was as she continued to trudge across the sand. She squinted, shielding her eyes with her hand to get a better look. Could it be? It looked like people waving at her and jumping up and down; they looked tiny as they were so far away. Ariana waved back and picked up her pace as she made her way towards them. It looked like they were also heading her way, and eventually, the distance between them narrowed, and Ariana's heart leapt for joy as she recognised Jack, Jessica and Pippy!

They ran towards one another, and Ariana leapt into Jack's open arms.

"Oh God, I've missed you!" he cried. "I was so worried about you! When I got here, I was all alone and then Pippy arrived in her bubble. We didn't find each other at first for a good while, and then together we found Jessica, and we have been looking for you for ages!"

His words came out all at once, in such a super-fast flurry, that Ariana just managed to keep up with what he was saying. Pippy was fluttering beside her, tugging at her hair and talking at the same time, elated that they had found her. Even Jessica was standing by laughing, as she watched Jack and Pippy fussing over Ariana, and she seemed pleased to see her too.

"Oh, guys I did worry about you all when we got separated!" said Ariana. "Especially you, Jack!" She looked directly into his smiling face; her eyes locked with his, her heart was racing, and she was beaming back at him, so relieved at finding that he was alright.

"Well, it's good to see we all survived the trials," said Jessica, tapping Ariana on the shoulder and smiling at her as Jack let her go.

Ariana took Jessica by surprise and gave her a big hug, and she held out her hands to Pippy who finally got Ariana's attention as she leapt onto her open palms. With wings fluttering, Pippy looked radiant with joy as she put her hands on her hips and asked,

"Haven't you noticed anything different about me yet?" Pippy did a twirl and gave a great big smile as she posed, waiting expectantly for Ariana's reaction.

Ariana looked from Jessica to Jack as they both shrugged their shoulders at her and looked at one another dubiously.

"Hmm, let me see…" Ariana lifted Pippy up as she inspected her. "Ah, I know! It's your wings! They look different…"

Pippy fluttered up in the air and clapped her hands in glee, "Yes! I have bigger and more beautiful wings that light up even brighter in the dark and take me even further when I fly. I never knew this was going to happen to me!" She twirled around again and again, laughing with joy as they admired her new wings.

"Oh, wow, that's great Pippy!" Ariana enthused as she laughed with Pippy, glad to see her so happy.

"There is a beautiful beach hut that we found," said Jessica, "where we can rest and catch up. I think we may have been sent here to eat and rest as food and refreshments are waiting for us in a more than comfortable setting. We found it just before we saw your bubble arrive. Come on, we'll show you." Jessica began leading the way.

"No bugs I hope?" Ariana asked tentatively as she remembered their cottage experience and shuddered at the memory.

"Yuk! No!" Pippy pretended to heave and they all laughed.

The Cocoon Within

"No, we don't think so, but let's find out," said Jack. He winked and grabbed Ariana by the hand as they hurried after Jessica, with Pippy fluttering along beside them, twirling and dancing in the air with her new wings.

***

"This is fantastic!" said Jessica as she lay on a sun lounger and sucked noisily on the straw in her glass that was full of delicious fresh tropical juice. They had found swimwear in the luxurious beach hut; it was as though everything had been thought of and each of them found something to wear that fit perfectly.

"It's utter paradise," agreed Ariana, as she did the same, relaxing on a sun lounger beside Jessica, enjoying the wonderful taste of the ice-cold juice that they had found in the kitchen, along with an array of fresh fruit and other delicacies, all laid out as though prepared ready for their arrival.

"This is bliss, I was due a beach holiday and this sure hits the spot!" Jack echoed their thoughts as he slurped his drink, before leaning back on his sun lounger, arms behind his head.

Pippy was lying next to Jessica, tiny arms and legs outstretched on a sun lounger that practically dwarfed her.

"Guys, I'm ready to talk about my trial now," announced Pippy. "I think we ought to share in turn." She had turned over and propped herself up on her elbows, one small leg wiggling around lazily as she faced them waiting for a response.

"I'm game," said Ariana, sitting up, "and I really want to hear about all of yours, too."

"Well, I can hear all of your wishes remember, so I know that you are all curious about each other's journeys," said Pippy, smiling at them with a superior expression on her pixie-like face before she began telling them her story.

"So, I had to face my greatest fear, which was losing my wings." She looked at them solemnly before continuing, "A wish-helper's wings mean everything to us; our wings have a special meaning, and not only do they ensure our survival, but they also secure our place in wish-helper society. My wings tell other wish-helpers of my ranking and proper place in the order of things. So, for a wish-helper to lose their wings, is a tragedy of the worst kind. They won't grow back and a wish-helper with no wings would be cast out from wish-helper society forever and would only be fit for foraging the forest floor for eternity," she paused and looked at them as though awaiting their reaction.

"Oh, oh that would be awful!" Ariana piped up quickly, shaking her head as she elbowed Jack, who had moved to sit beside her on her sun lounger.

"Awful, absolutely awful," Jack quickly added, with a forlorn expression on his face.

"Yes, quite tragic," Jessica agreed.

Pippy sighed dramatically before continuing, "My trial was not for the faint-hearted; I had to fight against the evil ones that chased me through a forest and there were other wish-helpers everywhere being chased too. Some were crying because they had already had their wings ripped off," she wiped a tear and gave a little snuffle, "they were everywhere, crying out for help, some were screaming in pain, but I didn't stop, I couldn't help them!" She buried her face in her tiny hands. Jessica looked at Ariana who motioned with her hands to Jessica to do something.

Jessica sat on the edge of her sun lounger and reached out her hand to pat Pippy on the back. "There, there, at least it's over now," she said, and she looked around at Ariana and shrugged her shoulders. Ariana realised that empathy was not one of Jessica's strengths, nevertheless, she gave Jessica a thumbs-up to encourage her, as they do say that practice makes perfect.

Pippy took her head out of her tiny hands and snuffled and wiped her eyes. "Thank you," she said, smiling up at Jessica before carrying on.

The Cocoon Within

"So, all I had was my little dart blower. I kept on flying with the others who hadn't been caught and blowing my dart gun at the evil ones as I tried to escape them. These evil ones were specialist wish-helper catchers, and they caught many of us in a net and we were all taken to their evil lair, where they tortured us and then started to pluck our wings off!" Pippy's face grew angry as she recounted her story, "and I had to watch my friends being tortured and have their wings plucked off and destroyed!"

"Oh no, but why did they want your wings?" asked Jack.

"To use in a potion; they snatch wish-helpers for their wings so they can crush them and make a mind-reading potion."

"Oh no!" cried Ariana.

"Oh yes and they show no mercy!" cried Pippy in anger as she passionately recounted the events of her trial. Pippy explained how the evil ones had stuck pins in her brain and in her wings, they had whipped her and stretched her arms and legs, whilst she screamed for mercy.

"So, what happened in the end?" asked Jack, as ever, keen to get to the outcome.

"After they tortured me, the evil ones dragged me to an altar, placed me face down and ripped off my wings!" Pippy began crying again, "It... it... was so painful, excruciating and humiliating!"

Jack, Ariana and Jessica looked at one another, lost for words, before Jessica continued rubbing Pippy's back gently, speaking kind words of encouragement and sympathy. Ariana was pleased that Jessica was getting better at being a shoulder to cry on.

"That must have been so awful, Pippy!" Jack empathised.

Pippy shot Jack a cross look, "It was more than awful, it was the worst thing that ever happened to me ever, ever, ever!" she cried.

They waited as Pippy composed herself and then she continued, "After they tortured me cruelly and ripped off my wings, they threw me into the ditch of uselessness, with all the other wingless wish-helpers. Everyone was crying and wailing in agony and gnashing

The Cocoon Within

their teeth, it was so awful." Pippy wiped her eyes and paused as she looked at them all one by one.

"What happened next, Pippy?" Ariana asked gently.

"I crawled out of the ditch. I asked others to come with me, but they were crushed in spirit because they let the ditch of uselessness cloud their minds and steal their hope. But I was determined, I just had to get out, because I know that all things are possible if you just believe."

Ariana thought about Pippy's words, they resonated with her and gave her hope as she thought about Granpey.

"It took me ages to climb out of the ditch of uselessness, I had no wings so I couldn't fly out. My hands and legs are too tiny to climb fast, and when I looked up, I couldn't even see the top of the ditch. I couldn't see the way out! I nearly gave up after hours and hours of climbing and I slipped three times, by the time I got to the edge of the ditch, I was covered in mud and exhausted. I don't even know how I did it, but I pulled myself over the edge finally."

"Well done, Pippy!" Ariana cried.

"Thank you," Pippy smiled at Ariana, "and then as I lay in the mud at the top of the edge of the ditch, catching my breath, I heard a voice speak to my mind."

"Oh my gosh! I heard a voice speak to me in my trial too!" Ariana enthused.

"Me too!" cried Jack in agreement.

They all looked at Jessica expectantly.

"What? I didn't hear a voice in my trial!" Jessica replied, annoyed.

"What did the voice say to you, Pippy?" Jack asked.

"The voice told me to get up and go and find some new wings! So, I did what the voice said, and I made my way back to the evil one's lair. I covered my face in mud too, so that I looked like a ground gremlin. I thought that if I was going to find new wings then there were going to be wings in the evil one's lair. I knew that would mean taking someone else's wings but if that was my destiny, then so be it." Pippy shrugged her shoulders and gave them a wide-eyed look.

"When I got to the lair, I crept in through a rat's hole. I could hear the blood-curdling screams from the torture chamber, but I carried on through the lair, searching and then I found a room full of wish-helper wings. They weren't just any old wish-helper wings, they were the highest order of wish-helper wings. The voice spoke to me again and told me to take these." Pippy twirled around for dramatic effect. "Otherwise, I never would have ever presumed to take higher-order wings. Legend has it that if the wings are ever removed from the highest order wish-helper, the wings can't be destroyed, but they can be transferred to another wish-helper but on one condition only," she said, with a look of amazement on her face.

"On what condition?" asked Jessica earnestly.

"Only if the wish-helper is worthy! The wings won't bond otherwise," Pippy replied, and raised her brows at them, her eyes were like saucers in her small face, "Don't you see? When I took the wings, they just bonded to my back seamlessly! It means I'm worthy and that I must have a special purpose! I am now a highest order wish-helper! A leader of wish-helpers!" Pippy fluttered off her lounger, twirled around and clapped her hands, "I just can't believe it!"

"Wow, that's amazing Pippy and I'm proud of your determination, though I wish there was something we could do to help the other persecuted wish-helpers," Ariana said, thoughtfully.

"Me too," Pippy agreed.

"Well, maybe there will be something we can do. Maybe when we get the Chalice of Fire, it might put all things right, who knows?" Jessica speculated.

"Hmmm, if we take a leaf from your book, Pippy, anything is possible," Jack added with a broad smile.

"If we believe!" agreed Pippy.

"Right, my turn, let me tell you what happened to me," said Jack, getting up from his sun lounger. He was wearing brightly coloured Bermuda shorts and flip-flops.

Ariana wondered who was responsible for the wardrobe get-up on this island. Though Pippy assured her that it was most likely benevolent beings that had been tasked with that responsibility, and Pippy had also said that they would know exactly what clothing earthly beings wore from all the different eras. Ariana chuckled to herself thinking that they must have got their eras mixed up as Jack definitely had that eighties look going on right now.

Jack paced in front of them slowly as he recounted the events of his own trial, and Ariana, Jessica and Pippy lay back on their sun loungers all ears.

"So, I too had to face my greatest fear," said Jack and he paused to look at them each in turn before he gulped and took a deep breath, "Just as Pippy said about her trial, my own was also not for the faint-hearted, I repeat this is not for the faint-hearted."

"Oh Jack, just get on with it will you? Tell us what happened!" Jessica waved her hands at him impatiently.

"When I left you guys, I travelled in my bubble far, far away and my bubble shot at speed into a forest and instead of landing on the forest floor, it continued right into the ground. I could see the darkness of the soil all around me and nothing else. I felt the fear begin to rise up inside me as the bubble continued deeper still through the earth and then it came to a stop. The bubble disintegrated away, and, in a panic, I waved my arms around, only to find I was restricted. My arms hit a wall to the left, to the right and above me, there was only about a foot or so gap and I realised that I was in a wooden box, buried in the ground."

Ariana's hand flew to her mouth. She knew Jack's greatest fear was being buried alive.

"No way! You were buried alive?" gasped Jessica.

"Yep, my absolute worst fear! I couldn't believe it. And I'm claustrophobic too, so I went into full-blown meltdown, six feet

The Cocoon Within

under, and no way out. I mean I have never yelled so loud in all my life; my throat went hoarse. I bashed against that coffin with all my might. I tried to find a weakness in the woodwork, my fingernails hurt, and I began to shake and have a panic attack and for the first time in my life, I thought I was going to die. I have no idea how long I lay there with tears streaming down my cheeks and my whole body shaking until I felt like I couldn't breathe. And then suddenly, I heard it… a still small voice in my mind that said, *"draw on the strength of your inner man."* When I heard the voice, I immediately froze, my heart was pumping with full-blown adrenaline, and I thought my heart was going to burst! I knew that it wasn't my own thought. No, I definitely heard that thought and it wasn't my own, but then whose was it? And just then the voice repeated itself only with urgency this time, *"draw on the strength of your inner man!"* And the second time I heard those words, I felt hope rise inside of me. I concentrated on the words, and I repeated them to myself out loud, and you'll never guess what happened next?" Jack sounded excited as he looked at them, eyes wide and with a great big grin on his face.

"No idea, tell us what happened next Jack?" asked Pippy before Ariana got the chance to even open her mouth.

They were all so enthralled by Jack's scary experience, after all, claustrophobic or not, no one wants to be buried alive! Pippy sat up on her lounger and leaned forward waiting for Jack to continue. Ariana looked over at Jessica and she looked super engaged in Jack's storytelling, so much so that she had hardly said a word.

"I don't know why I did it, but I held my hands out and pressed them firmly against the ceiling of the coffin and I shouted at it BREAK OPEN NOW! And guess what happened?" asked Jack, barely able to contain his excitement as he bounced around in front of them almost hopping from one leg to another.

"Oh my God, you've got powers?" declared Ariana excitedly, kind of half-asking at the same time.

"You bet your cotton socks I have!" Jack began doing a crazy dance and Pippy flew in the air, clapping her hands, twirling around and singing.

Ariana had noticed that Jessica didn't join in, and she seemed somewhat miffed.

"So, I suppose you blasted your way out of the coffin and the ground, right?" Jessica asked.

"Yep, as soon as I shouted, the lid of the coffin burst open and flew upwards through the earth with such fantastic force. After rubbing the soil from my eyes, I could see the sky from where I lay in the coffin. The force of the blast had literally created an opening all the way to the surface, a clear way out. I just lay there for a moment, stunned, and then I burst out laughing, I was in shock! Though once I processed what had happened, I felt absolutely elated, because moments earlier I thought that I had been about to die!"

Before anyone had a chance to say anything else about Jack's story Jessica piped up loudly, "Right, my turn everyone. I think my trial was much worse than everyone else's!"

Jack shrugged his shoulders and sat back down on his lounger. Pippy chuckled and Ariana took a long sip of her drink and wondered what was up with Jessica as she seemed pretty snappy all of a sudden, in fact, after Jack had mentioned his newfound powers, why wasn't she happy for him?

Jessica got up and stood where Jack had stood moments ago, taking centre stage. She flicked her beautiful long hair and placed her hands on her slender hips, she looked amazing as always, wearing a golden-coloured, shimmery, bikini. Ariana looked down at her own stripey blue and white one-piece and wondered where on earth Jessica had found the glamourous bikini, and why she got all the best outfits. Ariana shrugged to herself and concentrated on what Jessica had to say.

"After we separated in our own bubbles, I imagined that I would face some kind of a test that would involve fighting the evil giant beasts or the Tormenting ones, and I was ready for that. My bubble travelled some distance through space, and then to Earth at great speed, and finally to what looked like my childhood home, through the window and into my bedroom I landed, and then my bubble just disappeared. I looked around my old bedroom, and there hung my beautiful ballet outfit that I used to love to dance in. I had always felt like a little princess whenever I wore it. Photographs of me winning dancing awards and horse-riding championships hung on the wall, along with my many certificates. Numerous awards for beauty pageants that my parents had entered me for, were also dotted around the room. All those memories flooded my mind, and I felt a warm sense of pride and joy as I looked at all of my achievements throughout the years.

I went to the window and looked outside and there were dozens and dozens of the evil giants surrounding my home. They were looking up at me with angry faces, shaking their fists, lifting their Lifeblood swords at me and yelling and snarling. I started blasting them from my window, keen to get rid of as many as I could as there was no one to help me this time. I could see that some of the giants were up to something at one side of the house and then I heard the explosion, they had set fire to the house! The fire spread quickly, I couldn't jump out of any of the windows as the house was surrounded by the giant beasts waiting to capture me, so I had to find another way. I ran downstairs and got trapped in the fire, and I got badly burned as I ran through it. I remember screaming in agony, and flames licking my throat, my hair was singed, burned, gone!" Jessica buried her face in her hands for a moment, before she wiped her eyes and felt for her hair with her hands, then chuckled, "I still keep checking that my hair is alright. It was awful, anyway, I passed out and woke in a hospital with bandages all over my face and hands. When they removed the bandages, and I saw my face in the mirror, I was completely disfigured! Oh God... I feel sick just remembering!"

"Throw up in the sand over there if you have to," Ariana suggested, concerned that Jessica might actually throw up all over the picturesque veranda of the beach hut that they were all comfortably lounging on.

"No, no it's ok, I'm fine," replied Jessica as she felt her face with her hands and smoothed her hair again before continuing,

"The scarring was horrendous, I was unrecognisable, and I hadn't known before until that moment, that my greatest fear was losing my looks. There I've said it, I know it's rather shallow, but that's me, I care about being beautiful, it's all I've got, that's me."

"Hey, I like to look nice too, there is no shame in it," said Ariana, wanting to reassure Jessica. She felt an overwhelming sense of compassion towards Jessica. It was the first time that she had seen Jessica look remotely uncomfortable, she seemed rather perturbed by her experience, which of course anyone would be, but somehow Jessica seemed different because of it. Ariana couldn't quite put her finger on it.

"I agree, no shame in that," said Jack.

"Well, I always like to take care of myself," Pippy piped up, holding her little hairbrush and brushing her tiny ponytails. "And when I was covered in mud in that ditch, I looked far from beautiful, and I was not happy at all!" She preened her wings with her hands and turned back to listen to the rest of Jessica's story.

Jessica started pacing up and down in front of them as she continued,

"The next thing I knew, I was standing at the edge of a bridge, high up over a murky river. On the other side of the bridge, the land looked lush. full of plants and trees with thick foliage, and I felt a yearning, a strong desire within me to be on that side of the bridge. I looked behind me and the land where I stood was dry and barren, like a desert. When I turned back to look at the bridge there were two giant beasts in the middle of it, standing side by side, roaring at me, their bodies heaving in anger, arms flailing aggressively as they raised their Lifeblood swords as if taunting me to dare to approach them."

"What did you do?" Pippy asked eagerly as she leaned forward, keen to hear what happened next.

Jessica motioned with her hands as she spoke, "I drew my Lifeblood sword, and stepped onto the bridge towards them. As I got nearer, I saw on one of the giants' breastplates the words

'*Greatest Fear*'. I looked over at the other giant and on its breastplate was the word '*Identity*'." Jessica paused for a moment, and she looked at them, Ariana could see the vulnerability in her expression. "Guys, my heart was pounding as I faced those two beasts on that bridge, and for the first time, I actually felt afraid. I don't know why, because I had fought many of these giants before and slain them and escaped the edge of their swords."

Jessica was wide-eyed, confusion etched her face as she frowned deep in her own thoughts for a moment as she shook her head and continued,

"They bounded towards me, and each raised their sword to strike. I blocked each attack with my own sword and pushed them back. I fought hard and managed to defeat one of the giants and it lost its footing and fell to the river below. The other giant was too strong for me; it kept striking back harder, faster, stronger, to the point where it had me on my knees. I held my Lifeblood sword against its sword, as I fought for my life and as I just managed to push it backwards with all my might, the beast stood and raised its sword and with two great strikes it severed the bridge in half. We both hung onto the rope from the split bridge and pulled ourselves up onto our respective opposite sides of the river. The beast held my eyes for a moment before it raised its head and what sounded like a deep guttural victory cry escaped its lips, it looked back at me again and my eyes were drawn to the single word on its breastplate, '*Identity*'. The beast turned and ran through the thick foliage and out of sight. And in that moment, I just knew something symbolic had taken place, and I still yearned with all my soul to be on the other side of the bridge, but I had failed. I closed my eyes and when I opened them again, I was back in my bubble floating away. I put my hands up to feel my face and it was as smooth as a baby's skin, with no scarring, back to normal and my hair was intact, long and luscious as ever. I may have looked the same, but I didn't feel the same." Jessica stopped and her expression was one of confusion and disappointment.

Jack was the first to respond, "Hey if it makes you feel any better, after I had gotten out of my coffin experience, I thought everything would be alright, but it wasn't. I mean, great I had climbed out of the ground and escaped my greatest fear physically, but not mentally." He pointed to the side of his head for emphasis. "It's kind of embarrassing, but I consider you guys all to be in my circle of trust after everything we have been through together. In the next part of my trial, I found myself back in school, but instead of being my usual jokey self, you know, class clown," he grimaced, "I found myself fearful, jumping at the slightest thing, my experience had changed me in ways that I didn't like. Then similar to your experience, Jessica, two giants showed up in school, with the exact same words that your giants had written across their breastplates, and they were coming for me, so I had no choice but to fight them, but I felt myself paralysed with fear. Long story short, I only won the battle against them with help from the unknown voice that guided me again to use my inner strength, otherwise I think I may have been a goner."

Pippy flew off her sun lounger and clapped her hands for their undivided attention. "These trials have a hidden meaning, that's for sure, and I know that my own trial points to a special purpose. Remember, we are at a crucial time in Elopia right now, where not only have Go-betweens arrived for the first time in more than a thousand years but for the very first time, you, Jack, a Child of Mankind, have the gift of sight and have been able to enter our realm."

"So, what do you think my trial means?" asked Jessica, sounding a little worried.

"I don't know, but I think you need to be watchful for the words of wisdom imparted by the sacred beings," answered Pippy, giving Jessica a stern look and Jessica frowned as she dwelt on Pippy's words.

"Arry, we've not heard about your trial," said Jack and they all looked over at Ariana expectantly.

After a momentary pause, as Ariana had been trying to piece together the significance of all of their trials, she described her own very emotional and traumatic trial, leaving out no details. When she had finished telling all, she realised that her face was tear-stained. She looked at her audience and all three of them were open-mouthed, with not a dry eye in sight. Jack immediately got up and wrapped Ariana in a bear hug, the action brought on more tears from Ariana and as she was smothered in Jack's arms, she wept against his bare chest. She felt Jessica's arms encircle her shoulders and then Pippy's tiny arms around her neck.

"Group hug needed," said a rather emotional Jack, as they all stood there for a good five minutes, at least until Ariana had stopped crying.

What they didn't see were the eyes peering at them from the edge of the veranda, and the scrawny translucent body of a tormenting being that slinked away from its eavesdropping escapade, grinning smugly as it hurried along the beach before disappearing into the undergrowth.

6
A Tree and a Dark Place

They seemed to have forgotten about the book; it was the book that had awakened Ariana to her powers, to her identity. It was the book that had shown them the way to the Edge of Reason and now it was the book that had opened its pages to show them the battle, like watching a television show, but on the golden pages of the mystical book. Ariana had called the others to quickly join her, and together they had watched what the book wanted to show them. The book showed them Leo leading his celestial troops in battle, the ferocious leader in all his glory, slaying hordes of those demonic giants and tormenting spirits. There were hundreds and hundreds of the evil giants rising from the ground and the celestial beings in all forms were charging, Lifeblood sword clashing against Lifeblood sword, celestials and giants falling to the ground, beast versus humanoids and vice versa, destroyed by the edge of the sword, giant teeth and claws clashing against celestial flesh and bone. It was a momentous, ferocious battle to watch, and it didn't stop. After watching the pages turn with live battle scene after battle scene, eventually the book showed no more, and the golden shimmer from the pages dimmed. They all agreed that the urge to get moving was overwhelmingly strong and they quickly changed back into their suits of ultimate truth.

Ariana hoisted her rucksack over her shoulder, and they stood on the veranda of the beach hut for a moment as they deliberated on their next move, but before they had time to do anything, they heard the sound of the eagles' cries. Covering their ears, they followed Pippy as she flew to the beach and knelt on the sand covering her ears and they did the same. The eagles' cries got louder as they landed on the sand beside them before they chattered amongst themselves with the now-familiar whistles and clicks. Ariana felt the atmosphere change when in the presence of the eagles, an overwhelming sense of awe overcame her, and she knew the others felt it too.

The six voices of the eagles cried in unison, "Arise Celestial beings and Child of Mankind!"

Pippy, Jack, Jessica and Ariana stood up on the sand. They couldn't look directly at the eagles' faces, as the glow that surrounded their heads and emanated from their faces was dazzling. The eagles' eyes, the brightest of jade, penetrated the bright glowing light surrounding their faces and the eagles' fantastic plumage mesmerised them with their ever-changing shimmery feathers of gold, silver and bronze.

"Chosen One step forward, Wish-helper come forward," they commanded.

Ariana took a quick sideways glance at Pippy before stepping towards the eagles, squinting her eyes as she looked at them. Pippy hovered in the air beside Ariana, and they waited for the eagles to speak again.

"You have both proven yourselves worthy, behold the key."

Ariana felt something heavy in her right hand and looked down, but there was nothing visible and then she remembered that Pippy had said that the key was invisible. Ariana smoothed her hands over the key like a blind person would touch and feel an object to gauge its makeup. She felt a large irregular-shaped object, it felt like a medallion, and it had a chain attached to it, it felt like it had a large stone in its centre, set in some kind of heavy metal.

"It is more beautiful than they said it would be, put it around your neck," whispered Pippy.

Ariana felt for the chain and put the invisible key around her neck for safekeeping, then she looked at the eagles with eyes squinted and thanked them.

"Guard the key with your lives and return it to its rightful place," the eagles echoed to one another.

The eagles chattered amongst themselves for a moment with whistles and clicks before saying, "Child of Mankind, step forward, Go-between step forward." Jack and Jessica quickly stepped forward before giving each other a sideways glance. Ariana saw Jessica reach for Jack's hand, and they held hands as they awaited the words from the eagles.

"You fought your greatest fear with courage, I commend you. But the knowledge of your true identity is high, and you could not attain it."

Jessica nudged Jack, and he instinctively knew she probably had the same question as him, but after last time she no doubt didn't want to ask anything.

"If you please, am I allowed to ask a small question?" Jack asked tentatively, not wanting to arouse the wrong response from the mighty eagles.

The six faces of the eagles looked directly at Jack, and he had to shield his eyes from the glare, "Child of Mankind, in answer to your question, both you and Jessica the Go-between, remain on a journey to discover your true identity. Knowing in word alone is not sufficient, you must know deep within your inward parts." With that, the eagles began squawking loudly, their cries were excruciating. Pippy, Jack, Jessica and Ariana immediately covered their ears and fell to their knees as the birds opened their enormous wings, and as the eagles beat their wings, their golden talons pushed their huge bodies away from the ground, and they soared gracefully into the sky with their loud screeching gradually fading into the distance.

Ariana quickly pulled the book out of her rucksack; it was glowing again, and as if on cue the pages of the book flickered until they opened up to display the map, and it was as if the map came alive.

"Look, the book is showing us a pathway!" cried Ariana excitedly. Since the eagles had spoken, she felt a great sense of urgency and a renewed feeling of exuberance, prompted by a strong desire to move them all forward on their mission to retrieve the Chalice of Fire.

The others gathered around and together they deciphered the way to go, according to the directions from the map.

"It's time to get serious about this mission, Leo and the troops need us, our families need us, so let's do this!" Ariana was bold, and she wasted no time in leading the way. The others looked on in slight surprise before they turned and followed her lead.

Ariana trudged through the sand on the shoreline and headed inland, just as the book had shown them. She was ahead of the others and turned back to see Pippy fluttering a few metres behind her. Jack and Jessica were together following behind Pippy, and they looked deep in conversation with one another. Ariana frowned, why hadn't Jack come to be by her side, to walk and talk with her like he usually did? She felt momentary confusion; perhaps he had a change of heart? Maybe he preferred Jessica after all? She was beautiful, that was undeniable. And then there was the moment that Jack and Jessica had shared as they waited for the eagles' verdict when Jessica had reached for Jack's hand, that had surprised Ariana the most. She shook her head, she really needed to focus on the task at hand.

Pippy flew up to Ariana's face, her tiny hands outstretched. "Stop! Do not go any further!"

Ariana immediately froze. "What's wrong, Pippy?"

Jack and Jessica caught up with them, and Jack strode right past them before Pippy could stop him, and he started sinking fast into the ground.

Pippy looked at Ariana, "That's why I stopped you!" she said and flew over to Jack, grabbed hold of his collar and tried with all her might to heave him upwards.

"Guys, I'm sinking fast, help me!" cried Jack, sounding frantic as his chest began to slide into the ground.

Jessica ran and grabbed a long branch and held it out for Jack to seize hold of. By now he was up to his neck in the ground and Pippy was trying her best to help keep his head above the surface.

"Oh, what's the use of having powers if they are no good in a rescue situation!" cried Ariana in frustration as she tried to help Jessica pull the branch so they could drag Jack out of the weird quicksand that they couldn't actually see. The branch snapped and Jack barely had his mouth above ground level.

"No!" screamed Ariana and in desperation she yelled, "*BE LIFTED UP NOW!*" and she aimed her hands towards Jack just as he disappeared into the ground and Pippy had to let go of him. Jessica and Pippy both cried out in horror.

Ariana lifted her hands upwards and Jack burst through the ground, held by the powerful blue-white beams from Ariana's hands. She directed her hands over to the solid ground where they stood, and Jack was carried in the beams, safely to the ground.

He spluttered and coughed, wiping his eyes and face clear of the invisible quicksand, gasping, "I thought I was a goner. Oh my God, thank you, thank you!" They all gathered around and helped him to his feet.

"Wow!" Jessica looked directly at Ariana, with an amazed look on her face. "How did you learn to do that?"

"I don't know, though it happened in my trial unexpectedly," replied Ariana, rotating her hands and looking at them in wonder. "It was when I got really, really, angry, I mean I flew into a rage. It was when Jack and Granpey were being attacked by the giant beasts, my powers just took on a new dimension and I lifted up those beasts in the same way, and then I annihilated them. I didn't think about it, I just did it."

"Well, I'm glad you didn't annihilate me!" Jack piped up and he winked at Ariana.

"What about your powers, Jack? You said you had them in your trial; have you tried them since?" Ariana asked.

"I have been trying ever since and nothing, so maybe it was just in the trial, and I don't really have powers at all!" he shrugged his shoulders.

"Or maybe it has something to do with what the eagles said?" said Ariana, thinking of the eagles' words about both Jessica and Jack needing to know deep within, though that was probably for them to figure out for themselves.

Ariana caught Jessica looking at her own hands with a frown on her face, she was probably wondering if her powers could do that too.

"Hey, come on stop wasting time chattering!" Pippy snapped her tiny fingers, and surprisingly they made quite a loud sound. "We have to find another way. There is quicksand ahead of us as far as the eye can see," she declared. "Let me take a look for another way, wait here." And with that, Pippy flew out over the land until they could see her no more. Pippy's new wings were faster and stronger, and they carried her to new heights.

"I thought the book led us here?" Jessica frowned, "did we read the map wrong?"

"Let's take another look, Arry. We have trusted the book thus far and if it's a sacred book isn't it meant to help us?" Jack asked as he looked at Ariana thoughtfully.

"Yes, you're right, I thought we had followed the map correctly. Hang on, let's look again." Ariana pulled out the book and opened it up on the page with the map. They all peered at the map carefully. Jack traced their tracks on the page with his finger.

"See the direction arrows do point this way, so where did we go wrong?" he asked.

Ariana looked carefully at the direction arrows on the map. Jack was right, the arrows went all the way across this area, unbeknown to them, however, was the invisible quicksand but thank God Pippy could see it. Ariana peered closely as she continued to follow the arrows on the map.

"So, the arrows take us right across this land, but look at what this island is actually called…"

"Paradise Lost?" Jack guessed with a laugh.

Jessica and Ariana both shot him an ironic look, "No! It's called *Land of Sleight of Hand*," said Ariana.

"Oh God!" Jack slapped his forehead, "This just gets worse."

"What does it mean?" asked Jessica.

"Basically, this land isn't what it seems," he sighed.

"Guys look!" Ariana showed them on the map, "See the arrow that goes across this area? Look at where the arrow goes directly through." She stared at Jessica and Jack waiting for the penny to drop.

"It goes straight across this land; I don't see anything," replied Jessica, still looking at the map intently, and she sounded rather confused at Ariana's point.

Ariana jabbed her finger on the map, "Look, the tree! Don't you see? If you look carefully, you'll see that the arrow goes directly through that tree." Taking her finger off the map, she pointed to a gigantic tree several metres away from them that looked not dissimilar to a giant oak tree.

Both Jack and Jessica stared up at the huge tree, suddenly catching on.

"Right, so we took the wrong route when actually the tree is some kind of bridge or portal to take us over the land to avoid the quicksand!" Jack concluded.

"Or maybe not overground, perhaps a tunnel underground?" Jessica mused.

"Exactly!" Ariana grinned at them both.

The Cocoon Within

"Please! Not underground!" Jack had his hands together as if in prayer, and then they all burst out laughing.

Just then Pippy flew towards them asking, "What's so funny?"

"You don't want to know," Jack replied defeatedly, which set Ariana and Jessica off laughing again.

"You won't get any sense out of these two for the next five minutes at least, so let me fill you in," said Jack, showing Pippy what Ariana had discovered from the map.

She was in complete agreement and wondered how they could have missed that; they certainly needed to pay closer attention to the map's details next time. Pippy said that she had flown a great distance and there was nothing but quicksand everywhere she went, so this completely backed up what Jack had just shown her on the map, it had to be the tree.

"So where do you think the door is?" Jack asked the others as they all stared at the trunk of the giant tree.

The tree itself had to be more than three hundred feet tall, it was phenomenal. The trunk was surely around thirty feet wide. On closer inspection, the bark displayed beautiful shades of multicoloured browns, with hues of purple and violet. The branches and leaves of this fantastic tree were up high above, creating a vast canopy of foliage, only broken by sparse rays from the lesser sun and the greater sun, that managed to shine through the gaps and onto the forest floor.

"No idea where the door is," replied Ariana, "but it's funny that we didn't notice the tree before."

"I wonder if it's a tree that can move about?" said Jessica. "Remember when we first arrived in Elopia and we were followed by a tree?" She looked up at the vast leafy foliage. "I certainly wouldn't want to be chased by a tree of this size that's for sure!"

Pippy was examining the other side of the tree and she called to them, "Hey, I've found something, come here quick!"

The Cocoon Within

They all ran around to see what Pippy had found, and there on the tree trunk words had formed, and more continued to be etched into the bark as they watched, almost as though an invisible hand was carving words into the wood of the tree.

"Look, at what it says!" cried Ariana and they read the words aloud together:

'The way to the hidden land is not for the faint of heart,
Solve the riddle to pass through the gateway,
Otherwise, you'll remain in the vine, but the choice is divine,
You'll find that your mind may be all of a bind.'

Those words disappeared and new ones began etching in their place, and together they read them aloud:

'Is there an oaf that delights in your name? Think of a place but don't forget 'h'.

"So, the answer to this riddle will open the gateway? Guys, think, what could it be?" Ariana racked her brain and said, "It's the name of a place."

"Elopia!" cried Jessica.

"No, it hasn't got a letter 'h' in it," Pippy corrected.

"Earth?" Jack suggested tentatively.

"Guys look!" said Ariana, pointing at the tree.

They watched as the riddle disappeared from the tree trunk, and a sand timer appeared in its place. The sand timer slowly rotated until the sand began to fall through its narrow neck, starting the clock ticking, and the sand was falling fast.

"Perhaps it's an anagram?" Jessica suggested, looking first at Jack and then at Ariana.

"Hmm, good suggestion Jessica," he replied. "Hang on, so what did the riddle say again?"

"I think you might be right, Jessica," Ariana joined in, and repeated the riddle to herself as she tried to work it out, *'Is there an oaf that delights in your name? Think of a place but don't forget 'h'*. Just then, before Ariana could have a proper think, Jessica was turned upside down and disappeared into the tree's canopy as she let out a wail in shock.

"What on earth?" cried Ariana, unsure what had just happened to Jessica, and then she felt something tightening around her ankles. She looked down to see large vines binding them and several more vines coming towards her like snakes.

"Whoa! Jack, use your sword!" she shouted, drawing her Lifeblood sword and slashing the vines from her ankles.

Jumping back, she slashed the vines that were coming towards her and looked round to see Jack doing the same, in some kind of battle of the vines dance as he skipped and hopped out of their reach and kept slashing at them. Meanwhile, Pippy was able to easily outmanoeuvre the attacking vines, taking flight with her new wings. Ariana did a backflip and sprang up high, grabbing onto a large branch, she began to climb up towards Jessica. The vines were still coming for her, so she used one hand to slash at them with her sword.

"Jessica, use your powers to blast them and break free!" Ariana yelled. She couldn't even see Jessica anymore, the foliage was too thick, and Jessica had been dragged up too high.

"I can't! My hands are tied into the vines," Jessica cried; at least they could hear her.

Ariana began blasting the vines above her to try to create an opening to climb up through to see if she could reach Jessica, but every time she blew them away, new vines immediately formed in the same place, thicker and stronger.

"Oh, blast and darn it! This isn't working!" Ariana shouted, desperately. "Jessica! I can't get to you; it's no use, it's too thick. We will have to find another way!"

"Okay! I guess I will just have to wait up here then, I can't go anywhere!" Jessica yelled back.

Ariana leapt out of the tree to the ground. Jack was still fighting the vines, whilst Pippy continued dodging them.

"Arry! The hourglass, we are running out of time! Quick! Solve the riddle, maybe that will stop all these vines!"

"Oh yes, yes! *Is there an oaf that delights in your name? Think of a place but don't forget 'h'* It's an anagram! I've got it Jack *'an oaf delights, but don't forget h'* it has to be this place! SLEIGHT OF HAND!" Ariana cried at the top of her voice… and suddenly there was silence, and the vines instantly stopped their attack.

"I will see if Jessica can come down now," said Pippy, darting up high towards the canopy.

Jack and Ariana watched in wonder as the wood at the centre of the tree trunk began to swirl and spin around and around, reminding Ariana of a brightly coloured little wooden spinning top that she used to have as a child. Fixated on the colours of browns, purple and violet in the swirling wood of the tree trunk, she wondered what was going to happen next, and just then the swirling wood melted away, to reveal a large opening right the way through the middle of the tree trunk, that they could walk right through.

Pippy arrived shaking her head. "It's no good," she said, "she's locked into the canopy; the vines are intertwined around her body, and she can't break her arms free. I tried to help her, but it was no use and I couldn't even get to her Lifeblood sword, though that would probably have been too heavy for me, I wanted to try. Jessica said to go on without her and come back for her when we get the Chalice."

"No, we will have to come back for her sooner," argued Jack. "We don't know how long it will take us to get the Chalice and we need to think of a way to get her out of that tree." He frowned, his concern for Jessica was evident.

"I agree, and what about the crystal pendant?" asked Ariana, looking at Pippy hopefully. "Jessica could use that to get back to the river's edge and then to En Arias."

"I told you, they are thought-reading pendants. The pendant will know when Jessica is in grave danger, and by grave danger, I mean about to be killed, that's when it will activate, and she will be immediately transported back to the river's edge before any harm can come to her." Pippy rolled her eyes, clearly exasperated at having to explain again.

"But why didn't my pendant save me from the invisible quicksand then?" asked Jack, still frowning as he felt for his pendant which Ariana could see was still around his neck, so he did have a good point.

"It's like explaining to children sometimes!" groaned Pippy and rolled her eyes heavenward before continuing, which did elicit a chuckle from both Jack and Ariana. "The crystal pendants read the thoughts of any living being, which means that it would have read the thoughts of all of us and hence it identified that Ariana was going to try to save Jack with her powers after the branch snapped. If that hadn't worked, then the pendant would have transported you out of danger before your last breath."

Jack shuddered at Pippy's words and said, "Boy, am I glad that frog dude gave us these pendants!"

Pippy and Ariana looked at one another. "He wasn't a frog, he was a lizard humanoid being!" said Pippy, rolling her eyes again, and then they all burst out laughing.

Ariana was the first to get them moving again. "Come on, Jack, Pippy, let's go! We must continue with the mission. Jessica will be fine till we get back, she has the pendant which will protect her and as soon as we get the Chalice, we'll be back for her." She looked up at the tree and shouted, "Jessica, we've opened the gateway, and we need to get the Chalice, then we will come back for you. Remember the pendant will keep you safe!"

The Cocoon Within

"Guys, just complete the mission and get the Chalice, and I will see you all soon. Just don't forget that I'm up here!" Jessica yelled back at them courageously.

Ariana sighed and they looked at one another for a moment, none of them wanting to abandon Jessica, but they had to get the Chalice and who knew how long the gateway in the tree would remain open.

"I can stay with Jessica and wait for you both to return; at least that way she won't be on her own," Jack volunteered.

Ariana's heart melted at Jack's selflessness; he was such a kind and thoughtful soul. Yet at the same time, she wondered what benefit it would be for Jessica as he couldn't reach her, plus she would be separated from Jack again. Ariana couldn't stay as she was the only one who could take up the Chalice, and Pippy had the gift of seeing the invisible and she was the only other one worthy to take up the key if push came to shove, so she needed her by her side to complete this mission.

Ariana looked at Pippy who shrugged her small shoulders as she fluttered between them both.

"It's your decision, Jack, just find somewhere safe in the tree to stay hidden till we get back."

Ariana flung herself at Jack, wrapping her arms around him and he did the same, giving her a giant squeeze, before pulling back to look into her eyes. He stroked her face tenderly and lifted her chin before planting his lips firmly on hers. It was a tender and unexpected kiss, full of hidden meaning. Taken by surprise, Ariana looked at Jack and she felt his sadness at them being separated again, tears pricked at the corner of her eyes at the sight of his emotion.

"Don't get all sentimental will you, you'll be back and we'll all be together again soon," said Jack. Quickly turning to Pippy, he held out his hand to her, but she flew at his neck, wrapped her arms around him and gave him a big wish-helper hug.

"Right, off you go before I change my mind!" he winked at them both.

The Cocoon Within

As Ariana walked with Pippy fluttering beside her through the gateway in the centre of the giant tree trunk, she turned around and gave Jack one last look, and he raised his hand and blew her a kiss. Ariana beamed back at him, her eyes dancing with love, before the swirling wood closed the gateway behind them and she could see him no more.

"Jessica, I'm coming up!" yelled Jack.

"Jack! I thought you had all gone through the gateway in the tree, what happened?" she asked, surprised.

"I volunteered to keep you company!"

"Oh, Jack! You didn't have to, though I'm not complaining; perhaps we can play eye spy!" she suggested laughingly, as she tried to wriggle into a more comfortable position amidst the vines that crowded her entire body rather tightly.

Jack chuckled as he began climbing the giant tree. He could see what looked like a rather large opening in the tree quite high up, close to the great canopy, that would do as a nice resting place. He increased his speed as he reached for another branch to grab onto.

"Hey, this climbing malarky is quite fun, it takes me back to my childhood days when I built a makeshift tree house in the backyard," he said and began telling the story.

Jessica listened to Jack rambling on. At least with his chattering the time would pass quicker, though it was awkward being trapped in the vines and not being able to move properly, and the possibility of having all-over body cramps was not something she was looking forward to. She could hear Jack slashing at the vines, no doubt without success and she could hear him huffing and puffing, with a few expletives escaping his lips every now and then, with his growing frustration.

"Ariana did say that the vines just grew back stronger every time she cut them. Don't waste your energy, Jack."

"Yeah, I know, but I just wanted to try."

He positioned himself in the large opening in the tree where he could lean back nicely and relax for a minute. He felt a little tired after all the exertion of climbing, coupled with his futile efforts to hack the vines.

"I'm just going to close my eyes for a minute, Jessica."

"Alright, power nap it is, nothing else to do I guess while we wait," she sighed as she wondered how some animals managed to fall asleep whilst standing.

***

Meanwhile, Ariana and Pippy continued through the gateway until they were out on the other side of the tree. Ariana was surprised at the depth of the tree trunk; it was at least a walk of several metres. She shook her head in amazement, as they had literally walked into another world and it certainly was a portal or gateway to another realm. She looked down and realised she was standing on a giant mosaic steppingstone, and ahead of her were lots of the same steppingstones laid out in a network of pathways, all leading in different directions. The air was thick and humid, and they could hear gurgling and splashing noises that sounded some distance away, coming from far below. Ariana looked between the steppingstones and that's when she realised that the steppingstones were the only places of solid ground, and that between them was a sheer drop into what looked like a sea of blue volcanic lava. She froze on the spot.

"Oh, Pippy, what is this place?" she asked in trepidation as she continued to look around.

The sky above was not a clear blue sky, but a mixture of swirling colours of purple, violet and deep blue. There appeared to be a blood-red moon in the strange twilit sky and glimpses of unusual creatures of the night were flitting around making strange noises.

"I don't know," answered Pippy, fluttering beside Ariana. Her eyes were wide as she flipped around from side to side, staying alert for any danger, with her little dart gun at the ready. "But what I do know is that we are definitely in one of the darker realms."

"Great!" Ariana said with mock enthusiasm, her hands outstretched, ready for anything. "Ok, I guess we had better choose a direction and move forward."

She suddenly wondered why they couldn't at least have been allowed one of the Fearsome ones to come with them on this mission. Somehow a trainee Go-between and a small fairy with a tiny dart gun really didn't make for a formidable team in her view. Ariana smiled at her rather modest summation, and then mentally chided herself for underestimating their abilities. She stared for a moment at the multiple choices of mosaic steppingstones all around her and decided,

"Well, I guess it doesn't matter which one…" and she took a giant step onto the stone directly to her right.

As soon as she landed on it, there was a great sound of heavy stone moving, and Ariana felt the entire stone start to move downwards. Pippy fluttered beside her, wide-eyed and hands outstretched as she gave a dubious shrug. The giant stone continued to travel downwards into the dark abyss. They could see the great pillars of all the other steppingstones around them and feel the humid heat from the volcanic lava rising from the depths of the abyss. Suddenly the steppingstone came to an abrupt halt next to a landing strip that led to an archway with heavy, metallic double doors. Inscribed on the double doors were the words: *'The Accursed'*, and surrounding the words were strange symbols, accompanied by carved gargoyle faces with eerie expressions.

There was nowhere else to go but through the door and after a moment's hesitation, Ariana looked at Pippy and asked, "Ready?"

"I was born ready!" replied Pippy, smiling confidently.

Ariana pushed open the double doors and walked forward, but she immediately fell as though off a cliff's edge. Looking around her, she thought she must be free-falling through some kind of circular tower that appeared to be built of stone. Even Pippy was falling and rolling around in the air as she tried to gain her balance in flight, but it was no use. It was like there was some sort of force pulling them downwards and sucking them into a vacuum. Then they landed with a squelch in a sea of dark sludge.

"Eew, what is this awful smell?" said Ariana, pulling herself upright, thankful that the awful sludge was only waist-deep.

She saw Pippy's muck-covered wings sticking out beside her in the sludge and quickly stuck her hand in the gungy muck and pulled her out, before helping to wipe globs of the gunge free from Pippy's tiny body. Ariana felt for the key around her neck, grateful that it hadn't fallen off into this awful smelly muck. Somehow, her rucksack with the book inside had managed to remain intact on her back.

Pippy spat and coughed up mud, and then wiped her face with her tiny hands. "Great!" she exclaimed, "and I had just brushed my hair earlier today!" She crossed her arms as she sat in Ariana's palm and started cleaning her wings.

"Here let me help," offered Ariana and did her best to wipe away some of the muck with her hands, as Pippy flapped her wings and fluttered about joyously, sending mud flying off her small body and splattering right across Ariana's face.

"Oops sorry!" said Pippy, as her hands flew to her mouth to stifle her laughter.

"Oh, Pippy!" Ariana cried between chuckles, as she wiped her eyes.

Ariana waded slowly through the thick sludge and then she bumped into something buried in it. "There is something in here!"

"Uh-oh, that can't be good," said Pippy, her eyes were wide, and she began to fly higher to put some distance between her and whatever was in the sludge with Ariana.

"Hey! It's alright for you up there…" Ariana's voice trailed off as something began to rise out of the sludge just in front of her, so she backed up a few paces trying to put some distance between her and whatever it was.

The Cocoon Within

Ariana and Pippy watched in silence as a creature's head rose out of the muck, twisted to one side, and they heard the click of its bones. One mangled arm followed out of the sludge and then another. The sound of bones clicking into place continued until the being stood facing them at a slightly lopsided angle. Ariana looked at its face and watched as blobs of the muck slid down its cheeks, revealing cheekbones and glimpses of red, raw flesh. Ariana gasped; its eyeballs were sunk deep into the hollow holes of its skull. It looked like a walking skeleton with raw meat clinging to its bones, it was grotesque. Ariana sure hoped that neither she nor Pippy had ingested any small bits of body parts involuntarily when they had fallen into this hell hole. She looked up at Pippy who was pointing to her hands, frantically motioning to Ariana to blast the creature with her powers.

Ariana lifted her hands to aim and fire, but just then the creature shrieked, "Help… me."

Its amber eyes began to blaze and as Ariana looked into them, she was able to see a vision. She immediately sensed that the creature was showing her something. She saw a family on Earth, a regular family, a mum, dad, teenage daughter and a son about nine years old, a very happy family. The vision showed her the memories of this family as though playing home videos of their life together. Laughter, seaside holidays, family meals, the usual family arguments and then the making up, moving house and other key milestones in their lives. But there was something about the son. The vision moved on to follow him, and unbeknown to him, he was being followed by a dark presence. It had been following him all his life and Ariana recognised it as one of the Tormenting ones. She watched as it whispered sickly words into his ear; she watched as the son changed, got angry, threw tantrums and rebelled. As the son got older and more words were whispered in his ear, he listened to the lies, the dark words; he took drugs, he self-harmed and things only got darker. Ariana watched as the boy's life spiralled out of control; she watched as the boy went into a gun store and purchased a gun, and she watched as he walked into his home and at point blank range, shot his mother, his father, his sister and then himself. Ariana immediately turned her face away in horror.

The vision disappeared and the blaze died out in the creature's eyes. It started making a strange noise and gnashing its teeth. Ariana could hear its bones rattling as it crumpled back into the sludge. More creatures began to appear out of the mire, each one showing Ariana harrowing stories of untold acts of evil committed, tormented from birth, followed, hounded and whispered lies to. Each creature crumpled back into the muck, as though exhausted after showing her its vision, wailing and gnashing their teeth and rattling bones. Ariana was overcome by the stench of rotting flesh, somehow the place was saturated in evil, she could sense it, along with a deep sense of harrowing pain and regret, remorse and guilt, death and destruction.

"Pippy, I feel ill in this place. I have seen too much, I need to get out of here!"

Ariana wiped tears from her eyes with the back of her hand, before throwing up. She felt sick to her stomach, her insides repulsed at what she had seen and smelt. She looked at the gruesome disjointed bodies of the creatures as they slowly writhed in the muck, jostling for space to lie still once more, and Ariana realised that these creatures had once been humans, that had lived and breathed on Earth.

"Look over here!" called Pippy, holding onto some small metal railings in the wall, if you didn't look for them in this dark place, you could easily miss them, camouflaged by the wall itself. "And they go all the way up, see!"

Ariana was already wading her way towards the bottom rung. Stepping over the bodies in the sludge was quite tricky, but she made it and grabbing onto the bottom rung, she heaved herself up, until she was eye level with Pippy, smiling through her mud-stained little face.

"At least I found a way out," beamed Pippy.

"Thank goodness! I don't think I could take any more of the awful visions they were showing me!"

"What did they show you?" asked Pippy, frowning.

"Let's get out of this place first and then I'll tell you."

Together they hurried to the top of the tower, back through the double doors and onto the giant steppingstone, which carried them back up to where they had started.

"It looks like we have to choose another stepping stone. Pippy, you choose this time."

Ariana watched as Pippy deliberated, before choosing the one directly in front of Ariana.

"Ok here goes!"

The stone made a loud noise as it moved downwards and stopped in front of a ledge that led to another door, that looked like it was made of wood, and on the door was engraved the words: *'Kingdom of Principalities.'*

Ariana was just about to push open the door.

"Wait!" cried Pippy, as she flew in front of Ariana's face, gesturing emphatically with her tiny hands, "what did the Accursed ones show you?"

Ariana's face dropped and looking intently at Pippy she declared, "I saw their lives on Earth, everyday family lives. Then they showed me death, destruction, awful acts they committed, some were criminal, horrific." Ariana looked both repulsed and sad at the same moment, "I felt their regret and remorse, and something else… an air of horror and confusion, yes that was it, they were horrified by their own actions. They didn't realise at the time that they were being tormented into committing such acts of immense evil."

"They will remain in that place forever, there'll be layer upon layer of accursed ones down there, it goes on forever from the most ancient of ancient times," sighed Pippy, shaking her head.

"Where do they all come from?" Ariana asked, almost not wanting to know the answer.

"These are the souls of humans, they are entrapped here, in the dark realms," replied Pippy solemnly.

"After they die?"

"Yes."

"Is that what Eriat meant when she said that we are connected in more ways than we can understand?"

"Yes, when you truly become enlightened, understanding comes and you will see things as they really are."

Ariana was beginning to understand, but then what about the people who had died after living good lives? Those who hadn't been abusers, murderers or committed despicable acts of unspeakable evil; people who hadn't been tormented? Ariana thought back to when she and Jessica had encountered the Tormenting ones in class and the canteen. There had been students who had been overlooked by the Tormenting ones, as though they were invisible to them. Why were some students tormented and others left alone? It didn't make sense.

"Ariana, let us go forward. We need to get the Chalice," urged Pippy and clapped her tiny hands in front of Ariana's face, as her wings fluttered at a furiously fast pace, keeping her hovering in the air.

"Yes, yes, of course, let's go!" said Ariana, snapping out of her deep thoughts, but she still had questions. "One more thing, Pippy; do all humans end up here after they die?"

Pippy looked her straight in the eyes and frowned, "No, of course not! They are not all accursed when they die." Shaking her head, Pippy rolled her eyes heavenward, flew up to the door and pointed at it in frustration, "Come on, let's go!"

Ariana took a deep breath and pushed open the large wooden door and together they entered the Kingdom of Principalities.

***

Meanwhile, Jessica slowly and sleepily opened her eyes, suddenly remembering that she was still stuck up high in that giant tree. The realisation quickly dawned on her that the vines appeared to have grown thicker. She tried to move but could only wriggle feebly, the vines had bound her to the tree. She felt something in her mouth, and she used her tongue to manoeuvre the foreign objects around, before spitting out a bunch of soggy leaves! They must have fallen into her mouth whilst she slept. Jessica could feel the tickle of something on her face and as she rolled her eyes downwards, she could see leaves on her cheeks, but at least her eyes and mouth were not covered. She watched as a small blue and green striped caterpillar crawled across a vine, and stretched its flexible little body mid-air till its tiny multitude of feet reached a leaf sticking out from Jessica's shoulder. Jessica sighed as she watched the little caterpillar creep across her shoulder towards her neck. Just then her eyes were drawn to something in the sky; was it a bird? Jessica stared intently as it gradually came into focus, and she saw that it was something quite large flying straight towards her.

"Please not the eagles," Jessica muttered to herself and then she remembered that the eagles always make a loud screeching sound so it couldn't be them.

She squinted against the bright sunlight, and whatever it was came closer and closer until, at last, she could make it out, but could it actually be... a flying horse and chariot? She was stunned to see a majestic, giant flying horse approaching at pace through the sky. Its shimmery sleek coat was dark as night, and it pulled a shiny golden chariot behind it, in which stood a humanoid being. Jessica watched as the great black Pegasus beat its wings gloriously in the air, and what a vision it struck in all its majesty, as it galloped through the sky confidently, before pulling to a magnificent halt, mid-air beside her. Jessica gulped and tore her eyes away from the snorting Pegasus to look up at the rider of the chariot. She gasped as she was taken aback by the size of the being standing before her, as though she had been transported back in time, to the days of the Greek gods.

The Cocoon Within

The giant humanoid was handsome in form, like a Greek Adonis, he stood tall and proud, dressed in a sleek suit of armour as though for war, the contours of his large muscular body beneath could not be hidden. He wore a helmet much like a Roman soldier might have worn, though it shimmered as though made of precious metal. Jessica lifted her eyes to look at the face of the humanoid, it was covered in markings, not unlike those that Eriat had on her face. His eyes were a deep and piercing amber, set in a broad, rugged face that told of many battles. His skin was an unusual deep brownish red, like nothing Jessica had ever seen before.

He just stood there on his chariot staring intently at Jessica trapped in the vines, high up in the tree canopy. The Pegasus appeared impatient to continue in flight, as it snorted and its breath could be seen in the air, as it raised its glorious head up and down and pawed the air with one hoof. The rattling of its elegant bridle and the soft beat of its wings were the only sounds to be heard.

After a few moments of silence, during which Jessica began to feel rather disconcerted by the continued stare of this amber-eyed, handsome, though unusual-looking stranger, he said,

"I am Vedriece, Sky Warrior and High Commander of the troops from the Kingdom of the North, and who are you?" His voice was deep and authoritative.

"My name is Jessica... I am a Go-between," she replied not sure how much she should say, but she hoped that this handsome stranger was one of the good guys.

Vedriece looked at her thoughtfully before responding, "I had heard that Go-betweens had entered the realms," and with that, he stepped out of the chariot that held his rather unruly black Pegasus in place, unsheathed two Lifeblood swords, one from each hip, and Jessica watched in awe as he walked right across the space between them in the sky, as though on dry land, before adeptly slicing through the vines that entrapped her, allowing her to wriggle free at last.

"Oh, thank you so much!" Jessica was joyous, as she stood poised on a thick tree branch, using one hand to pull off the remnants of vines and leaves still hanging onto her body, and the other to grip onto a large overhanging branch, to keep herself steady. Vedriece held out his hand to her as he stood in the air firmly.

Jessica hesitated, "But won't I fall?" she asked, looking down. It was rather a long way down and though she had powers, which she knew she probably hadn't yet fully mastered, she would surely sustain a broken bone or two if she fell.

"No, you will not fall," Vedriece said, matter of factly and waited.

She took hold of his strong hand and stepped off the branch, and to her surprise she didn't fall. It was as though she had stepped onto solid ground, but there was nothing but sky all around them.

"I can walk on air! Wow!" she exclaimed, and in her excitement, she let go of Vedriece's hand and immediately started falling. She gasped and before she could cry out, she felt herself being pulled back up by the strong arms of Vedriece, as he held her from behind. As soon as he took her hand again, she could stand as if on solid ground.

"Lesson learned; if you let go of my hand, you will fall," he said with a deep, throaty laugh and his amber eyes blazed as he held her gaze.

Jessica blushed, and for the first time, she felt lost for words. She wasn't sure if it was because she was embarrassed or because she felt a strong attraction to this dark, handsome stranger.

Vedriece helped Jessica climb into the chariot, and as he took the reins of his unruly Pegasus, he turned his rugged face and looked directly into Jessica's eyes. His voice was deep and breathy as he said to her, "I am overcome by your beauty."

Jessica blushed again, what was it about his eyes? They were just so mesmerising. She didn't usually blush at compliments from the opposite sex, after all, she was used to getting a lot of attention, so she couldn't quite understand why Vedriece had such a powerful effect on her.

Those deep amber eyes continued to hold hers for a moment, and then he said, "Come with me to my city?"

Jessica wasn't sure if it was a statement or a question, but she replied immediately and eagerly, "Yes, yes, I would love to!"

And with a flick of the reins, Pegasus finally got his heart's desire to gallop across the sky once again.

Jack awoke from his slumber to a sound he couldn't quite identify; it was coming from above. He quickly pulled himself up, leaned as far as he could and looked upwards. He couldn't believe his eyes, so he blinked a couple of times to make sure he was awake. Was that a flying horse and chariot? And... oh my God... was... that Jessica? And who was that very tall and muscular stranger with her?

"Jessica!" Jack yelled in disbelief, as he watched the horse and chariot fly past.

Jessica turned around, her hair swishing aside, as she held onto the sides of the chariot and laughed, "Jack! This is fantastic! I am going for a ride with Vedriece, but don't worry, I'll be back soon!" She waved to Jack with a huge grin on her face, and as she turned away, leaving Jack open-mouthed, Pegasus sped through the sky until they were nothing but a small dot far in the distance.

Jack sat back in the hole in the tree. "Unbelievable!" he said, "she left me, she actually just left me! I stayed behind for her, and she just left me!" He shook his head in utter disbelief as he talked to himself aloud. He was dumbfounded, he just couldn't believe that Jessica would do something like that and go off with a complete stranger! They were supposed to stay together. Unless she had been forced? Yes, that's got to be it... but no... that can't be right, as Jessica had been smiling and waving goodbye happily. Perhaps the stranger had put her under some kind of magic spell? That was entirely possible. Jack reasoned with himself, before pondering what he should do next. He could stay and wait in the tree for the others to return and tell them that he had lost Jessica, but done absolutely nothing about it, or he could try to follow them through the portal in the tree and tell them about Jessica so that together they could hatch a rescue mission. Yes, he quite liked the sound of that! And without further ado, he began the climb down from his resting spot in the giant tree.

7

The Dark Valley

"How do I look?" Jessica twirled around, wearing the gown that Vedriece had suggested she try on.

Since being rescued by him from her entrapment in the giant tree, they had flown a great distance in the chariot, with Pegasus taking them high in the sky before swooping to land in Vedriece's tremendous kingdom. He had spoken of his kingdom with great pride, saying he had a great many things to show her that would be remarkable to her eyes, and he hadn't been wrong. He also told her that he wanted to lavish many a fine gift upon her, as her ravishing beauty was to be celebrated and admired by all. Jessica told him everything that had happened to them all so far, finding the books, escaping the giants and Jack being a Child of Mankind. It was a mystery as to why Jack could even enter the realm of Elopia. She told Vedriece about their trials, and about the eagles giving Ariana the invisible key because apparently, she was the Chosen One. Vedriece told her that actually, that was not true; she, Jessica was the true Chosen One, not Ariana. He told her that the eagles were evil spirits and not sacred beings. Vedriece also said that Leo and Eriat were using them all to get the Chalice of Fire for their own dark purposes and that she was not to trust them.

Jessica twirled around in front of Vedriece in her fantastic gown, which was encrusted with sparkling precious stones from each of the seven realms. He told her that they sparkled ten times brighter than the purest diamond from the earthly realm and that the gown was made from the purest purple silk ever found in all the realms, formed by the rarest of all the known celestial silkworms.

"Come, my beauty, let me take you to meet the fair maidens of my kingdom, they will prepare you for our evening ceremony of feasting and dancing to celebrate your arrival and you will have enjoyment of all your heart's desire. Every need or greed is yours to have; in this kingdom, we satisfy our heart's desire, and there is much joy amongst all. I want you to be the one to rule beside me, Jessica, for you alone are the Chosen One, every knee bows to me in this kingdom and they will bow to you also, for I am all-powerful."

Jessica was mesmerised by Vedriece, his words melted her heart and she felt she could disappear into his blazing amber eyes as they held her gaze and she felt entranced by him. Jessica strode towards Vedriece, holding his gaze as she looked up at him lovingly and as she put her hand in his, she felt a warm glow from within, and her heart pounded furiously in her chest just by being near him. Jessica was certain that she had found true love, and all thoughts of Jack, Ariana, and Pippy were gone from her mind.

***

Ariana pushed open the door and walked through with Pippy following behind as they entered the Kingdom of Principalities. Not knowing what to expect, Ariana had her sword unsheathed and Pippy held her little dart gun at the ready. She crept silently and Pippy fluttered at her side. Looking around, they saw that they were in a dimly lit stone corridor. It seemed like they were in an underground tunnel, purpose-built, with space that was high enough for even the tallest of humanoids to stand upright and walk with ease.

Both Pippy and Ariana visibly relaxed when they realised that they were alone in the tunnel.

"Look," whispered Pippy, pointing to Ariana's left.

Ariana looked and noticed a door. She scanned along the tunnel and up ahead were lots of doors, on both sides of the tunnel. She looked back at the door closest to them; it had words etched on it. They both edged closer to read what it said, *'Generational Curses.'*

Pippy had an angry look on her face that spoke volumes, and she shook her head and little fist at the door. Ariana strode to each door to read what was inscribed on them and Pippy followed.

The next door said,

'Pestilence and Plagues' and the next, *'Infirmity and Malady'*, the next *'Fear and Terror'* and on and on. *'Necromancy'*, *'Sorcery'*, *'The Dark Arts'*, *'Rage, Addiction and Violence'*, *'Temptation'*, *'The Seven Deadly Sins,'* *'Mutilation'*, *'Madness and Terror of the Mind'*, and *'Diseases of the Flesh'*.

Ariana felt her anger kindling with each door she read, knowing that this place held so much evil. She was beginning to understand that there was a connection here to the sufferings of the people on Earth, and she suddenly remembered Miriam and Eddie Marskall, and the Tormenting ones whispering evil thoughts and instructions into their minds.

Shaking her head, Ariana looked at Pippy's mud-covered face and said, "I want to look inside one of these rooms, I really want to understand what this all means."

Pippy flew directly up to her, placed her tiny hand on Ariana's shoulder and held her gaze, warning her, "Once you have seen, it can never be unseen."

Ariana paused for a moment with her hand on the door that said, *'Diseases of the Flesh.'* She took a deep breath, and a sideways look at Pippy, and then she quietly turned the handle of the door and slowly pushed it open. Not knowing what to expect, they both peered tentatively around the door.

What they saw was a myriad of activities in a giant-sized cave that seemed to stretch on and on as far as the eye could see. There were multitudes of Tormenting ones everywhere, busy running around collecting things from different sections of what looked like an organised mass production line, and after they had collected their items, they hurried to another part of the cave, where some further activity was taking place and then they disappeared through a door, above which was a sign that read, *'Commission and seek authority.'*

The Tormenting ones were so engrossed in what they were doing, queuing in line to collect their items and following through each stage of the production line, it allowed Ariana and Pippy to slip inside the huge cave unnoticed.

"What are those?" whispered Ariana, as she saw a group of creatures ambling towards them, of all different shapes and sizes and covered in mud. She was about to draw her Lifeblood sword.

"They are Ground Gremlins, put your sword back and don't say a word," Pippy whispered.

The Ground Gremlins were covered in mud from head to toe, and from what Ariana could see, they appeared humanoid in form, yet they were hunched and the way they moved was strangely awkward. As they got closer, Ariana could see that their hands were more like claws and they had tails; they had mud-covered, matted feathers or fur on their bodies, Ariana couldn't tell which, and their noses were hooked rather like a bird of prey's beak and their eyes were small and beady. They ambled awkwardly over in a group and stopped in front of Ariana and Pippy; some of them were making strange, chattering noises as they stared at them bleakly and blinked their tiny beady eyes before the one closest to them said,

"Well don't just stand there, take one of those carts and get to work!" the creature gave a jeering look before continuing past them, and the rest of the group followed.

Ariana realised they were all holding onto a rope which was attached to a cart that they were dragging along. The cart was full of jars. Pippy and Ariana watched the group amble towards one of the production lines, where they began to offload the contents of their cart to a waiting group of Ground Gremlins that began opening each jar, before scooping something from the production line into the jars, which were then placed on a conveyor belt, which then went on to the next section, where Tormenting ones were waiting.

The Ground Gremlin that had spoken to them turned back to look at them and shouted, "Hurry up and bring more jars!"

Ariana and Pippy looked around and saw that there was some kind of cart station at one side of the cave, where groups of Ground Gremlins took carts full of jars and hurried them over to the different rows of production lines.

"Come on Pippy, let's make like a Ground Gremlin," Ariana whispered as she grabbed Pippy by the hand and together, they began ambling along towards the carts, trying their best to imitate the way the Ground Gremlins hobbled along.

Ariana was thankful that the mucky sludge that they had fallen into in the Accursed pit, was serving a purpose as a viable disguise. Much as she would rather have a good wash to get rid of the mucky, sticky stench, it could be the very thing that saved both of their lives right now.

Ariana and Pippy joined the back of the disorderly queue with the other Ground Gremlins, and they watched as the Gremlins pushed and shoved one another to get to the carts first. Looking at the jars, Ariana could see that inside each jar something was moving, she couldn't quite make out what it was. Keen to get a closer look, she jostled between the Gremlins with the same amount of force that they were dishing out, bumping her and Pippy aside to try to get a cart first. Finally, Ariana managed to squeeze in between two Gremlins and grab hold of the rope that was attached to one of the carts, which she yanked firmly. The crowd of Gremlins quickly moved aside to let her through with her cart, but not without jeering at her, as though envious that she had gotten a cart before them. One of them shoved Pippy as she made her way through them towards Ariana, calling her a pip-squeak of a Gremlin and making that strange chattering noise. Pippy shoved the Gremlin back and then quickly joined Ariana and grabbed hold of the rope and together they slowly ambled off towards one of the production lines.

When no one was looking, Ariana stopped and pretended she was organising the jars to fit in the cart properly, so that she could have a look at what was inside them. She picked up a jar and held it up so that she could take a better look, she could barely see anything in the jar, but just then she saw something tiny moving. She peered closer and spotted the tiniest little wormlike creature, wriggling and stretching upwards from the bottom of the jar. Its white little body was so thin it was almost like a fine hair. As Ariana twisted the jar around, she could see there were many more fine hair-like tiny white worms inside and they looked like they were floating in a breeze inside the jar as they swayed from side to side, twisting and turning.

"What are these?" Ariana asked as she tapped on the glass with her finger and she almost dropped the jar at the instant reaction of those fine, threadlike worms. They responded with lightning speed, bulging to at least ten times their size and shooting out from the top of their wormy heads, large, orange-coloured globules that attached themselves to the glass, like giant suckers. She peered at the strange globules and could see what looked like tiny razor-sharp rows of teeth all along the underside of them as they gripped onto the glass.

"What do you think you're doing? Put that down and bring those parasites here!" the same Ground Gremlin shouted at them again, and for a second time, Ariana nearly dropped the jar.

"We're coming," cried Pippy as Ariana quickly put the jar back in the cart, but not before scanning the other jars, which all seemed to hold tiny, strange amoeba-like creatures, some swimming in a type of fluid, and others stuck to the sides of the jar or flattened at the bottom of the jar, writhing and wriggling, or morphing into something or other. They were all rather gruesome-looking living organisms, that Ariana realised were no doubt diseases in the making.

Together, Ariana and Pippy hurried over to the production line with their cart. They copied what the Ground Gremlins were doing and started loading the jars onto the conveyor belt. They watched as each jar moved along and then stopped in front of a Tormenting one that scooped something out of a large, bulbous glass container. The Gremlins had crowded around to watch and some of them were making that strange chattering sound and others appeared to be laughing, whilst shoving each other aggressively as they jostled for the best viewing position. Ariana and Pippy joined the throng of Gremlins to see what the Tormenting ones were doing. As they wriggled their way through the Gremlins to the front, Ariana gave as much shoving and pushing as she got from them and finally, she reached a good spot.

She watched the Tormenting one put the lid back on a jar and pop it back onto the conveyor belt and it disappeared along to the next section. The Tormenting one blinked its big amber eyes in its oversized grey alien head and paused for a moment as a giant ugly grin spread across its grey almost translucent face. It blinked again and reached its scrawny greyish clawed hand across to grab another jar, unscrewed the lid, looked inside and its grin grew wider, its expression conniving as it picked up its ladle and dipped it into the large glass bulbous container.

Written on the container, as though inscribed into the glass itself, were the words, *"Mutating cells."* The Tormenting one appeared to get rather excited by what it was about to do, as it began chuckling, and its eyes grew wide in anticipation. It looked over at its audience of Ground Gremlins who seemed to be just as excited, cheering him on. The Tormenting one scooped and then lifted the ladle, which looked like it held a purple potion that fizzed and then he poured it straight into the jar, whilst the Ground Gremlins roared a cheer which prompted the Tormenting one to perform a little dance, slap its scrawny thigh and shake back its oversized head in laughter. Before finally screwing the lid back on the jar which contained the writhing organism that seemed to take on a much more violent disposition as it slapped itself against the jar furiously. The Tormenting one then placed the jar onto the conveyor belt once more and it disappeared down the line to the next section.

Ariana had seen enough to know what evil was being conjured up in this place behind the door of *"Diseases of the flesh."* The next thing to know was where and how these were being spread.

Ariana and Pippy withdrew from the crowd of cheering Gremlins, grabbed their empty cart and ambled across the cave to see if they could find out where the jars ended up. They followed the conveyor belt as it carried the jars to a waiting Tormenting one that was seated on the other side of the conveyor belt, waiting for the jars. Ariana and Pippy stopped to watch as it picked up a jar, unscrewed the lid, and turned to its array of condiments on its workstation, which reminded Ariana of the Chemistry lab at school with its test tubes and pipettes and other utensils used for mixing and testing various concoctions.

They watched as the violent little organism writhed and splurged around, and almost leapt out of the jar, until the Tormenting one stopped it mid-air, with a quick gesture of its hand as though casting a spell on the tiny creature, which immediately slipped obediently back into the jar as though put to sleep. The Tormenting one reached for what looked like a vial from its array of condiments, popped the lid off with its claw and then tipped the contents into the jar and the organism shrunk in size until it could hardly be seen. The lid was returned to the jar and the jar was placed back on the conveyor belt once more, moving along to another Tormenting one that was standing at the front of a long queue as they all waited their turn.

It appeared rather excited as it waited for the jar to arrive and snatched it from the conveyor belt, whipped it open and stuck its long dark claw inside the jar and its dark claw changed to a purple colour as the tiny organism was sucked into its claw like a straw. The Tormenting one threw back its head, its expression joyful as though experiencing a moment of ecstasy. The jar tumbled to the floor and rolled around and the Tormenting one held up its purple claw and began to grin excitedly before it hurried along to the door with the sign above it that said, *'Commission and Seek Authority.'*

There were jars all over the floor which several Ground Gremlins were gathering and taking away through the door underneath the sign that said, *'Commission and Seek Authority'*. Ariana and Pippy glanced at one another, both with the same thought in their heads. They gathered some empty jars and put them in their cart and followed behind a couple of Ground Gremlins as they pulled their cart of empty jars through the open doorway. The doorway led to another cave, where they were met by two Tormenting ones that stood as sentries. They each held what looked like a spear in their hand and they crossed their spears, stopping the two Ground Gremlins in front of them. There appeared to be some dialogue between them. Ariana couldn't quite hear what the exchange was about, though she took the opportunity to scan around the cave to see what was going on.

She could see that the Tormenting ones that had sucked the parasites through their claws were lined up in various queues, and at the front of each queue stood a Tormenting one that looked to be in some sort of trance-like state, with amber eyes fixed, yet blazing just like the accursed ones. Ariana watched as a clear vision emerged from one of the Tormenting one's blazing eyes, almost like a movie projector showing a film. The vision showed the cosmos zooming by, and then planet Earth came into sight. The vision raced towards Earth at lightning speed, bursting through Earth's atmosphere, passing continents, soaring across oceans and then towards an island, and speeding towards the island, which got bigger and bigger as it zoomed along streets and houses, and then to a hospital, zooming through the corridors and into a hospital room, and finally, it stopped right in front of a tiny baby in a hospital incubator. The baby looked premature, and there were feeding tubes attached to its tiny body, and beside the cot were its parents staring lovingly, yet their deeply furrowed brows displayed evident concern, at the tiny baby that they couldn't yet hold.

The Tormenting one with the blazing eyes then spoke to the other Tormenting one that was standing directly opposite it, that had been watching the vision attentively, *"Locate the Child of Mankind, seek authority, speak the words of darkness to the mother, deliver the parasite into the blood of the child, and complete the commission."* As it spoke the instructions, its words floated into the open mouth of the Tormenting one standing opposite who chuckled as it received its commission, threw its head back in ecstasy, and then ran through what looked like a giant pulsating wormhole at the back of the cave, similar to the one that Ariana, Jack and Pippy had gone through at the river's edge.

"Imbecile of a Gremlin! Speak when spoken to!"

The Cocoon Within

Ariana felt a jab in her side as she reacted by jerking sideways to avoid being stabbed by the Tormenting one's spear. She immediately looked at the Tormenting one that was pointing the spear at her, its face was scrunched into an angry scowl, its large, saucer-like, amber eyes blazed and then they squinted as they looked at her more closely.

"You are a funny-looking Gremlin," it said and then it looked from Ariana to Pippy, and Ariana saw a large blob of sludge slide down Pippy's face, revealing her true features, as the sludge slid to the ground.

Ariana watched the Tormenting one's face change as realisation dawned. *"INDTRUDERS!"* it yelled in fury, and its face looked as though it were about to burst. Every Tormenting one in the cave immediately stopped what they were doing and turned to look at Ariana and Pippy.

Pippy quickly flew up high in the cave, and Ariana somersaulted backwards and then blasted as many of the Tormenting ones as she could before she raced back through the door that they had come in by. Pippy was already out of the door and flying across the huge cave towards the exit. The production line was busy and none of the others had noticed the kerfuffle, until Ariana heard another one of the Tormenting ones yelling, *"INDTRUDERS! STOP THEM!"* and the sound of a loud horn, which Ariana instinctively knew was no doubt an alarm call to summon help.

Ariana raced after Pippy, easily blasting any Tormenting ones out of the way that tried to stop her. She dashed through the exit after Pippy and kicked the door shut behind her, and together they raced through the tunnel and past all the other doors, with no idea where it would lead them next. They sped along and were faced with a maze of tunnels to choose from, each going in different directions. They could hear the shouts of pursuers behind them, so they had no time to lose. Ariana chose to go straight ahead, leading the way, and they continued as fast as they could until they reached a door at the end of the tunnel which had a sign on it that said, *"Upper Levels."*

Ariana opened the door and both she and Pippy shot through and then closed the door behind them. It could be bolted shut from the inside, so Ariana quickly slid the bolt across the door to stop anyone else from opening it. They paused at last, relieved that they had managed to escape, catching their breath whilst looking around in the dark, with Pippy casting the only illumination from her glowing body and wings.

"Oh, great, now we are in a tower!" Ariana said as she looked up, and eyed the metal rungs that they would need to climb to reach the top, which she hoped led to a way out.

The clattering sound of their pursuers could be heard at the door. Pippy quickly flew upwards with Ariana making a hasty grab for the metal rungs as she pulled herself up and climbed each rung with speed. On and on they went, and Ariana could hear the door being bashed in. She looked down and saw that a giant was in hot pursuit, but it was awkward for it in the small space, so it couldn't catch up with them quickly. More giants barged through, trying to clamber over one another to chase after them through the narrow space of the tower, but they hindered one another which gave Ariana and Pippy the chance to get to the top first. This opened up to another rather narrow tunnel with more tunnels leading off from one another.

"Quick, through here!" cried Pippy as she grabbed hold of a metal grid that covered a vent. "They won't be able to catch us if we go through here."

Ariana quickly grabbed the other side of the metal grid and pulled it off easily. Pippy flew inside and zipped down the chute, and then Ariana climbed in feet-first before placing the metal grid back in place. She could hear the sound of the giants reaching the top of the tower, and just in time, Ariana let herself fly after Pippy down the chute.

Having escaped the pursuing giants, Ariana and Pippy travelled along the chute which ended up taking them all the way to a narrow vent. Ariana had to leave her rucksack behind, but not without removing the sacred book first. As they thrust their way through the vent, they could hear music and the sound of many conversations as though a large party was on the other side of the wall. They slowly slid along the vent and came to an end, where there was a metal grill, through which they could watch what was going on without being seen. When Ariana peered through the holes in the grill, she could see humanoids and all sorts of unusual beings, that were dancing, eating, drinking and chatting animatedly with one another. It looked like a party was in full swing.

"Pippy, it looks like there is some sort of a celebration going on."

"Let me see."

Ariana felt Pippy climb over her shoulder and across her hair. "Ouch, mind my hair will you!" she cried.

"Sorry!" said Pippy, chuckling as she untangled herself from Ariana's curls before peering through the holes in the grill. "It's a banquet!" she observed, "and I bet it's a celebration of the entrapped! And is that…? Yes, I think it is! What is she doing here?" Pippy exclaimed in surprise.

"Who?" asked Ariana, peering through the holes to see who Pippy was talking about.

"I think it's Jessica!" Pippy exclaimed.

"Jessica? Could it be? Where? I can't see her," said Ariana, scanning the crowd looking for Jessica.

"Look at the stage, at the back, there are two thrones, and I think Jessica is seated on the left throne, in a purple dress!"

Ariana pushed her face closer to the grill and strained to look through the small gaps. As she pressed her eye up closer to the grill, after a moment, she caught a glimpse of the woman seated on one of the thrones on the stage, as dancers waltzed by. She wore a silky purple gown that sparkled so brightly, she couldn't quite see the woman's face. Ariana moved her head slightly to try to get a better look, as some more dancers sped by and then a gap between dancers at last! Ariana looked at the woman's face, highly made-up in colourful shades; she looked at the features, the eyes, the long lush dark hair, that stunning face… it was none other than… Jessica!

Ariana looked at Pippy in shock, "If Jessica is here, then what on earth has happened to Jack?" she asked with a look of concern on her face as she contemplated all sorts of things that might have happened to him.

Pippy shrugged her little shoulders, "I don't know, but I imagine that Jessica is under some sort of spell."

They watched as two Tormenting ones on either side of the stage, each blew a large horn loudly. The music stopped and the crowd began to quieten, signifying an imminent announcement. Ariana drew her attention to the audience or the guests, as one would expect at any kind of party. Some of the guests were great, beastly creatures, with horns and fangs, and fearsome gazes. Others were gruesome-looking humanoids, not unlike the giants, with drooling mouths, and markings etched on their faces, their claw-like hands clutching silver and golden goblets as they swigged back their drinks and looked on at the stage with anticipation. Ariana also noticed a group of female humanoids; they appeared quite beautiful and were dressed seductively, and adorned in jewels of what looked like gold, silver and precious stones. Even their hair sparkled with jewel-encrusted tiaras and beads. Their faces were made up, and their stark make-up made Ariana think of the geishas that she had read about in history lessons. The group of female humanoids were seated at a large table at the front, near the stage and appeared to be enjoying themselves as they ate, drank and laughed amongst themselves. Ariana looked for the entrances around the great hall; stationed at each archway that led in and out of the hall, was at least one armoured giant, like a towering sentry on guard.

"Pippy, who are the beautiful celestials at the front table? They seem out of place amongst all the beasts," Ariana asked curiously.

"They must be the renowned harem of beauties called the Fair Maidens of Sin. Rumour has it that the Fair Maidens were snatched by the Destroyer when they were but young buds and they were since corrupted. They collude to bring in new abductees and they are responsible for spawning his grotesque offspring."

Ariana could see that Pippy's face had contorted with disgust. Even underneath the remaining layer of mud that still covered parts of her face, her expression was clear and said it all.

Just then, one of the female humanoids got up from the table, she appeared more senior than the others and she walked confidently and had an almost regal air about her. She walked up the few steps that took her onto the stage. Ariana noticed that many of the beasts eyed the female humanoid as she took to the stage, their expressions gleeful, appreciative, excited even, and some licked their lips as drool slithered from their grotesque mouths, as they watched her strut onto the stage, her voluptuous body barely encased in the silvery dress she wore that clung to her like a second skin. Ariana couldn't take her eyes off her either, she oozed seduction, and it was mesmerising, her deep V-shaped plunging neckline revealing the cleavage of her large golden-brown bosom, her dress split showing strong and toned legs that seemed to go on forever. A hushed silence descended on the entire room as all eyes were on the silvery, mermaid-like humanoid, and as though she knew that she commanded the attention of the entire room, she scanned the audience with her deep violet eyes set in her beautiful golden brown glowing face. She shook the blue-green tresses of her hair and Ariana heard her own involuntary sharp intake of breath as she realised that the tresses were shiny, slithery, little individual serpents that were hissing and flickering their small, forked tongues as they moved in wave-like slow motion.

"Greetings, fellow followers and principality dwellers, tonight we celebrate all that we have achieved and all that we are going to achieve, according to our prophecy; momentous things are coming! But first dear in-dwellers let us bow to our great leader and king!" and with that, the silvery-serpent haired humanoid flung her arm outwards sharply, her eyes grew bright and fiery, and a broad grin spread across her face as she took a deep bow.

The Cocoon Within

Everyone's gaze turned to the left of the room to watch as a giant being entered, and a hushed silence filled the air as every creature in the room bowed low. The great statuesque being was like a giant-sized Hercules, he strode across the room, with the thuds of his feet reverberating across the floor. Dressed in a sleek suit of armour, his huge muscular body was accentuated by the close-fitting armour, his broad, rugged, battle-scarred face was also covered in raised skin markings, and his unusually deep reddish skin looked taut, yet almost leathery. He exuded an energy of a different kind, powerful, yes there was no doubt about that, but what Ariana was picking up was what she could only describe as an atmosphere or energy that surrounded this being, of intense physical and mental strength. It was as though he was shrouded in an energy that was driven by an intense rage almost akin to a wildfire burning that grows ever intense and cannot be extinguished. Yet what struck Ariana the most about this giant being, was his deep, piercing amber eyes, they somehow seemed ever so slightly familiar to her, almost as though she had seen them somewhere before.

"The Destroyer!" Pippy cried as her hands flew to her mouth.

Ariana looked at Pippy and said, "So we are in the Destroyer's kingdom? And he has got Jessica, possibly even Jack too. Do you think he knows about us?"

"He will know about us, he might not know that we are here, but if he has put Jessica under a spell then she would have told him everything." Pippy's voice lowered to a whisper, "Ariana you must protect the invisible key, that is what he will be wanting, so that he can get the Chalice of Fire, and he will want to destroy you too because you have an important part to play in the restoration of all things."

Ariana thought that she should feel fear at Pippy's words, but she didn't, and then she remembered the words the Gnetic leader spoke about Higher Order Celestials not feeling fear. Though she was really glad about that, how would she even complete such an otherworldly mission if she felt afraid every minute? But what was bothering her which she knew was attached to her greatest fear just like in her trial, was Jack's whereabouts, she needed to know that he was safe. Ariana instinctively felt for the invisible key, it sat heavy and secure around her neck, whatever happened, she would make sure that the Destroyer did not get his hands on the key. Ariana felt a fiery determination rise from deep within her inner self and she knew without a shadow of a doubt, that she had to complete her mission and set all things right.

"So, what's the plan?" Pippy's question snapped Ariana out of her thoughts, somewhat taken aback by the fact that Pippy was expecting her to have a plan.

"We need to hide the book somewhere and come back for it when we get the chance," said Ariana, looking around the narrow vent for somewhere to stash the book.

"I saw an opening in the wall further back," offered Pippy, "and I think the book might just fit. Here, give it to me and I'll try and hide it there." Pippy took the book and managed to push it into the opening in the wall.

"There, it fits nicely, no one would find it unless they were looking for it, we just have to remember how to find it."

"What's that scratching noise? Listen," there was a scratching noise echoing through the vent and it was getting louder.

"I'll take a look," Pippy glowed and flew back along the vent whilst Ariana lay there waiting for her, watching earnestly for Pippy to come back.

As the scratching sound became louder and more furious, Pippy flew back down the vent to Ariana, her hands waving furiously and an expression of complete desperation on her face.

"Go, go, go! We have to get out now!" Pippy cried. "They have sent the hordes of Drakken to flush us out!"

Ariana whacked the grill open and pulled herself out of the vent and onto the floor in the hall. With Pippy following close behind her, they slid behind the rows of tables at the back of the room, slipping underneath the nearest table, they were hidden beneath the table cover.

"What are the Drakken?" Ariana whispered as she crouched under the table and tried to peep through a small gap.

Pippy used her little dart gun to slash an opening in the table cover. "Behold, the hordes of Drakken," she said, holding the gap in the cloth open for Ariana to look through.

Ariana put her eye to the gap in the cloth and watched as creature after creature appeared, no doubt emerging from the vent that they had just escaped from. The creatures were about the size of a small dog, but as they crossed the room, they grew larger, transforming to the size of a horse. Each creature was muscular and heavy set; they were covered in thick dark fur with a row of sharp spiny spikes all along their backs, heads and tails, resembling that of a lizard. Yet their faces were also canine in shape, with rows of large razor-sharp jagged teeth, much like that of a shark. Bright green eyes burned in their broad, heavy-set faces and their muscular shoulders gave a show of great strength, their clawed feet were wide and strong. One of the Drakken who appeared to be the leader of the pack walked through the parting crowd and stopped in front of the Destroyer, who was on the stage with Jessica seated on his left and the silvery-dressed humanoid standing on his right.

"My Lord and master," said the large Drakken beast, bowing low before continuing, "We have intruders, and they are amongst us, we followed them here and even now…" The Drakken sniffed the air, and his gaze scoured the crowd, his green eyes blazing, a dark and evil expression of fury etched on his face, "I can smell them!"

The Destroyer's expression hardened, and then he turned to look at Jessica. "I believe your friends have come looking for you, my beauty!"

Jessica turned her gaze to him and smiling, she stretched out her hand to reach for his. "There is no one but you, my wonderful Vedriece, you are the only friend and love that I need."

The Destroyer threw back his head and his deep throaty laughter rumbled loudly across the room. His audience joined in with gleeful shouts and laughter.

"Find them and bring them to me!" bellowed the Destroyer, before turning towards the crowd, his deep coarse voice echoed as he spoke loudly to them, "My followers, dine! Feast! Meet every need and every greed to your heart's content! Tonight, we celebrate what is to come!" He snapped his fingers and the music resumed, the crowd cheered and raised their goblets in agreement and the celebrations continued. The Drakken raced in between the crowd, weaving in and out of the tables, sniffing out every square inch of the hall. The crowd didn't care, they continued laughing, drinking and eating, some of the great beasts began dancing with the Fair Maidens of Sin, who seemed to be enjoying the attention, as they gyrated seductively, swinging their hair and draping their scantily clad bodies around the beasts. One or two of the beasts threw a fair maiden or two over their shoulders and carried them off through one of the archways, with laughter and shouts of excitement as their intentions were clearly to indulge their every wanton desire.

Ariana watched as the Drakken headed towards the tables at the back of the hall.

"They will soon be upon us," Pippy whispered.

"I will blast them with my powers. There will be an all-out fight, but we have no other choice. When I start blasting, you fly up high and away, make your escape, I will catch you up when I can. If our lives become endangered, we have our crystal pendants, remember?"

Ariana heard the sound of growling close by, and she knew that their table was surrounded by the Drakken, they had sniffed them out.

"On three, I will strike first!" said Ariana, looking at Pippy who nodded her small head solemnly.

"In case it goes sour, I just want to say, it has been a pleasure knowing you," said Pippy, with a feeble smile as she gulped and held her tiny dart gun at the ready.

Ariana smiled and held up one finger, then two, and then she mouthed the word *'three'*. As she held out her hands and blasted the power from them, the tablecloth immediately disintegrated, and Ariana came face to face with the Drakken.

Three Drakken stared back at her, with snarling faces, their bright green eyes blazing furiously at her. The Drakken were fearsome-looking giant beasts, their tails thrashed about wildly as they lunged at her like attacking dogs. Yet Ariana felt no fear, she felt anger rising inside her, a rage that seemed to involuntarily surge outwards as though to match her attacker's stance and empower her to meet fury with fury. It was the same outraged feeling that she had experienced in her trial when Granpey and Jack had been hurt by the giants, and when Jack had almost drowned in the quicksand, it just seemed to propel her into action.

Ariana blasted the three attacking Drakken in one swoop and they immediately disintegrated, but more came with the same ferocious fervour. Out of the corner of her eye, Ariana saw Pippy slip away, so she rolled out from under the table, blasting the ever-increasing approaching hordes. As she sprang to her feet and leapt backwards onto the table, drawing her Lifeblood sword in one hand, she slashed at the Drakken on one side of her, with expert strikes, and she blasted the Drakken on her other side with her free hand. Ariana fought consistently, so absorbed in her own activity, that she was oblivious to her own stealth and speed with which she moved. The Drakken fell one by one, they simply could not overpower her, for she outmatched their ferocious physical strength, with the speed of her own agility and celestial power.

Suddenly, Ariana felt herself being lifted high into the air; she tried to use her powers, but she was immobilised by a powerful beam. She turned her gaze towards the source of the beam, it was the Destroyer. The music had stopped and all eyes were on her. The Destroyer raised both his hands; one held her up in a powerful beam and the other held Pippy similarly up high, they were trapped.

"Oh, celestial being, your powers have limits you know, I could destroy you with the flick of my finger, for I am all-powerful!"

roared the Destroyer, holding her gaze, his deep piercing amber eyes blazing.

The crowd roared in agreement, some jeering, with goading remarks, "destroy her! Her kind is not welcome here!"

"All in good time, my followers, but not yet!" Just then, the Destroyer's eyes flared, and amber rays shot from his eyes and struck the crystal pendant from Ariana's neck. As it fell to the floor, he turned his gaze to Pippy and did the same. Ariana watched as Pippy's pendant dropped to the floor too. The Destroyer's amber gaze shot rays towards Ariana, and she felt both ankles become encased and her wrists too, as she floated downwards towards one of the giant sentries that wheeled a large, crisscrossed pole and her wrists and ankles immediately stuck to it as though by a magnetic force. Another giant wheeled forward an identical pole, and Pippy floated down and was instantly stuck to it, trapped in the same way as though a magnetic forcefield held her in place.

The crowd roared with laughter and the Destroyer's deep voice bellowed loudly. He grabbed Jessica in his arms and swung her around, she threw back her head in laughter and then he released her. He turned to the silvery humanoid, drawing her close with one giant hand, and he kissed her deeply, the snakes in her hair hissing, their slithering forked tongues flickering. He threw her over his shoulder and grabbed a goblet held out to him by one of the Fair Maidens and he sauntered off the stage and into the waiting crowds, and through the same archway that the other beasts had carried off their Fair Maidens, leaving Jessica to slump back onto her throne as though in some kind of a daze. Ariana and Pippy, trapped on the criss-crossed poles, were wheeled across the hall by the sentry guards, through the crowd as they were spat upon, jeered at and hissed at.

"You are not welcome here celestial!" shouted the crowd as they were wheeled by. One gruesome-looking humanoid, covered in protruding blobs of skin all over its face, spat the remark at Ariana as she passed by. She stared at its strange, gross-looking face and saw lots of small wriggling maggots squeeze through the blobs of skin on its face, each maggot had a tiny, evil-looking face, with blinking eyes that peered out from the blobs of skin on the creature's face. The tiny maggots opened their minuscule mouths and echoed the creature's words in harmony, their voices tight and squeaky, "You are not welcome here celestial!" As she was wheeled by, Ariana turned her head to continue watching the spectacle of a creature, and as she observed it, she pondered that although she and Pippy had been captured, and were being carted away somewhere by the sentries, at least they were still alive, and being alive meant an opportunity for escape.

***

Jack leaned against the wall; he couldn't believe that he had thrown up, yet again! He was so glad that Ariana and the others hadn't been there to witness another of his embarrassing moments. Jack smiled to himself at the thought, as he took a few deep breaths and allowed his mind to wander over the ordeal that he had just been through. The fact that he had managed to solve a new riddle from the giant tree all by himself, whilst fighting off those pesky vines, and just in the nick of time too, so that he could dash through the portal in the tree. That had made Jack feel pretty capable of successfully finding Ariana and Pippy. Well, that was at least until he had fallen into the Accursed pit, where he had been traumatised by the living dead that he had encountered. Jack shuddered as he replayed the gruesome events in his mind, it had been just like a scene out of a horror movie, and he swore he would live to rue the day that he had decided to climb down from that giant tree to search for Ariana and Pippy.

He wiped some of the sludge from his face as he thought about what he should do next. After all, he didn't even know if Ariana and Pippy were alright, they could be trapped somewhere or injured, maybe even separated from one another or captured. It was pretty clear that he was definitely in the darker realms, and God only knew what kind of things lay in wait for him. He wondered if he should turn back and try to make his way back to the relative safety of the tree and wait for Ariana and Pippy to return as originally planned.

The Cocoon Within

After pondering what to do, he chided himself for being a coward and reminded himself that he had been given inner strength by the eagles, who were sacred beings after all, so they should know what they were doing. That must mean that they gave him enough inner strength to cope with whatever was to come his way. Yes! That was it, he was going to go forward, and Jack decided in his mind, that he had all the strength he needed to find Ariana and Pippy, come what may.

8
Fear No Evil

"At least we are still alive," Ariana said as she hung upside down, still attached to the criss-crossed pole that the giant sentry had hooked to a huge rail on the ceiling. She looked over at Pippy who was in the same predicament, and they were not alone. The room that they had been taken to and so ungraciously strung upside down in by the giants, appeared to be a great holding cell or dungeon, with captive upon captive, strung upside down, hanging from the ceiling in the same way as Ariana and Pippy. The room was dim, with bleak, flickering lanterns, that gave off a low level of visibility, which was better than complete darkness Ariana supposed. As she looked around at the other captives hanging from the ceiling, she noticed most of them seemed half-asleep, barely conscious. They were celestial beings, humanoids of all different types and creatures like wish-helpers, that had no doubt been captured by the Destroyer and his followers.

"What do you think is wrong with them all?" Ariana asked, as her roaming eyes moved along the rows of victims, and then met Pippy's gaze enquiringly.

"Maybe they have been here for a long time and the dark and evil atmosphere has overcome them? celestial beings are most sensitive when out of their own atmosphere for a long duration," Pippy sighed and shook her head as she scanned the room.

The Cocoon Within

Ariana looked to her left, where a small wish-helper was hanging limply beside her. "Excuse me?" she said, trying to get its attention, "Hello? Excuse me, hello?" louder this time. The little wish-helper's eyes began to slowly open, as though being woken from a deep sleep. "Over here! Hello, why is everyone so drowsy?" Ariana asked directly, looking intently at the little wish-helper who now looked rather surprised at the question, and slightly disoriented.

The wish-helper yawned loudly and some of the others began to stir from their slumber. "Hello, have you just arrived here?" asked the little wish-helper, yawning again. "Sorry I am just so tired; I have been trapped here for so long now that I can barely keep awake."

Just then, the door at the far end of the room was flung wide open, and in walked two giant beasts, amber eyes blazing in their heavy-set wide faces, mouths open displaying their ferocious-looking rows of sharp teeth. Their heavy, large muscular frames moved with surprising agility, as they walked with purpose along the rows, inspecting each upside-down victim with their gaze. One of the giants walked along Ariana's aisle, looking with intent at victims hanging on each side, and then it stopped not far from the wish-helper beside Ariana. It was staring intently at a female humanoid, hanging limply and appearing life-less. Lifting one large, gnarled greenish-coloured hand, the giant grabbed the hair of the humanoid and lifted her head. The giant moved its face closer, and it peered at the humanoid's face as though studying its every contour, and then without warning, the giant raised its other hand, and with lightning speed it gashed the humanoid's neck with precision, slicing it open as dark blue blood gushed out of the wound. The giant's blazing eyes lit up and it immediately planted its huge mouth over the wound to drink the blood, and the sound of the beast gulping the lifeblood from its victim could be heard.

Ariana's sharp intake of breath made the giant pause and stop its grotesque blood-guzzling, and it looked around sharply, midnight blue blood dripping from its blood-stained teeth, and its blazing amber eyes met Ariana's gaze that displayed a look of disgust. The giant immediately let go of the humanoid's hair and her head flopped about as the dark blue blood continued to ooze from her wound and onto the floor. The giant strode purposefully to Ariana until its face was close to her upside-down face, and it made a growling sound. Full of anger, its blazing eyes looked deep into Ariana's eyes, but it didn't say a word.

Suddenly, a loud guttural sound came from the doorway, it was the other giant, it had a humanoid draped limply over its shoulder.

"What are you doing?" the giant shouted at his comrade, his deep voice coarse and harsh. "Bring the sacrifice for the feast and leave the Chosen One as we have been instructed fool!"

"Grrr! Then let me take her small friend as a morsel for my own delight," the giant looked from Ariana to Pippy with an evil expression of glee. Angered by the giant's request, Ariana twisted her body as much as she could, she tried to get free with all her might but the invisible bonds on her wrists and feet were like iron, and she couldn't raise her hands to use her powers.

"No! Imbecile! We were instructed not to touch either of them, we are to just bring more sacrifice for the feast, now hurry up!" yelled the giant, as his victim on his shoulder groaned and tried to raise her head.

The rebellious giant gave Ariana and Pippy a hard stare and then turned and unhooked the humanoid, easily put her over his huge shoulder and sauntered towards the door. With a dripping trail of the humanoid's blood staining the floor, both giants left, locking the door behind them.

Pippy let out a huge breath, before frantically wailing, "This is not what I signed up for! I knew I would have to go to the darker realms for this mission, but I draw the line at this abomination! He slashed her throat and sucked the lifeblood from her, right in front of our very eyes! And we were helpless. We have been sent here with no help, how can we just sit by and watch these atrocities being carried out in this dark and evil place? It would have been better to have drowned in the Accursed pit than witness this evil!"

Ariana turned to the little wish-helper that was beside her. She was quietly snuffling, and Ariana realised that she was crying. "Hey, don't cry, look I know it's awful, but we can't help her now; what we can do is try to find a way to help everyone else."

"I know," snuffled the little wish-helper, "but it is just so sad, I have seen so many come to this place, and be taken by the evil ones and they never come back, never!" She continued snuffling, "And the thing is they are tortured and eaten, some are eaten alive, but if they are lucky, they are killed in their sleep first like what you just saw, she was one of the lucky ones." The little wish-helper continued crying softly.

"See, see! I told you! It's worse than I thought, and we could be next!" Pippy was becoming hysterical.

"Pippy stop it! Just calm down and pull yourself together. We have to think of a way to get out of these bonds and help everyone escape this place. Losing our heads will not help anyone."

Her words seemed to have the desired effect on Pippy, as she quietened down though she continued to mutter to herself at the predicament they were in.

Ariana tried to rack her brains as to how and with what they could break these bonds. Just then the little wish-helper spoke to her,

"Are you really the Chosen One?" asked the little wish-helper, her teary eyes were wide as she looked at Ariana hopefully.

"Yes, she is!" Pippy jumped in before Ariana even opened her mouth. "She came from Earth as the legend foretold. The Mighty One sent for her and she is worthy to take up the invisible key, which she was given by the sacred beings, and she has come to help us destroy the evil one and set all things right!" Pippy had a proud look on her face as she waited for the little wish-helper's reaction.

The little wish-helper's eyes lit up, "Did you say she has the invisible key?" she asked, looking dumb-founded.

"Yes, that's exactly what I said," answered Pippy, rolling her eyes, wondering why on earth she had asked her that when she had just told her a moment ago, that Ariana had the key.

The Cocoon Within

Realising that Pippy was irritated with her for asking, the little wish-helper explained, "Oh, I'm sorry it's just that, if she is the Chosen One and she also has the invisible key, then she ought to be able to unlock anything using the key, because from what I heard, the Chosen One can activate the key's unlocking power, and that means anything including... shackles of bondage." The wish-helper looked over at Ariana, whose ears had pricked to attention at the suggestion that she could use the key to help them escape.

"Woah, so you are saying I have the power to use the key to unlock these invisible bonds holding us captive right? So, how do I do that?" Ariana asked eagerly, suddenly feeling confident that they would be getting out of this place sooner rather than later.

The little wish-helper explained, "Before I was captured and brought to this place of desolation and despair, I used to be a wish-helper at Abratoria's Abratorium, the place of all things invisible. I loved working there, and my master was full of wisdom and knowledge of the mysteries of all things invisible. One thing he taught me was the legend of the invisible key and that all its power lay in the mind of one worthy to take up the key. According to legend, the Chosen One was worthy and would access the key's power through the mind. His exact words to me were, *'the worthy one, thinketh it, speaketh it, and maketh it cometh to pass'*."

Pippy was suddenly attentive, "Ariana, you did it before with your powers when you made the fire by the river, remember?" Pippy seemed to have shrugged off her earlier hopelessness and her eyes were now bright and excited.

Ariana considered Pippy's words, but the difference was that her hands had not been restricted when she had started the fire by the river. But perhaps the invisible key would generate the power for her, even though her hands were restrained. After all, she was the Chosen One, and if the key was powerful enough to unlock the way to the Chalice of Fire, then it must be powerful enough to break these shackles.

"Ok, I'm going to try thinking it and speaking it. Give me a minute."

Ariana thought she ought to give it her all. She focussed her mind, reminding herself that her Suit of Ultimate Truth gave her enhanced abilities, and that included enhanced thinking, which she had noticed since wearing the suit, her thinking had become much clearer and sharper. And even though she hadn't been able to hear Leo anymore, which she supposed the reason for that to be something that she wasn't meant to know, just yet, though she didn't know why, she just felt it deep within. Ariana closed her eyes and she started to visualise in her mind, and as she moved her wrists, the invisible chains of iron began loosening, and the more she moved her wrists, the freer they felt.

"Oh, my goodness, the key is glowing!" Pippy cried excitedly. Ariana opened her eyes at Pippy's words, though she was still bound. "Don't stop! Keep going," cried Pippy earnestly.

"Don't forget to speaketh," reminded the little wish-helper as she smiled encouragingly at Ariana.

"Right, here goes," Ariana closed her eyes and resumed visualising moving her wrists and she could feel that the invisible shackles were loosening, *"Shackles be broken!"* cried Ariana with fervour, and suddenly her hands were free! She heard a cheer escape from both Pippy's and the little wish-helper's lips, and she opened her eyes and lifted her hands, they were really free! Suddenly she fell from the criss-cross pole to the ground, completely free from the invisible shackles that had held her prisoner.

Ariana quickly stood up and danced around in glee, so happy to be free. It didn't matter that she had a bruise or two, she looked upwards and put a thumbs up to Pippy and the little wish-helper, both were smiling broadly and Ariana beamed back at them, proud that her first attempt had worked, so quickly too.

"I'm going to try to break your shackles too, be ready to fly, ok?" Ariana called up to them and they both did a very enthusiastic, upside-down nod in response.

Ariana closed her eyes and visualised the shackles breaking free from Pippy and the little wish-helper's wrists and ankles, *"Shackles be broken!*" cried Ariana once more, and she felt as though a surge of power was in the words that she spoke. She couldn't explain it, but she just knew that there was power in her words and that the key had somehow activated it. She opened her eyes and to her delight, both Pippy and the little wish-helper fluttered down towards her, their excited little faces so joyful, and considering that moments earlier, one had been borderline hysterical, and the other crying in despair, their positive transformation was all the encouragement Ariana needed to initiate a plan of escape.

"Chosen One, can you help us too?"

They all looked up at the sound of the small voice, and a tiny celestial creature with a humanoid face and torso and spotted legs and tail like that of a leopard gave a small upside-down wave and a beseeching look.

"And me too, please set me free!" a deep voice bellowed, "I am fierce and battle-ready, and I can help to lead everyone out of here."

They turned around to look at a great celestial humanoid that had spoken, hanging upside down. They could see that he was tall and mighty, and he had a strong and muscular physique. He wore a suit of armour, like a gladiator as though from the military; his muscular biceps looked large and powerful. His skin was dark ebony, with well-worn, deep battle scars criss-crossing his arms and face. He had a strong, broad face, with piercing blue eyes the colour of the sea, and a broad nose that rested between chiselled cheekbones. Although he was upside down, it was clear to Ariana that his features were quite striking, and they commanded the attention of any onlooker. He looked like a powerful warrior, and Ariana immediately thought that she would most definitely want him on her side, going up against any enemy.

Many of the celestial beings began to awaken from their slumberous state, and as they hung upside-down, some yawned and eyes began to open drowsily, some groaned and others talked softly amongst themselves, as they slowly came to life. But Ariana was holding the upside-down, blue-eyed gaze of the ebony-skinned stranger, as she contemplated how on earth they could all escape unnoticed, and whether the best plan of action would be for a handful of them to go first to find a way out, defeat as many of the enemy troops as possible, and then come back for the others.

Ariana felt a small tapping on her arm, it was the little wish-helper. "I know where they stashed the celestial's Lifeblood swords," she said. "We could take a group and retrieve as many of them as possible so that we are armed for battle."

Ariana looked into the little wish-helper's eyes and saw great courage and loyalty in her gaze. She turned to look next at Pippy, the great warrior and the other beings, and it suddenly dawned on her, that each and every one of them was looking to her, not only to release them from their entrapment, but for instructions and leadership. Ariana felt a strong sense of allegiance from them all, to go forward in a group escape attempt, regardless of the risk.

Ariana paused a moment as she contemplated a plan, "celestial beings, do you all have natural powers to fight against the enemy?" There were many affirmative upside-down nods and positive responses. "So, we can fight with or without Lifeblood swords, right?"

"Yes, but the strike of a Lifeblood sword annihilates the enemy swiftly at first strike if used correctly and can penetrate even the toughest armour," said the blue-eyed warrior. "Combined with one's powers, then we are unstoppable against the giant beasts. If not for the Destroyer, none of the celestial warriors that are here would have been captured," he finished emphatically.

"Ok, here goes, let me set the battle-ready warriors free first and together we will get the Lifeblood swords, and make a way for escape and then we will come back for the rest of you," said Ariana, gaining mumbles of acceptance from the upside-down crowd. She focused her gaze across the crowd as she looked at each of the celestial warriors, then she closed her eyes and held them in her mind's eye, imagining their shackles breaking, "Shackles break free from all the celestial warriors!" she cried.

Ariana heard thuds to the ground, and opening her eyes, she found to her delight and that of Pippy and the little wish-helper, that one by one, every celestial warrior had dropped to the ground, amid cheers from the crowd, their shackles broken.

The ebony, blue-eyed warrior stood tall before Ariana, Pippy and the little wish-helper and dusted himself off. As the rest of the warriors got up and stood beside him, they were a mighty and fearsome-looking group.

"I am Badari, the great warrior and commander from the land of Minasha in the fifth realm, and these are my battle-ready warriors. We are at your service, and we are ready to pledge our allegiance," he said, sweeping his arm towards the other warriors, and they each placed their right hand firmly on their chest in a sign of salute.

"I am Ariana, and they call me the Chosen One, from the highest order of celestials in the seventh realm." There was murmuring from all the crowd, in response to this statement.

Pippy stepped forward and bowed, "And I am Pippy, a wish-helper, from Elopia in the sixth realm."

The little wish-helper also stepped forward and bowed before speaking, "I am Alorra, wish-helper, also from Elopia in the sixth realm."

Pippy turned to look at the little wish-helper with a stunned expression on her face, "I can't believe it! You are one of the Elopians taken captive at the last great war!" she exclaimed.

"Yes, and there are many more of us. Elopians raise your hands!" Alorra called to the crowd.

They all looked over at the upside-down crowd of celestials, and one by one, they waved their hands, calling out their names, signalling their Elopian heritage. Ariana lost count, there were so many.

Pippy rushed over to Alorra and embraced her in a big hug, vowing, "We will rescue every last Elopian from this place, or I will die trying. We will not leave anyone behind!"

Ariana could hear the emotion in Pippy's voice, as tears sprung in Alorra's eyes and she nodded at Pippy in gratitude, before the two embraced once more.

Badari urged them, "Come, let us retrieve the Lifeblood swords," and he signalled to some of his warriors to remain behind, stationed by the door, for a surprise attack on any returning beasts.

"Pippy, can you remain here too, in case any of the beasts return, you can quickly come and find us and alert us?" Pippy nodded at Ariana's instructions. "Alorra, show us the way to the Lifeblood swords."

Ariana's eyes met Pippy's and the unspoken understanding between them spoke volumes, filled with concern that each other should remain safe. Ariana paused and held Pippy's gaze for a moment before giving her a nod and a reassuring smile, then turned and headed towards the door with the others.

Ariana used the power from the key to unlock the door of the holding cell, as she visualised and then commanded the door to be unlocked, though she felt sure that she could have blasted the door with her own powers, but that would have made way too much noise and the giants would no doubt come running. Badari and his warriors led the way out of the holding cell. They stayed in the corridor and waited until Alorra and Ariana were both out too, before closing and bolting the door back in place.

Alorra signalled for them all to follow her and she flew quickly along the corridor, zigzagging swiftly around corners and along more stone corridors that were lit by flaming torches, before stopping outside a large door.

"They are in there," she said, pointing at the door as she hovered mid-air and watched as Ariana slowly turned the door handle and discovering that it was unlocked, she tentatively pushed it open.

Badari strode forward, his huge powerful frame filled the doorway as he confidently took the lead and made sure the room was clear of any danger. Then he silently handed out Lifeblood sword after sword, until they each carried four swords, apart from

Alorra who could only manage to carry one in both hands. They hurried silently back towards the holding cell, and as they raced past one of the corridors, they could hear screams of agony mixed with cries of delight and jeering laughter, that sounded like a great crowd were torturing and taunting victims. Ariana dared not begin to imagine the evil that was taking place behind the closed door of that room, and she felt all the more determined to rescue every last captive from this evil place.

Back in the holding cell, Ariana used the key to break every shackle and there were hundreds of captives now standing free before them. As Ariana looked at their grateful faces, she saw a renewed vigour and energy in them. Gone was the drowsy lifelessness, replaced instead with hope and a great determination for freedom. With Lifeblood swords held in the hands of the great warriors, their faces fierce and invigorated, the entire being of each warrior oozed a readiness for battle. There was a silence among them all and it was filled with an unseen energy, it was the calm before the storm.

Badari and his troops were getting ready to go in force, to try to storm their way out and lead everyone with them to safety.

"Badari, we need a plan," said Ariana. "I think we should send out spies first and set up an ambush at the room where we know that many of the enemies are torturing captives, so we can fend them off for as long as possible to give everyone the best chance to escape, and we need to know where the quickest way out is before we bring everyone with us so that we are not running blind," she said vehemently.

Badari held Ariana's concerned gaze for a moment before turning to the warrior at his right, "Agar, you will take the strongest twelve with you and position yourselves, hold the torture room door and ambush the beasts if they break free." Agar saluted, and Badari turned to Ariana and nodded.

"If I can unlock anything with the key, surely, I can also lock anything I choose to, right?" Ariana asked Alorra.

"Yes, I believe that you can."

"Great, then I will use the key to lock the door where the beasts are torturing captives. It looks like it is made of heavy iron, so it might hold them off for a good while."

Badari and his warrior troops all nodded affirmatively.

"Hey!" a small voice piped up, "I am a route-finder, it is my gift, I can find a way out quicker than anyone because I move at many times the speed of any celestial being in all the realms!"

Everyone turned to where the small voice was coming from, but Ariana couldn't see who had spoken.

"Come forward!" she called.

A tiny little humanoid stepped forward and everyone watched as the little celestial being stood apart from the crowd. Ariana looked down at the little pint-sized being, surprised at how small he was, no bigger than a cat or a small dog in height, dressed in red and gold armour, with a sword at his side and shield on his back. Ariana looked at his face, which had a bold expression and large green eyes stared back at her. She thought he looked just like a miniature human, but with blue skin that shone.

"I am Oliad, route-finder from the nomad tribes of Gelius, in the north of Elopia, at your service!" and pint-sized Oliad took a deep bow.

Ariana smiled, "Nice to meet you, Oliad. If you can travel at such speed as you mentioned, then you can certainly have the job of seeking a way out of this evil place!" Ariana looked at Badari and he gave her a nod.

Badari stepped forward, "Fellow friends and freedom fighters! Yes, that is what you are now, freedom fighters! Be vigilant and stay close, help your fellow brothers and sisters as we unite in this battle for our freedom. We have the Chosen One with us, so let us take our stand with confidence and in the name of the Mighty One, may we go in strength and power!" the air was filled with the sound of agreement from all. "Oliad, go with haste, find the way of escape and return for the rest of us. Agar, take the twelve, and I will stand guard with the others here until Oliad returns."

Oliad ran so fast that they didn't even see him move across the room and out of the door.

"Wow! He wasn't joking about being many times faster than the rest of us!" Ariana said in surprise.

Badari laughed, "Yes, route-finders may be one of the smallest creatures, but they are also one of the fastest, so fast that they can move about unseen, you will only see them when they stop running."

Ariana left with Agar and the twelve warriors, and she used the key to secure the door where there was much noise from the giant beasts amid cries of anguish from their victims. Ariana longed to storm in and rescue those being tortured, but Agar stopped her, telling her to stick to the plan, so as not to jeopardise the lives of so many others. He reassured her that once they got many out safely, he would return to rescue any remaining. As Ariana left Agar and the twelve and ran back to the holding cell, she allowed herself to think of Jack, she was worried about him, but she couldn't let the worry overwhelm her, she continued to hope for the best, if she could get to Jessica and break her out of the trance or spell that she was under, then she could tell her where Jack was. Yes, that was what she needed to do, rescue Jessica, get the book and find Jack.

***

Jack stared at the giant steppingstones that surrounded him and contemplated which one to choose. Well, he had to pick one, he couldn't stay in this sweltering place forever, standing there like a scared lemon on this giant stone with nothing but a huge abyss of volcanic fury beneath him. Jack gulped and took a deep breath, "Well here goes…" he muttered to himself as he took a giant step forward and then changed his mind and instead leapt towards the giant stone on his left. Misjudging the distance, he lost his footing and gasped as he grabbed onto the edge of the giant stone with both hands, clinging on for dear life. Sweat poured down his face and his heart pounded furiously like a loud drum as he desperately tried to pull himself up, but he just couldn't seem to lurch himself forward onto the steppingstone. After several attempts, he felt his arms begin to weaken from the strain of holding himself up. Panicking, Jack couldn't see how he could survive this moment, and thoughts of Ariana and his parents flooded his mind. Remembering the crystal, which was still around his neck, he really hoped that it would work because he thought he would probably fall very soon into the scorching abyss.

But just then something strange happened, a voice, a still small voice, clear as day, said,

'Strength in the inward parts Jack, command it…'

Before Jack even had time to think, he gulped involuntarily, followed by a loud burp, and then he heaved deep within his stomach, yet he didn't feel sick. And it was as though time stood still and he felt his mouth open, and Jack watched in amazement as words floated out of his mouth, and he heard himself speak the words aloud as though someone or something had taken control of him. Still clinging to the edge of the steppingstone, with the words floating in front of him, he heard himself mutter the words aloud,

"Be released in my true identity!"

Was that really his voice? He sounded different. Jack felt his body begin to float, as though he was levitating and not of his own accord, he let go of the edge of the steppingstone and floated safely to a standing position, gently landing on top of it. He shook his head, stunned, "What just happened?" he asked himself aloud, and then he felt the great towering stone moving upwards with the mighty sound of mortar against mortar. The stepping stone came to a halt and Jack stood face to face with two giant wooden doors. As he stared at the doors, words began to etch on them, as though an invisible hand was scrawling on the wood, and Jack read the words, *'Place of Utter Darkness'*. With nowhere else to go but forward, he took one last look at the swirling sea of hot blue lava in the abyss beneath him, before taking hold of both door handles, and pushing the giant doors wide, he stepped forward into the unknown.

The Cocoon Within

***

Meanwhile, Oliad, the Route-Finder, reported back to Ariana and the others,

"The good news is that there are few sentries on guard around the Destroyer's kingdom, so we can easily overpower them, for there are many more of us than them. Having scoured the kingdom, many of the great beasts are intoxicated, they are all celebrating and are distracted, indulging their desires in the various bed chambers of the fair maidens of sin. We must take the opportunity now; the small celestials can be led out easily through a narrow tunnel which has an opening just large enough for them to fit through, this will take them to the outer boundary. There is a weakness in the outer boundary that they can squeeze through one by one. Once outside of the boundary, they will be in the deep wilderness, but legend has it that if you continue north there is a portal that takes you directly to the fifth realm, and from there you can make your way back to the edge of the sixth realm, and on to Elopia. Larger celestials, you will need to make your way to the West Wing of this kingdom and fight your way out, we have the advantage of numbers," Oliad crossed his arms proudly.

"I can lead the smaller celestials to the boundary, and then I will come back," Oliad continued and looked directly at Ariana. "You will need me to help you navigate the way to the Mountain of Peace."

"Thank you Oliad," said Ariana, appreciating any help on offer. Feeling more confident now that they were seeing the beginnings of a plan, she turned to Badari and said,

"Badari, I will need to go back to the great banquet hall and retrieve the sacred book."

"I will come with you."

"No, no you go and fight with the others, they will need your strength and I will be quicker on my own," Ariana was resolute, she knew the way back and she would be fast, she also wanted to look for Jessica, she didn't want to leave her behind and she could also find out where Jessica had last seen Jack.

"We will follow you, Pippy," said Alorra and a crowd of a multitude of wish-helpers gathered around Pippy.

"Why me?" asked Pippy, forgetting for a moment about her new wings and what they signified.

"Are you not a leader of wish-helpers? And besides, your wings tell us your rank, so we need you to lead us all home," Alorra's little face looked puzzled for a moment as she stared up at Pippy who was somewhat larger than her in size.

"Oh, ahem, yes pardon me, sorry I forgot myself for a moment, it must be the evil atmosphere in this place!" Pippy clapped her hands and addressed the crowd of wish-helpers, "I am Pippy, leader of wish-helpers from Elopia in the sixth realm and I shall lead us home, stick close and follow my instructions!"

There were positive murmurings from the crowd of wish-helpers in response and Pippy turned to Ariana who said,

"I am so proud of you Pippy. You know, I think this is your destiny." Ariana smiled broadly, though she was surprised to feel the prickle of tears at the corner of her eyes, as Pippy flew at her, wrapped her arms around Ariana's neck and smothered her with a big wish-helper hug, before releasing her, and giving a silent salute.

Ariana watched as Pippy flew over to Oliad with the crowd of wish-helpers following behind her, and all the small-sized celestials joining too, keen to find their way to freedom at last. Two of Badari's warriors opened the heavy door and went ahead of them, as Pippy and Oliad led the crowd of what looked like possibly a hundred or more little celestials out.

Badari looked solemnly at Ariana, before placing one hand firmly on his left chest, giving an affirming salute, as he turned to the crowd of warriors and celestials, many armed for battle with Lifeblood swords, and he led them out.

Ariana stood for a moment in the empty holding cell, looking up at all the empty cross bars that had held so many captive. She felt proud to be a part of helping to set everyone free, and now she only hoped that it wasn't too late for Jessica and Jack; with that thought in mind, she raced for the door.

***

Bugger it! Jack couldn't see a thing; trust him to pick a stepping-stone that took him to the *Place of Utter Darkness*, of all places it had to be a place of darkness! Why him? Jack, who suffers from claustrophobia, was all alone in this damned place, and shrouded in complete blooming darkness, with no idea what else could be lurking in this place with him. Darn it, he just stubbed his toe on something, grrr! Jack had been taking small steps along, trying to edge his way forward, not really knowing what else to do, as he couldn't see a darn thing and he was worrying if he would ever make it out of this place and find the others and now to have stubbed his toe, this just about took the biscuit!

He bent down to tentatively try to feel what it was that he had bumped into, and his hand felt something hard. He slowly moved his hand over it and suddenly felt something sharp jab his finger, "Ouch!" he cried before quickly covering his mouth.

"What's going on now? I can't keep using my energy on your nonsense!" a voice said, sounding rather irritated.

Jack froze on the spot and before he could even contemplate the fact that he wasn't alone, the darkness began to fade as a dim light emitted and grew slowly brighter until it lit the entire place.

Jack blinked, as his eyes adjusted to the light, and he saw that he was in a cave, and he certainly wasn't alone. The light was coming from the large bulbous tail of a creature that reminded him of a platypus. Jack blinked again as he continued staring at the creature that was on the other side of the cave. He felt something tapping his leg and he looked down at what looked like a small dinosaur, with prickly-looking spines all across its back; that must have been what he'd pricked his finger on.

"Hello, my name's Blod, what's yours?" the little dinosaur creature asked as it looked at Jack with its miniature T-Rex features and small, piercing yellow eyes.

"Erm… Jack… pleased to meet you," Jack couldn't believe he was talking to what looked like a miniature dinosaur. Well, on the bright side, it could be worse, he supposed, rather this than the Accursed Pit any day.

"Nice to meet you, Jack, and that's my friend, Wissle," Blod said, continuing to stare up at Jack, his eyes unblinking.

Jack looked over at Wissle, the platypus-looking creature, which seemed to be grumbling and muttering to itself.

"Oh, never mind, Wissle, he is always grumbling about something or other. So, what brings you to the place of utter darkness then?" asked Blod, with his unwavering stare, which Jack was beginning to find a little disconcerting, and he hoped that he wasn't going to turn on him and try to eat him. After all, didn't dinosaurs eat man?

Blod and Wissle listened as Jack told the story of coming to Elopia accidentally, but kind of on purpose, as they had been following the guidance of the sacred book, whilst escaping from the giant beasts. Jack told them how he was desperately seeking his friends, Ariana, Jessica and Pippy the wish-helper, and how they had all gotten separated after their encounter at the giant tree.

"Hang on, so you're telling us that your so-called friend Jessica just upped and left you, and flitted off with some chap she hardly knew, after the two of you were abandoned by Ariana, the one you have a thing for, and Pippy, without so much as a second thought for yours or Jessica's welfare?" Wissle surmised as he cocked his strange, large grey bill to one side, and with one eyebrow raised, he looked at Jack with an expression of disbelief and something akin to disgust.

"No, no, it wasn't like that!" Jack started, feeling a little put out that Wissle had drawn such a cruel conclusion. "What I meant was…"

The Cocoon Within

Blod raised his tiny dinosaur hand, stopping Jack mid-flow, "We understand perfectly what you meant, and to conclude, you would like our help to find your friends!"

Blod looked at Wissle whose face immediately creased into a frown, and he started grumbling something about helping others always ending up being a disaster.

"That settles it then," said Blod, "we will help you find your friends. No one knows the place of utter darkness better than the two of us, this will be a piece of cake for us as they say on Earth, or what's the other saying they like to use... a walk in the park, yes that's it!"

Blod looked especially cheery as he began planning their next steps, "So, we can lead you safely past the hordes of Drakken and into the hall of chambers, as we got wind of intruders in the West Wing of Vedriece's kingdom, so that is where your friends will be for sure. The place of utter darkness leads directly into the heart of Vedriece's kingdom. It's all connected you know and it's all going on around here. Nothing escapes our attention, nothing!" cried Blod as he gave Jack that unnerving stare without blinking.

"Oh... er... thanks," Jack wasn't sure if he should trust these two oddities, but he didn't have a choice, so he supposed he ought to go along with it. Worst comes to worst, he still had his crystal pendant, and he had his Lifeblood sword, which he would use if push came to shove.

***

Meanwhile, Ariana had no trouble retrieving the sacred book from its hiding place in the wall, in the vent where she had stashed it because everyone in the great hall was too busy enjoying themselves. Most were drunk, intoxicated and playing vicious and boisterous games, whilst others were stuffing their faces with food, or off in one of the numerous bed chambers where laughter and drunken screams of illicit delight could be heard. The Destroyer was nowhere to be seen, which was good, because he was her real concern, as she had encountered firsthand how his power could overcome her, so she didn't want to come face to face with him again.

Ariana scanned the great hall for Jessica, but she was nowhere to be seen. She looked around wildly, time was of the essence, and she was torn between needing to go back to the others and not wanting to leave Jessica behind. Then she saw her, the flash of her purple gown as she left the hall and went into one of the bed chambers. Ariana followed swiftly, weaving in and out of the large stone pillars. Using them as cover, she peeped around the open door of the room and saw Jessica seated at a vanity table next to a four-poster bed, and she was alone. Ariana slipped into the room and placed the sacred book on a small side table, as she bolted the door behind her.

Jessica's hand paused mid-air holding a hairbrush that she had been stroking through her hair.

"Is that you, my love?" she called with excitement as she swivelled around on the chair and faced Ariana.

"Jessica it's me, Ariana, I have come to rescue you, you must come with me…" her voice trailed off as Jessica's face transformed from excitement to fury and she threw the hairbrush at Ariana with such force, that she ducked to avoid being hit and it smacked into a standing mirror which instantly shattered.

"Jessica!" cried Ariana, but Jessica raced at her, with her hands outstretched like claws, intent on scratching Ariana's eyes out. They locked in a physical fight; Ariana elbowed Jessica in the neck, making her splutter as she choked in shock for a moment before she tried to come at Ariana again scratching like a wildcat, but Ariana's quick reflexes held her at bay, They tussled, Jessica was twisting and lurching as she screamed that she was the Chosen One and not Ariana. Ariana deflected every attack with precision, like a martial arts expert she effortlessly defended and blocked every move that Jessica made. Ariana pushed Jessica to the floor, her hair was wild from fighting and her face still enraged, as she ranted about being fed lies by Ariana, Leo and Eriat!

"Jessica, stop! It's not true. You have been put under some sort of spell you have to snap out of it!"

Jessica ran at her again, this time with a piece of the broken mirror in one of her hands and she slashed viciously at Ariana, missing her by inches as she dived from side to side to avoid her strikes, thrusting Jessica away from her.

"Enough! Get back!" cried Ariana as she held her hands out to Jessica, encasing her in a beam of her power, her own anger now kindled.

Jessica froze on the spot, the broken piece of mirror dropped from her hand, shattering into small pieces on the floor. Ariana lifted Jessica in the powerful beams from her hands and then lowered her hands to lay Jessica softly on the bed. Ariana watched as Jessica shook her head in confusion.

"Where am I? What's going on?" Jessica looked at Ariana beseechingly.

Ariana was at her side. She stroked Jessica's hair back away from her face and asked, "Are you back with me now? Are you ok, do you remember whose side you are on?" Ariana stared intently into Jessica's eyes, checking that the real Jessica was back.

"What do you mean?" Jessica asked, bewildered.

"Put it this way, you were under some sort of a spell, and you were convinced that you were in love with the Destroyer, and you attacked me just moments ago when I came to rescue you, but I think I somehow broke the spell with my powers."

Jessica laughed and covered her mouth with her hand, before shaking her head in disbelief. "Love!" she laughed again. "Me? Not yet and it would certainly take some guy, but where is Jack and Pippy?"

"Wrong answer," Ariana frowned. "I was hoping you would tell me where you last saw Jack. You're still somewhat disoriented so maybe it will come to you soon. Look, we have no time to lose, so I can't bring you up to speed now as we have to get going. Pippy is ok, but we have to fight our way out of this evil place, are you ready? And do you remember where your Suit of Ultimate Truth and your Lifeblood sword are?"

The good news was that they found Jessica's Suit of Ultimate Truth and her Lifeblood sword, so she was battle-ready and back to her old self. Together Ariana and Jessica had made it unnoticed through the great hall, and they raced down the corridors, to make their way to join the others at the West Wing, where Oliad had told her the best way of escape was, which would lead them straight to the outer boundary, but they would have to fight their way out. Ariana hoped that Badari and the other celestials had already secured the exit, but if not, then they would join them in battle, they just had to get everyone out.

As Ariana and Jessica rounded the corner, approaching the torture chamber where Agar and the twelve warriors had been taking a stand in case the great beasts emerged. One of the twelve lay wounded in the hall and there was debris everywhere with the bodies of slain beasts strewn across the hall.

Ariana ran to the warrior's side, crouching beside him. "Where are you hurt?" she asked as she looked for signs of injury. He was holding his arm over his chest area.

"Here," he replied, taking his hand from his chest.

Ariana could see that his armour was penetrated and beneath glistened blue blood from a deep wound. His breathing grew shallow, and Ariana quickly laid her hands over the wound.

"Be healed and restored right now!" she cried and watched as her hands glowed brightly and then after a few moments, they dimmed and returned to normal. When she removed her hands, the wound was completely healed. She stood and helped the warrior to his feet.

"You have the gift of healing, thank you! You truly are the Chosen One!" he bowed in gratitude.

"What happened to the others?" she asked.

"They fought the great beasts and slayed many with the edge of the sword, and they led the beasts away so that we could rescue the captives that were still alive, not all made it." The warrior inclined his head to the open door of the torture chamber, where the brave warrior had fought with his comrades against the evil beasts.

Jessica and Ariana went to the doorway and looked on in horror at the mass of blood-soaked body parts strewn about the room. There were all sorts of bloodied torture weapons, and lastly, several beings with eyes gouged out and dismembered limbs hanging from their bodies, were lying on the floor. Ariana recognised one of the victims as the female humanoid whose throat had been slit earlier by one of the beasts. She turned her face away, sickened and angered at the pure evil committed in this place.

"Come! Let us find the others!" the warrior urged them, and together they raced through the corridors towards the West Wing.

They joined the battle at the West Wing. The huge doors were open and celestials were running for their freedom, as Badari and his battle-ready warriors fought to hold off the great beasts, alongside many of the freed captives. The sound of Lifeblood sword clashing mightily against Lifeblood sword rang out. Ariana watched as Jessica threw herself into combat, wielding her Lifeblood sword with precision as she thrust it into the chest of a giant beast. The beast fell and she twisted her sword to slice the head off another beast to her right just in time, and its decapitated body collapsed.

Ariana saw movement in her peripheral vision and in a split second she used her powers to blast the hordes of Drakken as they leapt towards her, and they were destroyed in an instant as her powerful rays took them out. More and more of the Drakken continued to come for them and Badari and his warriors struck them over and over with their swords. Both Ariana and Jessica used their powers to blast the ever-approaching Drakken; celestials turned back from the open doors and fought the Drakken using their powers. They were winning this battle, the upper hand was theirs, beast and Drakken fell by the might of their swords and powers, till there were just two standing. Badari leapt in the air, holding two Lifeblood swords he struck the beast and Drakken, simultaneously slaughtering them both.

"For our Freedom!" cried Badari loudly and the crowd cheered. "Everyone out, run to the boundary and make good your escape!"

Everyone ran, making their way outside, through the boundary. Ariana stood, her suit covered in the blood of the Drakken, catching her breath. They had done it they had rescued so many captives!

"Come on Jessica, Let's…"

Suddenly, there was an almighty scream. Ariana and Badari turned, but it was too late. Lifted on high was Jessica with blood pouring from her mouth. Ariana looked on in shock, her eyes trailed down to the long razor-sharp knife-like claws that protruded from Jessica's stomach, and she watched the blood pouring from the deep wounds. In confusion and horror, Ariana looked at the face of the perpetrator who was standing there lifting Jessica's mutilated body up high with his knife-like claws. Ariana's legs buckled in shock, and she collapsed to the floor.

"Chosen One, you have again caused the death of a much loved one. I warned you that you are no match for me, but did you listen? No! So instead, you will feel my wrath!" The voice of the dark one was blood-curdling.

Ariana looked at the **deep sunken, piercing amber eyes, set in a giant face,** one that she could never forget, of raw flesh and bone, with two giant coiled horns on its head, its massive muscular body had the appearance of red, raw, rotting flesh, every sinew and muscle was visible and as its face emitted fury, flames of fire encased its being, but it wasn't consumed. The grotesque creature threw Jessica to the floor and her lifeless body rolled and came to a standstill in front of Ariana. Ariana cradled Jessica in her arms, stroking her hair, tears streamed from her eyes as she looked at Jessica and over and over again, Ariana cried,

"Be healed now, I command you!" as she lay her hand on Jessica's chest. "Be healed, I command you to be healed!" Ariana wept furiously, oblivious to everything around her as she wept for

Jessica, for her mother and father, who had been slain by this same evil beast, and it was all her fault! It was her fault that Jack was lost, and it was her fault that they should all die at the hands of this evil beast. She had failed Jessica and she had failed everyone.

Ariana felt her arm being gripped and she was being pulled away from Jessica, it was Badari. "Come away, there is nothing you can do for her now," his voice was firm.

"Why can't my powers heal her? It's my fault she's dead, it's all my fault!" cried Ariana through her tears.

"Silence, Chosen One! You are not permitted to speak. I am Vedriece, Lord and Master over all things, and I am all powerful, you will yield to my command!"

Ariana looked into the great beast's piercing amber eyes, and she felt her sorrow begin to morph into anger. She could feel the rage building within, and her hand instinctively reached for her Lifeblood sword. She immediately felt the strong grip of Badari's hand on hers and frowning, she turned her face towards him and watched as he shook his head at her. It was a clear message and Ariana understood that retaliation against this all-powerful beast was useless. Frustration and hopelessness overwhelmed her senses for a moment and then she suddenly remembered words that Leo had spoken, "*We need the Chalice of Fire to end this war and set all things right.*" Ariana was grateful for being reminded that there was still hope; all they needed to do was retrieve the Chalice of Fire and defeat the enemy once and for all. That wouldn't bring Jessica back, but at the very least, her death wouldn't be in vain.

"Bring out the captive!" cried the great beast, suddenly his whole being began to change, the horns, the rotting flesh, melted away and in its place stood, his humanoid form, the Destroyer! Ariana clenched her fists as she stared at him with vengeance in her eyes. Vedriece and the Destroyer were one and the same, the same evil one that had cruelly slain Ariana's parents and now Jessica too!

Two giant beasts strode purposefully to the back of the West Wing and thrust open two doors. They pulled out a crossbar that was flanked by two small, strange-looking creatures, one of them resembled a small dinosaur and shackled to the crossbar was none other than Jack!

"Jack!" Ariana ran forward towards him, evading Badari's grasp.

"Arry, oh my God Arry, are you alright?" Jack strained, as he instinctively tried to free his arms to embrace her, but he couldn't.

"Get back!" cried one of the giants, as it flung its large, clawed hand out to push Ariana backwards, but she was too quick, and she retaliated by halting its huge hand mid-air with her powers.

"No! You stand back! I can slice off your hand in an instant with my sword, beast!" Ariana spat her words back at the giant.

She felt herself immediately lifted and thrust onto the floor by the Destroyer's beams of power and she rolled backwards as Badari reached her side. "Stay calm, Chosen One, bide your time," he whispered, as he helped her up.

"Arry! Oh, please don't hurt her! Oh no, Jessica… is she…?" begged Jack distraught, as he looked from Ariana to Jessica's lifeless body.

"Silence!" Vedriece, the Destroyer, one and the same, commanded loudly before he lifted Badari in his powerful beams and set him shackled, onto a crossbar that was brought out by another pair of giant beasts.

Ariana mouthed the words 'I'm sorry' to Badari, whose expression was staunch in the face of his recapture, as he met her eyes and held her gaze with a reassuring look of strength.

Ariana's mind raced. She couldn't bear to lose Jack or see anything happen to Badari. They had been so close to escape, though at least they had freed all the captives, who should by now be on their way through the deep wilderness, and as far away from this place of enslavement as possible.

"Chosen One, your great commission has changed, I know that you are in possession of the invisible key," the Destroyer gave her a mirthful stare and laughed mockingly. "You will go to the Mountain of Peace and bring me the Chalice of Fire. If you are not successful, then your friends will be slain and be warned, it will be a slow and painful death, there will be no mercy!"

The Destroyer summoned more of his beasts and called two of them forward. "Accompany the Chosen One as far as the edge of the Mountain of Peace and wait for her to retrieve the Chalice. Do not return here without the Chalice. Now go and bring to me what is rightfully mine!"

The beasts sauntered over to Ariana like great, grotesque, ogres and flanked her as she stood before the Destroyer. Ariana realised that Badari was right, she needed to bide her time, she had no more cards to play at this moment; the evil one was holding all the cards, but once she had the Chalice, she would have the upper hand. She just needed to think of a cunning plan to thwart the Destroyer, as she had no doubt in her mind that he would kill them all, even if she were to hand over the Chalice of Fire.

9

The Sacred Mountain of Peace

Ariana's heart sank as she walked beyond the boundary, with the two great beasts flanking her on each side, and there, she saw hundreds of the captives that they had helped escape, now recaptured and held entrapped in some sort of great forcefield. As Ariana looked at their faces, she felt she would forever be haunted by their expressions of fear and defeat. She had let them down, every last one of them, she had no idea if they would all face torture or death before her return, but she couldn't let that happen, she had to do something. Still reeling from the shock of Jessica's death, Ariana also contemplated their return to Earth without Jessica. How in the hell could they break the news to her parents, what could they possibly say? She shook her head in disbelief, no this can't be how this all ends, somehow, they had to bring Jessica back. Back from the dead? Is that even possible? And words that Pippy had spoken, came to Ariana in an instant, quickening her senses, *'Just remember nothing is impossible if you would only believe.'* Perhaps it is possible, the eagles will know! That's it, she would need to find the sacred eagles and ask them how to bring Jessica back.

Ariana felt a hard smack on her shoulder, jolting her out of her thoughts, "Chosen One! Move forward!" It was one of the beasts that had struck her, she hadn't realised that she'd stopped walking. She gave the beast a dark look and continued forward. The other beast seemed preoccupied with crushing small creatures from the wilderness floor and thorny thickets and eating them. Ariana could hear the cracking of bones as the beast crunched on a small creature that it had captured. She knew that she could easily slay these two beasts with her powers or use her skill with her Lifeblood sword. The more she thought about it, the more it dawned on her that the Destroyer knew that she could easily slay them, so why bother sending them with her? What was his reason for that? It didn't make much sense to her, none the less she decided that she would carry on walking with them to the edge of the Mountain of Peace as instructed, moreover, if she killed the beasts then she could jeopardise Jack and Badari's safety.

Ariana trudged on silently, her thoughts with Jack and Badari, she also noted that she hadn't seen Pippy and the wish-helpers with the others that had been recaptured, so hopefully they were well on their way northbound, to the portal that would take them out of the darker realms and on to freedom.

"Stop here!" growled one of the giant beasts loudly, drool dripping from its jaw as it ambled over to a great stone in the middle of the wilderness.

Ariana stopped in front of the huge stone as commanded and looked up at its smooth rock face. The stone had the appearance of granite, and it had a sparkling sheen to it that was covered in symbols and markings. She wondered what the unusual markings meant.

"Use the key to unlock the portal!" ordered the giant beast, its angry amber eyes holding Ariana's gaze.

She complied and placed the medallion of the invisible key directly against the rock face and commanded the portal to open. She heard an unlocking noise as though a mechanism was triggered, and in an instant the rock face faded, and was replaced by a silvery swirling vision, like a whirling waterfall.

"Move onwards!" the other beast commanded as it shoved Ariana forward.

As Ariana walked through the portal, she expected to be taken on a rollercoaster ride like before, but it was different this time. It was like she had stepped out of one world, directly into another, and as she looked around, the seemingly never-ending barren wilderness that had surrounded them, was nowhere to be seen. The terrain had changed in an instant after stepping through the portal. Where the land had been dry, on the other side of the portal, it was now a lush landscape, bursting with life and full of fantastic-looking great trees and grasslands, silvery, shimmery and colourful. Where the creatures had been desert dwellers scurrying about in thorny thickets, there were large, silvery, strong, muscular herds of deer, in groups, eating the lush colourful vegetation that stood bright and shiny. Stunning birds flew up above in the expanse of sea blue sky, glorious creatures of all kinds darted to and fro, animals and insects all completely wonderful to behold, a stark contrast to the deep and barren wilderness that they had just left, and Ariana couldn't imagine paradise being any more beautiful than this.

The two beasts had followed her through the portal, and they stood there looking around at the abundant life surrounding them. The great and stunning silvery deer, standing tall and proud, ears pricked, huge, majestic antlers in the air, their beautiful eyes fixed on the beasts.

"Mine for the taking!" bellowed one of the beasts as it made a dash for the largest stag, raising its great claw-like talons to strike the majestic creature, but instead of making contact with the stag and tearing it in two, its claws struck an invisible barrier. Confused, the beast struck again with its other clawed hand, and again with both hands, but it met with the same invisible barrier.

"Fool! Do you not remember our instructions?" cried the other beast with disdain.

His comrade turned to him with grotesque features creasing into a scowl of injured pride and disappointment, "The urge to maul and devour was stronger than our master's words, when he told us we have no jurisdiction this side of the portal."

"Silence! Before you say too much!" snapped the other beast as he turned to Ariana, "This is as far as we go. We will wait for you here, hurry and return with the Chalice!" he commanded gruffly, and

The Cocoon Within

his eyes followed Ariana as she turned and walked into the silvery forest that was beckoning her.

Ariana thought about what the beast had just revealed, as she walked across the silvery forest floor. So, in a nutshell, the beasts cannot harm the creatures on this side of the portal. She saw it with her own eyes, the beast had struck out but been blocked by an invisible barrier. It reminded Ariana of that time back on Earth when they had encountered the great horde of beasts surrounding her home, and an invisible barrier had prevented them from reaching her and the others. Though they eventually broke through the barrier, perhaps that was what the Destroyer was planning, a way to break through the barrier here, but why? What is it about this place that he wants other than the Chalice of Fire? Ariana took stock of her surroundings, perhaps the clue was all around her. As she continued on, now out of sight and earshot of the two beasts, she realised that as she walked, it was as though she was floating across the beautiful forest floor. She looked down and the silvery grass shimmered and swayed and as she took a step forward, she felt it again, it was like she was walking on a cushion of air that just lifted her gently along.

"This feels amazing!" she muttered to herself as she turned and to her surprise, there was a group of about five or six glistening, silvery deer following behind her.

"I agree, it really is amazing," a small voice replied.

Ariana stared at the deer suspiciously, but they were chewing on the silvery grass and staring right back at her, so perhaps it wasn't the deer that had spoken. Somewhat bewildered, she swivelled around to try to see where the voice had come from, and lo and behold from behind a glorious-looking oak tree, the speaker stepped forward.

"Oliad! Oh, am I glad to see you!" Ariana knelt and swept pint-size Oliad into her embrace, giving him a great big hug.

"Oh erm, well that was wholly unexpected, though it's always nice to be… erm appreciated!" He appeared a little embarrassed at receiving such an affectionate greeting.

Ariana quickly filled him in on everything that had happened. Her eyes became teary as she told of Jessica's fate, and how both Jack and Badari were captured and being held to ransom for the Chalice of Fire.

"How did you find me?" she asked him.

"I followed you and the beasts, and I ran in as soon as the portal opened and stayed hidden until I could get you alone," he beamed at her proudly.

Keen to put Jessica out of her mind for now, so she could focus on the task at hand, as there was no way in hell that she could lose Jack too, she pressed on, "Ok, so what's the plan, route-finder? Which way to get the Chalice of Fire?"

"Follow me!"

Together they continued through the silvery forest and the deeper they went, the more wondrous their surroundings became. Glorious rivers of living, shimmering waters ran along both sides of the forest, and swarming shoals of magical flying fish leapt in and out of the crystal-clear waters. Everything around them was a myriad of beauty and shimmering colours, such as Ariana had never seen before; precious stones sparkled in every rock they passed, and flowers were blossoming and blooming in shimmering shades of golds, and silvers, amongst other unusual sparkling colours. Stunning trees were saturated with heavy succulent fruit, that was being eaten by beautiful creatures, some were small bear-like creatures with shimmering silvery fur and others looked like snow leopards but with fantastic wings, whilst others were giant-sized, gentle, slow-moving silky creatures with sparkling fur and large doe-like eyes.

"This place is unbelievable, and there is a wonderful feeling here too. Do you feel it, Oliad? It's just such an amazing feeling, and I have never felt like this before. I am positively glowing inside and out, which is quite bizarre considering all that has happened."

The more Ariana walked through the forest, the more glorious she felt, she had experienced nothing like it in her life.

"It's the peace, we are getting closer to the Mountain of Peace. Legend has it that the aura from the mountain can shroud you in such heightened, glorious peace, that it can put you into the deepest and most wonderfully peaceful slumber."

"Wow, well much as I love to sleep, we really need to get that Chalice and rescue all of the others. Oliad, do you think the evil one will destroy them all before we return with the Chalice?" she asked, just wanting everyone to be alright, especially Jack.

Oliad gave her a solemn look, "I don't know, but it won't stop us from trying!"

Together they continued for what seemed like hours, on and on through the ever-changing, glorious forest of paradise. It was hard not to get distracted by the amazing creatures surrounding them; the urge to simply watch and enjoy their beauty and bask in the ambience of the forest was almost overwhelming. Ariana had to stop Oliad a few times from lying down on the forest floor, as he began yawning and stretching, his face radiating peace and he kept telling her how much he yearned to sleep.

"Stay with me, Oliad!" Ariana cried as she held his tiny hand and pulled him along. "Come on, Oliad, get up!"

As though he had taken some kind of sleeping potion, Oliad sparked out, his little body wasn't going to budge anywhere, and the only response Ariana got from him was the sound of his snoring.

"Oh, bugger it!" she cursed and picked him up as if he was a little baby, then threw him over her shoulder, as he stretched and yawned and snuggled comfortably, resting his head on the ends of her curls as though they were a comfy pillow.

"Hmm, so which way to the Mountain of Peace now?" Ariana asked herself as she looked ahead, but the only thing that she could see through the trees was what looked like a waterfall. It was as though there was nothing else behind the trees, but an entire wall of falling water.

"You have to go straight through," a voice spoke to her mind.

She didn't know how she knew, but she just knew that it was the deer speaking to her! Ariana turned around to see the small herd of silvery deer standing just behind her, chewing the silvery grass and staring at her with their beautiful eyes. One of them took a few steps forward and she heard its voice again in her mind,

"Walk through the wall of water," the deer nodded its head and pawed at the ground with its hoof.

"Thank you," she replied and still carrying Oliad on her shoulder, she walked through the trees and looked up at the immense wall of water gushing like a powerful waterfall that sparkled and shimmered with all sorts of beautiful colours. The wall of water was so expansive that as far as her eye could see, there was nothing else, so it appeared to be where the forest ended. She stood for a good five minutes at least, staring up at the immense and very impressive waterfall, listening to the cascade of gushing water, before taking a giant step into the shimmering wall of water.

Why wasn't she wet? How very odd! Ariana stood in the middle of the gushing water, yet she wasn't even the slightest bit wet. She lifted her free hand and held it under the falling water, holding onto Oliad with her other hand. He still slept peacefully on her shoulder, and she could feel the sensation of the water streaming onto her hands and through her fingers, yet her hand remained dry, what a phenomenon! She shook her head in awe.

"So much that we don't understand," Ariana muttered to herself, shaking her head as she pondered the mystery of everything she had encountered thus far. She continued forward through the vast wall of water, and as she walked, she felt a strange sense of oneness with the water. She could sense the life beat of the water and she knew that it was alive. Ariana tried to fathom the connection to the water that she was experiencing, but she couldn't. It dawned on her, that she could only feel and experience, and she was very aware that she didn't have the knowledge to understand it.

She took another step forward and realised that she had stepped out of the wall of water to the other side. Her heart pounded in awe at the sight in front of her, in all its glory and magnificence stood none other than the Great Mountain of Peace. It was all that she had imagined and more, immense and all-encompassing. The entire mountain looked like it was shrouded in clouds of great mist, yet it sparkled brightly through the mist and appeared to be covered in all sorts of dazzling precious stones. Ariana had to squint her eyes because the glare from the rock face of the mountain was so bright.

The feeling of extreme peace was overwhelming, giving way to such euphoria or could it be that she had reached a state of nirvana? Ariana wasn't sure, and she wondered if this was what nirvana felt like. She had never fully understood what that word meant, but she imagined how she felt at this moment could be something akin to it.

She searched for a secluded spot to lay the sleeping Oliad down, until her return from the mountain, hopefully with the Chalice of Fire in her hands. She found a small cluster of rocks under a beautiful shimmering tree that stood out from the rest with its vivid rustic red and golden leaves that shone brightly. She lay him down gently on a bed of silvery grass between the rock cluster and placed the book beside him for safekeeping till she returned.

"There that should do just fine," she said and stood back to survey the area. She felt sure that she would remember this spot. Besides, there was only one tree with those unusual red and golden leaves, and it was right by the wall of water, which was the way she would need to come back anyway, once she had the Chalice in her possession.

"Right here goes!"

Ariana felt for her Lifeblood sword at her side. She wasn't sure if she would need it in this place, she didn't know what to expect. Considering the peaceful aura of the mountain and her own state of being right now, and if the mountain had this effect on all beings, then surely there would be no conflict in this place. Ariana felt for the invisible key, it was secure around her neck. She took one last look at the cluster of rocks under the special tree, hoping that Oliad would be safe there, and then she stepped forward, alone, into the unknown, towards the great glistening mountain that was beckoning her from afar.

Despite everything, Ariana found herself enjoying the walk through this fascinating, and dazzling land, it was just so peaceful, everything felt, well... perfect. It was perfectly warm and sunny, just the right temperature, not too hot and not too cold. All her inner fears and worries seemed to have faded into the recesses of her mind, no longer plaguing her in the now, instead being replaced with a feeling of overwhelming peace and serenity. The sounds of the creatures all around were very soothing to the ears and the mind. It was a joy to stop and watch the herds of silvery deer pass by and see the winged leopards, as well as other intriguing animals of all sorts of indescribable beauty, in the trees, on the grass, flying up high, leaping out of streams. It was a myriad of beauty and colour, all laced with that silvery sheen that emanated peace and tranquillity. Even walking along on the silvery grass was a pleasure. It was that wondrous, floating feeling with every springy step that she took and looking down at the grass itself, each blade appeared to wave gently, as it sparkled and glowed beautifully like a work of glorious art. As Ariana continued across the landscape, wonderful trees lined the rolling hillside and the sun beat warmly over the land. It was all she could do to resist the urge to lie on the soft grass and run her fingers through each blade and just admire the abundant and magnificent-looking flowers that seemed to go on forever across the entire landscape.

As Ariana continued forward, she could see something up ahead, but the sunlight was hindering her view. Squinting, she held her hand above her eyes to block the rays of the sun so that she could get a better look. She thought she could see three white horses, standing in a row, watching her, waiting for her. She hurried forward; she felt so very peaceful in this place, and she trusted the feeling, she knew that she was where she was supposed to be. She didn't know how she knew, she just did, and she thought that it must be something to do with what the eagles had said about the trials, and even Eriat had said something about understanding through discovery.

Suddenly, as she approached, Ariana realised that they weren't horses, they were Pegasus, flying horses! Ariana pondered what the plural for Pegasus was, as she stared at them in awe. One of the winged horses was of the purest white colour, its coat was so dazzlingly white, that Ariana had to blink several times at the glare. The other was a silvery colour, sparkling and glistening brightly, and the other was pearlescent, an indescribable coat of many colours in one. Each of the winged horse's body language and movement demonstrated its energy and as Ariana admired their sheer beauty before her, she heard a voice in her mind,

'Choose the right one.'

She looked at each of the flying horses; the pure white one stared back at her as it shook its head and pawed at the ground. The silvery-coloured, sparkling one raised its head several times and kicked out with its back legs and whinnied, as it looked at her. Last but not least, the pearlescent horse with its coat of many colours, reared up onto its hind legs and spread its wings wide. The other two horses were forced to move aside and give it space. Its tail flicked as it snorted and brought its forelegs back to the ground, and its jade eyes flashed brightly and appeared to change colour, as they met Ariana's eyes, and held her gaze with its unwavering stare.

Ariana walked directly up to the pearlescent horse, and it obediently lowered itself for her to climb onto its back. As she held tightly to this wonderful creature's mane, it galloped and pushed itself up into the air, with its great wings beating gracefully, and together they soared high into the sky. Looking down, she watched as the other two horses simply melted away and disappeared, as though they hadn't been real all along.

Admiring the beautiful scenery below, with every stride this wonderful Pegasus took through the clouds, Ariana experienced such a heavenly feeling, that she wondered if this place on the other side of the waterwall where the Mountain of Peace existed, was actually paradise. Were there humanoids, celestial beings that dwelt here? Perhaps she would find out. Pushing through the sky, breaking through clouds, Pegasus flew with ease, his majestic, pearlescent wings shimmering and shining as they gracefully beat a swift pace across the expanse of sea blue sky. As they approached the magnificent mountain, Ariana couldn't take her eyes off its sparkling beauty. She squinted as the surface of the mountain appeared to shine and twinkle in the sunlight, and she felt her heart respond with joyous awe.

"Absolutely fantastic!" Ariana heard her own involuntary words and shaking her head in amazement, she looked down at the glorious coat and mane of the pearlescent Pegasus. She could feel the creature's strength beneath her, as he snorted and galloped through the air, great wings lifted high, as they cut across the sky's expanse with ease. Ariana took in the scenery as Pegasus swooped in for landing, though not on the mountain peak itself, but about three-quarters of the way to the top. Bracing herself for the landing, she heard the thud of his hoofs as they touched down, and she supported her body weight as she leaned forward and then back again. Pegasus continued forward and Ariana surveyed the land; it seemed strange to think that they were so high up on the mountain. The mountain rock face was even more dazzling up close, and she could see that it was covered in clusters of precious stones that twinkled and shone, and it was mesmerising to look at.

Pegasus continued straight towards the rock face. Ariana heard her own sharp intake of breath as his head disappeared into the dazzling rock, and then his neck and she flinched as she braced herself to hit the mountain face, but instead, he carried her straight through, as though it didn't physically exist.

Mouth wide open in shock, Ariana blinked and rubbed her eyes, as she looked at the magnificence all around her. They had entered a new land, a place within the mountain itself. It was a stunning landscape, like the one she had just travelled through to get to the mountain, but it was literally buzzing with life and not just creatures, there were humanoids and celestials of the most dazzling kind.

Pegasus stood still and then he lowered himself to the ground, her cue to dismount. Ariana climbed off Pegasus and turned and stroked his mane before looking into his flaming jade eyes.

"Thank you," she whispered.

Pegasus rose and lifted his head up and down and snorted and whinnied in response, before turning around and going straight back the way he had come. Ariana took in the scene before her, she was in such a beautiful place, filled with streets that looked like they were made from gold, and glorious mansions lined the streets that seemed to go on forever. Each mansion had its own wonderful garden, and there were celestial families with their children, spending time together, laughing and smiling and enjoying life. Wherever Ariana looked, everyone was happy and smiling, as they shared food. Some were walking and talking together, celestial children were out and about playing in the golden paved streets. Creatures of all kinds, sentient beings were with one another in harmony. Ariana strolled along the golden street and enjoyed the sun shining on her face as she looked around at everyone and everything, and everyone she passed, stopped to greet her with a smile, they beamed and radiated kindness, goodness and love. Each being's face glowed and she sensed a level of intelligence in them all, that she couldn't explain. It was as though they could see into her soul when they looked at her, and yet she felt accepted and strangely, she felt loved.

Turning to look at a movement that had caught her eye, she saw a great being striding with purpose towards her along the golden path. It was a great humanoid creature that appeared to be carved out of sheer white marble; its strides were heavy and strong, and it had large wings held slightly open at its side. Its body was muscular like a great athlete, with broad shoulders and torso, and a striking star-shaped symbol in the centre of its chest, but the being was faceless. Its large oval-shaped head was completely smooth and devoid of any features. The great being strode purposefully until it faced Ariana and then it spread its wings and knelt on the ground with one knee, striking a formidable pose before her. Ariana stared, open-mouthed at the being, not quite sure what to do or say.

"Chosen One, you are welcome here, you have been summoned, come with me."

Ariana tried to figure out how the being spoke without a mouth. Its voice was crystal clear with the most beautiful tone that was unlike any voice she had ever heard. The great being rose to its feet, its muscular white body with a faceless head and giant wings, fascinating to watch. So smooth and agile as it moved, yet heavy-looking, like marble, the smoothness of its skin was quite radiant. It proceeded forward purposefully, the heavy thud of its feet on the golden path reverberated loudly; all the other celestials and humanoids on the path respectfully moved aside to let him pass, stopping to watch as he strode by. The great faceless being didn't look back to see if Ariana was following, but she hurried after him. On and on the great being went with the loud thud of his footsteps guiding Ariana as she continued taking in her surroundings.

What appeared to be a gigantic castle of glistening, shiny white marble, stood tall and majestic at the end of the path of gold. Ariana followed closely behind the great faceless being as it strode directly up to the towering arched doors of the castle, beside which stood two sentries that were identical faceless winged beings just like the one Ariana was following. The sentries nodded to their fellow being and pushed open the heavy white marble doors and the great faceless being strode through them with Ariana hurrying behind.

The doors closed behind them, and Ariana found herself standing in front of a group of twelve celestial beings that appeared to be seated on floating thrones that looked like bright white orbs formed into a circle. All around them stood great marble statues that looked like Greek gods and goddesses, poised as though ready for battle with weapons drawn.

Ariana was speechless; overwhelmed with awe, she fell to her knees, her face to the floor and she began weeping involuntarily. What was happening to her? Ariana's mind raced, it was like she wasn't in control of herself, yet at the same time, she felt in control. Astonishingly, kneeling before the twelve beings and weeping, felt right, and she began to experience a strange feeling inside her gut, spasms, as though something deep within her was being released, upwards and through her oesophagus and out of her mouth. With her face to the marble floor, she tried to look at what she was regurgitating but there was nothing on the floor. As Ariana tried to grapple with what was happening to her, she heard one of the twelve speak, its voice was ethereal,

"She needs to purge from within."

Ariana looked up from her kneeling position on the floor and watched as one of the twelve floated towards her on its glowing orblike throne. The magnificent aura of the being was so great that Ariana felt an immediate physical sensation of peace and calmness wash over her, and the spasms in her gut stopped. The face of the being glowed brightly, violet eyes stared into the depths of Ariana's very soul, and the sheer beauty of the being's aura moved Ariana to weep once more.

"What is happening to me?" she asked as she wept uncontrollably.

The beautiful glowing being held out her palm towards Ariana, and said loudly,

"*Strongholds of mankind... BE RELEASED!*"

Ariana felt the spasms in her gut return, but this time they were stronger, so strong that she felt something moving inside her being pushed or pulled through her stomach, along her throat and towards her mouth! She spat and spluttered as the physical sensation of something large gushing upwards as though carried along in a river of fluid, almost made her choke. She felt something large and heavy slide out of her mouth and onto the marble floor. Spewing residual blobs of fluid from her mouth, Ariana coughed and wiped her lips with the back of her hand, and then she saw that what had emerged from within her was alive and wriggling on the floor, covered in what appeared to be a transparent sac, surrounded by body fluids. Ariana continued to watch as it wriggled furiously as though trying to fight its way out of the sac that was restricting it.

"What the?" Ariana stuttered as she peered closer to try to see what it was that had emerged from deep inside her. She thought she ought to be horrified, but she wasn't; perhaps it was because of this place, or the peaceful being with the beautiful aura.

Suddenly the sac broke.

"Wahhh, wahh, waaahhhh!" the sound of the tiny baby crying grew louder, as it wriggled, and its face grew red with fury.

"A baby!" Ariana was shocked, a baby had emerged from within her... gut? She had learned about the birds and the bees, but this sure beat anything she had learned in biology lessons!

Stunned, Ariana continued to watch as the being with the beautiful aura held out her hand once again and a great dazzling white ray of light emitted and shrouded the baby, which immediately grew and grew in the space of mere seconds, Ariana watched as the baby changed in age, from baby to toddler to child of about nine or ten years old, and she recognised the child as herself.

"Inner child, come forward," said the beautiful being.

Ariana watched her inner child walk forward obediently and stand before the beautiful being.

"Speak of your pain," commanded the beautiful being with eyes full of compassion, as she held the gaze of the inner child.

Ariana watched in amazement, as her inner child began wringing her small hands together until they turned red, and her little face began to pucker as though she was about to cry.

"I... I... I don't like feeling like this," the inner child hiccupped and snuffled as she tried to hold back her tears, but one by one little droplets began to roll down her cheeks.

"How are you feeling, my child?" asked the beautiful being softly, encouragingly.

After snuffling and hiccupping some more, she blurted out her reply, "I don't like feeling like I don't belong!" and suddenly the

The Cocoon Within

floodgates opened, and the inner child began bawling uncontrollably.

The beautiful being gazed at the inner child in contemplation for a moment before her orb-like throne hovered low enough so that she could hold out her arms to the inner child, who ran and almost fell into the beautiful being's arms.

Ariana watched the exchange. Bizarrely, she was surprised to feel like she was intruding on an intimate and personal moment. The beautiful being held the inner child close, stroking her hair, soothing the child's tears away, and she visibly relaxed in the embrace of the beautiful being, becoming calm and peaceful. Stepping out of the embrace, the inner child was sufficiently calmed, and she began to talk more confidently about her feelings.

"I feel upset because it's my fault that my mummy and daddy got killed," she said amid more snuffles.

"Why is it your fault, my child?"

"Because I overheard Daddy telling Mummy that they had to protect me because I am the Chosen One and that the evil one would be coming after me."

Ariana's heart plummeted at her inner child's revelation. She didn't even remember overhearing a conversation like that when she had been a small child. She looked at her inner child and felt confused, how could she not be aware of what she had been harbouring within since childhood?

"And now it's my fault that Jessica is dead, just like my mummy and daddy," the small child's lips quivered. "And... and... I only have Jack and Granpey left and what if they die too?" Tears began streaming down the inner child's face again and unable to hold back her emotions, her lips crumpled.

"Fear not my child, for the Mighty One is on your side. He has brought you thus far and is with you. You will never be forsaken; do you believe this?"

The beautiful being didn't wait for the child to answer, instead, she held out her palm, which emitted rays of glorious light that surrounded the inner child, and said,

"Be released from tormenting guilt and inner fear by trauma, right now, disperse and leave this child forever!" the being's voice rang out with great authority as she spoke her command.

Ariana felt a great rushing wind blow past her and suddenly it whooshed towards her inner child whose hair blew upwards, and then the child appeared limp as the wind twirled her around and around. Ariana could see something emerging from the inner child's mouth, something almost translucent, with a greyish tinge. She recognised a clawed hand, and then a rather squashed oversized grey head appeared, somehow squeezing its way through her inner child's mouth. Ariana felt sickened as she watched the shrivelled creature flop onto the ground, and then another followed, climbing its way out of her inner child's mouth, also shrivelled and rather flattened, it slid to the floor.

The two creatures, Tormenting ones, lay on the floor immobile, while the inner child continued to swirl around faster and faster, shrinking to become a tiny baby once more, encased in a sac, which flew towards Ariana as it continued to shrink in size, before it disappeared into Ariana's open mouth, back to where it had come from. As she coughed and spluttered in reaction to what had just happened, Ariana watched as the beautiful being held out her hands to the Tormenting ones as they lay still on the floor and the moment the great light from her hands touched the creatures, they instantly disintegrated, with no trace of them ever having been there.

The beautiful being turned to Ariana, her gaze was so glorious to behold, that Ariana had to avert her eyes.

"My child, you have been purged of deep inner pain and torment," the beautiful being continued to hover on her orb-like throne, which moved towards Ariana.

"Thank you," she replied, not knowing what else to say. She thought she ought to show gratitude, even if she didn't quite understand what all this meant.

"My child, do you believe that you will never be forsaken?"

Ariana's heart leapt at the beautiful being's words, as though the words themselves had lifted her very soul, she felt loved, strengthened and so alive.

"Yes, yes, I do believe!" Ariana responded with fervour.

Just then the great faceless being with wings strode heavily across the room towards Ariana and the beautiful being hovered upwards, her orb-like throne taking her back to the circle of celestial beings.

"You are worthy to take up the Chalice of Fire, follow me," said the great faceless being, then he turned and walked forward, leading Ariana past the circle of twelve, through a great archway and towards a maze of corridors.

The great faceless being stopped there and turned towards Ariana. Oddly she knew that he was looking at her, she thought that perhaps he had eyes behind the smooth marble that was his face, but that they were just not externally visible. She shrugged and stared up at the great being, waiting for his instructions and as she looked at his impressive statuesque form, she pondered the end result of all of this, and she felt a longing for home, for Granpey and for Jack.

"Now you must go forward alone, you are deemed worthy by birthright, but you must prove yourself worthy of your identity," he said, spreading one giant wing wide, and inclining his head in the same direction.

Ariana perfectly understood that the rest of this journey to retrieve the Chalice of Fire was up to her. After a momentary pause, she stepped forward and walked straight along the stark marble corridor and followed it to the end, where she turned and stared back at the great faceless being; raising her hand she gave a wave, before she disappeared around the corner.

Not knowing quite what to expect after her strange, yet liberating encounter with the beautiful being, Ariana continued forward along the stark white marble corridor that seemed to go on forever, turning corner after corner, which led to yet another and another identical corridor. Well, if anything, it gave Ariana time to think and reflect on what had just happened. The only thing that made sense to her right now was that she felt free and clear-headed in a deeper way than ever before. It was as though she had been released from a dark cloud deep within her that she had been carrying around for years, but that she didn't know had been affecting her so deeply until now. On reflection, that made a lot of sense because how could you know what true inner freedom felt like, if you had never experienced it in the first place?

As she continued to walk along the stark white corridors, she concluded that she now understood that she was here for a reason, that she was the Chosen One for this moment in time and she was destined to walk this path for the good of others. Suddenly, as she reached that moment of clarity, the walls of the corridor where she stood faded away, the entire space completely transformed, and as she looked around her, she realised that she was now standing on the summit of the mountain.

She had to squint at the dazzling brightness that suddenly encompassed the mountain summit, and as her eyes adjusted to the light, she saw before her, three great lampstands, and on each lampstand stood a chalice. Behind each lampstand was a great humanoid creature with wings, each holding a bronze rod in its right hand, and their faces were covered with what looked like a helmet of crystal and gold, shaped much like a medieval knight's helmet. They each hovered in the air behind their lampstands, looking like fearsome and mighty protectors, their bodies partially covered in crystal and golden armour with a great star emblazoned on the breastplate that shone brightly. Their bronzed mighty arms and legs were covered in that familiar five-fold symbol. The beings looked heavy set, muscular and strong, like gladiators ready for battle.

Ariana just stood and waited, she wasn't sure what she was supposed to do, but she did know that one of the three chalices was the Chalice of Fire, but which one? And were these beings going to let her just walk right up and take it? After contemplating for a moment what her next move should be, Ariana took a step forward towards the lampstands and immediately one of the beings was in front of her blocking her path, holding its bronze rod horizontal like a barrier.

"Higher Order Celestial, confirm your identity," said the winged being, its voice deep and authoritative.

"I am the Chosen One, here to take up the Chalice of Fire," Ariana replied hoping that was enough.

"Confirm your identity," repeated the being, holding its position, not moving an inch and appearing like a statue apart from the fact that it had spoken.

"I am Ariana, Chosen One, Higher Order Celestial of the Seventh Realm."

"Confirm your identity."

"Damn it! What do you want me to confirm?" losing patience, Ariana yelled.

The being flipped its rod so fast to strike Ariana, but she already fielded the blow with her Lifeblood sword which clashed loudly against the bronze rod. She still didn't know how she did that, her combat skills were furiously fast to the point where she didn't even know how she was doing it. As Ariana engaged in battle with the being, he struck and dived faster and faster but she out-matched him with speed and skill, using her sword to block every strike of his bronze rod. Ariana saw the other two beings flank her and joined in the attack, but she began to move faster and faster blocking all three beings with supersonic speed.

Ariana leapt backwards out of their reach, dropping her sword, she blasted her powers from her hands and all three beings did the same blasting their own powers, which met hers, and the blue-white rays of light from each of them joined together and formed a star-shaped pinnacle of light that pulsated like a bright sign on the mountain summit. It was like a Eureka moment for Ariana, as she stared at the great pulsating star-shaped light, she realised this was what they were looking for. After a moment the three beings turned and retrieved their bronze rods from the ground where they had dropped them and took their positions back behind the lampstands. Ariana watched as the star-shaped light remained up above them and continued to pulsate brightly.

"Chosen One, it is your time to take up the Chalice of Fire," announced one of the beings as he thrust his bronze rod vertically against the ground which made a loud noise.

Ariana stepped forward and looked at each chalice in turn. The first one was large and looked like it was made from crystal with gold markings of a five-fold symbol, a lion and star covering its exterior. The next one, also quite large, looked like it was made of gold and had the same markings engraved on its exterior, and the last one looked like it was made up of a combination of many precious stones, it was small, yet it had silvery markings of a five-fold symbol, a lion, star and an eagle covering it entirely. Ariana looked from one cup to the other, but her eyes were drawn to the last one, the smallest one. She looked up at the beings, they gave nothing away, she grabbed the small dazzling Chalice and the moment that she took hold of it and lifted it from its stand, flames of fire blazed from inside the Chalice and a great rumbling sound like thunder could be heard all around them. Still holding the Chalice in her hand, she felt the ground begin to shake beneath her feet as though an earthquake had taken a grip of the place.

"What's happening?" cried Ariana as she looked at the beings searchingly, quickly placing the Chalice back on the stand hoping the shaking would stop, but it made no difference, so she picked it back up again, holding it tightly.

"It is time for the great awakening!" the three beings declared in unison before they elevated themselves upwards with a few strokes of their wings and flew off into the distance.

Great! Left alone up here when everything seems to be falling apart! *"Thanks a lot!"* Ariana called loudly after the disappearing beings as they flew further and further away, knowing full well that they couldn't hear her.

As the ground continued to shake, the lampstands broke apart and the two remaining Chalices fell to the ground, smashing to pieces, revealing themselves as the fakes that they were. Then suddenly, the mountain top disappeared and Ariana was back in the stark white corridor. Still feeling the trembling of the ground beneath her, she ran with the Chalice held tightly and she noticed that the flames had fizzled to a small smouldering glow within the cup itself. She only hoped that everyone was alright and that she had definitely taken the right Chalice, though she didn't understand why the ground was shaking as though everything would soon come crashing down. She had to get out of here and get the Chalice to Leo and rescue the others. Ariana ran down the corridor, steadying herself against the walls as she felt the ground shaking beneath her.

10

The Great Awakening

Ariana didn't understand what was happening! From the moment she had taken the Chalice from its stand, everything began to shake as though a tremendous earthquake was about to destroy the entire place. She had tried putting the Chalice back on the stand, in the hope that the great shaking would stop, but it made no difference. Holding onto the Chalice, Ariana ran back through the maze of corridors as fast as she could. Her heart was pounding with the rush of adrenaline as she raced through each corridor and back into the hall where the great faceless being and the twelve celestials had been.

Amidst the ground shaking furiously, Ariana could see that the twelve celestials were elevated high up on their thrones and together they appeared to be creating some sort of light force that was filling the room. She could hear the sounds of screaming and chaos outside, and a crashing noise of what sounded like bricks and mortar falling. The great faceless beings were nowhere to be seen. Ariana heard a loud noise and she turned swiftly to her right to see what it was. She watched in shock as the giant statues glowed with the light force from the twelve Celestials, and they began to break away from their podiums with the movement of their marble limbs, stone becoming a living, moving entity. The great warrior statues came alive, each one with sword and shield, some were riders atop giant winged horses, that flew out of the great open doors and into the chaos outside. Ariana watched in amazement as the last of the great statues came alive and thudded its giant sandal-clad feet past her, as it strode towards the open doorway. Resembling the image of a Greek god, the huge statue's muscular legs and great torso loomed larger than life, and it clutched a giant sword and shield, and looked ready for battle.

Turning to the twelve, she looked at them hoping for guidance. The beautiful being hovered towards her.

"My child, a great and mighty battle rages on through the realms, you must be ready to slay all who try to take the Chalice of Fire from your hands. You are the Chosen One and you must fulfil your destiny and bring victory for mankind and the seven realms."

Ariana knew that she needed to get the Chalice to Leo, to stop the Destroyer and end the war and set all things right, but what of Jack? If she didn't take the Chalice to Vedriece, then Jack and Badari would be killed and all the captives too. But if she handed over the Chalice, he would kill them all anyway, of that she was certain. She needed to come up with a plan, and she needed to get to Oliad and the book!

Ariana drew her Lifeblood sword and raced out of the great castle. She didn't expect to see so much destruction; the ground was shaking and buildings were falling apart. There were celestial beings using their powers to uphold buildings and others were holding up protective forcefields over their homes. Many celestials and their families were running out of the mountain to escape the unstable land and others departed on great winged horses, soaring into the sky to escape the danger. Ariana ran through the crowds, trying to keep her balance as she fled and grabbed the cloak of a celestial being nearby.

"What is happening? Why is the ground shaking like this? And why is everyone leaving?" Ariana asked the stranger beseechingly.

"The sacred land has been penetrated by dark forces! Those that can fight must go to the lower levels and hold back the evil ones and stand our ground, and the mothers and young must flee to safety," replied the being, turning to go.

"Wait! Why is the ground here shaking? What is happening?" Ariana cried.

As the stranger ran from her grasp, he turned and yelled above the noise, "It's the protection of the Twelve Arc Celestials!" Then he ran towards a Pegasus, leapt onto its back and galloped along the golden path and flew through the mountain wall.

With everything crumbling around her and celestials fleeing in every direction, Ariana gripped the Chalice tightly and sped along the golden path, stumbling in the wake of the tremors underfoot, and weaving in and out of everyone rushing frantically along the path. This was a far cry from the peace and serenity of this place that she had encountered less than an hour ago. Ariana decided that her most pressing concern was to find her way back to Oliad and the book; she only hoped that he was alright.

As she ran, she sheathed her Lifeblood sword, and then she heard galloping beside her and a familiar whinny. It was the pearlescent Pegasus of many colours! He had come for her! Ariana's heart soared with joy at the sight of him and she literally leapt onto his back, as he flew up above the crowds and straight through the mountain face.

"Boy, am I glad to see you!" she shouted, not sure if he understood her, but she patted his neck vigorously, hoping that he could sense her appreciation.

Looking down, Ariana's heart sank as she saw hordes of giant beasts and the Drakken slaying the beautiful deer and creatures of paradise. They were everywhere, shedding blood, devouring the sacred creatures, mauling them and fighting celestials to the death. Ariana could see the great Greek god-like statue slaying the giants, like they were toy soldiers, but more and more of the beasts were emerging from the ground in droves. Ariana's sharp intake of breath said it all, as more celestials flew through the sky on their great winged horses to join the battle, while others raced on foot, with swords drawn or powers at the ready, yet still they were outnumbered.

Ariana wondered how the beasts had broken through the forcefield because the ones that had accompanied her, had revealed in no uncertain terms that they had no jurisdiction this side of the portal. So, what had happened to change that? She saw the great faceless beings fighting the giants, smashing them with their huge wings and crushing them with their heavy bodies, this was a bloody war, and it didn't look like it was about to end anytime soon. Ariana's eyes scoured the land for the red and golden leafed tree, where she had left sleeping Oliad but surely the chaos would have woken him, and then perhaps he had gone into hiding? She might never find him, but at least she could try. Ariana spotted the tree in the distance; it stood out with its bright glowing leaves and she nudged Pegasus to turn towards it, swooping in for landing close by. She leapt off Pegasus and ran to the tree, scouring the undergrowth and the cluster of rocks, but Oliad was nowhere to be seen and neither was the book.

"Oliad! Oliad!" she called as she desperately looked about, and then she saw a movement in the silvery undergrowth on the far side, opposite the red and gold tree.

"Oliad! Oh, Oliad, you're hurt!" she cried, brushing aside the leaves to get a good look at him.

"They took the book, I'm so sorry…"

"It's ok, Oliad, let me help you." She lay her hands over the wound in Oliad's side, from which protruded a sharp and bloodied branch, *"Be healed right now!"* Ariana's hands glowed that great blue light which grew intense before fading again. Stepping back, she watched as Oliad felt his side, which was now free of the branch and completely back to normal.

Jumping up, he gave Ariana the biggest hug. "Thank you! Thank you so much! "He cried, jumping up and down, waving his arms about and kicking his legs, "I am fine, perfectly back to normal!" he said with wonder, before quickly becoming sombre and frowning with concern.

"What is it? Are you still hurt somewhere?" Ariana dashed back to his side.

"No, no I'm fine, it's the book, it's my fault, they took it and that's why they had the power to bring all of this devastation to this sacred land. So, now they have two books and if they find the third one and get the Chalice of Fire from you, then we will have no hope."

Before Ariana could begin to reply, out of nowhere, leaping towards her with great jaws wide open and ready to attack with force, came the Drakken. Ariana flung the Chalice at Oliad and yelled at him to run through the portal, as she back-flipped out of the Drakken's reach. Landing feet first with outstretched hands, she blasted the Drakken with her powerful beams, as more came racing towards her, their thick, long matted dark fur appeared like the death of night as they ran, heavy claws scraping the beautiful silvery grass, their terrifying faces lunging forward, and the sound of their rumbling heavy breathing mixed with growls as they approached at pace, eager to devour any living thing that crossed their path.

Ariana blasted each and every one of them with ease. Spreading her arms wide, she shot her powerful rays at them one by one, and each Drakken disintegrated mid-air as they leapt with their great jaws snapping as they tried to reach her. Ariana didn't wait around for more to come, she ran past the battling beasts and celestials, heading in the direction of the portal, hoping that Oliad had made it through. She knew that he could run without being seen so his chances of survival were very high and at least the Chalice should be safe for now.

Ariana ran through the waterwall and onwards towards the portal, past the bloodied carcasses of the beautiful silvery deer, tears of sorrow and anger pricked at her eyes. All around she could see that it looked like the entire herd had been slaughtered. Beautiful, sacred, innocent creatures that had not harmed a soul. Ariana drew her Lifeblood sword and struck giant beast after giant beast, slaying each beast in her path with the edge of her sword, before racing through the portal.

The Cocoon Within

Stopping dead in her tracks, Ariana's heart raced furiously, as she took in the scene in front of her. She had crossed the portal and was back in the deep wilderness, but standing before her, appeared to be Vedriece's entire army, ready and armed for battle. Some were astride the Drakken, riding atop them like horses, bearing armour and shields, with sword and spear in hand.

Jack and Badari were kneeling on the ground, and two great beasts each holding a Lifeblood sword stood behind them.

Vedriece stood tall like a great muscular Greek god. "Chosen One, I see you have failed the mission," his deep voice drawled with sarcasm. "Yet you have the audacity to return empty-handed, despite my command to return with the Chalice!" his deep laughter rang out loudly. "Bring the captive!" he ordered as he watched Ariana closely when one of his giant beasts stepped forward and threw Oliad to the ground as he clutched the Chalice.

Ariana's heart sank as she watched Oliad climb to his feet, his head hanging low as though in shame, and then he slowly lifted his eyes to look at Ariana and said, "I'm sorry, I'm so sorry... ha ha ha ha ha!" Oliad began laughing uncontrollably, hysterically.

Ariana frowned in confusion. Had Oliad betrayed her? Suddenly his features began to change, and his pint-size body grew taller. He began to swirl around as though caught in a furious whirlwind and all the while his body was changing and morphing into something, but into what? Ariana heard her own sharp intake of breath as the whirlwind stopped and Oliad was no more and in his place stood none other than the silvery serpent haired humanoid, her blue-green serpent tresses hissed in united symphony and swayed, as the voluptuous being thrust her arms in the air, holding up the Chalice, her great bosom shook and the skin on her slender golden arms glistened enticingly, as she continued laughing manically, and the crowds of the army standing behind her joined in with victorious cheers.

"There is none more powerful than our kingdom! We rule with the depths of great dark power! And we shall slay all who oppose the kingdom of Vedriece; all will bow before him and yield to his reign!"

Her blue-green serpent tresses hissed and swayed wildly, as she strode to Vedriece and wrapped her arms around him. His giant hands gripped her and then he kissed her deeply, before raising her hand with the Chalice in the air, and the crowd cheered once more.

Ariana was still reeling from the shock of Oliad not being Oliad; had he ever been real? And now she had given the Chalice over to the enemy! She had failed the mission completely. Jessica was dead, Jack, Badari and the captives would no doubt be killed too and so would she, and what of Granpey and the others back on Earth? Ariana's mind raced, as she tried to think of a way out of this. Oh, where were Leo and Eriat when she needed them? There was no point trying to use her power because Vedriece would simply subdue her with his own power like last time, though he hadn't killed them yet, so perhaps they still stood a chance at escape. Something glinted on the ground by her feet, she looked down and saw it was one of the pendants that the Gnetic had given them! She silently stepped over the pendant to hide it from sight, she could use it to save Jack at least. If the giant beast were to attempt to slay him with its Lifeblood sword, he could use it to escape death.

"Bring the sacred books!" cried Vedriece, and a giant beast ambled forward carrying both books.

Another beast flung a lifeless Oliad to the ground in front of Ariana. Realising that the serpent-haired humanoid had somehow mimicked Oliad's form, she crouched beside him and lifted his small hand, but there was no movement, his head flopped to the side, eyes glazed and still. It was clear that little Oliad was yet another poor casualty of the evil Vedriece's reign of terror. Ariana closed his small eyelids with her palm as a tear trickled down her cheek, and she quickly took the opportunity to grab the pendant from the ground. No one saw her, except Jack. Their eyes met and she could see the yearning in his eyes, yearning for them to escape their captors, yearning that no more innocents should lose their lives. A yearning for good to triumph over all this evil.

Ariana watched as Vedriece began to speak in a language she could not understand, as though casting some kind of spell. His giant arms spread wide, the books glowed and elevated in the air, circling around and around one another as Vedriece's voice rose and he appeared to be in some kind of a trance, his features flashing between his true self of raw flesh and bone and his humanoid self. His skin glowed a deep, fiery, reddish hue, which intensified and appeared as though at any moment he might burst into flames. Yet on and on he chanted at the swirling books, and then with his hands he drew the Chalice of Fire up and out of the hands of the serpent-haired being, her blue-green tresses of snakes swaying as the Chalice hovered out of her hands until it was beneath the swirling books, and then suddenly a great fire arose out of the Chalice. Purple, white, orange and red flames flared up from it, the flames licking at the books as Vedriece continued chanting, but the books were not consumed. On and on this went until finally Vedriece threw his hands down in fury and yelled with frustration and the books and the Chalice fell to the ground loudly.

"Cursed be these darned books! It won't work! The Chalice's power is not activated!" Vedriece's face was full of fury, and he turned to Ariana. "Yes of course! Only the Chosen One is worthy to take up the Chalice of Fire, only she can activate its power! Bring her to me!" he commanded.

"Jack, quick catch!" Ariana threw the pendant to Jack, he caught it, and he quickly grasped hold of Badari, just as the beasts thrust their Lifeblood swords at them, but at that exact moment, both Jack and Badari disappeared.

Relieved that the pendant had done its job and that both Jack and Badari were safe, Ariana took her chance and back-flipped out of reach of the beasts and Drakken that were darting towards her, and she went straight through the portal out of the deep wilderness and back onto the battleground.

Vedriece may have the Chalice, but he couldn't use it without her, so she needed to make darned sure that she didn't get caught. She raced through the battleground, blasting any beasts in her path and leaping over carcasses, she made her way to the thick of the forest and found a hiding place she could spy from. Vedriece and his army were already through the portal, tipping the scales in his favour with his hundreds of warrior beasts and Drakken. Ariana watched the bloody war with horror as she saw the great faceless being getting smashed by a beast with a giant club, pieces of his marble face shattering and flying across the silvery forest that was once a place of paradise but was now a bloody battleground. Another faceless being came to rescue his comrade, knocking the club from the giant's hand and stomping on the giant's face and body. Another great beast ran with a club in hand and smashed the great faceless being's legs in two and Ariana watched with sadness as it fell to the ground, immobilised.

The great stone warriors were fighting hard, pushing the enemy back, stomping on beasts and slashing them with the edge of their swords, stabbing, thrusting their blades, and smashing them with shields. Ariana was willing them to succeed in destroying Vedriece's entire army, but that's when he struck, with his great power he simply raised his hands and shot his power one by one at each of the great stone warriors and Ariana gasped as they smashed to pieces in an instant. The remaining celestials continued to fight to the death with powers and Lifeblood swords. Both giants and celestials fell by the edge of the sword and by the might of celestial powers, but the balance was in the favour of the evil ones and as their terror reigned, so the sky began to darken, and where there had been bright sunlight, suddenly the sky was shrouded with dark grey clouds.

Ariana looked at the sky in wonder and she hoped that Jack and Badari had made it safely back to En Arias. Racking her brains on how to get the Chalice back before every celestial here was killed or taken captive, Ariana watched as she saw beasts taking celestials in chains back through the portal. Her heart sank as it seemed that they were losing this fight.

She had no time to dwell on her thoughts as she saw a flash of blue-green tresses flying towards her, sword in hand ready to strike. Ariana drew her Lifeblood sword with lightning speed and struck her opponent's blade in defence, fielding off the attack. The sound of Lifeblood sword clashing against Lifeblood sword rang loudly, as though performing a tremendous dance they tussled with the might of their swords. The serpent-haired humanoid had a look of warped glee on her face as she wielded her sword and struck again and again. Her eyes glinted brightly as she laughed and smirked at Ariana, taunting and goading her with every strike. Ariana leapt about like a gymnast, avoiding every sword thrust, and finally pushing her opponent to the ground as she struck her own Life Blood sword against her smirking serpent-haired enemy's sword, which went flying and landed afar and out of reach.

With unexpected precision, the serpent-haired being flipped herself to a crouching position, raised her hands and blasted rays of power at Ariana, who flew backwards and landed against a tree. For a fleeting moment, Ariana thought that the impact would have hurt more than it did before she quickly ran at her opponent and shot her powers in retaliation. As her serpent-haired enemy flew backwards to the ground, suddenly Ariana felt herself being lifted into the air, immobilised, captured once again by none other than Vedriece himself. Striding towards her, face full of fury, he flung his arm outwards, and she flew backwards and slammed against a tree. Ariana winced in pain at the impact as she slid to the ground. She heard the heavy footsteps of Vedriece thud across the ground until he was towering over her. With one blast of his powers, her wrists were encased in a forcefield; she tried to lift her hands to use her powers, but she couldn't move them, she was trapped again.

"Take this half-breed out of my sight! I will slay every celestial being this side of the portal and then she will activate the power of the Chalice for my pleasure and my victory!" Vedriece commanded as he looked at her with disgust, *"I WILL HAVE MY VENGEANCE!"* he yelled with fury and his face flashed back and forth between his humanoid form to his true evil form, of raw flesh and bone. "Kill them all! Every single last one of them, every sacred being in this place, do not let a single one live and breathe!" Vedriece yelled at his horde of giant beasts that had crowded around their master, before he strode off furiously, smashing trees with his bare hands, breaking them apart. And then he began blasting everything in his sight with his powers of darkness. Vedriece's serpent-haired maiden followed after him, and together they strode back onto the battlefield and joined the violence.

One of the beasts sauntered over to Ariana, grabbed her by her feet, dragged her across the ground and flung her over to a group of captives. She bashed into one of the captives as she landed.

"Sorry," she said and twisted around awkwardly.

She looked at the faces of the captives beside her and she recognised some of the celestials from within the mountain, that only a few hours earlier had been peacefully enjoying their time together amongst their families. Some were mothers with children, and they were huddled together, tear-stained faces saddened by the destruction and death all around. Ariana looked around at the devastation, as the fighting and slaughter continued; bodies of innocent celestials strewn across the silvery grass, beautiful creatures injured and crying out in pain. She watched as a silvery fawn bleated pitifully as it stood beside its dead mother who lay still, lifeless, and a giant beast dragged the carcass of a great silvery stag by its antlers, across the beautiful grass that was now stained with blood and death.

Meanwhile, the battle raged on in front of them all. Ariana watched the captives' defeated expressions of lost hope, as more and more giant beasts entered the portal, there were far too many of them and they outnumbered the celestials. Ariana felt the indignant rage begin to build within her, so much so that she emphatically wanted to stop this horror and slaughter of the innocents once and for all. Just then, Ariana remembered that she could use the invisible key to unbind her hands and the others too… but where was it? Realising that it was no longer around her neck, Ariana's heart sank, it must have fallen off when she had fought the serpent-haired maiden! Looking around wildly, she tried to think where it might have fallen. If she could just get to the spot where they had fought, then she could at least try to feel around on the ground for it with her feet, but how would she ever find it if she couldn't see it?

Just then, Ariana saw one of the giant beasts coming towards them. It threw its heavy shield to the ground, its angry eyes intent on the captives. The beast was covered in blood, no doubt the blood of celestials slain by its hands. Its large, distorted face looked more terrifying than ever with blood oozing from its jaws. It stood in front of them all before grabbing hold of one of the small celestial children that had been captured with its mother. The beast yanked it from its screaming mother's arms. Ariana was horrified as the beast lifted the child to its mouth, biting its arm, tearing a chunk of its flesh and devouring it in front of everyone's eyes as blood streamed from the screaming child's wound.

Ariana jumped up and yelled at the beast to let the poor screaming child go. She struggled in vain to release her hands and all of the bound captives yelled and screamed in distress as they too furiously tried to break free so they could rescue the child. The beast's angry amber eyes seemed to dance in manic delight at the screams and cries of both the child and all the captives. As the beast was about to take another bite of the terrified child, a great black panther leapt out of nowhere, lunging straight for the beast, tearing into its face and neck as the child dropped to the ground. Another black panther appeared, and Ariana recognised them both, the Fearsome ones!

"Allies are on their way, quickly release the captives with the invisible key before we are seen, and I will lead them to safety," growled one of the panthers.

"I haven't got the key! I lost it in battle with the serpent-haired maiden!" Ariana cried despondently as she tried to lift her wrists to show the panther. She was desperate to heal the poor wounded child.

Then came a familiar voice, "But I have the key!"

Ariana shrieked in delight when she realised who it was, "Pippy! Oh, Pippy, you're alright and you came back for us!"

Pippy threw herself at Ariana and gave her an affectionate wish-helper hug, before placing the invisible key against Ariana's wrists. Ariana quickly commanded the release of her own hands and raced over to the wounded child, she lay her hands on the child and healed her. After releasing all the captives, Pippy and Ariana stayed behind, and one of the Fearsome ones led the captives carefully through the portal without being observed as the war raged on all around them.

"Oh, Pippy, am I glad to see you! Did you manage to get the other celestials and wish-helpers to safety?" Ariana asked hopefully as they stayed hidden behind a rock cluster out of sight of three raging beasts that seemed to have now noticed the missing captives and were heading in their direction. The remaining Fearsome one, leapt out at the beasts striking all three in succession as it ferociously attacked with a fatal bite to each beast with ease. Ariana watched as four great Drakken ran to attack the Fearsome one, who let out a mighty growl, swaying his head as he did so, and from his mouth, great blue-white rays of power bolted with speed and struck each of the Drakken with a fatal blow.

Hope arose within Ariana as she witnessed the power of the Fearsome one, and she suddenly felt confident that the tables were about to turn in this war.

"Yes," said Pippy, "I took all the small captives safely to the portal to the fifth realm, and the Fearsome ones were stationed at each end of the portal to guard entry, so they were escorted safely home." Pippy had a proud look on her face, "It was a long and arduous journey across the wilderness, but everyone made it safely, we didn't lose a soul."

Looking Pippy directly in the eyes, Ariana's proud smile held so much meaning. "I am so proud of you, Pippy, you truly are a great leader of wish-helpers!"

Pippy beamed, fluttering and replied, "It was my destiny. I knew it the moment these wings bonded to me, I knew my dreams had to be fulfilled, but where is the Chalice of Fire?" She looked at Ariana's empty hands with concern.

"The serpent-haired maiden killed Oliad and took the Chalice, but I don't know what she has done with it. Vedriece tried to use it, but he found out he couldn't activate its power and that only I could do that, so he will come for me."

"What about Jack and Jessica and the others?"

Ariana hung her head, tears filling her eyes as she replied, "Jessica... didn't make it. Jack and Badari escaped by the power of the pendant back to the river's edge, but the rest of the captives were recaptured in the wilderness. Pippy, we have to save them! I let them all down... and most especially, Jessica."

Before Pippy could respond, they heard a loud growl as the Fearsome one called them to hurry over. "Get on my back, we have to retrieve the Chalice of Fire, we are running out of time!"

The ground was still shaking, but suddenly it erupted into more furious rumbling and the ground on which they were standing began to crack.

Ariana and Pippy didn't need to be asked twice. Ariana leapt onto the panther's back, with Pippy tucked in front of her, gripping onto the panther's neck. To their surprise, he raced through the midst of the battleground and as he darted with incredible agility through the fighting crowds of stone warriors, giant beasts, hordes of Drakken and celestials, Ariana realised that they were surrounded in a protective forcefield. The Drakken tried to attack on one side and the giant beasts on the other, but neither could penetrate the shield of the Fearsome one.

"Use your weapons and look for the Chalice!" commanded the Fearsome one.

Pippy used her tiny dart gun stunning the enemy as they weaved in and out of the battleground, safe on the back of the Fearsome one. Meanwhile, Ariana took every opportunity to slash and jab at the giant beasts with her Lifeblood sword whilst scouring the crowds for the serpent haired maiden and Vedriece to see if she could spot the Chalice.

Suddenly the ground shook again and more great cracks opened up. As beasts and celestials alike fell through the open ground, the Fearsome one leapt over a gaping hole and headed for the portal, as beasts and celestials raced through the portal to escape the quaking ground. On the other side of the portal, in the barren wilderness, the fighting continued.

As Ariana scanned the chaos, it suddenly dawned on her that Vedriece was nowhere to be seen, but surely, he was looking for her, because without her the Chalice was useless to him. Where could he have taken the Chalice? Back to his kingdom perhaps? Maybe he had hidden it in his own chamber, somewhere safe where no one could get to it?

Ariana and Pippy held tightly to the Fearsome one as he continued to dash throughout the wilderness, growling, scowling and destroying any giant beasts in his path; one strike of his mighty claws or bite to the throat was sufficient to inflict a fatal wound, the beasts did not stand a chance against him. The celestials continued to fight hard, though they were still outnumbered and one panther, though mighty, was not enough to tip the balance.

A loud crashing noise that sounded like an explosion erupted in the distance, but it didn't stop, it continued on and on, louder and louder.

"What is that?"

"The sacred mountain has to be protected, the twelve Arc Celestials have seen to that, but there are consequences for the abomination committed on sacred land because innocents have been slain, there is no time to explain, our priority now is to retrieve the Chalice of Fire."

The Fearsome one continued to run with great speed across the battleground, easily dodging past the warriors and beasts and leaping over the dead that lay on the ground, as the battle raged on around them. He raced away from the battle, taking them deep into the wilderness until the cries of fighting could no longer be heard. Here the landscape changed somewhat; there were plenty of strange, dry-looking trees that grew together, creating twirling loops of thick branches like a twining aged wisteria tree, they weaved in and out of one another, creating rows and rows of avenues, a fortress even, that looked thick and impenetrable. The only way into this place was by a great wooden door embedded neatly in the centre of the fortress.

As the Fearsome one approached the door, Ariana could see that there were words engraved on it, *'At your own peril knock and seek the Omniscient.'* Pippy looked up at Ariana having also just read the words.

"I can't go in there," said Pippy, resolutely; her face said it all.

"Well, I'm not sure that I want to go in there either," replied Ariana, looking down at Pippy and making a face.

The Fearsome one stopped outside the door of the fortress. Ariana hopped off his back and she noticed that the only sound in this eerie place was the sound of Pippy's little wings flapping furiously fast as she hovered beside Ariana.

The Fearsome one turned to look at Ariana and Pippy, his great panther face emanated superior strength, and remarkably alert jade eyes locked with Ariana's, she felt the jolt of fear from his gaze, but it was different this time. The fear didn't penetrate her heart like before, though she felt it, the fear had no effect on her. She was beginning to understand her identity, her true self, her celestial identity. Eriat was right, about understanding coming to them through discovery.

"Chosen One, this is the only way to quickly discover where the Chalice lies."

Ariana took a deep breath and nodded. She needed to be the brave celestial, one without fear, the Chosen One.

"Keep out of sight and wait for us," Ariana instructed, and Pippy gave her a quick hug before fluttering high up into a nearby tree and settling there to wait for them.

Stepping past the panther, Ariana raised her hand to knock at the door, but before she could knock, the door slowly opened by itself making a loud creaking sound. Ariana looked up at Pippy, who bobbed in the air from her place in the nearby tree, with her beautiful wings fluttering brightly; she gave a great smile of encouragement and motioned with her hands for Ariana to go forward. Ariana looked at the Fearsome one and he growled at her and inclined his head as he rose and followed.

Together, Ariana and the Fearsome one walked through the open door, leaving Pippy behind. They heard the door close behind them. Inside the strange fortress, the twining branches were everywhere, creating a large interior passageway. As they walked along it, they could see more passageways to the left and right. Ariana wondered at the size of the inner fortress of this place and who or what resided here.

They continued along the passageway in silence. Ariana took a sideways glance at the Fearsome one, he looked magnificent, his silky, thick black glossy fur shimmered, and his face looked intent on their purpose as he picked up the pace, taking the lead. Ariana followed suit and then she began to run after him as she watched his speed increase. Suddenly, he leapt as though pursuing a target, crashing into the twining walls and appearing to pounce on something. As Ariana hurried to his side, she saw his claws digging into something, as though he had captured it, his body looming over it aggressively, but there was nothing there.

"Take us to the one with the stolen gift of Omniscience!"

Then a voice replied, "Oh great Arc Celestial, please do me no harm, I am a mere worker here, I am but a servant and I have nothing to offer you."

At that moment, what had been invisible became visible, and lying beneath the panther was a creature that appeared to have two upright legs of a bovine nature, and a humanoid upper body and face, though atop his head were two large horns that coiled backwards. The creature was dwarfed by the great panther as he lay terrified beneath him and begged for mercy.

The Fearsome one roared loudly in the face of the creature, displaying his great canines and Ariana could see a blue-white light swirling within his jaws.

"Alright! Alright! I will take you!" the creature cried, trembling in fear and conceding to the request without hesitation this time.

They followed behind the creature as it trotted along the passageways, weaving along the corridors, left, then right and on and on, like a maze until they finally came to a wooden arched door. The creature bowed and gave a little smirk before hurrying away, his little hoofs making a clattering sound as he ran.

The Fearsome one scowled in his direction before turning to Ariana and saying, "Be warned, as we enter the presence of a Necromancer, take no sustenance offered, do not ingest anything from this place. I will speak and you will only speak when I give you the nod."

"Understood."

Just then the door opened by itself, and Ariana followed the Fearsome one into the room, and the door closed behind them.

She was surprised to enter a rather warm and cosy-looking room, complete with a central fireplace, where a great fire was burning, and above which were numerous pots with some delicious smelling food simmering away. Assuming the being that was hovering over the pots with a wooden spoon was the Necromancer, whose back was turned to them, Ariana noted the attire of a long purple cloak, sparkly black shoes with a little kitten heel, and long wavy dark hair with grey flecks. She noted the feminine traits of this Necromancer.

"Take a seat and make yourself comfortable, Chosen One."

Ariana looked to the Fearsome one and he nodded and resumed his inspection of the room. She took a seat in one of the armchairs in front of the wide table which faced the fireplace, and she took the opportunity to scan the room. The entire walls of the room were made up of floor-to-ceiling bookcases, with no doubt hundreds of books on each shelf. From the ceiling hung dried herbs, and what looked like cured or dried animal parts amongst other paraphernalia. She noticed an unusual-looking bird on a stand in one corner of the room, preening its feathers; it resembled a hawk of some kind, with a very bright purple shock of feathers on its wings and tail. Every now and then it stopped its preening, raised its head and watched them closely with its sharp yellow eyes.

The Necromancer turned around, wooden spoon in hand, and Ariana stared open-mouthed as her mind tried to reconcile what she was seeing. The Necromancer was both male and female, right down the middle, a being that was male on one side and female on the other. Ariana watched with fascination as the Necromancer held the wooden spoon up and licked the sauce, and seemingly overjoyed at the taste, proceeded to suck the flavour of the sauce right off it, before placing the spoon on the side, taking a seat opposite them and folding their hands in front of them on the wide table which was covered with an array of condiments, note pads and writing instruments.

"Ah, welcome to you both! I knew you were coming! And may I extend my apologies for the less than receptive welcome from Peapod, he is rather jittery and prone to fibbing, doesn't like to help a soul and will only do so when threatened… well… never mind… here you are at last." The Necromancer beamed broadly, displaying large white teeth, and lipstick-covered lips on the feminine side, and a moustache and beard surrounding his lips on his masculine side, which was rather an oddity to behold.

The Fearsome one finished prowling across the room and joined Ariana opposite the Necromancer. "You know why we are here," he growled.

"Well, yes of course, after all… I am all-knowing," the Necromancer purred in her feminine voice, turning sideways in the chair so that the masculine side was hidden.

"By illegitimate means!" cried the Fearsome one scowling at her.

"No need to lose your temper… can I offer you some golden tea perhaps? Or a slice of my best pumpkin and sea snail pie? It's to die for!" Looming over the table to gaze with one eye at Ariana, she fluttered her eyelashes and smiled encouragingly, before clicking her fingers.

Ariana smiled back and watched, rather bemused, as the teapot levitated across the table by itself, and the cups and saucers did the same along with the pumpkin and sea snail pie. Next, a knife hovered in the air, before it thrust into the pie, cutting a neat slice, and placing it on a small side plate with a spoon, and then it floated over to hover under Ariana's nose enticingly. The pie did smell good, and Ariana wondered what the harm could be in having one small bite. Just then the Fearsome one whacked the plate of pie across the room with his paw and jumped on the table, sending everything flying.

"Show us where the Chalice of Fire is!" he roared. "We have no time for games with the dead!"

At once the masculine side turned to face the panther, his face red with anger and his eye bright with fury. "How dare you enter my domain and threaten me and my other half and make demands of us! Why should we tell you anything?" he shouted furiously at the panther.

Ariana heard the clink of crockery and looking down she could see that the broken cups and saucers were floating towards the trash by themselves; either that, or something invisible was clearing them away.

The Fearsome one roared loudly at the Necromancer, the sight of which made him fall back in his chair and compose himself.

"Well, I suppose I'm open to negotiation, what do you think my love?" the Necromancer proceeded to have the oddest conversation between her feminine self and masculine self, until both halves disagreed, debated, argued, and then finally came to an agreement.

"We will show you where the Chalice of Fire lies, on one condition."

"Speak of it!"

"I want this one to give up something." This time the feminine side turned around to peer at Ariana. Looking Ariana dead in the eye she made her request, "You will lose something you desire, for the greater good, there will be no bloodshed, nor life lost, but you will forfeit your heart's desire in your next season of life," she said and continued to stare at Ariana with her one unwavering eye, waiting for an answer.

Ariana looked across at the Fearsome one, but to her dismay, he gave her the nod. She wondered what she would have to forfeit, but at least no one would come to any harm and if it was for the greater good, she supposed she ought to.

"I accept," she reluctantly confirmed, and the Necromancer sprang from the chair and leapt about dancing and jumping for joy.

"Now the Chalice!" roared the Fearsome one, bringing the celebrating Necromancer to a halt.

The feminine side pouted as she sat back down, then turned face forward, and both halves began chanting in their masculine and feminine voices. As the chanting grew more urgent, with both hands in the air making circular motions, suddenly a picture appeared between the palms of the Necromancer's hands, like a projector displaying a scene from a movie.

As Ariana and the Fearsome one watched closely, they saw Vedriece carrying the Chalice in a dome-shaped glass case, fire dazzled brightly from within the Chalice, though it appeared secure inside the case of glass. They watched Vedriece stride through the corridors of his Kingdom, passing row upon row of closed doors, and it suddenly dawned on Ariana that she recognised the corridor of doors, when he finally stopped in front of a door marked, 'The Dark Arts'.

Pushing the door wide, Vedriece walked inside, and behind him followed the serpent-haired maiden. The room they entered was lit by flaming torches on the dark walls which were covered in strange writings, that appeared to be etched in blood. In the centre of the floor was a diagram of a large triangle with a huge sleeping eye in the middle of it. As Vedriece stepped towards the triangle, carrying the Chalice in the glass case, the giant eye immediately opened, and flames licked the edges of the triangle. They saw movement by the surrounding walls, and there appeared long cloaked figures, they hovered forward, away from the walls and surrounded the flaming triangle. Ariana could not see their faces, just darkness inside the hood of their cloak. The cloaked figures began chanting, and as they did so, Vedriece held up the Chalice in its case and it floated to the centre of the triangle, held high within some sort of swirling force, and there it remained, as the cloaked figures continued to chant, and Vedriece and the serpent maiden turned and left the room, and the door closed behind them.

The vision disappeared as suddenly as it had appeared, and the Necromancer flopped lifeless in the chair.

"Is she dead, I mean he... er... are they dead?"

The Fearsome one scowled in the direction of the Necromancer and turned to Ariana, saying, "I only wish that were the case, but this is what happens when a gift is stolen. It is merely a corrupted transplant, and it devours the spirit. Come, we must go, now that we have what we need!" and with that, the Fearsome one turned and leapt to the door, which immediately opened.

"Wait!" Ariana hurried over to the bookshelf. She had noticed one of the books glowing on the shelf and she felt as though it was calling to her. She pulled the book free; it was identical to her own sacred book! Turning around to face the Fearsome one in excitement at her discovery, she cried, "Look! It's the third book! The missing sacred book!"

Just then the Necromancer moaned and started to come to.

"Quickly, Chosen One! We must leave now and bring the sacred book; it has no place here."

They ran down the many corridors, Ariana holding onto the sacred book as they twisted and turned through the avenues of twining branches until they finally reached the door out of the fortress. They were surprised that the door opened of its own accord, and they fled through it, out into the deep wilderness. Half expecting to be set upon by some creatures of doom, Ariana was relieved to find that they were alone. She looked upwards for Pippy

The Cocoon Within

in the nearby tree where they had left her, but she was nowhere to be seen.

"Pippy, Pippy! Where are you?" called Ariana as she looked about wildly.

"Chosen One! We must leave now!"

"I can't leave without Pippy!"

"Sometimes a sacrifice has to be made, for the greater good, for the sake of the lives of many others," replied the Fearsome one, solemn but resolute. "We go now, or we risk the lives of many, including those back on Earth, the middle land."

Ariana was torn as she met the staunch gaze of the Fearsome one, suddenly becoming aware in her inner being of his utter wisdom, and she knew that she had to make the decision to go. Jumping onto his back, she took one last look up at the trees for Pippy, but just then she heard and felt the deep growling of the Fearsome one. She immediately knew something was amiss and as she looked ahead, she could see a vague movement in the distance, but it was dark and gloomy in the depth of the wilderness and hard for her to make out the figures.

As the Fearsome one continued to growl loudly and spit with fury, body erect and poised for attack, Ariana jumped off his back and stood beside him, ready to use her powers and draw her Lifeblood sword. She watched closely as the moving figures approached and as they got nearer, she heard them begin to moan and wail, accompanied by the sound of crunching and clicking bones with every movement, as the creatures came into full view. They were covered in what looked like mud, that slid from their bodies as they moved, revealing red raw flesh over bones. Sunken eyeballs, deep in their sockets glowed amber within their skulls that were covered with peeling flesh.

"The Accursed!" growled the Fearsome one, just before the rotting creatures began to run towards them.

Unsure how to tackle these unexpected attackers, Ariana drew her Lifeblood sword with speed and slashed at three of the Accursed ones that threw themselves at her, their mangled arms reaching for her throat. Jumping backwards, she realised that her Lifeblood sword had no effect, it simply passed through them making no impact. Leaping out of their reach, she fled and sheathed her sword as they made chase.

"Use your powers!" roared the Fearsome one. Blue-white rays of power shot from his mouth at a group of raging Accursed ones and they immediately disintegrated.

Ariana backflipped out of reach and faced the Accursed that were running at her. Holding out her hands, she blasted them with her powers, and they disintegrated in an instant. Together Ariana and the Fearsome one annihilated all the Accursed attackers until none remained.

"Good work, Chosen One! Only your celestial power will destroy the undead, the Accursed."

"Thanks for the heads-up," said Ariana, pausing to catch her breath. She felt exhilarated from the battle, yet she couldn't help but think about what she had learned about the Accursed, that they had once been humans that had walked the earth, tormented by the evil ones.

"Are you looking for this one?" asked the Necromancer.

The Fearsome one turned around, growling angrily. The Necromancer had Pippy! The bird of prey with the shock of purple feathers had Pippy tightly in its talons as it rested on the Necromancer's arm.

"Don't you hurt her!" cried Ariana furiously. "Pippy, are you alright?"

"I'm not hurt, I'm alright," cried Pippy bravely, as the Fearsome one prowled around the Necromancer, spitting and snapping viciously.

"Now, now, I have no wish to harm her, but my dear hawk will tear off her wings and rip her to shreds if you so much as lay a finger on me or my other half," and with that the bird of prey flew out of

The Cocoon Within

reach and up into the nearby tree taking Pippy with it. "I only ask that you return to me that which was so ungraciously taken without my permission!" the Necromancer's masculine face snapped angrily.

"Grrrrr, nothing would give me more delight than to tear you to pieces, you, thieving scourge of the seven realms!" The Fearsome one threatened.

Ariana was about to relinquish the book into the hands of the Necromancer, she just couldn't stand by and watch Pippy perish, she just couldn't. Suddenly out of nowhere, they heard the sound of a great horn blowing. Spinning around, Ariana was confused, but her confusion quickly turned to elation as she saw none other than Jack riding atop a large lizard-skinned horse! And right beside him also riding on such a horse, was Badari!

"You're alive! Oh, Jack, I just knew it! I knew you'd be alright!" Ariana cried with glee as her heart skipped a beat at the sight of him, looking handsome as ever in his Suit of Ultimate Truth, and a great smile of joy at seeing Ariana, written all over his face.

"Arry, I am so happy to see you, I was so worried about you, Badari will tell you! I couldn't think about anything but you, I needed to know if you were safe, and now at last I do!"

Suddenly, the invisible army of the Gnetic became visible, a formidable troop of riders stood behind Jack and Badari, strong and mighty warriors of the Gnetic, armed and battle-ready.

Ariana looked up at Pippy in the tree still in the clutches of the hawk, but not for long, as one of the Gnetic warriors became visible in the tree, gripping the hawk by its wings and taking it by surprise, so that it released Pippy and she immediately flew down to Ariana and Jack, unscathed.

"Jack!" Pippy flew at him and flung her arms around his neck before kissing him on his cheek, "We missed you!"

"I missed you both too!" Jack leapt off his lizard horse, strode purposefully towards Ariana and wrapped her in his strong arms, giving her the biggest hug ever. Ariana wrapped her arms around him and reciprocated the hug, snuggling into his shoulder, so relieved that she had her Jack back.

Suddenly, they heard an almighty roar, it was the Fearsome one, he had chased the fleeing Necromancer who ran back inside the fortress and slammed the door closed.

"Come, we must go and retrieve the Chalice from the place of the Dark Arts, we have no time to lose!"

Ariana and Jack leapt onto the Fearsome one's back, and off they all went in search of the Chalice. With the might of the Gnetic behind them, they rode in the direction of the battleground and Vedriece's kingdom.

Ariana held tightly to Jack as they rode. She had given him the sacred book that she took from the Necromancer, and Badari had helped him strap the book to his back for safekeeping. With Pippy flying beside them, they travelled, with the mighty Gnetic warriors riding alongside, united in their mission to win the war against the Destroyer and his kingdom of darkness.

They heard the sound of the battle, long before they saw it. The clash of mighty Lifeblood sword against Lifeblood sword, the roar of beast and celestial alike, the battle cries mixed with the cries of the dying and wounded, the smashing of skulls and armour, bone and flesh, and the rumbling of the ground beneath them all as warriors thudded and galloped into battle.

"We must head to the kingdom of darkness to retrieve the Chalice! May the protection of the Mighty One be with you!" cried the Fearsome one as he bid the Gnetic farewell and watched as they stormed into battle. He turned and headed for Vedriece's kingdom carrying Jack and Ariana, with Pippy in flight beside them.

"I will come with you in case you need my help," Badari yelled as he urged his lizard-like horse on. It strained at the reins as it lunged forward, keeping in step with the Fearsome one.

When they arrived at Vedriece's kingdom, the place appeared deserted, with no sign of giant beasts or Drakken.

Badari was first to dismount. "They must all be at the battleground," he said, patting his lizard-horse and looping its reins to a low-hanging tree branch.

As he approached the wide-open gates, Badari cut a fine, strong and mighty figure as he walked through them, Lifeblood sword at his hip, the ebony skin of his battle-scarred face and muscular arms shimmering as he strode forward. Jack and Ariana hopped off the Fearsome one and followed after Badari, whilst the Fearsome one took in the surroundings, pacing the perimeter, before joining them at the great doorway to the kingdom itself.

"I can fly in first and scout for any danger?" Pippy suggested as she hovered between them.

"No, I will go first and check for the enemy," said Badari, a true celestial warrior, conditioned to lay down his life for others. He withdrew his Lifeblood sword and was already through the open door, turning, he motioned to them to follow.

Jack and Ariana unsheathed their Lifeblood swords and together they followed Badari, with Pippy fluttering alongside them and the Fearsome one taking up the rear, cautiously keeping watch for an attack from behind.

They passed through the West Wing, where Ariana expected to see the bodies of the dead where they had fought and lost Jessica, but she wasn't there, in fact, there were no dead bodies anywhere to be seen. Ariana looked at Jack and she knew he was thinking the same as her. Where was Jessica's body? What had happened and was she really dead? A small window of hope bubbled in Ariana's heart, perhaps it had been an illusion? But then what about the others that had been slain?

As they continued weaving along corridor after corridor, Pippy remembered the way to the corridor with the many doors of evil, and she flew ahead as she navigated the way. Everywhere they turned was empty, no guards, just the bodies of those slain lay by the torture chamber, in their earlier attempt to escape the kingdom. It was as though the entire kingdom was deserted.

Pippy stopped outside a door and she fluttered up and down, pointing furiously to it. They hurried to her side and read the words on the door, *The Dark Arts*. Badari reached out to grasp the door handle, but he could not take hold of it; each time he tried to open the door, the handle passed through his hand as though it were a hologram that he could not physically take hold of.

"Stand aside!" instructed the Fearsome one and they all moved aside and watched as he leapt at the door, to force it open, but he too could not physically touch the door, and he simply landed back on the ground of the corridor; it was as though the door did not exist.

The Fearsome one turned to look at Ariana, "Chosen One, only you can take up the Chalice of Fire. Try the door."

Ariana stepped forward and took hold of the door handle; she looked at them in surprise as she was able to clutch it in her hand.

"Be careful!" warned the Fearsome one. "There is foul play afoot, sorcery, be on your guard and bring back the Chalice."

Ariana felt Jack's hand on her shoulder and she turned into his arms. As they embraced, she heard his whisper, *"I love you Arry, make sure you come back."*

As Jack stepped back, Pippy threw herself at Ariana, wrapping her tiny arms around her neck and hugging her, before fluttering to rest in Jack's hands.

Ariana looked at Pippy's worried face and she saw the concern in Jack's eyes. She looked at Badari the warrior, standing tall, his expression serious and intent, and the Fearsome one, that would give his life for her, for them all. She suddenly felt an overpowering sense of gratitude for the lives of each and every one of them standing before her. She smiled at them, and she felt brave, she wasn't afraid, she had to retrieve the Chalice for all their sakes, and with that, she turned the door handle, opened the door and walked through into *The Dark Arts*.

Hearing the door shut loudly behind her as though someone or something had slammed it shut, Ariana quickly took stock of her surroundings. Just like the vision that the Necromancer had shown them, there were six, hooded entities standing in the centre of the dark room, which was lit by flames on the ground and torches of fire on the walls, with strange writings on the wall that appeared like they were etched in blood. The hooded entities were chanting, and as Ariana looked more closely at the ground, she could see that there was a large eye on the floor in the centre of the flames that formed a triangular shape, and suspended above the eye in the middle of it all was the Chalice of Fire, enclosed in what looked like a glass case.

Somehow, Ariana had to get the Chalice of Fire, but what should she do? Walk right up and take it? She doubted that would work. As she stood there taking in the scene, racking her brain on what to do next, she thought she ought to try using her powers. Holding her hands out to the hooded entities, she blasted her powers at them, but she flew back against the walls each time she tried that, and they just continued chanting as though she was not there.

She unsheathed her Lifeblood sword and ran at one of the entities, slashing at it with her sword but it just went through them as though they were holograms, unscathed they continued to chant.

"Oh bother, I may as well just go for it!" she said, and with that, Ariana somersaulted in the air, leaping over the flames and as she stretched out her arm to grab the Chalice of Fire, her whole body just froze, suspended over the eye with the Chalice, unable to move a muscle.

Realising that she was trapped, her mind raced furiously, and she wondered how on earth she was going to get herself out of this mess. She tried to speak, yell for help but she couldn't. She managed to roll her eyes downwards to look at the great eye amid the flames and there in the depths of the eye, she could see a reflection of what was happening to her. As the hooded entities' chanting grew more intense, she could see her suspended body in the reflection of the eye; she was glowing bright blueish white, her entire being was dazzling, and the fire in the Chalice was growing more intense.

Ariana started to feel the power within her flowing like a river through her entire venous system. As the power continued to flow around her body, and the fire in the Chalice burned ever more brightly, spasms of pain flooded her senses, uncontrollable pain and she just knew that the power was being drained from her inner being, but she couldn't cry out for help, she was immobilised, even her lips, she just couldn't move her mouth! Despite the pain, all Ariana could think of was that it couldn't end this way, and she wasn't even thinking about herself, there were so many people and celestials, innocents that needed her to succeed, to get the Chalice out of the hands of the evil one and save the world and all the realms, she just couldn't die here, not now, not like this!

"It's been too long; something must have happened!" cried Jack as he paced up and down the corridor, frustrated that Ariana had to go into that place alone, unprotected, not knowing what she would face.

The Fearsome one growled as he paced and swiped at the door to no avail. Pippy was beside herself with worry for Ariana, and Badari was at a loss as to what to do.

Suddenly Jack heard a voice in his mind, *'Take the book to Ariana, hurry Jack!'* He immediately stopped his frantic pacing.

"Quick Badari! Help me take the sacred book from my back!" he cried, and Badari ran to his side, unstrapped the book and handed it to him.

"You have had word?" The Fearsome one asked.

"Yes! a still small voice spoke to my mind and told me to hurry and take the book to Arry. That means I must be able to open the door too!" he replied and without waiting, Jack burst through the door with the sacred book.

Seeing Ariana suspended in the air, her veins bright blue, her face white as the power was being sapped out of her body, downwards straight through to the eye on the ground. As flames simultaneously flowed from the Chalice to the eye, Jack cried out not knowing what to do to stop it, and then he heard it again,

'Take the book to Ariana, hurry Jack!'

The Cocoon Within

Without a moment's hesitation, Jack jumped over the flames and into the centre of the triangle, standing on the eye, he held the sacred book against Ariana's right hand, her left hand was still outstretched touching the Chalice the way she had been when frozen in motion. Just then her eyes which were closed, suddenly shot open, and she let out a deep breath. A sound like an explosion blew open the door and blasted the hooded entities against the wall, into the darkness once more. The flames on the ground instantly died out, the eye closed and Ariana and the Chalice dropped to the floor, the glass case smashed to pieces, freeing the Chalice.

The Fearsome one, Badari and Pippy hurried into the room as Jack helped Ariana to her feet, and she grabbed the Chalice at the same time.

"Are you alright Arry?"

"Yes, yes, I'm fine, oh thank you, Jack, you came just in time! I thought I was a goner, and all was lost!"

"Look, your hands are glowing!" cried Pippy.

Ariana looked down at her hands as she held the book in one hand and the Chalice in the other. Her hands were dazzlingly bright, glowing with power so much so that blue and white sparks were floating from her hands.

"The legend is true!" Badari affirmed.

"The Chosen One shall release untold power to restore all when the Chalice and sacred books are united!" the Fearsome one finished. "Now come, we have a war to end!"

Together, they raced out of the Destroyer's kingdom. Badari mounted his lizard-horse, and with both Chalice and sacred book safely in Ariana's hands, they headed for the battleground.

The sight that met their eyes at the battleground was not what they were expecting; celestial troops were defeated, injured, and many dead. Ariana looked on as the Gnetic continued to fight bravely alongside the remaining celestials, but they were cruelly outnumbered as the ground shook and a multitude of giant beasts emerged one after another, heaving themselves expertly from the rubble, armed with Lifeblood swords, and battle-ready, teeth bared, claws out, prepared to destroy and mutilate anything in their path.

Furious, the Fearsome one immediately left their side and ran into battle, fiercely defending his comrades as he mauled, and sunk his teeth into one beast after another, roaring his great power to annihilate any enemy in his way. Badari then rode into the fury of the battle, Lifeblood sword raised, he struck down the hordes of Drakken as they came at him, leaping off his ride, he fought beast upon beast.

Ariana turned to Jack and Pippy, "I have to stop this war, I'm not sure how but I am going to use my powers with the Chalice and the sacred book. Look, my hands are still glowing so this must mean something."

As hordes of Drakken came charging towards them, Ariana lifted the Chalice of Fire in the air with one hand and the sacred book in the other, her hands glowed ever brighter and great sparks of power shot from them like fireworks, blasting the Drakken away.

Suddenly, she saw Vedriece lifted up in the sky, fire encompassed him, and he flew over the fighting crowds towards Ariana. His face flashed between his true form and his humanoid form, glimpses of the beast that he was with rotting flesh and great horns, sickening Ariana to the pit of her stomach, as a flashback of her father's murder passed across her mind.

As Vedriece hovered in the sky in front of her she saw a great eye appear on his forehead with a triangular sign etched around the eye in flames, and there appeared around him the six hooded entities with nothing but darkness inside their cloaked hoods, faceless, formless beings, they began chanting, words that Ariana could not understand.

"Chosen One! You think you are all-powerful! You think that you can conquer me! Think again, I have already stolen much of your power, and that of the Chalice, you are no match for me! *YIELD!*"

The Cocoon Within

As Vedriece, the ultimate Destroyer yelled in fury, he raised his grotesque hands of rotting flesh in the air, and Ariana felt her body freeze again. She felt like she was being choked, and she watched helplessly as her body lit up with her power, which began swirling around her insides like the force of a river that was squeezing her power out of her body. Suddenly the blue-white rays of power shot from her hands directly to the eye on Vedriece's forehead and the fire from the Chalice did the same as the chanting from the hooded entities increased. As Ariana scanned the view, searching for Jack, she saw that everyone including him, appeared to be frozen, motionless.

Ariana's heart raced furiously, was this how it was all going to end? As she struggled to accept their fate, it was then that she saw something bright in the distance. It looked like something was moving towards them. It looked like a great star, shining bright, and as she watched this star in the distance behind Vedriece, as it grew closer, she could see that it wasn't just a star, something was moving with it.

Her eyes were getting weak as she felt her power being drained away and, blinking, she strained to focus. Suddenly her heart leapt in realisation, and she felt her strength returning at the sight before her! It was an army, a great and mighty army. The Arc Celestials! What a sight to behold! Ariana's heart leapt again with a mixture of great relief and exceeding awe at the sight of them approaching. An army of many chariots soared through the sky, and mighty winged horses with warriors astride them, Arc Celestials, strong and mighty, with giant wings in flight, battle-ready, glowing with celestial power. She saw a large army of the mighty ones with the bronze rods, just like the ones that she had fought on the great mountain summit. And as the army approached with speed, up above them she could now clearly see the great bright and dazzling star, just like on the mountain summit.

At the forefront of the army, leader and Commander was none other than Leo, magnificent and mighty, running towards them, looking fierce with his great shimmering silvery-gold mane shrouding his glorious features. Giant silvery-gold wings spread wide, as he soared majestically through the sky, the great lion warrior with his flaming mane, his strong, muscular body pounding through the sky. Surprisingly, astride Leo's back sat Eriat, dressed for combat, with a dazzling rod of bronze in her hand, and flanking Leo on each side were the two great leopards, the Fearsome ones.

The army of Arc Celestials descended on the giant beasts and hordes of Drakken and when they fought, they fought as one, in power like no others. It was stunning and humbling to watch the great and mighty force of the Arc Celestials in combat. Many of the giants fled, racing towards Vedriece's kingdom, fleeing into the wilderness, as the Arc Celestials descended upon them, slaying them with the might of their swords and powers in one fell swoop.

Ariana watched in great awe, her heart pounding, as Leo gave an almighty roar and set upon Vedriece, claws striking him, sending him flying to the ground and breaking the curse of sorcery. Eriat leapt to the ground and engaged in direct combat with Vedriece, who was taken by surprise, a mixture of both fear and fury seemed to cross his evil features.

Ariana and everyone who had been immobilised were now free from the sorcery of Vedriece and his hooded entities, the latter of which had disappeared as quickly as they had appeared. As Ariana stood holding onto the Chalice of Fire and the sacred book, she looked on in amazement as Eriat moved with lightning speed and agility, her powers in combat were second to none. She used her bronze rod and powers to entrap Vedriece in a forcefield, then turning she called out to Leo,

"The Chalice! Now!"

"Arc Celestials, Chosen One! It is time!" Leo called.

Ariana quickly lifted the Chalice of Fire high in her right hand and she held the sacred book in her left hand. Her hands still glowed with blue-white power, dazzling brightly. She watched in awe as every Arc Celestial also raised their hands to the sky, and their rays of power united with the great bright star in the sky. Ariana watched as the powers from her own hands did the same, and the Chalice of

Fire was also lifted up by her beams of power. She watched as it was taken up high to meet the star in the sky.

Then suddenly, the sacred book floated from her hand and stopped in the air in front of her, glowing brightly, the pages flicked open and stopped at the centre page. Great golden words floated off the pages, like a running river.

Ariana recited the words aloud and it was as though they came from deep within her,

"The Chalice of fire is released by the united blood of two worlds, as it was spoken at the beginning of time, go forth and take all that seek evil and let them be bound once more. I command them into a thousand depths of darkness, that their reign of torment over all peoples and lands shall cease. Set the captives free to return home, for I the Chosen One of both worlds release this power to set all things right."

As Ariana finished speaking, she felt the rumbling of the ground beneath them begin to intensify, and suddenly a great fireball erupted from the Chalice in the sky, and like a volcano, out poured a lava-like fiery substance, which seemed to be directed by the rays of power from all the Arc Celestials. For the first time, Ariana witnessed great rays of power emerge from Leo's roaring mouth, channelling the lava substance that gushed like a white-hot river as it trapped Vedriece in its grip. He struggled to free himself in vain and the lava took him deep into a gaping hole in the ground. The lava began to flood the ground, running through Vedriece's kingdom, like a great tsunami, dragging every evil beast and creature with it, deep into the ground. Ariana, Jack and Pippy watched as the ground closed, swallowing its victims into the furthest depths underground.

A great cheer erupted amongst the crowds of celestials, signifying their victory at this bloody and dark war's ending. Jack and Ariana embraced each other, relieved that it was all over and that Vedriece's evil reign of terror had finally been halted.

Ariana turned to Pippy, smiling. Pippy hovered in front of her, joyous eyes dancing, before she flung herself at Ariana and gave her the biggest wish-helper hug ever.

"We did it! We stopped the war!" cried Pippy. "Thank you for everything!"

"No, thank you, Pippy, I couldn't have done any of this without you."

Just then Leo and Eriat walked towards them and Ariana experienced that feeling of their greatness as they approached. She felt humbled and awestruck in their presence.

"Well done Chosen One," Eriat's eyes met Ariana's and she held her gaze stoically, the fivefold symbol on the centre of her forehead glowing starkly, "you have proven yourself to be worthy of your identity."

Ariana thanked Eriat and was just about to ask about Jessica as she was still very much in her heart. Ariana didn't understand how she could come from Earth yet perish here in a different realm.

Reading her thoughts, Eriat spoke comforting words to Ariana, "You will see Jessica again."

As Ariana pondered Eriat's words with joy, she watched as Leo said to Jack,

"Child of Mankind, you were given the gift of sight for good reason, though bravery is not natural for a human, therefore today, I commend you for your courage." Jack beamed as Leo raised his giant paw to rest on his shoulder in approval, but as soon as he touched him, Jack disappeared!

Open-mouthed and in shock, Ariana was about to speak, when Leo moved to stand in front of her. "My child," he said, "you are the Chosen One, you have fulfilled your destiny this time and now it's time for you to return," and as if in slow motion, Leo raised his paw to place it on her shoulder.

Ariana looked for Pippy and there she was hovering in the background, smiling at Ariana, waving goodbye. And as she felt Leo's great paw touch her shoulder, she felt herself mouth the words, "Thank you," before suddenly everything went black.

***

Her eyes felt like they were stuck together. She tried again to open them, but they just felt so heavy. Then finally, she managed to open one eye and then the other. It was hard to focus at first, but after blinking a few times, her eyes adjusted, and she realised that she was lying in bed.

Looking around the stark white unfamiliar room, she saw that there was a TV on the wall opposite the bed she was lying on, and a window to her right. What was that bleeping noise? She turned around, accidentally pulling a tube from her arm, and an alarm sounded. Confused for a moment, until it suddenly dawned on her that she was lying in a hospital bed. God, was she alright? She moved her arms and legs slowly; they still worked, which was a good sign, though they felt a bit heavy. What about her face?! She raised her hand to feel her face and hair, oh thank God, everything seemed intact.

The hospital room door opened and in walked two very anxious-looking people. Ariana stared at them for a moment and then came the recognition. Could it be she was dreaming?

"Mum? Dad? Is that really you? Am I dreaming?" This was ethereal, she must be dreaming!

Her mother rushed to her bedside, exclaiming, "Darling, you've had an accident, a nasty bump to the head and you have just woken from a coma, you were in a coma for two weeks, sweetheart."

Ariana stared into her mother's eyes, her beautiful face, older than she remembered from the old photos, but just as beautiful. Ariana's heart pounded furiously as she tried to reconcile this, it seemed so real.

"Doctor, I think she might have amnesia, can you come and take a look at her please?" Ariana looked over at her father as he spoke briefly to the doctor before coming to her bedside and peering at her face intently.

"Darling, it's your dad, how are you feeling? Do you know your name sweetie?"

"You're alive?" Ariana stroked her father's face, and he turned to look at her mother, a rather worried expression on his face.

"Of course, we are alive, what makes you say that?"

"It's just that you both died in a car accident, well that's what I had thought until I went to Elopia and found out the truth, and Granpey looked after me. Granpey? Oh, where is Granpey? Is he alright?"

"Calm down, poppet, Granpey is fine, he is just outside waiting to come and see you, it's only two visitors at a time so as not to overwhelm you."

Ariana visibly relaxed, so everyone was alright, maybe the whole thing was a dream, and she had somehow mixed her dream up with reality whilst in a coma. That must mean reality would fully come back to her memory soon, she hoped.

The doctor examined her and asked her some questions, what her name was, where she lived, her favourite food, her school, and her best friend's name, she got all those answers right, so she was sure that she must be alright.

"Can I see Granpey, please?"

"Of course, you can! Colin, send him in won't you honey?"

Ariana's dad gave her a big hug before he dashed off to send Granpey in, and Ariana's heart soared at the sight of her beloved Granpey as he hobbled in, using his favourite walking stick, and sat down in the chair her father had just vacated. Ariana put her hand in Granpey's and beamed up at him, she was surprised to see a glimmer of tears in his eyes as he looked at her lovingly.

"Aye, look at ya lass, getting yourself made a fuss of like this, eh? Sleeping for two weeks solid with no one knowing if or when you'd come back to us! But mark my words, I said to Colin and your mam that you'll be right as rain in no time, and so you are lassie, so you are." Granpey squeezed her hand, clearly overjoyed to see her.

"I love you, Granpey and I'm glad you're alright."

"Eh, lass, no need to be getting mushy, nowt wrong with me, you just get your strength back so we can have you home sharp."

After spending a wonderful afternoon with Granpey and her mum and dad, they left long after visiting hours were over, due to a kind nurse who turned a blind eye. Ariana spent time mulling over everything, from her dream, which she had thought was reality, but it wasn't, to her parents who she thought were dead, but they had been alive and with her and Granpey all along! She shook her head; it was amazing what a bump to the head could do!

The following morning, as Ariana lay in the hospital bed, the more she thought about it, the more she struggled to comprehend that everything she had experienced had been a dream. She shook her head in wonder; she remembered every detail like it was yesterday! Both Jessica and Jack had been there in her dream. Eriat, Leo, Elopia, the giant beasts, the Destroyer and the great battle, and Pippy! Dearest Pippy, who journeyed with her through the darker realms and fought by her side in the great battle, how could it be that they were all just figments of her imagination?

Ariana shook her head once more, and she pressed the little button on the hospital bed remote control and listened to the sound of the hydraulics moving slowly till she was propped in a more upright position. She felt fine, she didn't even feel as though she had been in a coma for two weeks. It was strange that the dream had felt like her reality but thank God her parents were alive and well, and Granpey too, it was all so wonderful.

Just then, Jack walked in carrying a cup of tea, and in his other hand, he held her rucksack. "Here you go," he said, smiling as he put her rucksack on the chair next to her bed and then he pulled the hospital tray over, adjusted its position across Ariana's lap and set her cup of tea on the tray.

"I thought you might want your rucksack; they brought it in with you after the accident and I had locked it away in one of the hospital

The Cocoon Within

lockers just outside your room. It's got your phone and keys in there, and I brought your charger so you can get it charged."

"Thanks, Jack," Ariana smiled at him and sipped her tea.

"Oh, by the way, there is a very unusual book in there too, looks really old, do you remember where you found that?" Jack asked rather absent-mindedly, whilst he unravelled the cable of her mobile phone charger.

Ariana immediately froze at his words. Her hand began to shake, and the teacup wobbled, splashing some tea on the tray.

"Oh, here let me help you, you're probably a little weak still and I should have thought of that sorry." Jack was by Ariana's side, and he gently took the teacup from her and set it down on the tray. "Are you ok? You look pale all of a sudden, do you want me to fetch the nurse?" He stared at her intently and his eyes roved across her face with concern.

"No, no, I'm fine, just a little hungry. Would you mind seeing if you can get me something to eat, a little sandwich perhaps?"

Jack jumped up. "Of course," he said, "I'll get you a nice sandwich and some fruit." He beamed at her and dashed out of the room in search of food.

Ariana quickly grabbed the rucksack and there inside was the sacred book! She stared at it, she was gobsmacked, and her mind raced. How could it be a dream if the book was here?! She pulled the book out of her rucksack and passed her hands over the cover, allowing them to feel the raised symbols as though they were braille. And then she saw it, a faint glimmer of the pages, they were glowing! Ariana opened the book and the pages flipped by themselves and stopped at the centre page. There on the centre pages of the book she watched as the words that were in an unknown language, transformed before her very eyes, becoming words that she could understand.

She read them,

The Cocoon Within

The Cocoon within is where the power lies,
Let it burst forth O' Go-Between, Celestials rise and know your worth.

Rise and overcome evil with good,
Rise and run with Lions and maketh all things right,
Leave not one out of your sight.

And then it hit her, it hadn't been a dream at all! It had all been real, every last moment of it! Though clearly Jack remembered nothing of their otherworldly adventure to Elopia, and her mother and father's past had been rewritten. All things had been set right! Ariana let the book slip from her hands onto her lap and she looked at her palms, wondering if she still had her powers. As she studied her palms, they began to glow, it was that familiar bright blue-white light that shimmered, as though emanating deep from within the veins in her hands. As she mulled over the words in the book, she realised that the words were right, the power had lain within her all along. It was the cocoon of power that had been hidden within her until the book released it. Turning her hands over, she watched them glow, and Ariana marvelled at all that had happened before she was drawn back to the present.

"It's time for your medication." Ariana looked up as a nurse walked into the room, she was smiling at Ariana, but she appeared rather nervous.

"Oh yes, of course, thanks, I…" Ariana's smile trailed off as she saw a movement out of the corner of her eye. And there it was, that all-familiar greyish, translucent looking being with its oversized head, bulging great amber eyes staring intently at the nurse, focussed on its target, it rubbed its clawed hands together in glee. And as it grinned, it cupped its hands at the nurse and blew a cloud of words into her ear. Then it held up its hand and inspected one gnarled index finger, that glowed a deep purple. Ariana lifted her hands to face the Tormenting one, she knew what she had to do, but just then Jack walked in, and he wasn't alone, he was with Jessica.

Jessica was alive! She was alright!

"Hi Ariana, it's so good to see you awake and well. Jack has been so worried about you!" Jessica swished her long dark hair aside as she turned to look at Jack lovingly and he returned her stare and smiled, before doing the unexpected. He bent his head down to kiss Jessica passionately on the lips!

Ariana was open-mouthed in shock, distracted by Jack and Jessica's arrival, she didn't even notice the Tormenting one jab the nurse in the arm with its sharp claw as the purple fluid pumped from its gnarled finger into her veins. Nor did she notice the nurse stumble slightly before hurrying out of the room.

She continued to stare open-mouthed as Jack took Jessica's hand, brought it to his mouth and kissed it, before turning towards Ariana and handing her a cheese and onion sandwich, which he had got from the hospital kiosk.

"Sorry, they didn't have any fru… Arry? Are you alright?" Jack quickly pulled up a chair and sat down close to Ariana's bedside, peering at her with concern.

"You look white as a sheet like you've just seen a ghost or something! Are you feeling ok? Do you want us to get the nurse?"

Ariana grappled with her reaction to what she was seeing, Jack and Jessica… an item? He had always been her Jack. He had told her he loved her; those had been his last words to her before they left the great battle. What had changed? And suddenly Ariana remembered the words of the Necromancer, and her hand flew to her mouth in horror. She had lost him to Jessica, Jack had been her heart's desire, and she hadn't even truly realised it till now!

"Are you alright?" Jessica put her hand on Ariana's shoulder, but she shrugged her hand away and composed herself as best she could.

"No, no, it's alright, I just had a sudden wave of nausea. I think it's the medication, but it's passed now, though I do feel rather tired. I think I just need a nap."

After some time back and forth, convincing Jack and Jessica that she was fine and would much rather get some rest, they both reluctantly conceded and left hand in hand. Closing the door behind them, leaving her to her thoughts at last. She was suddenly grateful for the silence so that she could think.

Everything hadn't been a dream; she really had gone to Elopia with Jack and Jessica. On the plus side, completing the mission to get the Chalice and end the war had set things right; her mum, dad and Jessica were alive and safe. Though at the sacrifice of Jack's love. It was worth it, and she could live with that, as long as Jack was happy and everyone that she cared about was safe and well, that was the main thing. Though deep in the pit of her stomach, she felt an ache, a longing that she was unaccustomed to, and she realised that her heart was aching for Jack, her best friend and confidant, her lost love. To Ariana, he would always be her Jack.

Sighing deeply, she shook her head, pausing for a moment before remembering the Tormenting one that she had seen just a moment ago with the nurse, looking around the room, there was no trace of the intruder, it had no doubt long gone. Ariana only hoped that the nurse was alright.

As she contemplated the truth of all she had experienced being real, Ariana's heart began to pound as she looked down at the book. The pages of which were glowing again, and as she read the transforming words, she suddenly felt hope rising on the inside of her. A hope that just maybe she could reverse the curse of the Necromancer, as the book called to her once more,

Come O Chosen One,
Come and run with Lions,
For all is not as it seems,
Your destiny is sure,
And your path is straight,
Come meet the one who has set you at the gate.

*Available worldwide online
and from all good bookstores*

www.mtp.agency

@mtp_agency

www.ingramcontent.com/pod-product-compliance
Lightning Source LLC
LaVergne TN
LVHW041621060526
838200LV00040B/1372